英文不要學，只要聽，
本書由名美籍播音員錄音，
中文說得比中國人好，
英文說得比美國人好。

隨時隨地聽，自然學好英文。
中英文一起聽，
同時學會中文和英文。

不需要專心聽，
只要嘴巴跟著老師
唸唸有詞即可。

背了會忘是自然的，
要持之以恆。

# 字彙的重要

## 字彙和思想

字代表思想,是思考的工具。如果你的字彙有限,思想範圍必定較狹窄,和別人溝通也有困難。除非努力加強字彙,否則就沒辦法廣博又深入地思考,走向成功之路。

## 字彙和留美入學許可

專家指出,字彙能力和人的智力關係密切。美國各大學研究所的入學審查委員很注重字彙能力。字彙能力強,證明智慧較高,同時也顯示閱讀廣泛。托福和 GRE 考試中,字彙都佔了很大的比重,不可忽視。

## 閱讀是長期的方法,但收效慢

雖然閱讀是增強字彙的根本方法,但卻相當緩慢。對於有心想要在短時間內增進字彙的人,除了閱讀外,本書從幾方面教您最有效、最直接的方法。

## 學習意思相近的字群

經由閱讀得來的字彙有個嚴重的缺點——沒有組織。閱讀時碰到的新字,似乎和別的字沒什麼關聯。這當然不表示我們可以小看閱讀對增進字彙的幫助。不過有另一種方式能使字彙增加得更快,就是把意思相關的字組織起來,然後再加以研讀。

## 學習源自希臘文和拉丁文的字

槓桿原理使人花極少的力氣,得到極大的功效。同樣的法則也可用於學字彙。如果讀了相當豐富的希臘和拉丁字首和字根,就得到單字的槓桿力量。適度了解每個字首字根,可幫助你學會很多它所產生的單字。在關於希臘、拉丁字的章節裏,將介紹重要字首字根,有無數的單字都由它們構成。

## 學習由法文、義大利文、西班牙文借來的字

因為英文借用了相當多的法文、義大利文，和西班牙文，所以在書報雜誌中都會碰到外來語。這些字被認為是英文字彙的一部分，而且往往是文章中的關鍵。要是不了解一般的外來語，是字彙嚴重的缺憾。

## 學習造衍生字

如果你剛學了一個新字 fallible（易錯的），但不知道如何形成衍生字，那麼你僅僅增加了一個單字。

但是如果你知道怎麼形成衍生字，你所增加的單字就不只一個，而是好幾個，像 fallible, infallible, fallibly, infallibly, 和 fallibility, infallibility。

本書將教你如何形成、拼出衍生字，那麼你每學一個新字，就增加了很多字彙。

## 練習新的字彙

在身體成長的過程中，肌肉的運動是必須的。同樣地，在增加單字的過程中，字彙的練習是必須的。

為了有效地學會新字，必須儘早經常使用它們。本書有很多富挑戰性的反覆練習和測驗，會給你充分的機會來練習各種字彙。但是你自己仍應多加練習。

讀和聽的時候注意字彙，說和寫的時候適時用新的單字。如果你想讓生字真正成為自己的一部分，這些是必須的步驟。

**編者 謹識**

# 目 錄　CONTENTS

## 第三章 認識拉丁字首、字根以增加字彙

### ■ 第一部份 拉丁字首

## ■第二部份　拉丁字根

## 第四章　認識盎格魯‧撒克遜字首以增加字彙

## 第五章　出自希臘羅馬神話的字彙

## 第六章　出自法文的英文字彙

## 第七章　出自義大利文的英文字彙

## 第八章 出自西班牙文的英文字彙

## 第九章 字彙的舉一反三 ── 衍生字

## 第十章 關係字及類比字

# 一封感人的來信

學習出版社，您好：

　　我是貴社出版書籍的愛用者，畢業於台大電機系，入伍服預官役，於今年六月一日退伍。退伍後打定出國繼續深造的心意，首先面臨的就是托福及 GRE 測驗，在一個偶然的機會下，在書局發現貴社 Vocabulary Fundamental～22000 這一系列的字彙進階書，其內容紮實，循序漸進的編排方式甚合我的需要，於是直接到許昌街門市購買了 Vocabulary 5000 及 Vocabulary 10000 兩套，以此二套書來準備托福考試，果然於 8 月 1 日的托福考試中獲得 610 分的理想分數；接下來為了 GRE 考試的需要，我又購買 Vocabulary 22000 這一套及 GRE 字彙進階一書，經過充分研讀之後，於 10 月 11 日充滿信心的走入考場。前幾天我收到了 GRE 成績單：語文 570，計量 800，分析 760，總分 2130，這個成績是我原先作夢都不敢夢到的，尤其語文部分 570 分更可說貴社的書籍功不可沒。目前我正在進行美國碩士班的申請，在欣喜之餘，特地提筆向貴社致上我最誠懇的謝意，並盼望貴社本著一貫的高水準，繼續造福有志學好英文的莘莘學子。

最後謹祝

　　編安

　　　　　　　　　　　　　　　　　　　　　　××× 上

# 第一章
# 以中心思想方式記憶單字

　　增強字彙有效的方法是研讀相關的字群。根據這個方法，譬如可先讀一群和「貧窮」有關的生字，然後再讀和「財富」有關的字，你很快就會發現，同時讀幾個相關的字，比讀不相關的生字表有用得多。

　　本章共分二十組字群，每組都是中心思想相同的字，每個中心思想下，都有很多重要的生字，並有定義和例句。這些例句都是特別造的，以幫助你牢記定義和各個生字的用法。

　　儘管有這一切設計，要是你不照著做，還是達不到讀本書所能產生的效果。擴充字彙是件划算且富挑戰性的工作，它需要不斷的努力和想像。以下是幾項建議，能使你由本章獲益良多。

1. 仔細注意每個例句，然後至少在心中自己造個相似的句子。
2. 用頭腦多反覆練習，而不要機械化地練習。複習你失誤的字。
3. 在適當的場合中，儘快特意使用你的新字，例如和朋友聊天、課堂討論、寫信或作文都可用。只有練習運用生字，它們才會成爲你的一部分。

　　本章收集歸納的字群，均爲日常重要或考試常考的字彙。內容包括有關 skill（技巧），poverty（貧窮），wealth（財富），fear（恐懼），courage（勇氣），concealment（隱藏），disclosure（揭發），agreement（一致），disagreement（不一致），eating（吃），size, quantity（大小，數量），weakness（衰弱），strength（強壯），neglect（忽視），care（謹慎），residence（居住），disobedience（違抗），obedience（順從），time（時間），necessity（需要）等二十個 groups，現在讓我們一組一組來討論。

【Group 1】

# 有關 *Skill*「技巧」的字群

Group 1~20

**apprentice**[6]〔ə'prɛntɪs〕*n.* 學徒；徒弟

—— person learning an art or trade under a skilled worker; learner; beginner; novice; tyro

Young Ben Franklin learned the printing trade by serving as an *apprentice* to his half brother James. 小班・富蘭克林藉著到他同父異母的哥哥詹姆士那裡當學徒，而學會了印刷手藝。

**aptitude**[6]〔'æptə‚tjud〕*n.* 才能；資質；性向

—— natural tendency to learn or understand; talent; bent

【記憶技巧】
*apt* (fit) + *itude* (n.)

Eric is clumsy with tools; he has little mechanical *aptitude*.
艾瑞克不擅長使用工具；他沒什麼機械方面的才能。

**craftsman**〔'kræftsmən〕*n.* 工匠；技工；精於某一門工藝的人

—— skilled workman; artisan

To build a house, you need the services of carpenters, bricklayers, plumbers, electricians, and several other *craftsmen*. 要蓋一間房子，你必須請木匠、泥水匠、水管工人、電工，還有許多其他專門的技工。

**dexterity**〔dɛks'tɛrətɪ〕*n.* 靈巧；熟練

—— skill in using the hands or mind; deftness; adroitness

You can't expect an apprentice to have the same *dexterity* as a master craftsman. 你不能期望一個學徒做得像卓越的技工一樣靈巧。

**adroit**〔ə'drɔɪt〕*adj.* 靈巧的；熟練的 (*ant.* **maladroit**, **inept**)

—— expert in using the hands or mind; skillful; clever; deft; dexterous

Our *adroit* passing enabled us to score four touchdowns.
我們熟練的傳球，使我們能得到四個觸地球的分數。

**ambidextrous** 〔͵æmbə'dɛkstrəs 〕*adj.* 雙手很靈巧的；熟練的
—— able to use both hands equally well

Jack is an *ambidextrous* hitter; he can bat right-handed or left-handed.
傑克是一位雙手都很靈巧的打擊手；他可以用右手或左手打擊。

**versatile**[6] 〔'vɝsətḷ , 'vɝsətaɪl 〕*adj.*
多才多藝的；多方面的
—— capable of doing many things well; many-sided; all-around

【記憶技巧】
*versat* (turn) + *ile* (*adj.*)
（可轉向各方面發展，表示擁有很多才藝）

Leonardo da Vinci was remarkably *versatile*. He was a painter, sculptor, architect, musician, engineer, and scientist.
李奧納多・達文西是出名的多才多藝。他是畫家、雕刻家、建築師、音樂家、工程師，也是一位科學家。

Exercise：選出正確答案

1. If you have musical _____, you should not have too much trouble in learning to play an instrument.
   (A) aptitude
   (B) ineptness

2. In the olden days, a boy learned a trade by serving as a(n) _____ to a master craftsman.
   (A) artisan
   (B) apprentice

3. Ralph has been on the baseball, track, and soccer teams. He is a(n) _____ athlete.
   (A) maladroit
   (B) versatile

4. Since my right hand is injured, how can you expect me to write? I am not _____!
   (A) ambidextrous
   (B) adroit

5. The _____'s dexterity with tools is the result of years of experience.

    (A) tyro                     (B) craftsman

> 【解答】
> 1. A    2. B    3. B    4. A    5. B

## 【Group 2】

# 有關 *Poverty*「貧窮」的字群

**indigence**〔ˈɪndədʒəns〕*n.* 貧窮

—— poverty

By hard work, many Americans have raised themselves from *indigence* to wealth.

許多美國人藉著辛勤的工作，從貧困中擢升爲富裕。

**economize**〔ɪˈkɑnəˌmaɪz , i- 〕*v.* 節省開支；節儉

—— cut down expenses; be frugal

Consumers can *economize* by buying their milk in gallon containers. 消費者可以購買加侖裝的牛奶而節省開支。

**impoverish**〔ɪmˈpɑvərɪʃ〕*v.* 使成赤貧

—— make very poor; reduce to poverty

The increase in dues is only 10 cents. It will not *impoverish* any member. 會費只增加十分錢，不會使任何會員變窮的。

**destitute**〔ˈdɛstəˌtjut , -ˈtut〕*adj.* 窮困的；缺乏的

—— not possessing the necessities of life such as food, shelter, and clothing; needy; indigent

The severe earthquake killed hundreds of people and left thousands *destitute*. 強烈的地震造成數百人罹難，使數千人一無所有。

**frugal**〔'frugḷ〕*adj.* 1. 節儉的；節省的　2. 簡單便宜的

—— 1. avoiding waste; economical; sparing; saving; thrifty

2. small;, plain and not costing very much

An allowance of $200 a week for lunches and fares isn't much, but you can get by on it if you are *frugal*.　一星期二百元的午餐及車費津貼不算多，但是如果你節省一點，還是可以過得去。

The old man had nothing to eat but bread and cheese; yet he offered to share this *frugal* meal with his visitor.　那個老人只有麵包和起司可吃，但是他把自己簡單便宜的食物與訪客共享。

## 【Group 3】

# 有關 *Wealth*「財富」的字群

**avarice**〔'ævərɪs〕*n.* 貪婪；貪心

—— excessive desire for wealth; greediness

People who suffer from *avarice* spend much less and save much more than they should.

貪心的人花的比他們應花的少，而省的則是比他們應省的多。

**dowry**〔'daʊrɪ〕*n.* 嫁妝

—— money, property, etc., that a bride brings to her husband

With his wife's *dowry*, the young attorney was able to open a law office.　這年輕的律師靠他太太的嫁妝，開了一家律師事務所。

**means**[2]〔minz〕*n. pl.* 金錢；財富

—— wealth; property; resources

To own an expensive home, a yacht, and a limousine, you have to be a person of *means*.

要擁有一幢昂貴的房子、一艘遊艇，和一部豪華轎車，你得很有錢。

**opulence** 〔ˊɑpjələns 〕 *n.* 富裕；豐富
—— wealth; riches; affluence
Dickens contrasts the *opulence* of France's nobility with the
indigence of her peasants.
狄更斯比較法國貴族的富裕與其農民的貧窮。

**covet**[6] 〔ˊkʌvɪt 〕 *v.* 垂涎；貪圖（尤指屬於他人的東西）
—— desire; long for; crave, especially something belonging to
another
Peter *coveted* his neighbor's farm but could not get her to sell it.
彼得貪圖鄰居的農場，但卻沒辦法使她賣掉這個農場。

**fleece** 〔 flis 〕 *v.*【喻】詐騙（某人） *n.* 羊毛
—— (literally, to remove the wool from a sheep or a similar
animal) deprive or strip of money or belongings by fraud;
charge excessively for goods or services; rob; cheat; swindle
If your brother paid $4,000 for that car, he was *fleeced*. The
mechanic says it is worth $1,500. 如果你弟弟花四千美元買那部車，
那他就被騙了。技工說那部車只值一千五百美元。

**hoard** 〔 hord 〕 *v.* 貯藏；積聚
—— save and conceal; accumulate; amass
Tom had a reputation as a miser who *hoarded* every
penny he could get his hands on.
湯姆將能得到手的每一分錢都貯藏起來，所以有守財奴之稱。

**affluent** 〔ˊæfluənt 〕 *adj.* 富裕的；豐富的
—— very wealthy; rich; opulent
The new hospital wing was made possible by a gift of $500,000
from an *affluent* contributor.
有一位富有的捐助人捐獻了五十萬美元，使醫院能增建新的側翼。

**financial**[4]〔 fə'nænʃəl , faɪ- 〕*adj.* 財務的；金融的
—— having to do with money matters; monetary; pecuniary; fiscal
People who keep spending more than they earn usually get into
*financial* difficulties.
凡是開銷一直大於收入的人，經常會陷於財務困難。

**lavish**〔'lævɪʃ 〕*adj.* ( ↔ sparing ) 1. 慷慨的；大方的；揮霍成性的
2. 過多的；過度的
—— 1. too free in giving, using, or spending; profuse
　　2. given or spent too freely; very abundant; more than enough;
　　　profuse
The young heir was warned that he would soon have nothing left if
he continued to be *lavish* with money.
這年輕繼承人被警告說，如果他再揮金如土，將會很快破產。
Vera's composition is good, but it doesn't deserve the *lavish* praise
that Linda gave it.
維拉的作文不錯，但卻不值得琳達過度的稱讚。

**lucrative**〔'lukrətɪv 〕*adj.* 可獲利的；賺錢的
—— profitable; moneymaking
To run a restaurant is a *lucrative* business. 經營餐廳是賺錢的生意。

## Exercise：選出正確答案

1. As the world's most _____ nation, the United States has spent
billions to aid the needy peoples of other lands.
　(A) destitute　　　　　　　(B) affluent

2. France was impoverished in the eighteenth century by the
_____ spending of her royal family.
　(A) frugal　　　　　　　　(B) lavish

3. The child _____ her sister's broken doll, though her own was new and beautiful.
   (A) coveted             (B) lavished

4. The bride came with a large dowry as her parents were people of _____.
   (A) means             (B) indigence

5. The nation will be in serious financial trouble unless it _____ at once.
   (A) fleeces            (B) economizes

---
【解答】
1. B    2. B    3. A    4. A    5. B
---

## 【Group 4】

## 有關 *Fear*「恐懼」的字群

**craven** 〔'krevən〕 *n.* 懦夫

—— coward

A hero risks his life to help others; a *craven* runs from the scene.
英雄冒著生命危險去幫助別人；而一個懦夫卻臨陣脫逃。

**trepidation** 〔,trɛpə'deʃən〕 *n.* 驚恐；惶恐

—— nervous agitation; fear; fright; trembling

I thought Carol would be nervous when she made her speech, but she delivered it without *trepidation*.
我本以為卡蘿演說時會緊張，但發表時，她卻一點也不害怕。

**cower** 〔ˈkaʊə〕 *v.* 畏縮；退縮

—— draw back tremblingly; shrink or crouch in fear; cringe; recoil

Brave men defy tyrants, instead of *cowering* before them.

勇者公然反抗暴君，不在他們面前畏縮。

**intimidate**[6] 〔ɪnˈtɪmə‚det〕 *v.* 威脅；
脅迫（某人做某事）

—— make fearful or timid; frighten;
force by fear; cow; bully

> 【記憶技巧】
> *in* (in) + *timid*（膽小的）
> + *ate* (v.)（「威脅」會使
> 人膽怯）

The younger boys would not have given up the playing field so quickly if the older boys hadn't *intimidated* them. 要不是那些較大的男孩脅迫他們，這些小男孩是不會這麼快就放棄這球場的。

**apprehensive** 〔‚æprɪˈhɛnsɪv〕 *adj.* 憂慮的

—— expecting something unfavorable; afraid; anxious

Several *apprehensive* parents telephoned the school when the children were late in getting home from the museum trip. 當孩子們到博物館參觀，遲遲未回家時，憂慮的父母親紛紛打電話到學校。

**dastardly** 〔ˈdæstədlɪ〕 *adj.* 懦弱的；卑鄙的

—— cowardly and mean

It was *dastardly* of the captain to desert the sinking vessel and leave the passengers to fend for themselves.

拋棄沉船並丟下乘客讓他們自己謀生，這就是船長的懦弱。

**timid**[4] 〔ˈtɪmɪd〕 *adj.* 膽小的

—— lacking courage or self-confidence;
fearful; timorous; shy

> 【記憶技巧】
> *tim* (fear) + *id* (adj.)（會
> 害怕，表示個性是「膽小
> 的」）

If the other team challenges us, we should accept. Let's not be so *timid*! 如果有其他隊伍向我們挑戰，我們應當接受。絕不能如此膽怯！

【Group 5】

# 有關 *Courage*「勇氣」的字群

**exploit**[6]〔'ɛksplɔɪt〕*n.* 功績
—— heroic act; daring deed; feat
Robert E. Peary won worldwide fame for his *exploits* as an Arctic explorer. 勞勃特‧艾德文‧皮瑞以他北極探險家的功績而聞名於世。

**fortitude**〔'fɔrtə,tjud〕*n.* 堅毅
—— courage in facing danger, hardship, or pain; endurance; bravery; pluck; backbone; valor
The captain showed remarkable *fortitude* in continuing to lead his men despite a painful wound.
那位艦長不顧傷痛繼續領導手下，顯示出非凡的堅毅。

**audacious**〔ɔ'deʃəs〕*adj.* 1. 勇敢的　2. 無禮的
—— 1. bold; fearlessly daring
　　2. too bold; insolent; impudent
Risking serious injury, the outfielder made an *audacious* leap against the concrete wall and caught the powerfully hit ball.
冒著受重傷的危險，外野手勇敢地跳向水泥牆，接下那個猛力擊出的球。
After we had waited for about twenty minutes, an *audacious* freshman came along and tried to get in at the head of our line.
在我們等大約二十分鐘後，一位無禮的新生走來，試圖插進隊伍的前頭。

**dauntless**〔'dɔntlɪs〕*adj.* 無所畏懼的；勇敢的
—— fearless; intrepid; very brave; valiant
The frightened sailors wanted to turn back, but their *dauntless* leader urged them to sail on.
受驚的水手們想掉頭走，但他們勇敢的領導者激勵他們繼續航行。

**indomitable**〔ɪnˋdɑmətəbḷ〕*adj.* 不屈不撓的；不認輸的

—— incapable of being subdued; unconquerable; invincible

Columbus had an *indomitable* belief that he would reach land by sailing west. 哥倫布有個不屈不撓信念，認為向西航行就可到達陸地。

**plucky**〔ˋplʌkɪ〕*adj.* 勇敢的

—— courageous; brave; valiant; valorous

Though defeated, our team put up a *plucky* defense against their taller and huskier opponents.

雖然戰敗，我們的隊友依然勇敢地防禦他們高大、強壯的敵手。

**rash**[6]〔ræʃ〕*adj.* 輕率的；魯莽的（↔ deliberate）

—— overhasty; foolhardy; reckless; impetuous; taking too much risk

When a person loses his temper, he may say or do something *rash* and regret it afterwards.

一個人生氣時，可能說出或做出衝動的事，之後又後悔。

Exercise：選出正確答案

1. If you think you can _____ us by shaking your fists at us and shouting, you are mistaken.

   (A) cower                      (B) intimidate

2. Usually, the hero of a western movie performs a number of unbelievable _____s.

   (A) exploit                 (B) trepidation

3. When the opposing team took the field they seemed _____, but we were able to defeat them.

   (A) indomitable           (B) timorous

4. Who would have thought that a(n) _____ girl like Olga would have the impudence to interrupt the principal?

　(A) audacious　　　　　　　(B) timid

5. It would be _____ to drop out of school because of failure in one test.

　(A) dauntless　　　　　　　(B) rash

---
【解答】

1. B　　2. A　　3. A　　4. B　　5. B

---

【Group 6】

# 有關 *Concealment*「隱藏」的字群

**alias**〔'elɪəs〕1. *n.* 化名；別名　2. *adv.* 又名

── 1. assumed name

　　2. otherwise called; otherwise known as

Inspector Javert discovered that John Smith was not the mayor's real name but an ***alias*** for Jean Valjean, the ex-convict.

調查員傑佛特發現，約翰・史密斯不是市長的真名，而是前科犯吉恩・法耶的化名。

Jean Valjean, ***alias*** John Smith, was arrested by Inspector Javert.

吉恩・法耶，又名約翰・史密斯，被調查員傑佛特逮捕。

**enigma**〔ɪ'nɪgmə〕*n.* 謎；難題

── riddle; mystery; puzzling problem or person; puzzling statement

I have read the first homework problem several times but can't understand it. Maybe you can help me with this ***enigma***. 我把家庭作業第一題看了許多遍，還是不懂。也許你可以幫我解這個難題。

**lurk** 〔 lɜk 〕 *v.* 潛伏

—— be hidden; lie in ambush

General Braddock's troops, marching in columns, were easy
targets for the Indians *lurking* behind trees. 布雷達克將軍的軍隊以
縱隊方式前進，容易成為潛伏於樹後印地安人的目標。

**seclude** 〔 sɪ'klud 〕 *v.* 隔絕；隱居；躲藏

—— shut up apart from others; confine in a place hard to reach;
hide

To find a quiet place to study, Bruce had to *seclude* himself in the
attic. 布魯斯得躲在閣樓上，才能找到一個安靜的地方讀書。

**clandestine** 〔 klæn'dɛstɪn 〕 *adj.* 祕密的

—— carried on in secrecy and concealment; secret; concealed;
underhand

Before the Revolutionary War, an underground organization,
known as the Sons of Liberty, used to hold *clandestine* meetings
in Boston. 獨立戰爭以前，一個以自由之子為名的地下組織，常在波士
頓舉行祕密會議。

**latent** 〔'letn̩t 〕 *adj.* 潛在的

—— present but not showing itself; hidden but capable of being
brought to light; dormant; potential

A good education will help you discover and develop your *latent*
talents. 好的教育能幫你發現並發展潛在的才能。

**stealthy** 〔'stɛlθɪ 〕 *adj.* 隱密的；偷偷摸摸的；鬼鬼祟祟的

—— secret in action or character; sly

The burglar must have been very *stealthy* if he was able to get past
the two watchmen without being noticed.
能逃過兩個守夜者而不被發現，這小偷一定是非常隱密。

## 【Group 7】

# 有關 *Disclosure*「揭發」的字群

**avowal**〔ə'vauəl〕*n.* 公開宣稱；坦白承認
—— open acknowledgment; frank declaration; admission;
confession
The white flag of surrender is an ***avowal*** of defeat.
投降的白旗是公開宣稱戰敗。

**apprise**〔ə'praɪz〕*v.* 通知；告知
—— inform; notify
The magazine has ***apprised*** its readers of an increase in rates
beginning January 1. 這雜誌告知它的讀者，自一月一日起調漲費用。

**divulge**〔də'vʌldʒ〕*v.* 洩漏
—— make public; disclose; reveal; tell
I told my secret only to Margaret because I knew she would not
***divulge*** it. 我只把我的祕密告訴瑪格麗特，因爲我知道她不會洩漏。

**elicit**〔ɪ'lɪsɪt〕*v.* 引出；誘出
—— draw forth; bring out; evoke; extract
By questioning the witness, the attorney ***elicited*** the fact that it was
raining at the time of the accident.
律師藉由詢問目擊者，而引出事實是事故發生時正在下雨。

**enlighten**[6]〔ɪn'laɪtn̩〕*v.* 啓蒙；教導
—— shed the light of truth and knowledge upon; free from
ignorance; inform; instruct
The new student was going in the wrong direction until someone
***enlightened*** him that his room is at the other end of the hall.
這新學生走錯了方向，直到有人指點他，說他的房間是在走廊的另一端。

**manifest**[5] (ˈmænəˌfɛst ) 1. *v.* 顯示；表露　2. *adj.* 明顯的

—— 1. show; reveal; display

2. plain; clear; evident; not obscure; obvious

> 【記憶技巧】
>
> *mani* (hand) + *fest* (strike)
>
> ( 拍打雙手是一種表達 )

My art teacher told my parents that I have failed to *manifest* any interest in her subject.

美術老師告訴我父母親，對她的科目我顯示不出任何興趣。

It is now *manifest* that, if I do not do my work, I will fail the course. 現在很明顯的是，如果不用功，我這個課程就會不及格。

**overt** (ˈovɝt ) *adj.* 公然的

—— open to view; not hidden; public; manifest

The teacher didn't believe that Ned was annoying me until she saw him in the *overt* act of pulling my hair.

直到老師看見奈德公然扯我頭髮時，才相信他騷擾我。

## Exercise：選出正確答案

1. Do you understand Catherine? I don't. She is a complete _____ to me.

(A) alias　　　　　　　　(B) enigma

2. The witness _____ information not previously disclosed.

(A) divulged　　　　　　(B) apprised

3. The speaker's enigmatic remarks _____ the audience.

(A) enlightened　　　　　(B) confused

4. The companies were suspected of having entered into a(n) _____ agreement to fix prices.

(A) covert　　　　　　　(B) overt

5. A student's _____ talents sometimes show themselves when he participates in after-school clubs and activities.
  (A) manifest　　　　　　(B) latent

【解答】
1. B　　2. A　　3. B　　4. A　　5. B

【Group 8】

# 有關 *Agreement*「一致」的字群

**accord**[6] 〔 ə'kɔrd 〕 *n.* 一致；協調
—— agreement; harmony

【記憶技巧】
*ac* (to) + *cord* (heart) ( 做事符合心裡的想法，就是「一致」)

Though we are in *accord* on what
our goals should be, we differ on the means for achieving them.
雖然我們在目標上是一致的，但在達成的方法上卻不同。

**compact**[5] 〔 'kɑmpækt 〕 *n.* 協定
—— agreement; understanding; accord; covenant
The states bordering on the Delaware River have entered into a *compact* for the sharing of its water.
德拉威河鄰近的各州締結共用河水的協定。

**compromise**[5] 〔 'kɑmprə‚maɪz 〕 *n.* 妥協；和解
—— settlement reached by a partial yielding on both sides

【記憶技巧】
背這個字要先背 promise ( 承諾 )。

At first, the union and management
were far apart on wages, but they finally came to a *compromise*.
起初工會與資方對薪資的看法迥異，但他們終於達成和解。

**accede**〔æk'sid〕*v.* 同意

—— (usually followed by *to*) agree; assent; consent; acquiesce

When I asked my English teacher if I might change my topic, he readily *acceded* to my request.

當我問英文老師是否可以換題目時，他馬上同意我的要求。

**conform**[6]〔kən'fɔrm〕*v.* 遵守；追隨

—— be in agreement or harmony with; act in accordance with accepted standards or customs; comply

【記憶技巧】
*con* (together) + *form*
（形狀）（全部的形狀都
一樣，形成一致性）

When a new style in clothes appears, women usually hasten to *conform*. 新款式的服裝出現時，女士們經常迅速地追隨。

**correspond**[4]〔ˌkɔrə'spɑnd〕*v.* 通信；符合；相當於

—— be in harmony; match; fit; agree; be similar

The rank of second lieutenant in the Army *corresponds* to that of ensign in the Navy. 陸軍少尉的官階相當於海軍少尉。

【記憶技巧】
*cor* (together) + *respond*
(answer)（相互回信，即
「通信」）

**dovetail**〔'dʌvˌtel〕*v.* 密合；吻合

—— to fit together with, so as to form a harmonious whole; interlock with

Gilbert's skill as a writer *dovetailed* Sullivan's talent as a composer, resulting in the famous Gilbert and Sullivan operettas. 吉伯特寫作的技巧配合蘇利文作曲的才能，產生著名的吉伯特與蘇利文輕歌劇。

**reconcile**[6]〔'rɛkənˌsaɪl〕*v.* 使和解；調停

—— cause to be friendly again; bring back to harmony

【記憶技巧】
*re* (again) + *concile* (make friendly)（使兩人再度回復友好狀態，就是「使和解」）

After our quarrel, my brother and I refused to talk to each other until Mother *reconciled* us.
我跟弟弟發生口角後，直到母親調停才彼此說話。

**relent**〔rɪ'lɛnt〕*v.* 變寬容；變溫和

—— become less harsh, severe, or strict; soften in temper; yield

The Mayor has banned all lawn sprinkling because of the water shortage. However, if the reservoirs fill up, he may *relent* somewhat.
市長因缺水而禁止草地澆水。不過如果水庫填滿了，他可能會寬容一點。

**compatible**[6]〔kəm'pætəbḷ〕*adj.* 相容的
（↔ incompatible）

—— able to exist together harmoniously; in harmony

【記憶技巧】
*com* (together) + *pat* (suffer) + *ible* (*adj.*)
（能彼此容忍的）

Miss Evans knows that Arthur and I can't be on the same committee. We're not *compatible*.
伊凡斯小姐知道亞瑟跟我不能在同一個委員會裡。我們互不相容。

**consistent**[4]〔kən'sɪstənt〕*adj.* 前後一致的（↔ inconsistent）

—— keeping to the same principles throughout; showing no contradiction; in accord; compatible

By bringing up an unrelated matter you are not being *consistent* with your previous statement that we should stick to the topic.
你提出一件不相干的事，與你先前所說我們應堅守主題的聲明不一致。

## 【Group 9】

## 有關 *Disagreement*「不一致」的字群

**altercation**〔ˌɔltɚ'keʃən〕*n.* 爭吵

—— noisy, angry dispute; quarrel; wrangle

The teacher halted the *altercation* by separating the two opponents before they could come to blows.

老師在敵對的雙方未互毆前拉開他們，停止了爭吵。

**cleavage** (ˈklivɪdʒ ) *n.* 分歧

—— split; division

Our party hopes to repair the *cleavage* in its ranks so that it may present a united front in the coming elections. 我們政黨希望能補救各階層間的分歧，以求在即將來臨的選舉中呈現統一的陣線。

**discord** (ˈdɪskɔrd ) *n.* 不一致；不和；爭執 ( ↔ accord, harmony )
—— disagreement; conflict; dissension; strife

Billy Budd put an end to the *discord* aboard the *Rights-of-Man*. He was an excellent peacemaker.

比利・巴德結束人權號上的爭論。他是一位傑出的和事佬。

**discrepancy** ( dɪˈskrɛpənsɪ ) *n.* 矛盾；不符合
—— difference; disagreement; variation; inconsistency

Eighty students came to the dance but only seventy-four tickets were collected at the door. Can you account for this *discrepancy*?

八十位學生參加舞會，但是門口只收到七十四張票。你能解釋這不合之處嗎？

**friction**[6] (ˈfrɪkʃən ) *n.* 摩擦
—— conflict of ideas between persons or parties of opposing views; disagreement

> 【記憶技巧】
> *frict* (rub) + *ion* (n.)

At the budget hearing, there was considerable *friction* between the supporters and the opponents of higher taxes.

在預算聽證會上，增稅贊成者與反對者之間有相當大的摩擦。

## litigation 〔͵lɪtə'geʃən 〕 *n.* 訴訟

—— lawsuit; act or process of carrying on a lawsuit

Some business disputes can be settled out of court; others require *litigation*. 有些商業爭端可以庭外和解，有些則需提起訴訟。

## antagonize 〔 æn'tægə͵naɪz 〕 *v.* 使對立；引起⋯的反感

—— make an enemy of; arouse the hostility of

The official *antagonized* the leader of his own party by accusing him of cowardice.

那官員譴責自己黨內的領袖懦弱，而與之對立。

## dissent 〔 dɪ'sɛnt 〕 *v.* 反對

—— differ in opinion; disagree; object

The vote approving the amendment was far from unanimous; six members *dissented*.

贊同修正案的選票離全體一致的情形還遠得很；有六個成員反對。

## embroil 〔 ɛm'brɔɪl 〕 *v.* 使捲入（紛爭）

—— involve in conflict

Motorists who disregard traffic regulations eventually become *embroiled* with the law.

忽視交通規則的汽車駕駛人最後總會捲入法律紛爭。

## estrange 〔 ə'strendʒ 〕 *v.* 使疏遠

—— turn (someone) from affection to dislike or enmity; make unfriendly; separate; alienate

A quarrel over an inheritance *estranged* the brothers for many years. 有關繼承問題的爭論使他們兄弟疏遠了許多年。

## wrangle 〔'ræŋgl̩ 〕 *v.* 爭吵

—— quarrel noisily; dispute angrily; brawl; bicker

When I left, two neighbors were quarreling noisily. When I
returned an hour later, they were still *wrangling*.

我離開的時候，兩位鄰居吵得正兇。當我一小時後回去，他們還在吵。

## irreconcilable〔 ɪ'rɛkən,saɪləbl̩ 〕*adj.* 不能和解的；不相容的

—— unable to bring into friendly accord or understanding; hostile
beyond the possibility of reconciliation; not reconcilable

It is doubtful whether anyone can make peace between the
estranged partners; they have become *irreconcilable*.

是否有任何人能化解不和的股東們尚存疑；他們已經互不相容了。

## at variance〔 ət'vɛrɪəns 〕*adj.* 衝突的；不和的

—— in disagreement; at odds

Cynthia is an independent thinker. Her opinions are often *at
variance* with those of the rest of the class.

辛西亞是一個獨立的思考者。她的看法往往不同於班上其他人。

## Exercise：選出正確答案

1. The teacher did her best to ＿＿＿＿ the two friends who had
   quarreled, but without success.

   (A) reconcile　　　　　(B) alienate

2. If the express-train and the local-train schedules ＿＿＿＿, you
   can change trains without losing time.

   (A) relent　　　　　(B) dovetail

3. Both sides must give in a little. Otherwise there can be no
   ＿＿＿＿.

   (A) compact　　　　　(B) litigation

第
一
章

4. Our dog and cat get along without friction. They are _____.
   (A) compatible             (B) irreconcilable

5. There is no reason for you to _____ yourself in their altercation.
   (A) embroil                 (B) acquiesce

> 【解答】
>
> 1. A    2. B    3. A    4. A    5. A

## 【Group 10】

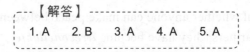

### 有關 *Eating*「吃」的字群

**condiment**〔ˈkɑndəmənt〕*n.* 調味料

—— something (such as pepper or spices) added to or served with food to enhance its flavor; seasoning

There is a shelf in our kitchen for pepper, salt, mustard, ketchup, and other *condiments*.

廚房裡有個擺胡椒、鹽、芥末、蕃茄醬,及其他調味料的架子。

**glutton**〔ˈglʌtṇ〕*n.* 貪吃者

—— greedy eater; person in the habit of eating too much

I had a second helping and would have taken a third except that I didn't want to be considered a *glutton*.

我吃了兩份,要不是不願被看成貪吃者,我會叫第三份。

**devour**[5]〔dɪˈvaʊr〕*v.* 狼吞虎嚥

—— eat up greedily; feast upon like an animal or a glutton

> 【記憶技巧】
>
> *de* (down) + *vour* (swallow)(把東西直接吞下去,就是「狼吞虎嚥」)

The hikers were so hungry that they *devoured* the hamburgers as fast as they were served.

健行者們餓得很，以致於漢堡一來，就開始狼吞虎嚥。

## slake〔slek〕*v.* 解（渴）

—— (with reference to thirst) bring to an end through refreshing drink; satisfy; quench

On a sultry afternoon you may find a long line of people at the drinking fountain, waiting to *slake* their thirst.

在悶熱的下午，你可以發現飲水機旁排了一行等著解渴的人。

## edible⁶〔'ɛdəbḷ〕*adj.* 可食用的

—— fit for human consumption; eatable; nonpoisonous

> 【記憶技巧】
> *ed* (eat) + *ible* (*adj.*)

Never eat wild mushrooms even though they look *edible*. They may be poisonous.

即使野生蘑菇看似可以吃，也絕對不要吃。它們可能有毒。

## luscious〔'lʌʃəs〕*adj.* 美味的；甘美多汁的

—— delicious; juicy and sweet

The watermelon was very *luscious*. Everyone wanted another slice. 西瓜很可口。每個人都想再來一片。

## palatable〔'pælətəbḷ〕*adj.* 美味的；可口的；怡人的 ( ↔ unpalatable )

—— agreeable to the taste; pleasing; savory

The main dish had little flavor, but I made it *palatable* by adding condiments. 主菜沒什麼味道，不過我加了調味料使它美味可口。

## succulent〔'sʌkjələnt〕*adj.* 多水分的；鮮美多汁的

—— full of juice; juicy

The steak will be dry if you leave it in the oven any longer. Take it out now if you want it to be *succulent*. 牛排在烤箱裡擺太久汁液會乾掉。如果你想要汁多味美的牛排，現在就把它拿出來。

**voracious** 〔 vo'reʃəs 〕 *adj.* 貪吃的；狼吞虎嚥的

—— having a huge appetite; greedy in eating; gluttonous

John would not be overweight if he were not such a *voracious* eater. 約翰如果不這麼貪吃的話，就不會超重了。

Exercise：選出正確答案

1. Mother put garlic on the shopping list because she needs it to
   _____ the roast.
   (A) slake          (B) season

2. Please leave some of that pie for the rest of us. Don't be
   _____.
   (A) gluttonous      (B) luscious

3. These oranges are not too succulent. They have too much
   _____.
   (A) pulp           (B) juice

4. We always have plenty of food on hand when my uncle comes
   for dinner. He has a(n) _____ appetite.
   (A) inedible       (B) voracious

5. Some customers prefer their food served _____ so that they
   may add condiments themselves.
   (A) palatable      (B) unseasoned

【解答】
1. B    2. A    3. A    4. B    5. B

# 【Group 11】

## 有關 *Size, Quantity*「大小；數量」的字群

**gamut**〔'gæmət〕*n.* 整個範圍；全部

—— entire range of anything from one extreme to another

After the test I thought at first I had done very well, then quite well, and finally, poorly. I ran the *gamut* from confidence to despair. 考試後起初我想自己考得很好，後來認為不錯，最後是差勁。我經歷了從自信到失望的全部歷程。

**iota**〔aɪ'otə〕*n.* 些微

—— (ninth and smallest letter of the Greek alphabet) very small quantity; infinitesimal amount; bit

If you make the same mistake again, despite all my warnings, I will not have one *iota* of sympathy for you.
如果你不顧我的警告，再犯同樣的錯誤，我就會一點也不同情你。

**magnitude**[6]〔'mægnə,tjud〕*n.* 重要；大小；【地震】震級

—— size; greatness; largeness; importance

Shopping for clothes can be a small matter for some, but a problem of the greatest *magnitude* for others.

> 【記憶技巧】
> *-itude* 表抽象名詞的字尾。

逛街買衣服對某些人而言是小事，但對某些人來說，卻是最重要的問題。

**pittance**〔'pɪtn̩s〕*n.* 微薄的薪水；少量

—— meager wage or allowance; small amount

At those low wages, few will apply for the job. Who wants to work for a *pittance*?
很少人會去申請那個低薪的工作。誰會想為微薄的薪水工作？

**superabundance** 〔͵supərə'bʌndəns 〕 *n.* 過多；極多

—— surplus; excess; great abundance

Our committee doesn't need any more help. We have a
*superabundance* of helpers.

我們的委員會不需要任何更多的協助。我們有太多的幫手。

**inflate** 〔 ɪn'flet 〕*v.* 使膨脹；使充氣

—— expand; puffs; well with air or gas

Since the football has lost air, we shall need a pump to *inflate* it.

這個橄欖球氣漏了，我們需要一個打氣筒灌脹它。

**colossal** 〔 kə'lɑsḷ 〕*adj.* 巨大的

—— huge; enormous; gigantic; mammoth; vast

The game will be played in a *colossal* sports arena with a seating
capacity of more than 60,000.

這場球賽將在一個可容納六萬多人的巨型運動場舉行。

**commodious** 〔 kə'modɪəs 〕*adj.* 寬敞的

—— spacious and comfortable; roomy; ample; not confining

Even during change of classes there is no crowding because the
halls and stairways are *commodious*.

即使在換教室的時候也不擁擠，因為走廊跟樓梯都很寬敞。

**infinite**[5] 〔'ɪnfənɪt 〕*adj.* 無限的

—— without ends or limits; boundless;
endless; inexhaustible

> 【記憶技巧】
> *in* (not) + *fin* (end) +
> *ite* (*adj.*)（沒有終點
> 的，就是「無限的」）

In our science lesson tomorrow we shall consider whether space
is bounded or *infinite*.

在明天的科學課，我們將思考太空是有限還是無限的。

## infinitesimal 〔͵ɪnfɪnə'tɛsəml̩ 〕*adj.* 微小的

—— so small as to be almost nothing; immeasurably small; very minute

If there is any salt in this soup, it must be *infinitesimal*. I can't taste it. 如果湯裡有鹽的話，一定很少，我吃不出味道來。

## inordinate 〔 ɪn'ɔrdn̩ɪt 〕*adj.* 過度的；過分的

—— much too great; not kept within reasonable bounds; excessive; immoderate

Frank kept my book for such an *inordinate* length of time that I shall never lend him anything again.
法蘭克借我的書太久了，我再也不會借他任何東西。

## picayune 〔͵pɪkə'jun 〕*adj.* 微小的

—— concerned with trifling matters; petty; small; of little value

The trouble with your studying is that you spend too much time on *picayune* details and not enough on the really important matters.
你讀書的問題是花太多時間在小細節上，眞正重要的事情，所花的時間卻不夠多。

## puny 〔'pjunɪ 〕*adj.* 微不足道的

—— slight or inferior in size, power, or importance; weak; insignificant

The skyscraper dwarfs the surrounding buildings. By comparison to it, they seem *puny*.
這摩天大樓使周圍的建築物顯得矮小。比較之下，它們顯得微不足道。

### Exercise：選出正確答案

1. A lavish spender can run the _____ from affluence to indigence in no time at all.

   (A) magnitude           (B) gamut

2. This _____ sofa can accommodate four people comfortably.
   (A) commodious　　　　　　(B) puny

3. We could have had several more guests for dinner. There was a _____ of food.
   (A) pittance　　　　　　　(B) superabundance

4. The spare tire needs to be _____ a bit. It has too much air.
   (A) deflated　　　　　　　(B) inflated

5. Though we were told to keep our reports within reasonable bounds, one student turned in a report of _____ length — thirty pages!
   (A) infinitesimal　　　　　(B) inordinate

```
【解答】
1. B    2. A    3. B    4. A    5. B
```

## 【Group 12】

## 有關 *Weakness*「衰弱」的字群

**infirmity**〔ɪnˈfɝmətɪ〕*n.* 虛弱

—— weakness; feebleness; frailty

On leaving the hospital, the patient felt almost too weak to walk, but he soon overcame this *infirmity*.
離開醫院時，病人覺得虛弱得幾乎走不動，但他很快就克服了虛弱。

**debilitate**〔dɪˈbɪləˌtet〕*v.* 使虛弱（↔ invigorate）

—— impair the strength of; enfeeble; weaken

The patient had been so *debilitated* by the fever that he lacked the strength to sit up.
這病人因發燒而一直很虛弱，以致於連坐起來的力氣都沒有。

**enervate** (ˈɛnɚˌvet ) *v.* 使無力
—— lessen the vigor or strength of; weaken; enfeeble
*Enervated* by the heat, we rested under a shady tree until our strength was restored.
熱得沒力時我們坐在一棵陰涼的樹下休息，直到力氣恢復爲止。

**incapacitate** (ˌɪnkəˈpæsəˌtet ) *v.* 使不能
—— render incapable or unfit; disable
Ruth will be absent today. She is *incapacitated* by a sore throat.
露絲今天將缺席。喉嚨痛使她不能出席。

**decadent** ( dɪˈkedənt ) *adj.* 墮落的；頹廢的；衰微的
( ↔ flourishing )
—— marked by decay or decline; falling off; declining; deteriorating
When industry moves away, a flourishing town may quickly become *decadent.* 當工業移走時，一個繁榮的城鎮可能很快就會衰微。

**decrepit** ( dɪˈkrɛpɪt ) *adj.* 老弱的 ( ↔ sturdy ) ；破舊的
—— broken down or weakened by old age or use; worn out
Bill rode past the street on a horse that looked *decrepit* and about to collapse. 比爾騎著一匹看起來旣老弱又快倒了的馬經過街上。

**dilapidated** ( dəˈlæpəˌdetɪd ) *adj.* 破舊的；快要倒塌的
—— decayed; falling to pieces; partly ruined or decayed through neglect
Up the road was an abandoned farmhouse, partially in ruins, and near it a barn, even more *dilapidated.* 沿那條路走下去，有一間部分毀壞的廢棄農舍，而農舍附近有一個穀倉，荒廢得更厲害。

**flimsy** 〔'flɪmzɪ 〕 *adj.* 薄弱的；脆弱的

—— lacking strength or solidity; frail; unsubstantial

Judy understands algebra well, but I have only a *flimsy* grasp of the subject. 茱蒂精通代數，但我對這個科目的理解卻很薄弱。

**frail**[6] 〔 frel 〕 *adj.* 虛弱的（↔ robust ）

—— not very strong; weak; fragile

To be an astronaut, you must be in robust health. It is not an occupation for a *frail* person.

要成爲太空人，必須身體強壯健康。虛弱的人不適合這個行業。

## 【 Group 13 】

# 有關 *Strength*「強壯」的字群

**bulwark** 〔'bʊlwək 〕 *n.* 堡壘；保障

—— wall-like defensive structure; rampart; defense; protection; safeguard

For centuries the British regarded their navy as their principal *bulwark* against invasion.

幾個世紀以來，英國認爲他們的海軍是抵禦侵略的主要堡壘。

**citadel** 〔'sɪtədḷ 〕 *n.* 城堡；堡壘；要塞

—— fortress; stronghold

The fortified city of Singapore was once considered unconquerable. In 1942, however, this *citadel* fell to the Japanese.

人們一度認爲新加坡這個設防的城市是無法征服的，然而在一九四二年，這個要塞卻落入了日本之手。

**forte**[4] 〔 fort , for'te 〕 *n.* 專長

—— strong point; that which one does with excellence

I am better than Jack in English but not in math; that is his *forte*.

我的英文比傑克強，但數學就不一樣了；那是他的專長。

**vigor**[5] 〔ˈvɪgɚ 〕 *n.* 精力；活力

—— active strength or force; strength; force; energy

【記憶技巧】
*vig* (lively) + *or* (*n.*)
（表現得很活潑的樣子，表示充滿「活力」）

The robust young pitcher performed with his usual *vigor* for seven innings, but he weakened in the eighth and was removed from the game. 那位強健的年輕投手以他常有的精力表現了七局，但八局時他力氣減弱並且被換了下來。

**invigorate** 〔 ɪnˈvɪgəˌret 〕 *v.* 使精力充沛；使增添活力

—— give vigor to; fill with life and energy; animate; strengthen

If you feel enervated by the heat, try a swim in the cool ocean. It will *invigorate* you.

如果你熱得感到無力，試著在涼爽的海水中游泳，它將增添你的活力。

**cogent** 〔ˈkodʒənt 〕 *adj.* 有說服力的；強而有力的

—— convincing; forcible; compelling; powerful

Excuses for not handing work in on time vary. Some are flimsy, as, for example, "I left it at home." Others are more *cogent*, such as a physician's note. 不按時交作業的理由不盡相同，有些比較薄弱，如：「我放在家裡。」有些則較有說服力，例如一張醫生證明。

**dynamic**[4] 〔 daɪˈnæmɪk 〕 *adj.* 充滿活力的；有力的

—— energetic; active; forceful

【記憶技巧】
*dynam* (power) + *ic* (*adj.*)

If you elect Jessica, you may be sure she will present our views forcefully and energetically. She is a very *dynamic* speaker.

如果選潔西卡，你能確定她可以強而有力地表達我們的觀點，因為她是一位很有活力的演說者。

第
一
章

## formidable⁶ (ˋfɔrmɪdəb!) *adj.* 可怕的；難以對付的

—— exciting fear by reason of strength, size, difficulty, etc.; hard to overcome; to be dreaded

【記憶技巧】
分音節背
for-mi-da-ble。

Our hopes for an easy victory sank when our opponents took the field. They were much taller and huskier, and they looked *formidable*.

當對手一出賽時，我們輕鬆得勝的希望就降低了，他們高壯很多，而且看起來不好對付。

## impregnable (ɪmˋprɛgnəb!) *adj.* 牢不可破的；堅固的

—— incapable of being taken by assault; unconquerable; invincible

Before World War II, the French regarded their Maginot Line as an *impregnable* bulwark against a German invasion.

二次大戰前，法國人認爲他們的馬其諾防線是對付德國侵略的堅固堡壘。

## robust⁵ (roˋbʌst) *adj.* 強壯的 ( ↔ frail, feeble )

—— strong and healthy; vigorous; sturdy; sound

The lifeguard was in excellent physical condition. I had never seen anyone more *robust*.

那個救生員的身體狀況良好，我不曾看過任何比他更強壯的人。

## tenacious (tɪˋneʃəs) *adj.* 緊握不放的；固執的；頑強的

—— holding fast or tending to hold fast; not yielding; stubborn; strong

After the dog got the ball, I tried to dislodge it from her *tenacious* jaws, but I couldn't.

那隻狗拿到球後，我試圖把球從牠緊咬不放的口中取下，但是卻辦不到。

## vehement (ˋviəmənt) *adj.* 激烈的；強烈的

—— showing strong feeling; forceful; violent; furious

Your protest was too mild.  If it had been more *vehement*, the dealer might have paid attention to it.

你的抗議太溫和了，如果當時你能再激烈點，業者可能就會注意。

## Exercise：選出正確答案

1. It will not be easy to defeat the faculty players.  They are certainly not _____.
   (A) decrepit  (B) formidable

2. Eddie was quite _____ until the age of 12, but then he developed into a robust youth.
   (A) vigorous  (B) frail

3. I strongly doubt that you can beat me in handball.  That happens to be my _____.
   (A) forte  (B) bulwark

4. A sprained ankle may render you unfit for physical activities for several weeks, but a fractured ankle will _____ you for a much longer time.
   (A) invigorate  (B) incapacitate

5. Laziness, luxury, and a lack of initiative are characteristics of a _____ society.
   (A) vehement  (B) decadent

【解答】
1. A　　2. B　　3. A　　4. B　　5. B

## 【Group 14】

# 有關 *Neglect*「忽視」的字群

**default**〔dɪ'fɔlt〕1. *n.* 未履行；疏忽；棄權　2. *v.* 拖欠；缺席

—— 1. failure to do something required; neglect; negligence
2. fail to pay or appear when due

The Royals must be on the playing field by 4 p.m. If they do not appear, they will lose the game by *default.* 皇家隊必須在下午四點前到達比賽場地，如果他們逾時不到，將因棄權而輸掉這場比賽。

The finance company took away Mr. Lee's car when he *defaulted* on the payments. 李先生無法付款時，融資公司就拿走他的車。

**ignore**[2]〔ɪg'nor〕*v.* 忽視

—— refuse to take notice of; disregard; overlook

【記憶技巧】
*i* (not) + *gnore* (know)（當作不知道，就是「忽視」）

The motorist was given a ticket for *ignoring* a stop sign.

那位汽車駕駛人因無視於停車標誌，而被開了一張罰單。

**neglect**[4]〔nɪ'glɛkt〕1. *v.* 忽略；不顧　2. *n.* 疏忽；怠慢

—— 1. give little attention to; leave undone; disregard
2. lack of proper care or attention; disregard; negligence

【記憶技巧】
*neg* (deny) + *lect* (select)（不願做選擇，就是「忽略」）

Some of the students in the play *neglected* their studies during rehearsals, but after the performance they caught up quickly.

某些參加戲劇表演的學生排演時置課業於不顧，不過在演出後他們又即時趕上。

For leaving his post, the guard was charged with *neglect* of duty.

這位守衛因離開崗位而被控怠忽職責。

**heedless** 〔'hidlɪs 〕*adj.* 不注意的（↔ heedful, attentive）

—— not taking heed; inattentive; careless; thoughtless; unmindful; reckless

Before his injury, Mike used to jump from the stairs, *heedless* of the "No Jumping" sign. Now he pays attention to it. 受傷前，麥克總是從樓梯上跳下來，不在意「不准跳躍」的標誌。現在他會注意了。

**inadvertent** 〔ˌɪnəd'vɝtn̩t 〕*adj.* 不小心的；非故意的

—— (used to describe blunders, mistakes, etc., rather than people) heedless; thoughtless; careless

Unfortunately, I made an *inadvertent* remark about Irma's failure while she was present. 艾瑪在場時很不巧我輕率地提及她的失敗。

**remiss** 〔 rɪ'mɪs 〕*adj.* 疏忽的；不小心的（↔ scrupulous）

—— negligent; careless; lax

The owner of the stolen car was himself *remiss*. He left the keys in the vehicle. 是被竊的車主自己的疏忽，因為他把鑰匙留在車上。

**slovenly** 〔'slʌvənlɪ 〕*adj.* 邋遢的；不整潔的（↔ neat, tidy）

—— negligent of neatness or order in one's dress, habits, work, etc.; slipshod; sloppy

You would not expect anyone so neat in her personal appearance to be *slovenly* in her housekeeping. 你無法想像一個外表如此整齊的人，會在她的家務事上如此懶散邋遢。

## 【Group 15】

## 有關 *Care*「謹慎」的字群

**solicitude** 〔 sə'lɪsəˌtjud 〕*n.* 焦慮

—— anxious or excessive care; concern; anxiety

My brother's *solicitude* for his girlfriend ended when he learned that she was faking her injury.

我弟弟對於他女朋友的焦慮，在他得知她假裝受傷時結束。

## vigilance〔ˈvɪdʒələns〕*n.* 警戒

—— alert watchfulness to discover and avoid danger; alertness; caution; watchfulness

The night watchman who apprehended the thief was praised for his *vigilance*.

抓到小偷的那位夜警因他的警戒而受到讚揚。

## heed[5]〔hid〕*v.* 注意；留心

—— take notice of; give careful attention to; mind

Our teacher said that we might have a test, but I didn't *heed* her. That's why I was unprepared.

老師說我們可能有一次考試，但我沒注意她，這就是我沒準備的原因。

## scrutinize〔ˈskrutn̩‚aɪz〕*v.* 細察

—— examine closely; inspect

The guard at the gate *scrutinized* Harvey's pass before letting him in, but he just glanced at mine.

門口的守衛細察了哈維的通行證後才讓他進去，但是他只瞄了一下我的。

## discreet[6]〔dɪˈskrit〕*adj.* 謹慎的
　　( ↔ indiscreet )

—— showing good judgment in speech and action; wisely cautious

> 【記憶技巧】
> discreet 中間有兩個 e，就是每件事情要檢查 ( examine ) 兩遍，所以是「謹慎的」)

You were *discreet* not to say anything about our plans when Harry was here. He can't keep a secret. 哈利在這裡時你很謹慎，沒提及任何有關於我們計畫的事。他是不能保密的人。

**meticulous**〔 məˈtɪkjələs 〕*adj.* 嚴謹的;極注意細節的

—— extremely or excessively careful about small details; fussy

Before signing a contract, one should read it carefully, including the fine print. This is one case where it pays to be *meticulous.* 簽合約前,必須仔細地讀一讀,包括附屬細則在內,這是一件值得慎重的事。

**scrupulous**〔ˈskrupjələs 〕*adj.* 審慎的

( ↔ unscrupulous, remiss )

—— having painstaking regard for what is right; conscientious; strict; precise

Mr. Brooks refused to be a judge because his wife's niece is a contestant. He is very *scrupulous.* 布魯克斯先生拒絕當裁判,因為他太太的姪子是參賽者之一,他非常的審慎。

**wary**[5]〔ˈwɛrɪ , ˈwærɪ , ˈwerɪ 〕*adj.* 小心提防的;謹慎的

( ↔ foolhardy )

—— on one's guard against danger, deception, etc.; cautious; vigilant

General Braddock might not have been defeated if he had been *wary* of an ambush. 如果布雷達克將軍留心埋伏,他就不會被擊敗。

### Exercise:選出正確答案

1. For months before the arrest, the police had the criminal's activities under constant _____.

   (A) solicitude              (B) scrutiny

2. When Mother scolded Laura for the _____ appearance of her room, she promised to make it more tidy.

   (A) slovenly                (B) meticulous

第
一
章

3. If you _____ my advice, you will have no trouble.

(A) heed                      (B) ignore

4. The attorney warned my aunt that, if she failed to appear in court, she would lose the case by _____.

(A) vigilance             (B) default

5. Deborah is _____ about returning books to the library on time. She has never had to pay a late fine.

(A) scrupulous           (B) remiss

---

【解答】

1. B    2. A    3. A    4. B    5. A

---

## 【Group 16】

# 有關 *Residence*「居住」的字群

**denizen** (ˈdɛnəzn̩ ) *n.* 居民;棲息者

—— inhabitant; dweller; resident; occupant

On their safari, the hunters stalked lions, tigers, and other ferocious *denizens* of the jungle. 在狩獵旅行時,獵人們偷偷走近獅子、老虎,及其他叢林裡凶猛的棲息者。

**domicile** (ˈdɑməsl̩ , -saɪl ) *n.* 住所;家

—— house; home; dwelling; residence; abode

The announcement read: "The Coopers have moved and invite you to visit them at their new *domicile*, 22 Apple Street."

那告示上寫著:「庫柏一家人已搬離,邀請你至新居拜訪他們,蘋果街二十二號。」

**inmate**〔ˈɪnmet〕*n.* 入獄者；住院者

── person confined in an institution, prison, hospital, etc.

When the warden took charge, the prison had fewer than 100 *inmates*. 這典獄長接管時，監牢裡的犯人不及一百人。

**native**[3]〔ˈnetɪv〕1. *n.* 本地人；生於（某地）的人（↔ alien）
2. *adj.* 原產的（↔ foreign）

── 1. person born in a particular place
　　 2. born or originating in a particular place

The entire Russo family are *natives* of New Jersey except the grandparents, who were born in Italy.
所有羅素家成員，除生於義大利的祖父母外，都生於紐澤西。

Tobacco, potatoes, and tomatoes are *native* American plants that were introduced into Europe by explorers returning from the New World. 煙草、馬鈴薯及蕃茄，都是從新大陸歸來的探險者引進歐洲，原產於美洲的植物。

**nomad**〔ˈnomæd, ˈnɑmæd〕*n.* 遊牧民族

── member of a tribe that has no fixed abode
　　 but wanders from place to place; wanderer

*Nomads* have no fixed homes but move from region to region to secure their food supply. 遊牧民族居無定所，而是由一個地區移至另一個地區，以取得他們食物的補給。

**sojourn**〔ˈsodʒɝn〕*n.* 寄居；逗留

── temporary stay

On her trip home, Jane will stop in St. Louis for a two-day *sojourn* with relatives.
在回家的旅途上，珍會在聖路易寄居親戚家兩天。

**commute**⁵〔kə'mjut〕*v.* 通勤;定期往返

—— travel back and forth daily, as from a home in the suburbs to a job in the city

Hundreds of thousands of suburban residents regularly *commute* to the city. 數十萬郊區居民定期往返於城市與郊區間。

**migrate**⁶〔'maɪgret〕*v.* 1.(隨季節變化而)遷移 2.移居

—— 1. move from one place to another with the change of season
2. move from one place to settle in another

In winter, many European birds *migrate* to the British Isles in search of a more temperate climate.
許多歐洲的鳥類在冬天會遷移至不列顛群島,尋找更溫和的氣候。
Because they were persecuted in England, the Puritans *migrated* to Holland. 因為清教徒在英國遭受迫害,他們便移居荷蘭。

**nomadic**〔no'mædɪk〕*adj.* 游牧的;流浪的

—— roaming from place to place; wandering; roving

Most of the Indians of the North American plains are *nomadic*.
北美平原上的印地安人大多居無定所。

**abroad**²〔ə'brɔd〕*adv.* 到國外;在國外

—— in or to a foreign land or lands

After living *abroad* for a time, Robert became homesick for his native land.
在國外住一段時間後,羅伯特開始想念故土。

**Exercise**:選出正確答案

1. Many Northerners _____ to Florida in the winter.

   (A) migrate                (B) commute

2. On arriving in our country, most _____ have a strong desire
to learn English.
   (A) denizens          (B) immigrants

3. If you are affluent, you can have a summer residence in the
country as well as a permanent _____ in the city.
   (A) sojourn          (B) domicile

4. These are not _____ melons; they are shipped from abroad.
   (A) native          (B) foreign

5. The regulations permit _____ to receive visitors on
Wednesdays and Sundays.
   (A) nomads          (B) inmates

> 【解答】
> 1. A    2. B    3. B    4. A    5. B

## 【Group 17】

## 有關 *Disobedience*「違抗」的字群

**defiance**〔dɪ'faɪəns〕*n.* 違抗

—— refusal to obey authority; disposition to resist; state of
opposition

The union showed *defiance* of the court order against a strike by
calling the workers off their jobs.

工會叫工人停職，以示對法庭禁止罷工命令的違抗。

**infraction**〔ɪn'frækʃən〕*n.* 違反

—— breaking (of a law, regulation, etc.); violation; breach

Parking at the bus stop is illegal. Motorists committing this *infraction* are heavily fined.

在公車站停車是違法的，違規的汽車駕駛人將被嚴重罰款。

## insurgent〔 ɪn'sɜdʒənt 〕 *n.* 叛亂者；暴動者

—— rebel

When the revolt broke out, the government ordered its troops to arrest the *insurgents*.

叛變發生時，政府下令軍隊逮捕暴民。

## insurrection〔͵ɪnsə'rɛkʃən 〕 *n.* 叛亂；造反

—— uprising against established authority; rebellion; revolt

The *insurrection* was easily suppressed, with less than a dozen being slain on both sides.

那次叛亂很快被平定，雙方死亡人數不到十二人。

## malcontent〔'mælkən͵tɛnt 〕 *n.* 不滿者；反叛者

—— discontented person; rebel

The work stoppage was caused by a few *malcontents* who felt they had been ignored when the promotions were made.

罷工是由一些認為升遷時被忽視了的不滿者引起的。

## sedition〔 sɪ'dɪʃən 〕 *n.* 煽動叛亂

—— speech, writing, or action seeking to overthrow the government

The author of the pamphlet advocating the overthrow of the government was arrested for *sedition*.

那本倡導推翻政府小冊子的作者因煽動叛亂被逮捕。

## transgress〔 træns'grɛs 〕 *v.* 踰越；違反

—— go beyond set limits of; violate; break; overstep

Jack's previous record showed he had been an obedient student
and had never *transgressed* school regulations.

傑克先前的紀錄顯示，他一直是個順從的學生，從不違反校規。

**trespass**[6]〔'trɛspəs〕*v.* 侵入

—— encroach on another's rights,
privileges, property, etc.

The owner erected a "Keep Off"
sign to discourage strangers from *trespassing* on his land.

所有者豎起一個「請勿靠近」的告示，以防止陌生人侵入他的土地。

**insubordinate**〔ˌɪnsə'bɔrdn̩ɪt〕*adj.* 不順從的；反抗的

—— not submitting to authority; disobedient; mutinous; rebellious

Do as Mother says. If you are *insubordinate*, Father will probably
hear of it.

照母親說的去做，如果你不順從的話，父親可能會知道。

**perverse**〔pəˈvɝs〕*adj.* 任性的；倔強的

—— obstinate (in opposing what is right or reasonable); willful;
wayward

Though I had carefully explained the shorter route to him, the
*perverse* youngster came by the longer way.

雖然我仔細地跟他解說過較短的路線，那任性的年輕人還是走較長的那條
路來。

## 【Group 18】

# 有關 *Obedience*「順從」的字群

**allegiance**〔ə'lidʒəns〕*n.* 忠誠

—— loyalty; devotion; faithfulness; fidelity

Every school day, millions of children pledge "*allegiance* to the flag of the United States of America and to the republic for which it stands."

每個上學日,數百萬兒童宣誓「效忠美國國旗和它代表的合眾國」。

## acquiesce 〔͵ækwɪˋɛs 〕 *v.* 默許;默認;勉強同意

—— (used with *in*) accept by keeping silent; submit quietly; comply

Though I wasn't enthusiastic about Tom's plan to go fishing, I *acquiesced* in it because there seemed nothing else to do. 雖然我不熱衷湯姆釣魚的計畫,但是我勉強同意了,因爲似乎沒什麼別的事做。

## defer 〔 dɪˋfɝ 〕 *v.* 順從

—— yield to another out of respect; authority, courtesy; submit politely

Husbands as a rule do not decide on the colors of home furnishings but *defer* to their wives in these matters.

丈夫一般都不決定傢俱的顏色,而在這些事上順從他們的妻子。

## discipline[4] 〔ˋdɪsəplɪn 〕 *v.* 訓練

—— train in obedience; bring under control

Mr. Walker, who had been told that he was getting a *disciplined* class, was surprised to find it unruly.

別人告訴華克先生他將帶個訓練有素的班級,他很驚訝地發現它難控制。

## submit[5] 〔 səbˋmɪt 〕 *v.* 屈服 ( ↔ resist, withstand )

—— yield to another's will, authority, or power; yield; surrender

Though he boasted he would never be taken alive, the outlaw *submitted* without a struggle when the police arrived. 雖然這歹徒誇口絕不會被活捉,但是警察來的時候,他毫不反抗就屈服了。

第一章

**docile** (ˈdɑsḷ, ˈdɑsɪl) *adj.* 溫順的；聽話的
—— tractable; submissive; easily taught; obedient
Dan is easy to teach, but his brother is not so *docile*.
丹很容易教，但是他的弟弟就沒這麼溫順了。

**meek** ( mik ) *adj.* 溫順的（↔ arrogant）
—— submissive; yielding without resentment when ordered about or hurt by others; acquiescent
Only two of the girls protested when they were ordered off the field. The rest were too *meek* to complain.
那些女孩被判離場時，只有其中兩個人提出抗議，其餘的太溫順而不會抱怨。

**pliable** (ˈplaɪəbḷ) *adj.* 易受影響的；柔順的（↔ obstinate）
—— easily bent or influenced; yielding; adaptable
We tried to get Joe to change his mind, but he was not *pliable*. Perhaps you can influence him.
我們試著要喬改變主意，但是他不容易受影響。或許你可以影響他。

**tractable** (ˈtræktəbḷ) *adj.* 易駕馭的（↔ intractable, unruly）
—— easily controlled, led, or taught; docile
For his cabinet, the dictator wanted *tractable* men. Therefore, he appointed no one whom he could not control.
這獨裁者想要用易駕馭的人來組成他的內閣，因此他沒有任命任何他無法控制的人。

Exercise：選出正確答案

1. The lad was disciplined for being ＿＿＿＿ when speaking to his elders.
   (A) meek             (B) arrogant

第
一
章

2. Mrs. Farrell often leaves her children in my care because they
   are very _____ with me.

   (A) intractable           (B) docile

3. The insurgents have been ordered to yield, but they will not
   _____.

   (A) submit              (B) transgress

4. When I asked my sister to turn down her radio, she made it even
   louder. I couldn't understand why she was so _____.

   (A) pliable             (B) perverse

5. If a neighbor asks you to stop playing the piano after 10 p.m.,
   you should, as a matter of courtesy, _____ his wishes.

   (A) trespass on        (B) defer to

【解答】

1. B     2. B     3. A     4. B     5. B

【Group 19】

# 有關 *Time*「時間」的字群

**dawdle**〔ˈdɔdḷ〕*v.* 浪費時間；磨蹭；閒蕩

—— waste time; loiter; idle

My sister *dawdles* over the dishes. Mother gets them done without
wasting time.

我妹妹洗起盤子來慢吞吞的，母親則一點時間也不浪費就可以做好了。

**procrastinate**〔proˈkræstəˌnet〕*v.* 拖延；耽擱

( ↔ incessant, continuous )

—— put off things that should be done until later; defer; postpone

Most of the picnickers took cover when rain seemed imminent.
The few that *procrastinated* got drenched.

大部份野餐者在雨快下之前就躲了起來，少數耽擱者則淋成落湯雞。

## protract〔 pro'trækt 〕*v.* 延長（↔ curtail）

—— draw out; lengthen in time; prolong; continue; extend

We had planned to stay only for lunch but, at our host's insistence,
we *protracted* our visit until after dinner. 我們原本計劃只留下來吃午
餐，但在主人堅持下，又把我們的造訪延長至晚餐後。

## chronic[6]〔'krɑnɪk 〕*adj.* 1. 慢性的　2. 習慣性的

—— 1. marked by long duration and
　　frequent recurrence
　　2. having a characteristic, habit,
　　disease, etc., for a long time;
　　confirmed; habitual

【記憶技巧】
*chron* (time) + *ic* (*adj.*)
（持續長時間的，表示此
病是「慢性的」）

Carl's sore arm is not a new development but the return of a
*chronic* ailment.
卡爾手臂的疼痛並非新傷，而是慢性病的復發。

Rhoda is a *chronic* complainer. She is always dissatisfied.
蘿達的抱怨是習慣性的，她老是不滿。

## concurrent〔 kən'kɜənt 〕*adj.* 同時的

—— occurring at the same time; simultaneous

When the strike is settled, there will probably be an increase in
wages and a *concurrent* increase in prices.
罷工事件解決後，可能會經常加薪，同時物價也會上漲。

## imminent〔'ɪmənənt 〕*adj.* 迫近的

—— about to happen; threatening to occur soon; near at hand

By the sudden darkening of the skies and the thunder in the distance, we could tell that rain was *imminent*.

天色突然變暗再加上遠處的雷聲，我們知道快下雨了。

**incipient**〔 ɪn'sɪpɪənt 〕 *adj.* 開始的；初期的

—— beginning to show itself; commencing; in an early stage; initial

Certain serious diseases can be successfully treated if detected in an *incipient* stage.

某些嚴重的疾病如果早期發現，就可以成功地治療。

**intermittent**〔 ˌɪntə'mɪtṇt 〕 *adj.* 間歇的

—— coming and going at intervals; stopping and beginning again; recurrent; periodic

There were intervals when the sun broke through the clouds, because the showers were *intermittent*.

因爲陣雨是間歇下的，所以有時陽光可破雲而出。

**perennial**〔 pə'rɛnɪəl 〕 *adj.* 1. 永久的　2. 多年生的 ( ↔ annual )

—— 1. lasting indefinitely; incessant; enduring; permanent; constant; perpetual; everlasting

　　2. (of plants) continuing to live from year to year

Don't think that war has plagued only our times. It has been a *perennial* curse of man.

別認爲戰爭只折磨我們這一時代，它已成爲人類永久的禍害。

Some grasses last only a year. Others are *perennial*.

有些草只生長一年，有些則是多年生的。

**sporadic**〔 spo'rædɪk , spɔ- 〕 *adj.* 零星的

—— occurring occasionally or in scattered instances; isolated; infrequent

Though polio has practically been wiped out, there have been *sporadic* cases of the disease.

雖然小兒麻痺症實際上已徹底消除，但仍有零星的病例。

## Exercise：選出正確答案

1. That child is perverse. If you politely ask him to finish his telephone conversation, he will only _____ it.
   (A) curtail
   (B) protract

2. There are two excellent television programs scheduled tonight, but I can see only one of them because they are _____.
   (A) concurrent
   (B) imminent

3. If public utilities were to provide _____ service, the people would not stand for it.
   (A) continuous
   (B) intermittent

4. Hay fever is a(n) _____ sickness that affects millions of sufferers at certain times each year, particularly in June and September.
   (A) incipient
   (B) chronic

5. The complaints, _____ at first, have become quite frequent.
   (A) sporadic
   (B) incessant

【解答】
1. B    2. A    3. B    4. B    5. A

第
一
章

## 【Group 20】

# 有關 *Necessity*「需要」的字群

**essence**[6]〔ˈɛsn̩s〕*n.* 本質；精髓

—— most necessary or significant part, aspect, or feature; fundamental natural; core

【記憶技巧】
*ess* (to be) + *ence* (*n.*)
（存在的東西，即「本質」）

The union and management held a lengthy meeting without getting to the *essence* of the men's dissatisfaction —— low wages.
工會與資方召開漫長的會議，卻無法觸及工人不滿的核心——低薪。

**prerequisite**〔priˈrɛkwəzɪt〕*n.* 先決條件

—— something required beforehand

A mark of at least 75% in Basic Art is a *prerequisite* for Advanced Art. 基礎藝術得分在七十五分以上，是進修高等藝術的先決條件。

**entail**〔ɪnˈtel, ɛn-〕*v.* 需要

—— involve as a necessary consequence; impose; require

Can your family afford the extra expense that a larger apartment *entails*? 你的家庭負擔得起較大公寓所需的額外費用嗎？

**necessitate**〔nəˈsɛsəˌtet〕*v.* 使成為必要；需要

—— make necessary; require; demand

Mr. Brown told Ellen that her refusal to work *necessitates* his sending for her parents.
布朗先生告訴艾倫，因為她拒絕工作，使他必須派人去請她的父母來。

**oblige**[6]〔əˈblaɪdʒ〕*v.* 使有義務；使不得不

—— put under a duty or obligation; compel; force

If your friend were in trouble, wouldn't you feel *obliged* to go to his help? 如果朋友有困難，你不覺得有義務幫他忙嗎？

**obviate**〔ˊɑbvɪˌet〕*v.* 使不必要；排除

—— make unnecessary; preclude

Helen has agreed to lend me the book I need. This *obviates* my trip to the library. 海倫同意把我要的書借我，這使我不必跑圖書館。

**compulsory**〔kəmˊpʌlsərɪ〕*adj.* 義務的；強制性的

—— required by authority; obligatory

State law makes attendance at school *compulsory* for children of certain ages. 州法律規定到達一定年齡的小孩都有義務上學。

**gratuitous**〔grəˊtjuətəs〕*adj.* 不必要的；無理由的

—— uncalled for; unwarranted

Were it not for your *gratuitous* interference, the children would have quickly settled their dispute.
要不是你多餘的干涉，孩子們很快就會停止爭論。

**imperative**⁶〔ɪmˊpɛrɑtɪv〕*adj.* 必須的；緊急的

—— not to be avoided; necessary; obligatory; compulsory; urgent

If you have failed a subject you need for graduation, it is *imperative* that you go to summer school.
如果有一個必修科目不及格，你就必須去上暑期學校。

**incumbent**〔ɪnˊkʌmbənt〕*adj.* 使負有義務的

—— (with *on* or *upon*) imposed as a duty; obligatory

Dan felt it *incumbent* on him to pay for the window, since he had hit the ball that broke it.
丹覺得他有義務賠償這片玻璃，因為是他打球弄破的。

第
一
章

## indispensable [ˌɪndɪˈspɛnsəbḷ ]

*adj.* 不可或缺的 ( ↔ dispensable )

—— absolutely necessary; essential

We can do without luxuries and entertainment. However, food, shelter, and clothing are *indispensable*.

我們可以不要奢侈品及娛樂，但是食物、住所，及衣物，卻是不可或缺的。

## pressing [ˈprɛsɪŋ ] *adj.* 緊急的

—— requiring immediate attention; urgent

Before preparing for tomorrow's party, I have some more *pressing* matters to attend to, such as finishing my report.

在為明天的宴會做準備之前，我有一些更緊急的事情得辦，如完成報告。

## superfluous [ suˈpɝfluəs , sə- ] *adj.* 多餘的；過多的

—— more than what is enough or necessary; surplus; excessive; unnecessary

Since we already have enough food for the picnic, please don't bring any because it will only be *superfluous*.

我們野餐所需的食物已足夠了，請別帶任何東西來，因為那只會是多餘的。

Exercise：選出正確答案

1. Since our truck is small, we cannot take any _____ items.

   (A) obligatory          (B) dispensable

2. Remember that the visitors are our guests. It is _____ us to show them courtesy and respect.

   (A) gratuitous to        (B) incumbent on

3. To _____ the need to read the marks to the class, the teacher posted them on the bulletin board.

    (A) obviate             (B) entail

4. Fay tried to explain our plan but omitted the most significant part, so that I had to supply the _____.

    (A) essence             (B) prerequisite

5. The other team wanted our key man, but we couldn't let him go because he is _____.

    (A) superfluous         (B) indispensable

> 【解答】
> 1. B　　2. B　　3. A　　4. A　　5. B

# REVIEW ★

## Exercise 1：選出正確答案

(　) 1. Earl has always favored a Senior Dance; on that point he has never been _____.

    (A) consistent         (B) inconsistent

(　) 2. The food is served _____. You have to add the condiments yourself.

    (A) unseasoned        (B) seasoned

(　) 3. In my conversation with Lester, I _____ the information that he was born in Chicago.

    (A) divulged          (B) elicited

( ) 4. I was _____ by the first paragraph. Its meaning is quite manifest.

(A) enlightened (B) confused

( ) 5. There is little hope of _____ because our ideas on the main issues do not correspond.

(A) harmony (B) discord

( ) 6. Before Carol antagonized Margaret at the meeting, they had never been _____.

(A) at variance (B) in accord

( ) 7. It is quite _____ to find the house; it is in a secluded spot.

(A) easy (B) difficult

( ) 8. There has been much friction between the partners. As a result, they have become _____.

(A) alienated (B) reconciled

( ) 9. By _____ these rules, you are placing your entire future in jeopardy.

(A) heeding (B) ignoring

( ) 10. Kenneth, who was worried that he had failed the test, was the only one who got 100%. His _____, as you see, was entirely unnecessary.

(A) solicitude (B) vigilance

( ) 11. The petunia is not a(n) _____ plant because it lives only for one season.

(A) native (B) incumbent

(C) perennial (D) adaptable

(　) 12. Though everyone else has nearly finished, Fred has not yet started his report.　He is still _____.
(A) meek　　　　　　　　　(B) dawdling
(C) acquiescing　　　　　　(D) submissive

(　) 13. Lester was a(n) _____ child at home, but his teacher did not find him _____.
(A) obstinate…pliable
(B) rebellious…insubordinate
(C) submissive…disobedient
(D) intractable…docile

(　) 14. On a Detroit assembly line, you can see the whole gamut of automobile production from _____ to _____ stages.
(A) early…incipient　　　　(B) temporary…permanent
(C) imminent…final　　　　(D) initial…final

(　) 15. It is more difficult for a(n) _____ smoker to give up the habit than for a novice, but it can be done.
(A) affluent　　　　　　　(B) confirmed
(C) beginning　　　　　　　(D) disciplined

(　) 16. King George III considered the Declaration of Independence an act of _____.
(A) allegiance　　　　　　(B) authority
(C) sedition　　　　　　　(D) accord

(　) 17. Millie's mother is driving us to school, _____ the need for us to wait for the bus in the rain.
(A) necessitating　　　　　(B) obviating
(C) entailing　　　　　　　(D) protracting

( ) 18. According to the terms of the _____, the insurgents are
to be pardoned if they _____ their weapons.
(A) cleavage...surrender (B) compact...retain
(C) covenant...yield (D) exploit...return

( ) 19. The principal _____ the student for his _____
behavior.
(A) rebuked...defiant (B) reprimanded...vigilant
(C) commended...willful (D) censured...vigilant

( ) 20. The cruise has been planned to allow passengers a two-day
_____ on the island of Nassau.
(A) breach (B) sojourn
(C) altercation (D) abode

Exercise 2：下列各題中，選出與斜體字意義最相近的答案。

( ) 1. mild *seasoning*
(A) disagreement (B) weather
(C) temperature (D) condiment

( ) 2. *unrelenting* fury
(A) forgiving (B) unhurried
(C) unyielding (D) momentary

( ) 3. costly *litigation*
(A) treaty (B) lawsuit
(C) compromise (D) cleaving

( ) 4. *dissenting* opinion
(A) harsh (B) disagreeing
(C) foolish (D) hasty

( 　) 5. *stealthy* manner

　　　(A) sly　　　　(B) rude　　　(C) stylish　　(D) courteous

( 　) 6. *savory* dish

　　　(A) tasteless　(B) fragile　　(C) frugal　　(D) palatable

( 　) 7. frequently *at odds*

　　　(A) strange　　　　　　　(B) rash

　　　(C) at rest　　　　　　　(D) at variance

( 　) 8. *sumptuous* feast

　　　(A) luscious　　　　　　(B) lavish

　　　(C) succulent　　　　　　(D) refreshing

( 　) 9. widespread *dissension*

　　　(A) discord　　　　　　　(B) discussion

　　　(C) circulation　　　　　(D) accord

( 　) 10. never *apprised*

　　　(A) acknowledged　　　(B) informed

　　　(C) divulged　　　　　　(D) incensed

( 　) 11. *recurrent* absence

　　　(A) unusual　　　　　　(B) periodic

　　　(C) prolonged　　　　　(D) necessary

( 　) 12. *nomadic* life

　　　(A) native　　　　　　　(B) permanent

　　　(C) mutinous　　　　　　(D) roving

( 　) 13. *chronic* truant

　　　(A) defiant　　　　　　(B) potential

　　　(C) habitual　　　　　　(D) undisciplined

(   ) 14. frequent *transgressor*
    (A) violator    (B) commuter  (C) migrant    (D) traveler

(   ) 15. questionable *allegiance*
    (A) disloyalty  (B) sedition    (C) judgment  (D) fidelity

(   ) 16. temporary *abode*
    (A) home             (B) sojourn
    (C) breach          (D) occupation

(   ) 17. *procrastinating* manner
    (A) insolent         (B) postponing
    (C) compliant      (D) perverse

(   ) 18. *sporadic* outbreaks
    (A) perennial  (B) unruly     (C) frequent    (D) isolated

(   ) 19. serious *infraction*
    (A) revolt           (B) devotion
    (C) violation       (D) discrepancy

(   ) 20. *pressing* reasons
    (A) obstinate      (B) urgent
    (C) gratuitous    (D) superfluous

Exercise 3：下列各題中，選出意義與其他三者無關的答案。

(   ) 1. (A) bulwark    (B) defense   (C) rampart   (D) forte

(   ) 2. (A) miniature        (B) picayune
    (C) superfluous     (D) diminutive

(   ) 3. (A) robust         (B) commodious
    (C) sturdy         (D) vigorous

（　）4. (A) horde　　(B) multitude　　(C) swarm　　(D) iota

（　）5. (A) fussy　　　　　　　(B) slipshod

　　　　(C) slovenly　　　　　 (D) untidy

（　）6. (A) credible　　　　　 (B) heedless

　　　　(C) convincing　　　　 (D) cogent

（　）7. (A) tenacious　　　　　(B) weak

　　　　(C) unsubstantial　　　 (D) flimsy

（　）8. (A) gigantic　　　　　 (B) mammoth

　　　　(C) colossal　　　　　 (D) infinitesimal

（　）9. (A) decadence　　　　　(B) watchfulness

　　　　(C) vigilance　　　　　(D) alertness

（　）10. (A) unconquerable　　　(B) invincible

　　　　(C) impregnable　　　　(D) infallible

## Exercise 4：在下列空格中填入最適當的字。

1. The patient's hospital and medical bills, amounting to several thousand dollars, were covered by insurance. Otherwise, he would have been _____.

2. A student who is talented in one subject may have little or no _____ in another.

3. Two seniors _____ a monitor into letting them use the side exit, but they were stopped outside by a teacher.

4. If my savings are not enough for my college expenses, I shall need _____ assistance.

5. The Academy Award statuette known as an "Oscar" is the prize most _____ by movie stars.

6. The first year Mrs. Michaels had her gift shop, she lost money. Since then, however, she has developed it into a(n) _____ business.

7. Our nation's highest award for _____ is the Congressional Medal of Honor.

8. Since the matter is important, let's take time to think. We need a(n) _____ decision, not a rash one.

9. Imagine the _____ of that thief! He tried to commit a robbery directly across the street from police headquarters!

10. If you paid $130 for that camera, you were _____. I saw it in a department store for $50.

---

【解答】

Ex 1.　1. B　2. A　3. B　4. A　5. A　6. A　7. B　8. A
　　　　9. B　10. A　11. C　12. B　13. B　14. D　15. B　16. C
　　　　17. B　18. C　19. A　20. B

Ex 2.　1. D　2. C　3. B　4. B　5. A　6. D　7. D　8. B
　　　　9. A　10. B　11. B　12. D　13. C　14. A　15. D　16. A
　　　　17. B　18. D　19. C　20. B

Ex 3.　1. D　2. C　3. B　4. D　5. A　6. B　7. A　8. D
　　　　9. A　10. D

Ex 4.　1. impoverished　　2. aptitude　　　3. bullied
　　　　4. pecuniary　　　　5. coveted　　　　6. lucrative
　　　　7. valor　　　　　　8. deliberate　　9. audacity
　　　　10. fleeced

# 第二章
# 認識希臘字根以增加字彙

源於希臘文的英文字彙相當豐富，而且還在增加中。這些字有的是日常生活經常使用的，例如 authentic, chronological, economical, homogeneous 等，有的則用於專門的領域。或許你曾聽過醫藥方面的術語 antibiotic, orthopedic, pediatrician；科學方面的術語 astronaut, protoplasm, thermonuclear；政治方面的 autonomous, demagogue, protocol。

這些重要單字和本章列舉的單字，都是由希臘字根構成的。一旦你認得了一個特定的字根，就容易了解源自這字根的字的意義。例如你知道 **PAN, PANTO** 的意思是 complete 或 all，就很快了解 panacea 是「萬靈藥」，用於各種疾病，panorama 則是「全景」，pantomime「啞劇」，是全用手勢而不說話的表演。

以下是二十個希臘字根，請背下它們的意思，以便在碰到含此類字根的單字時，能夠迅速反應。

## 【Group 1】

## Aut, Auto — *self*「自己」

Group 1～20

**autobiography**[4]〔͵ɔtəbaɪˋɑgrəfɪ〕

*n.* 自傳

—— story of a person's life written by the person himself

【記憶技巧】

***auto*** (self) + ***bio*** (life) + ***graph*** (write) + ***y*** (*n.*)

（寫關於自己一生的書，也就是「自傳」）

In her *autobiography The Story of My Life*, Helen Keller tells how
unruly she was as a young child.

海倫・凱勒在她的自傳「我的一生」中，描述孩童時她如何的任性。

**autocrat** 〔'ɔtəˌkræt 〕 *n.* 獨裁者

—— ruler exercising self-derived, absolute power; despot

The *autocrat* was replaced by a ruler responsible to the people.

那獨裁者被一位對人民負責的統治者取代了。

**autograph**[6] 〔'ɔtəˌgræf 〕 *n.* 親筆簽名

—— person's signature written by
himself

> 【記憶技巧】
> *auto* (self) + *graph* (write)

The baseball star wrote his *autograph* for an admirer who came up
to him with a pencil and scorecard.

那棒球明星為一位帶著鉛筆及他身高體重卡片的球迷簽名。

**automation** 〔ˌɔtə'meʃən 〕 *n.* 自動化；自動操縱

—— technique of making a process self-operating by means of
built-in electronic controls

Many workers have lost their jobs as a result of *automation*.

許多工人由於自動化而失去工作。

**automaton** 〔 ɔ'tɑməˌtɑn , -tən 〕 *n.* 機器人

—— (literally, "self-acting thing") purely mechanical person
following a routine; robot

An autocrat prefers his subjects to be *automatons*, rather than
intelligent human beings.

獨裁者希望他的人民都是機器人，而不是聰明人。

**autonomy**[6] 〔 ɔ'tɑnəmɪ 〕 *n.* 自治權

—— right of self-government

> 【記憶技巧】
> *auto* (self) + *nomy* (law)

After World War II, many colonies were granted *autonomy* and became independent nations.

二次大戰後，許多殖民地獲得自治權，成爲獨立的國家。

### **autopsy** 〔'ɔtəpsɪ, 'ɔtɑpsɪ〕 *n.* 驗屍

—— (literally, "a seeing for one's self") medical examination of a dead body to determine the cause of death; postmortem examination

The cause of the actor's sudden death will not be known until the *autopsy* has been performed.

直到驗屍後，才能知道這位演員突然死亡的原因。

### **authentic**[6] 〔ɔ'θɛntɪk〕 *adj.* 眞正的；可靠的

—— (literally, "from the master himself") genuine; real; reliable; trustworthy

【記憶技巧】
*aut* (self) + *hent* (doer) + *ic* (adj.)（自己親手做的，就是「眞正的」）

When you withdraw money, the bank compares your signature with the one in its files to see if it is *authentic*. 你提款時，銀行會拿你的簽名與其檔案裡的做比較，以查對那是不是眞跡。

### **automatic**[3] 〔ˌɔtə'mætɪk〕 *adj.* 自動的

—— acting by itself; self-regulating

【記憶技巧】
*auto* (self) + *mat* (think) + *ic* (adj.)（可以自己動腦去想的，就是「自動的」）

You do not have to defrost this refrigerator because it is equipped with an *automatic* defroster.

你不必替這個冰箱除霜，因爲它配有自動除霜器。

### **autonomous** 〔ɔ'tɑnəməs〕 *adj.* 自治的；有自主權的

—— self-governing; independent

The Alumni Association is not under the control of the school. It is a completely *autonomous* group.

校友會不在學校的控制之下，它是一個完全有自主權的團體。

第二章

Exercise：請由 **Group 1** 中，選出最適當的字，填入空格中。

1. Some of the members want to censure the president for ignoring the club's constitution and behaving like an _____.

2. You are behaving like an _____ if you act mechanically without using your intelligence.

3. The distinguished scientist left the writing of his life story to others, for he had neither the time nor the desire to write an

   _____.

4. Elevator operators are not employed in buildings equipped with _____ elevators.

5. In the past, colonial peoples who asked for _____ were usually told that they were not ready to govern themselves.

> 【解答】
> 1. autocrat    2. automaton    3. autobiography
> 4. automatic   5. autonomy

## 【Group 2】

# Cracy —— *government*「政府；政體」

**aristocracy**〔͵ærə'stɑkrəsɪ 〕*n.* 1. 貴族政治；貴族統治的國家

　2. 貴族

—— 1. (literally, "government by the best") government, or country governed, by a small privileged upper class

　 2. ruling class of nobles; nobility; privileged class

Before 1789, France was an *aristocracy*.

法國在 1789 年以前是一個由貴族統治的國家。

When the Revolution of 1789 began, many members of the French *aristocracy* fled to other lands. 1789 年革命開始時，許多貴族逃往外國。

**autocracy** 〔 ɔ'tɑkrəsɪ 〕 *n.* 獨裁政治；獨裁國家

—— government, or country governed, by one individual with self-derived, unlimited power

Germany under Adolf Hitler was an *autocracy*.

阿道夫‧希特勒控制下的德國是一個獨裁國家。

Adolf Hitler

**bureaucracy**[6] 〔 bjʊ'rɑkrəsɪ 〕 *n.* 官僚政治

—— government by bureaus or groups of officials

> 【記憶技巧】
> *bureau* (office) + *cracy* (rule)

The Mayor was criticized for setting up an inefficient *bureaucracy* unresponsive to the needs of the people.

市長因設立了一個無能、不顧人民需求的官僚政治而受到批評。

**democracy**[3] 〔 də'mɑkrəsɪ 〕 *n.* 民主政治；民主政體；民主國家

—— government, or country governed, by the people; ruled by the majority

> 【記憶技巧】
> *demo* (people) + *cracy* (rule)（由人民來管理，就是「民主」）

France helped the Thirteen Colonies establish the first New World *democracy*.

法國幫助十三個殖民地建立新大陸第一個民主政體。

**plutocracy** 〔 plu'tɑkrəsɪ 〕 *n.* 富豪政治

—— government, or country governed, by the rich

If only millionaires can afford to run for office, we shall quickly become a *plutocracy*.

如果只有百萬富翁才負擔得起公職的競選，我們將很快變成富豪政治。

**technocracy** 〔 tɛk'nɑkrəsɪ 〕 *n.* 科技專家政治；技術主義國家

—— government, or country governed, by technical experts

Many are opposed to a *technocracy* because they do not wish to be ruled by technical experts.

許多人反對科技專家政治，因為他們不想被科技專家們控制。

"crat" 這個形式置於字尾，指「某種政府型態的支持者」、「某一集團的成員」；如果字母大寫時，則指「某一政黨的成員」。

## aristocrat 〔 ə'rɪstə‚kræt , 'ærɪstə‚kræt 〕 *n.* 1. 貴族  2. 主張貴族政治者

—— 1. member of the aristocracy; nobleman
   2. advocate of aristocracy

Winston Churchill was born an *aristocrat*; he was the son of Sir Randolph Churchill.

溫斯頓・邱吉爾一生下來就是貴族，因為他是藍道夫・邱吉爾爵士之子。

An *aristocrat* would like to see noblemen in control of the government.

主張貴族政治者會想要看到貴族控制政府。

## Democrat[5] 〔'dɛmə‚kræt 〕 *n.* 民主黨黨員

—— member of the Democratic Party

The Senator used to be a Republican but is now a *Democrat*.

這位參議員以前是共和黨黨員，但現在是民主黨黨員。

Exercise：請由 **Group 2** 中，選出最適當的字，填入空格中。

1. It was most unusual for a member of the _____ to marry someone who did not belong to the nobility.

2. If you believe that only the affluent are fit to govern, you must be a(n) _____.

3. In a(n) _____, the ruler has absolute and unlimited power.

第二章

4. How can you call yourself a(n) _____ if you do not believe in majority rule?

5. In a(n) _____, the governing class would consist largely of scientists and other experts.

--- 【解答】 -----------------------------
1. aristocracy    2. plutocracy    3. autocracy
4. democrat       5. technocracy

## 【Group 3】

## Dem, Demo — *people*「人民」

**demagogue**〔ˈdɛməˌɡɔɡ〕*n.* 蠱惑民心的政客；群眾煽動家
—— political leader who stirs up the people for personal advantage; rabble rouser

No responsible leader, only a *demagogue*, would tell the people that, if elected, he will solve all their problems.

沒有任何負責的領袖，只有蠱惑民心的政客會告訴人民，如果選上了，他將解決他們所有的問題。

**epidemic**[6]〔ˌɛpəˈdɛmɪk〕1. *n.* 傳染病　2. *adj.* 流行的
—— (literally, "among the people")
　　1. outbreak of a disease affecting many people at the same time
　　2. affecting many people in an area at the same time; widespread

> 【記憶技巧】
> *epi* (among) + *dem* (people) + *ic* ( 會在民眾之間互相感染，即「傳染病」)

The high rate of absence in the lower grades last spring was caused by the measles *epidemic*.

去年春天低年級學生的高缺席率是痲疹傳染病所引起的。

Federal aid was granted to the depressed area where
unemployment had risen to *epidemic* proportions.
聯邦的補助金被允許撥到失業狀況普遍流行的蕭條地區。

## democratize〔 dəˈmɑkrə‚taɪz 〕*v.* 使民主化

—— make democratic

The adoption of the 19th Amendment, giving women the franchise
to vote, greatly *democratized* the United States.
給予婦女選舉權的第十九修正案實行後，使美國大大地民主化。

## democratic³〔‚dɛməˈkrætɪk 〕*adj.* 民主的

—— based on the principles of democracy, or government by the
   people

A nation cannot be considered *democratic* unless its leaders are
chosen by the people in free elections.
除非一個國家的領袖是在自由選舉中由人民選出來的，要不然就不是一個
民主政體。

Exercise：請由 **Group 3** 中，選出最適當的字，填入空格中。

1. Millions of people died in the 14th century as the result of a(n)
   _____ known as the Black Death.

2. The election was _____ because some people voted more
   than once and others were prevented from voting.

3. An intelligent voter can distinguish the unselfish political
   leader from the _____.

4. To _____ the country, a new constitution was drawn up,
   giving equal rights to all segments of the population.

5. It is more _____ for a governor to be chosen by the people than to be appointed by the king.

---
【解答】
1. epidemic       2. undemocratic       3. demagogue
4. democratize       5. democratic
---

## 【Group 4】

# Pan, Panto — *complete*「全部」

**panacea**〔ˌpænəˈsiə, -ˈsɪə〕*n.* 萬靈丹

—— remedy for all ills; cure-all; universal remedy

Panacea

A two-week vacation is wonderful for fatigue but will not cure baldness or improve vision. It is no *panacea.* 兩星期的假期對疲憊恢復很有效，可是卻不能治療禿頭或改進視力，它並非萬靈丹。

**pandemonium**〔ˌpændɪˈmonɪəm, -ˈmonjəm〕*n.* 大混亂；群魔殿；地獄

—— (literally, "abode of all the demons," i.e., hell) wild uproar; very noisy din; wild disorder

The huge crowds in Times Square grew noisier as the old year ticked away, and when midnight struck there was *pandemonium.* 隨著舊的一年逐漸地消逝，時代廣場上洶湧的人潮越來越嘈雜，當半夜十二點一到時，簡直是亂成一片。

**panoply**〔ˈpænəplaɪ〕*n.* 全副盔甲；全套裝配

—— complete suit of armor; complete covering or equipment

The opposing knights, mounted and in full *panoply*, awaited the signal for the tournament to begin.

對方的騎士全部武裝並騎上馬，等待比武大會開始的信號。

第二章

**panorama** 〔ˌpænəˈræmə, -ˈrɑmə 〕 *n.* 全景

—— complete, unobstructed view

The top of the Empire State Building affords an excellent *panorama* of New York City and the surrounding area.

帝國大廈頂樓提供了一個俯瞰紐約市及其周圍地區全景的良好場所。

**pantomime** 〔ˈpæntəˌmaɪm 〕 *n.* 默劇

—— dramatic performance that is all signs and gestures without words

Not until *The Great Dictator* did Charlie Chaplin play a speaking part. All his previous roles were in *pantomime*.

查理・卓別林直到演出「大獨裁」一片時才開口說話，他以前都是演默劇。

Charlie Chaplin

**Pan-American** 〔ˈpænəˈmɛrəkən 〕 *adj.* 汎美洲的

—— of or pertaining to all the countries of North, South, and Central America

The *Pan-American* Highway links all of the countries of the Western Hemisphere from Alaska to Chile.

汎美公路連接從阿拉斯加到智利所有西半球的國家。

Exercise：請由 **Group 4** 中，選出最適當的字，填入空格中。

1. When Jackson scored the tie-breaking goal with five seconds left to play, _____ broke out.

2. Many regard education as the _____ that will cure all of society's ills.

3. The top of 3605-foot Mt. Snow in Vermont offers a fine _____ of the Green Mountains.

4. In a _____, the actors express themselves only by facial expressions, bodily movements, and gestures.

5. The warship's guns provided a _____ of protective fire to cover the landing of the marines.

---
【解答】
1. pandemonium 　 2. panacea 　 3. panorama
4. pantomime 　 5. panoply
---

## 【Group 5】

# Chron, Chrono — *time*「時間」

**anachronism**〔ə'nækrə,nɪzm̩〕*n.* 年代的錯誤

—— error in chronology or time order

It is an *anachronism* to say that William Shakespeare "typed" his manuscripts.

如果說威廉‧莎士比亞「用打字機打」他的手稿，那就犯了年代上的錯誤。

---
【記憶技巧】
*ana* (against) + *chron* (time) + *ism* (*n.*)（違反時間，即是「年代的錯誤」）
---

**chronicle**〔'krɑnɪkl̩〕*n.* 編年史

—— historical account of events in the order of time; history; annals

One of the earliest accounts of King Arthur occurs in a 12th-century *chronicle* of the kings of Britain.

有關亞瑟王最早的記載之一，發現於十二世紀的英國國王編年史中。

**chronology**〔krə'nɑlədʒɪ〕*n.* 年表；年代紀；（事件的）年代順序

—— arrangement of data or events in order of time of occurrence

Bruce named all the Presidents, but he made an error in *chronology* when he placed Ulysses S. Grant after Abraham Lincoln, instead of after Andrew Johnson.

布魯斯把所有總統的名字說出來，不過他把尤里西斯・辛普森・格蘭特放在亞伯拉罕・林肯之後，而非在安德魯・強森之後，犯了年代上的錯誤。

## chronological〔͵krɑnə'lɑdʒɪkḷ〕 *adj.* 按時間前後順序的

—— arranged in order of time

The magazines in this file are not in *chronological* order. I found the February issue after the October one. 這個檔案箱裡的雜誌沒照時間前後順序排，我在十月份雜誌後看到二月份的。

## synchronize〔'sɪŋkrə͵naɪz , 'sɪn-〕 *v.* 使顯示同一時間；使同步

—— cause to agree in time; make simultaneous

The clocks in the library need to be *synchronized*; one is a minute and a half behind the other. 圖書館內的時鐘需要調整到同一時刻。有一個鐘比另外一個慢了一分半鐘。

Exercise：請由 **Group 5** 中，選出最適當的字，填入空格中。

1. Can you list the events leading to World War II in their correct _____?

2. To speak of the ancient Greeks as using machine guns or cannon at the siege of Troy is a(n) _____.

3. The film begins near the climax and then goes back to the hero's childhood, violating the usual _____ order.

4. The townspeople used to _____ their timepieces with the clock outside the village bank.

5. The current World Almanac is a(n) _____ of last year's events.

## 【Group 6】

# Mania — *madness*「瘋狂」

**kleptomania**〔͵klɛptə'menɪə〕*n.* 竊盜狂；偷竊癖

—— insane impulse to steal

The millionaire who was caught shoplifting was found to be suffering from *kleptomania*.

那個因逛街時順手牽羊而被捉到的百萬富翁，被發現是竊盜狂。

**mania**〔'menɪə〕*n.* 1. 瘋狂　2. 熱衷

—— 1. madness; insanity

　　 2. excessive fondness; craze

For a student with an A average to quit school two months before graduation is sheer *mania*.

一個平均甲等的學生會在畢業前兩個月離開學校，實在是瘋狂。

Though I am still fond of stamp collecting, I no longer have the *mania* for it that I originally had.

雖然我還是喜歡集郵，但已經不像最初那麼熱衷了。

**maniac**〔'menɪ͵æk〕*n.* 瘋子

—— raving lunatic; madman; insane person

maniac

The deranged behavior of John's brother leaves little doubt that he is a *maniac*. 約翰的弟弟發狂似的行為證明了他簡直就是瘋子。

**pyromania** 〔͵paɪrəˈmenɪə 〕 *n.* 縱火狂

—— insane impulse to set fires

The person arrested for setting the fire had been suspected of *pyromania* on two previous occasions.

那位因縱火被捕的人，先前有過兩次縱火的嫌疑。

**maniacal** 〔 məˈnaɪəkl̩ 〕 *adj.* 發瘋的

—— characterized by madness; insane; raving

The customer protested in such a loud, violent, and *maniacal* manner that onlookers thought he had lost his sanity.

那位顧客如此大聲、激烈，發瘋似地抗議著，旁觀者還以為他神智不清了。

＊ 在字尾的 maniac 表示「有某種發狂衝動的人；發狂者」。

如 kleptomaniac「有竊盜狂者」，pyromaniac「有縱火狂者」。

Exercise：請由 **Group 6** 中，選出最適當的字，填入空格中。

1. The weird _____ shrieks and groans coming from the house led us to believe that a madman lived there.

2. My sister has a _____ for chocolates; she will finish a whole box in no time at all if not restrained.

3. A person who can't help taking things belonging to others is a _____.

4. Officials believe the recent series of small fires to be the work of a _____.

5. The spoiled child raved like a _____ when he didn't get his way.

【解答】
1. maniacal　　2. mania　　3. kleptomaniac
4. pyromaniac　5. maniac

## 【Group 7】

# Ped — *child*「小孩」

**encyclopedia**[6]〔ɪnˌsaɪklə'pidɪə〕*n.* 百科全書
—— (literally, "well-rounded rearing of a child") work offering alphabetically arranged information on various branches of knowledge

【記憶技巧】
***en*** (in) + ***cyclo*** (circle) + ***pedia*** (education)（包含所有學問的書，即為「百科全書」）

There are four different *encyclopedias* in the reference section of our school library. 我們學校圖書館裡的參考室有四種不同的百科全書。

**orthopedic**〔ˌɔrθə'pidɪk〕*adj.* 整形外科的
—— (literally, "of the straight child") having to do with *orthopedics*, the science dealing with the correction and prevention of deformities, especially in children

Patients recovering from broken limbs are housed in the hospital's *orthopedic* ward.
傷斷手腳而正在康復中的病人，會被安置在整形外科的病房中。

**pedagogue**〔'pɛdəˌgɑg , -ˌgɔg〕*n.* 教師
—— (literally, "leader of a child") teacher of children; schoolmaster

A new teacher usually receives a great deal of help from the more experienced *pedagogues*.
新老師通常能從更有經驗的教師那裡獲得很多的幫助。

**pedagogy** (ˈpɛdəˌgodʒɪ , -ˌgadʒɪ ) *n.* 教育學；教育方法

—— art of teaching

Mr. Brown's lessons are usually excellent. He is a master of
*pedagogy*. 布朗先生的課經常都上得很好，他是教育學的碩士。

**pediatrician** (ˌpidɪəˈtrɪʃən , ˌpɛdɪ- ) *n.* 小兒科醫生

—— physician specializing in the treatment of babies and children

When the baby developed a fever, Mother telephoned the
*pediatrician*. 當嬰兒發燒時，母親會打電話給小兒科醫生。

**pediatrics** (ˌpidɪˈætrɪks , ˌpɛdɪ- ) *n.* 小兒科；小兒醫學

—— branch of medicine dealing with the care, development, and
    diseases of babies and children

From the number of baby carriages outside his office, you can tell
that Dr. Enders specializes in *pediatrics*.
從診所外載嬰兒來看病的車數上看來，你就可以知道恩德斯醫師多麼精通
於小兒醫學了。

Exercise：請由 **Group 7** 中，選出最適當的字，填入空格中。

1. _____ deals with diseases that afflict the young.

2. Charlotte doesn't have to go to the library as often as I because
   she has a twenty-two volume _____ at home.

3. A teacher's professional training includes several courses in

   _____.

4. Until he was six months, the baby was taken to the _____
   every month.

5. The operation to correct the deformity was performed by a(n)
_____ specialist.

【解答】

1. Pediatrics    2. encyclopedia    3. pedagogy
4. pediatrician    5. orthopedic

【Group 8】

# Ortho — *correct*「正確的」

**orthodontist**〔͵ɔrθə′dɑntɪst〕*n.* 牙齒矯正醫師

—— dentist specializing in *orthodontics*, a branch of dentistry
dealing with straightening and adjusting of teeth

A student who wears braces on his teeth is obviously under the
care of an *orthodontist*.

牙齒上戴著牙套的學生，很明顯地正在接受牙齒矯正醫師的治療。

**orthography**〔ɔr′θɑgrəfɪ〕*n.* 拼字法；正確的拼字

—— (literally, "correct writing") correct spelling

American and English *orthography* are very much alike.

美語與英語的拼字方式非常相像。

**orthopedist**〔͵ɔrθə′pidɪst〕*n.* 整形外科醫師

—— physician specializing in the correction and
prevention of deformities, especially in children

A deformity of the spine is a condition that requires the attention
of an *orthopedist*.

脊椎骨的畸形需要整形外科醫師的照料。

**orthodox** 〔'ɔrθə,dɑks 〕 *adj.* 正統的；公認爲正確的；傳統的

—— (literally, "correct opinion") generally accepted, especially in religion; approved; conventional; conservative

There was no religious liberty in the Massachusetts Bay Colony. Roger Williams, for example, was banished because he did not accept *orthodox* Puritan beliefs. 麻薩諸塞灣殖民地那裡沒有宗教自由，例如羅傑‧威廉斯就因爲不接受正統的清教徒信仰而被驅逐。

**unorthodox** 〔 ʌn'ɔrθə,dɑks 〕 *adj.* 非正統的；異端的

—— not orthodox; not in accord with accepted, standard, or approved belief or practice

Vaccination was rejected as *unorthodox* when Dr. Jenner first suggested it. 當金納博士最初提出預防接種時，被視爲異端而拒絕了。

Exercise：請由 **Group 8** 中，選出最適當的字，填入空格中。

1. It is _____ for a girl to ask a boy for a dance.

2. Phyllis has won the spelling bee again. She excels in _____.

3. The youngster's leg deformity has greatly improved since he has been under the care of this _____.

4. The infant gets up at 4 a.m. Naturally, we should prefer him to wake at a more convenient and _____ hour, such as 7 a.m.

5. Mrs. Early has been assured by an _____ that her daughter's teeth can be straightened.

---

【解答】

| | | |
|---|---|---|
| 1. unorthodox | 2. orthography | 3. orthopedist |
| 4. orthodox | 5. orthodontist | |

第二章

## 【Group 9】

# Gen, Genea — *race*「種族」

**genealogy**〔͵dʒɛnɪ'ælədʒɪ , ͵dʒini- 〕*n.* 家譜；家系；世系
—— (literally, "account of a race or family") history of the descent of a person or family from an ancestor; lineage; pedigree

Diana can trace her descent from an ancestor who fought in the Civil War. I know much less about my own *genealogy*.

黛安娜可以從一位參加南北戰爭的祖先開始追溯世系下來，而我對家譜的認識就少得多。

**genesis**〔'dʒɛnəsɪs 〕*n.* 起源；創始；發生
—— birth or coming into being of something; origin

According to legend, the Trojan War had its *genesis* in a dispute between three Greek goddesses.

根據神話上的說法，特洛戰爭起源於三位希臘女神的爭議。

**homogenize**〔ho'mɑdʒə͵naɪz 〕*v.* 使均質；使均勻
—— make homogeneous

If dairies did not *homogenize* milk, the cream would be concentrated at the top instead of being evenly distributed.

如果酪農場不把牛奶調勻，乳脂就會集中在上層，而不會平均分配。

**heterogeneous**〔͵hɛtərə'dʒiniəs , -njəs 〕*adj.* 異質的；各種各樣的
—— differing in kind; dissimilar; not uniform; varied

Many different racial and cultural groups are to be found in the *heterogeneous* population of a large city.

從一個大都市龐雜的人口中，可以發現許多不同種族及文化背景的團體。

**homogeneous** 〔ˌhomə'dʒɪnɪəs , ˌhɑmə- 〕 *adj.* 同質的；同種的；
類似的

—— of the same kind; similar; uniform

The dancers for the ballet were selected for similarity of height
and build so that they might present a *homogeneous* appearance.
芭蕾舞者經同等高度及體格的挑選後，才能呈現出類似的外觀。

Exercise：請由 **Group 9** 中，選出最適當的字，填入空格中。

1. The Swimming Club consists of intermediate and advanced
   swimmers, as well as a few beginners. It is a _____ group.

2. A family Bible in which births, marriages, and deaths have
   been recorded for generations can acquaint a person with his
   _____.

3. There are always lumps in the cereal when my sister Elizabeth
   cooks it. She doesn't know to _____ it.

4. When every house on the block has the same exterior, the result
   is a _____ dullness.

5. If you study the _____ of the modern automobile, you will
   learn that steam-driven cars were once more popular than
   gasoline models.

```
┌--- 【解答】 --------------------------------┐
: 1. heterogeneous    2. genealogy    3. homogenize :
: 4. homogeneous      5. genesis                    :
└--------------------------------------------┘
```

## 【Group 10】

# Meter, Metr — *measure*「度量」

## barometer〔bə'rɑmətə〕*n.* 氣壓計

—— instrument for measuring atmospheric pressure as an aid in determining probable weather changes

When the *barometer* indicates a rapid drop in air pressure, it means a storm is coming.

當氣壓計顯示出氣壓迅速下降時,便意味著暴風雨快來了。

## chronometer〔krə'nɑmətə〕*n.* 精密的計時器

—— instrument for measuring time very accurately

Unlike ordinary clocks and watches, *chronometers* are little affected by temperature changes or vibration.

精確計時器與普通的鐘錶不同,它不大受氣溫變化及震動的影響。

## diameter[6]〔daɪ'æmətə〕*n.* 直徑

—— (literally, "measure across") straight line passing through the center of a body or figure from one side to the other; length of such a line; thickness; width

> 【記憶技巧】
> *dia* (through) + *meter* (measure)(透過測量才知道「直徑」)

Some giant redwood trees measure 325 feet in height and up to 30 feet in *diameter*.

有些高大的紅木,高度有三百二十五呎,直徑長達三十呎。

## meter[2]〔'mitə〕*n.* 1. 計量器;儀表 2. 公尺;米

—— 1. device for measuring

2. unit of measure in the metric system; 39.37 inches

When water *meters* are installed, it will be easy to tell how much water each home is using.

當水表安裝好後,很容易看出每家用水量是多少。

A *meter* is 3.37 inches longer than a yard.

一公尺比一碼長三點三七吋。

**odometer**〔 oˊdɑmətɚ 〕 *n.* 里程表

—— instrument attached to a vehicle for measuring the distance traversed

All eyes, except the driver's, were fastened on the *odometer* as it moved from 9,999.9 to 10,000 miles. 當車上的里程表從九千九百九十九點九哩移動至一萬哩時，除了駕駛人，所有的眼睛都盯著它看。

**photometer**〔 foˊtɑmətɚ 〕 *n.* 光度計；測光表

—— instrument for measuring intensity of light

The intensity of a source of light, such as an electric light bulb, can be measured with a *photometer*.

光線來源，如一個電燈泡的強度，可由光度計測出。

**speedometer**〔 spiˊdɑmətɚ 〕 *n.* ( 車輛的 ) 速度計；里程計

—— instrument for measuring speed; tachometer

I advised Dad to slow down as we were in a 30-mile-an-hour zone and his *speedometer* registered more than 40.

我勸告父親車子開慢點，因為我們在時速限制三十哩的地區，而他車上的速度計卻顯示出已超過了四十哩。

**symmetry**[6] 〔ˊsɪmɪtrɪ 〕 *n.* 對稱

—— correspondence in measurements, shape, etc., on opposite sides of a dividing line; well-balanced arrangement of parts

【記憶技巧】
*sym* (same) + *metry* (measure) ( 兩邊測量出來的大小和形狀是相等的，就表示「對稱」)

As the planes sped by, we were impressed by the perfect *symmetry* of their V-formation.

當飛機飛過，我們對那完美對稱的 V 字形排列留下了深刻的印象。

Exercise：請由 **Group 10** 中，選出最適當的字，填入空格中。

1. Every apple in this package has a(n) ⎯⎯⎯⎯ of no less than 2 inches.

2. We couldn't tell how fast we were going because the ⎯⎯⎯⎯ was out of order.

3. Notice the ⎯⎯⎯⎯ of the human body. The right side is the counterpart of the left.

4. You can tell how many miles a car has been driven since the time of the purchase if you look at its ⎯⎯⎯⎯.

5. In the 100-⎯⎯⎯⎯ dash, the course is more than 100 yards long.

> 【解答】
> 1. diameter      2. speedometer      3. symmetry
> 4. odometer      5. meter

## 【Group 11】

# Ant, Anti — *against*「反抗」

**antagonist**〔æn'tægənɪst〕*n.* 敵手；反對者；反派角色
—— 1. one who is against, or contends with, another in a struggle, fight, or contest; opponent; adversary; foe
   2. main opponent of the principal character in a play, novel, or story

Japan was our *antagonist* in World War II.
日本在第二次世界大戰中是我們的敵人。

Brutus is the main character in William Shakespeare's *Julius Caesar*, and Antony is his *antagonist*. 布魯特斯在威廉‧莎士比亞著的「凱撒」中是主角，而安東尼則是主要的反派角色。

## antibiotic[6] 〔‚æntɪbaɪ'ɑtɪk 〕 *n.* 抗生素

—— substance obtained from tiny living organisms that works against harmful bacteria

> 【記憶技巧】
> *anti* (against) + *bio* (life) + *tic* (*n.*) (阻止生命的生長，即「抗生素」)

The *antibiotic* penicillin stops the growth of bacteria causing pneumonia, tonsillitis, and certain other diseases. 盤尼西林抗生素阻止了肺炎細菌、扁桃腺細菌，還有其他某些疾病細菌的生長繁殖。

## antibody[6] 〔'æntɪ‚bɑdɪ 〕 *n.* 抗體

—— substance in the blood or tissues that works against germs or poisons produced by germs

> 【記憶技巧】
> *anti* (反抗) + *body* (身體) (反抗侵入體內的病毒，即「抗體」)

When the body is invaded by foreign agents, such as bacteria or viruses, the *antibodies* go to work against them.
當身體被外來的作用物侵入，如細菌或病毒，則抗體就會發生作用去抵抗他們。

## antidote 〔'æntɪ‚dot 〕 *n.* 解毒劑

—— remedy that acts against the effects of a poison

By telephone, the physician prescribed the exact *antidote* to be given immediately to the poison victim.
醫生在電話中開了正確的解毒劑，立即給那位中毒的受害者。

## antipathy 〔 æn'tɪpəθɪ 〕 *n.* 反感；厭惡

—— feeling against; distaste; repugnance; dislike; enmity

A few of the neighbors have an *antipathy* to dogs, but most are fond of them. 有一些鄰居很討厭狗，但大多數都很喜歡。

## antiseptic〔͵æntə'sɛptɪk〕*n.* 殺菌劑；消毒劑

—— (literally, "against decaying") substance that prevents infection

The wound was carefully washed; then an *antiseptic*, tincture of iodine, was applied. 傷口被仔細地清洗，然後塗上消毒劑和碘酒。

## antitoxin〔͵æntɪ'tɑksɪn〕*n.* 抗毒素

—— substance formed in the body as the result of the introduction of a toxin (poison) and capable of acting against that toxin

We are injected with diphtheria *antitoxin* produced in horses because the *antitoxin* manufactured by our bodies may not be enough to prevent diphtheria.

我們注射從馬身上製造出來的白喉抗毒素，因為我們體內的抗毒素可能不夠來抵抗白喉。

## antonym[6]〔'æntə͵nɪm〕*n.* 反義字

—— word meaning the opposite of another word; opposite

"Temporary" is the *antonym* of "permanent." 「暫時」是「永久」的反義字。

【記憶技巧】
*ant* (opposite) + *onym* (name) ( 相反的名稱，也就是「反義字」)

Exercise：請由 Group 11 中，選出最適當的字，填入空格中。

1. Before each fight, the champion familiarized himself with the strengths and weaknesses of his _____.

2. Streptomycin, an _____ developed from living microorganisms, is useful in the treatment of tuberculosis.

3. The infection would not have developed if a(n) _____ had been used.

4. Mother has had an _____ to ship travel ever since she became seasick on a lake cruise.

---
【解答】
1. antagonist　　2. antibiotic　　3. antiseptic
4. antipathy
---

## 【Group 12】

# Onym, Onomato — *word*「字」

**acronym**〔ˈækrənɪm〕*n.* 頭字語；首字母縮寫詞

—— name formed from the first letter or letters of other words

The word "radar" is an *acronym* for *RA*dio *D*etecting *A*nd *R*ange.

雷達是由 RAdio Detecting And Range 的字頭所組成。

**homonym**〔ˈhɑməˌnɪm〕*n.* 同音異義字

—— word that sounds like another but differs in meaning

"Fair" and "fare" are *homonyms*.

"fair" 和 "fare" 是同音異義字。

**onomatopoeia**〔ˌɑnəˌmætəˈpiə〕*n.* 擬聲字

—— use of words whose sound suggests their meaning

Notice the *onomatopoeia* in these lines by the poet John Drydth:
"The double, double, double beat / Of the thundering drum."

注意由詩人約翰・德萊敦所寫的這幾行擬聲語："The double, double, double beat / Of the thundering drum."。

**pseudonym**〔ˈsudn̩ˌɪm〕*n.* 筆名

—— (literally, "false name") fictitious name used by an author; pen name

第二章

O. Henry is the *pseudonym* of William Sydney Porter.

「歐亨利」是「威廉‧悉尼‧波特」的筆名。

**synonym**[6] 〔ˈsɪnə,nɪm 〕 *n.* 同義字

—— word having the same meaning as another word

"Building" is a *synonym* for "edifice."

"building" 和 "edifice" 是同義字。

> 【記憶技巧】
>
> *syn* (same) + *onym* (name) ( 相同的名稱，也就是「同義字」)

**anonymous** 〔 əˈnɑnəməs 〕 *adj.* 匿名的；不具名的

—— nameless; of unnamed or unknown origin

When you write a letter to the editor, be sure to sign it. Responsible publications will not print *anonymous* letters.

當你寫一封信給編者，一定要簽名。負責的刊物是不會刊出匿名信的。

Exercise：請由 **Group 12** 中，選出最適當的字，填入空格中。

1. "Deer" and "dear" are _____.

2. If an author wishes to conceal his identity, he may use a(n) _____.

3. Anzac is a(n) _____ for *A*ustralian and *N*ew Zealand *A*rmy *C*orps.

4. I was embarrassed when the _____ test paper my teacher spoke about turned out to be mine. I had forgotten to put my name on it.

5. "Hiss," "mumble," and "splash" are good one-word examples of _____.

第二章

## 【Group 13】

# Derm, Dermato — *skin*「皮膚」

**dermatologist**〔͵dɝmə'talədʒɪst〕*n.* 皮膚科醫生

—— physician specializing in *dermatology*, the science dealing with the skin and its diseases

The patient with the skin disorder is under the care of a *dermatologist.* 那個有皮膚病的病人是由皮膚科醫生照顧。

**dermis**〔'dɝmɪs〕*n.* 眞皮

—— inner layer of the skin

The tiny cells from which hairs grow are located in the *dermis.* 長出頭髮的小毛孔是位於眞皮層。

**epidermis**〔͵ɛpə'dɝmɪs〕*n.* 表皮

—— outer layer of the skin

Although very thin, the *epidermis* serves to protect the underlying dermis. 表皮雖然非常薄，卻可用來保護下層的眞皮。

**taxidermist**〔'tæksə͵dɝmɪst〕*n.* (動物標本) 剝製師

—— one who practices *taxidermy*, the art of preparing, stuffing, and mounting the skins of animals in lifelike form

The lifelike models of animals that you see in museums are the work of *taxidermists.*

在博物館中，你所看到的生動的動物標本，都是剝製師的作品。

**hypodermic** 〔͵haɪpə'dɜmɪk 〕 *adj.* 皮下的

—— beneath the skin

A *hypodermic* syringe is used for injecting medication beneath the skin. 皮下注射器是用來注射藥物於皮膚下。

Exercise：請由 **Group 13** 中，選出最適當的字，填入空格中。

1. The _____ stretched the skin over a plastic cast of the animal's body.

2. Was the antibiotic taken by mouth or administered by _____ injection?

3. There are numerous tiny openings, or pores, in the _____, or outer layer of the skin.

4. It took three visits for the _____ to remove Bob's painful wart in the skin of his left sole.

5. The sweat glands are located in the _____, or inner layer of the skin.

```
--- 【解答】-------------------------------------
 1. taxidermist    2. hypodermic    3. epidermis
 4. dermatologist  5. dermis
```

【**Group 14**】

# Nom, Nem —— *management*「管理」

**agronomy** 〔 ə'grɑnəmɪ 〕 *n.* 農業經濟學

—— (literally, "land management") branch of agriculture dealing with crop production and soil management; husbandry

The science of *agronomy* helps farmers obtain larger and better crops. 農業經濟學幫助農夫們獲得更多很好的農作物。

## gastronome 〔'gæstrə,nom 〕 *n.* 美食家

—— one who follows the principles of *gastronomy* (literally, "management of the stomach"), the art or science of good eating; epicure; gourmet

Being a *gastronome*, my uncle is well acquainted with the best restaurants in the city.
我叔叔是個美食家,非常熟悉這個城市中最好的餐館。

## nemesis 〔'nɛməsɪs 〕 *n.* 1. 報應者;懲罰者(*Nemesis* 是希臘的復仇女神) 2. 強敵

—— 1. person that inflicts just punishment for evil deeds
2. formidable and usually victorious opponent

The fleeing murderer escaped the bullets of two pursuing policemen but ran into a third who proved to be his *nemesis*.
敏捷的殺人犯躲過了兩個追捕他的警察所射出來的子彈,卻遇到了第三個警察,懲罰他應得的報應。
We would have ended the season without a defeat if not for our old *nemesis*, Greeley High.
如果不是我們的強敵——格利中學,這一季我們就不會打敗仗了。

## astronomical 〔,æstrə'nomɪkḷ 〕 *adj.* 1. 天文學的 2. 龐大的

—— 1. having to do with *astronomy* (literally, "distribution of the stars"), the science of the sun, moon, planets, stars, and other heavenly bodies
2. inconceivably large

The first *astronomical* observations with a telescope were made by the Italian scientist Galileo.
最早用遠望鏡來觀察的,是義大利的科學家伽利略。
It is difficult to conceive of so *astronomical* a sum as one hundred billion dollars. 很難想像一千億如此龐大的數目。

Galileo

# economic⁴ 〔ˌikə'nɑmɪk〕 *adj.* 經濟的

—— having to do with *economics* (literally, "household management"), the social science dealing with production, distribution, and consumption

The President's chief *economic* adviser expects that production will continue at the same rate for the rest of the year.

總統的主要經濟顧問預期，在年底之前都能夠保持相同的生產速度。

# economical⁴ 〔ˌikə'nɑmɪkl̩〕 *adj.* 節省的

—— managed or managing without waste; thrifty; frugal; sparing

Which is the most *economical* fuel for home heating — gas, electricity, or oil?

哪一種燃料用於家庭暖氣最省錢——瓦斯、電力，還是石油？

第二章

Exercise：請由 **Group 14** 中，選出最適當的字，填入空格中。

1. The outlaw had engineered several successful robberies before encountering Sherlock Holmes, his _____.

2. Overproduction is a serious _____ problem.

3. Some museums and art collectors have gone to _____ expense to acquire paintings by the great masters.

4. Underdeveloped nations are trying to improve the yield and quality of their crops by applying the principles of _____.

5. The _____ cheerfully aided his dining companions in making their selections from the menu.

---

【解答】

| | | |
|---|---|---|
| 1. nemesis | 2. economic | 3. astronomical |
| 4. agronomy | 5. gastronome | |

【Group 15】

# Phan, Phen — *show*「顯示」

## cellophane〔'sɛlə,fen〕*n.* 玻璃紙

—— cellulose substance that "shows through"; transparent cellulose substance used as a wrapper

When used as a wrapper, *cellophane* lets the purchaser see the contents of the package.

用玻璃紙包裝使購買者能看到包裹內的物品。

## fancy³〔'fænsɪ〕*n.* 幻想

—— imagination; illusion

We must be able to distinguish between fact and *fancy*.

我們必須能夠分辨得出事實和幻想。

## fantasy⁴〔'fæntəsɪ〕*n.* 幻想

—— illusory image; play of the mind; imagination; fancy

Anne is not sure whether she saw a face at the window. Perhaps it was only a *fantasy*.

安不確定她是否在窗口看到一張臉,也許那只是幻想。

## phantom〔'fæntəm〕*n.* 幽靈;幻影

—— something that has appearance but no reality; apparition; ghost; specter

The *phantom* of the slain Caesar appeared to Brutus in a dream.

被殺害的凱撒靈魂出現在布魯斯特的夢中。

## phenomenon⁴〔fə'nɑmə,nɑn〕*n.* 1. 現象　2. 非凡的人或事物

—— (literally, "an appearance")

1. any observable fact or event

2. extraordinary person or thing; wonder; prodigy

【記憶技巧】

*phe* + *no* + *men* + *on*

第二章

Fever and inflammation are *phenomena* of disease.

發燒和發炎是生病的現象。

Philip is a *phenomenon* in math.　He always gets 100% on tests.

菲利浦在數學方面是個天才，他每次考試都得 100 分。

## phenomenal〔fə'namənḷ〕*adj.* 非凡的；傑出的；驚人的

—— extraordinary; remarkable; unusual

Young Mozart, a *phenomenal* child, began composing music at the age of 5.

年輕的莫札特是一個了不起的孩子，從五歲就開始作曲。

## fantastic[4]〔fæn'tæstɪk〕*adj.* 幻想的；異想天開的；怪誕的

—— based on fantasy rather than reason; imaginary; unreal; odd

Robert Fulton's proposal to build a steamboat was at first regarded as *fantastic*.

羅伯特‧富爾敦提出造一艘汽艇，起初被認為是荒誕的。

**Exercise：請由 Group 15 中，選出最適當的字，填入空格中。**

1. Babe Ruth was no ordinary hitter; he was a _____ .

2. Though these conclusions may seem _____ , I can show you they are based on reason.

3. If the apples are in a _____ bag, you can tell how many there are without opening it.

4. My prospects for passing English are good, but in French I don't have the _____ of a chance.

5. Mrs. Potter thought her daughter's performance was _____ , but I found nothing extraordinary or remarkable in it.

第二章

## 【Group 16】

# Therm, Thermo — *heat*「熱」

**diathermy**〔'daɪə,θɜmɪ〕*n.* 電療

—— method of treating disease by generating heat in body tissues by high-frequency electric currents

*Diathermy* may be prescribed for arthritis, bursitis, and other conditions requiring heat treatment.

對於關節炎、黏液囊炎,還有其他需要熱醫療的情況,都可用電療。

**thermometer**[6]〔θə'mɑmətɚ〕*n.* 溫度計

—— instrument for measuring temperature

During the hot spell, the *thermometer* reached 100 degrees on six days in a row.

在連續高溫天氣期間,溫度計一連六天都到達 100 度。

> 【記憶技巧】
> *thermo* (heat) + *meter* (measure)(測量溫度的,就是「溫度計」)

**thermostat**〔'θɜmə,stæt〕*n.* 自動調溫器

—— automatic device for regulating temperature

We set the *thermostat* to shut off the heat when the room temperature reaches 72 degrees.

我們設定了自動調溫器,當室溫達到七十二度,就會自動關閉暖氣。

thermostat

**thermal**〔'θɜml̩〕*adj.* 熱的;溫泉的

—— pertaining to heat; hot; warm

At Lava Hot Springs in Idaho, visitors may bathe in the *thermal* mineral waters.　在愛達荷的熔岩溫泉中,遊客可在熱礦泉水裡浸泡。

第二章

**thermonuclear** 〔͵θɝmo'njuklɪɚ 〕 *adj.* 熱核的

—— having to do with the fusion (joining together), at an extraordinarily high temperature, of the nuclei of atoms (as in the hydrogen bomb)

It is believed that the sun gets its energy from *thermonuclear* reactions constantly taking place within it.

大家相信太陽的熱能是從其內部不斷產生熱核反應得來的。

Exercise：請由 **Group 16** 中，選出最適當的字，填入空格中。

1. The room was cold because the _____ had been set for only 58 degrees.

2. If you have a _____ mounted outside your window, you don't need to go outside to learn what the temperature is.

3. The unbelievably intense heat required to start the _____ reaction in a hydrogen bomb is obtained by exploding an atomic bomb.

4. Drugs, hot baths, and _____ are some of the means used to relieve the pain of arthritis.

5. Hot Springs, Arkansas, derives its name from the numerous _____ springs in the vicinity.

---
【解答】
1. thermostat　　2. thermometer　　3. thermonuclear
4. diathermy　　5. thermal
---

第二章

【Group 17】

# Prot, Proto — *first*「第一」

**protagonist**〔proˈtægənɪst〕*n.* 主角

—— the leading ("first") character in a play, novel, or story

Brutus is the *protagonist* in William Shakespeare's *Julius Caesar*, and Antony is the antagonist.

布魯特斯在威廉莎士比亞的「凱撒大帝」中是主角,而安東尼則是他的對手。

**protocol**〔ˈprotəˌkɑl〕*n.* 1. 禮節　2. 草約

—— 1. rules of etiquette of the diplomatic corps, military services, etc.

　　2. first draft or record (of discussions, agreements, etc.) from which a treaty is drawn up; preliminary memorandum

It is a breach of *protocol* for a subordinate to publicly question the judgment of his superior officer.

一個下級官員公開質問上級的判斷是違反禮節的。

The *protocol* initiated by the representatives of the three nations is expected to lead to a formal treaty.

一般人期望由那三個國家代表所發起的草約,能成為一個正式的協定。

**protoplasm**〔ˈprotəˌplæzəm〕*n.* 原生質

—— (literally, "first molded material") fundamental substance of which all living things are composed

*Protoplasm* distinguishes living from nonliving things.

原生質成為生物和無生物的區別。

**prototype**〔ˈprotəˌtaɪp〕*n.* 原型

—— first or original model of anything; model; pattern

The crude craft in which the Wright brothers made the first successful flight in 1903 was the *prototype* of the modern airplane.

萊特兄弟在 1903 年初次試飛成功的原始飛機，是現代飛機的原型。

**protozoan** 〔͵protə′zoən 〕 *n.* 原生動物

—— (literally, "first animal") animal consisting only of a single cell

The tiny *protozoans* are believed to be the first animals to have appeared on earth.

一般相信小原生動物是最先出現在地球上的動物。

Exercise：請由 **Group 17** 中，選出最適當的字，填入空格中。

1. At the opening game of the baseball season in Washington, D.C., the President, according to _____, is invited to throw out the first ball.

2. The amoeba, a one-celled animal living in ponds and streams, is a typical _____.

3. Our Constitution has served as the _____ of similar documents in democratic nations all over the world.

4. The movie star will not accept a minor role; she wants to play the _____.

5. Living plants and animals consist of _____.

---

【解答】
1. protocol     2. protozoan     3. prototype
4. protagonist     5. protoplasm

## 【Group 18】

# Thesis, Thet — *set*「放置」

### antithesis〔æn'tɪθəsɪs〕*n.* 正相反；正好相反的事；對立

—— (literally, "a setting against") direct opposite; contrary

I cannot vote for a candidate who stands for the *antithesis* of what I believe.

我不能選一個贊成與我的信仰相反的候選人。

### epithet〔'ɛpə,θɛt〕*n.*（性質）描述詞；稱號

—— (literally, something "placed on" or "added") characterizing word or phrase; descriptive expression

In "crafty Ulysses" and "Richard the Lion-Hearted" the *epithets* are "crafty" and "the Lion-Hearted."

「足智多謀的尤里希斯」與「獅心理查」兩詞中的描述詞是「足智多謀」與「獅心」。

### hypothesis〔haɪ'pɑθəsɪs〕*n.* 假設

—— (literally, "a placing under" or "supposing") supposition or assumption made as a basis for reasoning or research

When Columbus first presented his *hypothesis* that the earth is round, very few believed it.

當哥倫布第一次提出地球是圓的假設時，很少人相信它。

### synthesis〔'sɪnθəsɪs〕*n.* 綜合；合成

—— (literally "putting together") combination of parts or elements into a whole

Only political parties can produce the *synthesis* or compromise of interest necessary to make representative government work.

只有政黨才能產生利益的綜合或妥協，而使代議政體運作。

**thesis**〔ˊθisɪs〕*n.* 1. 論點　2. 學位論文
—— (literally, "a setting down")
　　1. claim put forward; proposition; statement
　　2. essay written by a candidate for a college degree
Do you agree with Elbert's *thesis* that a student court would be good for our school?
你同意艾伯特認為學生法庭有助於我們學校的論點嗎？
Candidates for advanced college degrees usually must write a *thesis* based on original research.
要取得比大學更高學位的人，通常都必須寫一篇與原本研究有關的論文。

**synthetic**[6]〔sɪnˊθɛtɪk〕*adj.* 合成的；人造的
—— (literally, "put together") artificially made; man-made
Cotton is a natural fiber, but rayon and nylon are *synthetic*.
棉花是天然纖維，但人造絲和尼龍卻是合成的。

＊字尾是 is 的字，改成複數時，是將 is 改為 es。
　如：*antitheses, hypotheses, theses,* etc.

Exercise：請由 **Group 18** 中，選出最適當的字，填入空格中。

1. _____ rubber is superior to natural rubber in some respects and inferior in others.

2. Jonathan's bicycle, which he built himself, is a(n) _____ of usable parts from four old bicycles.

3. In the *Odyssey*, you will often find the _____ "wily" before Ulysses' name because he had a reputation for cunning.

4. A student who undertakes to write a(n) _____ must know how to do research.

5. Their leader, timid, complaining, and weak, is the _____ of what a leader should be.

【解答】
1. Synthetic  2. synthesis  3. epithet
4. thesis   5. antithesis

## 【Group 19】

# Aster, Astr, Astro — *star*「星星」

**aster**〔ˈæstɚ〕*n.* 紫菀

—— plant having small starlike flowers
Most *asters* bloom in the fall. 大多數的紫菀在秋天開花。

**asterisk**〔ˈæstəˌrɪsk〕*n.* 星號；星標（用以指示應注意的事物、註腳等）

—— (literally, "little star") star-shaped mark (*) used to call attention to a footnote, omission, etc.

The *asterisk* after "Reduced to $1.95" refers to a footnote reading "Today only."

在「減至一點九五元」後，有個星號標示著一個註腳，上面寫著「只限今天」。

**asteroid**〔ˈæstəˌrɔɪd〕*n.* 1. 小行星（運行於火星與木星軌道之間）
2. 海星；海盤車

—— 1. very small planet resembling a star in appearance
  2. starfish

Compared to planet Earth, some *asteroids* are tiny, measuring less than a mile in diameter.

跟地球這個行星比較起來，有一些小行星非常小，直徑還不到一哩。

If an *asteroid* loses an arm to an attacker, it can grow back the missing arm.

如果海星受到攻擊失去一條手臂，它可以再長出那隻失去的手臂。

## astrologer〔 ə'stralədʒə 〕*n.* 占星家

—— person who practices *astrology*, the false science dealing with the influence of the stars and planets on human affairs

An *astrologer* would have people believe that their lives are regulated by the movements of the stars, planets, sun, and moon.

占星家會使人們相信，他們的生命是受恆星、行星、太陽，和月球的運轉所控制。

## astronaut[5]〔'æstrə,nɔt 〕*n.* 太空人

—— (literally, "star sailor") traveler in outer space

> 【記憶技巧】
> *astro* (star) + *naut* (sailor) (航向星星的人，就是「太空人」)

Yuri Gagarin, the world's first *astronaut*, orbited the earth in an artificial satellite on April 12, 1961.

尤瑞‧蓋加林是全世界第一個太空人，1961 年 4 月 12 日在人造衛星中繞著地球軌道而行。

## astronomer[5]〔 ə'stranəmə 〕*n.* 天文學家

—— expert in *astronomy*, science of the stars, planets, sun, moon, and other heavenly bodies

Because the stars are so far away, *astronomers* measure their distance from Earth in "light years".

由於星星是如此地遙遠，天文學家都以「光年」來測量它們的距離。

## disaster[4]〔 dɪ'zæstə 〕*n.* 災難

—— (literally, "contrary star") sudden or extraordinary misfortune; calamity

> 【記憶技巧】
> *dis* (away) + *aster* (star) (這個字源自占星學，當星星不在正確的位置時，會造成「災難」)

The attack on Pearl Harbor was the worst *disaster* in the history of the U.S. Navy. 珍珠港事變是美國海軍史上最嚴重的一次災難。

Exercise：請由 **Group 19** 中，選出最適當的字，填入空格中。

1. Some _____ are regarded as pests because they feed on oysters.

2. _____ claim that a person's life is influenced by the position the stars were in at the moment of his birth.

3. _____ undergo a long and difficult period of training that equips them for the hazards of space travel.

4. Nations that continue to spend beyond their means are headed for economic _____.

5. A(n) _____ alerts the reader to look for additional information at the foot of the page.

--------【解答】--------------------------------
| 1. asteroids | 2. Astrologers | 3. Astronauts |
| 4. disaster | 5. asterisk | |
------------------------------------------------

## 【Group 20】

## Gram, Graph — *letter*, *writing*「字母；書寫」

**anagram**〔ˋænəˏɡræm〕*n.* 顛倒字母所成的字
—— word or phrase formed from another by transposing the letters
"Mota" is an *anagram* for "atom."
"mota" 是 "atom" 顛倒字母後所成的字。

## cartographer〔kɑr'tɑgrəfə〕*n.* 繪製地圖者

—— (literally, "map writer") person skilled in *cartography*, the science or art of map making

Ancient *cartographers* did not know of the existence of the Western Hemisphere. 古代的繪製地圖者不知道西半球的存在。

## cryptogram〔'krɪptə,græm〕*n.* 密碼

—— something written in secret code

Military leaders, diplomats, and businessmen use *cryptograms* to relay secret information.
軍事首長、外交人員，和商界人士都使用密碼來傳送祕密的消息。

## electrocardiogram〔ɪ,lɛktro'kɑdɪə,græm〕*n.* 心電圖

—— "writing" or tracing made by an *electrocardiograph*, an instrument that records the amount of electricity the heart muscles produce during the heartbeat

After reading Mrs. Hale's *electrocardiogram*, the physician assured her that her heart was working properly.
在讀了赫爾太太的心電圖後，內科醫生向她保證，她的心臟運作正常。

## epigram〔'ɛpə,græm〕*n.* 警語；雋語

—— (literally, something "written on," or "inscribed") bright or witty thought concisely and cleverly expressed

"The more things a man is ashamed of, the more respectable he is" is one of George Bernard Shaw's *epigrams*. 「一個人覺得慚愧的事越多，他就越值得尊敬。」是喬治‧蕭伯特的雋語之一。

## graphite〔'græfaɪt〕*n.* 石墨

—— soft black carbon used in lead pencils

"Lead" pencils do not contain lead, but rather a mixture of clay and *graphite*. 「鉛」筆並不含鉛，而是黏土和石墨的混合物。

**monogram** 〔'mɑnə͵græm 〕*n.*（由姓名首字母組成的）組合文字；花押字

—— (literally, "one letter") person's initials interwoven or combined into one design

Some of Dad's handkerchiefs are embroidered with his *monogram*.

父親的一些手帕是繡上他姓名首字母組成的組合文字。

**monograph** 〔'mɑnə͵græf 〕*n.* 專論；專題論文

—— written account of a single thing or class of things

For his thesis, the student plans to write a *monograph* on the life of an obscure 19th-century composer. 那學生計畫寫一篇有關十九世紀一個無名作曲家生平的專論，作為他的學位論文。

**stenographer** 〔 stə'nɑgrəfɚ 〕*n.* 速記員

—— person skilled on, or employed to do, *stenography* (literally, "narrow writing"), the art of writing in shorthand

A court *stenographer* has to be able to take down more than 250 words a minute.

一個法庭速記員必須能夠一分鐘寫下二百五十個字以上。

**graphic**[6] 〔'græfɪk 〕*adj.* 生動的；圖解的；平面藝術的

—— written or told in a clear, lifelike manner; vivid

The reporter's *graphic* description made us feel that we were present at the scene. 採訪記者生動的描述使我們覺得如臨現場。

**typographical** 〔͵taɪpə'græfɪk!̩ 〕*adj.* 印刷上的；排版上的

—— pertaining to or occurring in *typography* (literally, "writing with type") or printing

Proofs submitted by the printer should be carefully checked to eliminate *typographical* errors.

由印刷工人交出的校樣應該被仔細地檢查，以減少印刷上的錯誤。

Exercise：請由 **Group 20** 中，選出最適當的字，填入空格中。

1. Modern _____ use aerial photography as an aid in map making.

2. There is a(n) _____ account of the 1666 Great Fire of London in Samuel Pepys' *Diary*.

3. The patient's physicians cannot be certain that he has suffered a heart attack until they have studied his _____.

4. "Won" is a(n) _____ for "now."

5. I knew it was Annabel's stationery because her _____ was on it.

---
【解答】
---
1. cartographers　2. graphic　　3. electrocardiogram
4. anagram　　　5. monogram
---

# REVIEW

Exercise 1：選出正確答案

( 　) 1. It is not too _____ to make a selection from the box, since the contents are homogeneous.
(A) costly　　　　(B) easy　　　　(C) soon
(D) difficult　　　(E) inexpensive

( 　) 2. In an autocracy, all power is vested in the _____.
(A) noblemen　　(B) people　　　(C) wealthy
(D) clergy　　　 (E) ruler

( ) 3. Automation has made the clothes-washing process
_____.

 (A) unnecessary     (B) burdensome

 (C) unorthodox      (D) self-operating

 (E) democratic

( ) 4. A study of the ruler's genealogy will acquaint you with
his _____.

 (A) life      (B) descent     (C) beliefs

 (D) government    (E) education

( ) 5. An autopsy should reveal the true cause of the patient's
_____.

 (A) decease     (B) relapse     (C) complaints

 (D) dissatisfaction   (E) illness

( ) 6. We are forbidden to use _____, since our act is to be a
pantomime.

 (A) costumes     (B) words      (C) frowns

 (D) gestures      (E) smiles

( ) 7. A photometer measures _____.

 (A) light intensity     (B) distance traversed

 (C) atmospheric pressure   (D) speed

 (E) time

( ) 8. If the account is from an authentic source, you should not
_____ it.

 (A) believe     (B) settle     (C) doubt

 (D) read      (E) trust

( 　) 9. It is entirely normal for a child of two to be under the care
of a(n) _____.
- (A) orthodontist
- (B) demagogue
- (C) orthopedist
- (D) pedagogue
- (E) pediatrician

( 　) 10. Among the nations participating in the _____
conference were Myanmar and Pakistan.
- (A) Pan-African
- (B) Pan-American
- (C) Pan-Arabian
- (D) Pan-Asiatic
- (E) Pan-European

( 　) 11. An error is considered _____ if it appears in the printed
text but not in the author's manuscript.
- (A) graphic
- (B) authentic
- (C) anonymous
- (D) unavoidable
- (E) typographical

( 　) 12. A gastronome has a keen interest in _____.
- (A) good eating
- (B) crop rotation
- (C) the stars
- (D) soil management
- (E) maps

( 　) 13. The famous showman P.T. Barnum is remembered for his
_____ "There's a sucker born every minute."
- (A) cryptogram
- (B) epigram
- (C) anagram
- (D) monograph
- (E) acronym

( 　) 14. One of the topics studied in _____ is the rotation of
crops.
- (A) automation
- (B) gastronomy
- (C) taxidermy
- (D) husbandry
- (E) cartography

(    ) 15. "Buzz" and "hum" are not homonyms because they

_____.

(A) sound alike           (B) are opposites

(C) mean the same       (D) sound different

(E) are spelled differently

(    ) 16. All the novels we have studied this year have had a man as the leading character. It's about time we had a female

_____.

(A) antagonist      (B) prodigy           (C) gourmet

(D) protagonist     (E) phenomenon

(    ) 17. The following names all contain an epithet except

_____.

(A) One-Punch Nelson     (B) Ivan the Terrible

(C) Alexander the Great    (D) Wrong-Way Corrigan

(E) Henry Wadsworth Longfellow

(    ) 18. Antibodies work against _____.

(A) the body      (B) toxins           (C) the tissues

(D) antitoxins     (E) the blood

(    ) 19. Plutocracy is government by _____.

(A) the Army      (B) mobs

(C) the majority    (D) the affluent     (E) bureaus

(    ) 20. We associate asters with _____.

(A) the sea           (B) printed matter

(C) gardens         (D) outer space

(E) the aristocracy

第
二
章

## Exercise 2：選出與題前字意義相反的字

(　) 1. FANTASTIC:
  (A) imaginary　　(B) unorthodox　　(C) laughable
  (D) authentic　　(E) phenomenal

(　) 2. SYNTHETIC:
  (A) pliable　　(B) artificial　　(C) natural
  (D) original　　(E) fervent

(　) 3. PROTOTYPE:
  (A) model　　(B) robot　　(C) copy
  (D) electron　　(E) phenomenon

(　) 4. ANALYSIS:
  (A) hypothesis　　(B) comparison　　(C) symmetry
  (D) synthesis　　(E) antithesis

(　) 5. ANTAGONIST:
  (A) ally　　(B) adversary　　(C) rival
  (D) propagandist　　(E) opponent

(　) 6. FANCY:
  (A) illusion　　(B) ugliness　　(C) reality
  (D) fantasy　　(E) imagination

(　) 7. ASTRONOMICAL:
  (A) anonymous　　(B) infinite　　(C) colossal
  (D) prodigious　　(E) infinitesimal

(　) 8. SYNONYM:
  (A) acronym　　(B) homonym　　(C) alias
  (D) antonym　　(E) pseudonym

第二章

(    ) 9. ECONOMICAL:

       (A) unreal           (B) extravagant      (C) frugal

       (D) sparing           (E) judicial

(    ) 10. ANTIPATHY:

       (A) affection         (B) poverty         (C) enmity

       (D) affluence        (E) audacity

## Exercise 3：配合題（一）

(    ) 1. ortho             (A) child

(    ) 2. maniac           (B) all; complete

(    ) 3. gen, geno, genea    (C) madness; insane impulse; craze

(    ) 4. chron, chrono     (D) straight; correct

(    ) 5. crat             (E) government

(    ) 6. aut, auto        (F) race; kind; birth

(    ) 7. meter, metr      (G) people

(    ) 8. pan, panto       (H) advocate of a type of government

(    ) 9. mania           (I) measure

(    ) 10. cracy           (J) self

(    ) 11. ped             (K) time

(    ) 12. dem, demo      (L) person affected by an insane impulse

第二章

# Exercise 4：配合題（二）

( 　) 1. nom, nem　　　　(A) heat

( 　) 2. aster, astr, astro　(B) first

( 　) 3. therm, thermo　　(C) skin

( 　) 4. ant, anti　　　　(D) management, distribution, law

( 　) 5. derm, dermato　　(E) name, word

( 　) 6. gram, graph　　　(F) star

( 　) 7. onym, onomato　(G) show, appear

( 　) 8. thesis, thet　　　(H) against, opposite

( 　) 9. prot, proto　　　(I) letter, writing

( 　) 10. phan, phen　　　(J) set, place, put

【解答】

| Ex 1. | 1. D | 2. E | 3. D | 4. B | 5. A | 6. B | 7. A | 8. C |
|---|---|---|---|---|---|---|---|---|
| | 9. E | 10. D | 11. E | 12. A | 13. B | 14. D | 15. D | 16. D |
| | 17. E | 18. B | 19. D | 20. C | | | | |
| Ex 2. | 1. D | 2. C | 3. C | 4. D | 5. A | 6. C | 7. E | 8. D |
| | 9. B | 10. A | | | | | | |
| Ex 3. | 1. D | 2. L | 3. F | 4. K | 5. H | 6. J | 7. I | 8. B |
| | 9. C | 10. E | 11. A | 12. G | | | | |
| Ex 4. | 1. D | 2. F | 3. A | 4. H | 5. C | 6. I | 7. E | 8. J |
| | 9. B | 10. G | | | | | | |

# 第三章
## 認識拉丁字首、字根以增加字彙

### 第一部份：拉丁字首

### 【Group 1】

## Ab, A, Abs — *from*, *off*「從；離開」

The prefix *ab* (sometimes written *a* or *abs*) means "from," "away," or "off." Examples:

Group 1~24

| PREFIX | ROOT | NEW WORD |
|--------|------|----------|
| AB ("off") | + RUPT ("broken") | = ABRUPT ("broken off; sudden") |
| A ("away") | + VERT ("turn") | = AVERT ("turn away") |
| ABS ("from") | + TAIN ("hold") | = ABSTAIN ("hold from; refrain") |

**abrasion**〔ə'breʒən〕*n.* 擦傷；磨損

—— scraping or wearing away of the skin by friction

The automobile was a total wreck, but the driver, luckily, escaped with minor cuts and *abrasions*.

那輛汽車撞成一堆廢鐵，但是駕駛人很幸運的只以一點割傷與擦傷倖免。

**avocation**〔͵ævə'keʃən〕*n.* 副業；嗜好

—— occupation away from one's customary occupation; hobby

My uncle, an accountant, composes music as an *avocation*.

我叔叔是一位會計師，作曲是他的嗜好。

**abdicate**〔'æbdə͵ket〕*v.* 放棄

—— formally remove oneself from; give up; relinquish; surrender

The aging king *abdicated* his throne and went into retirement.

那年老的國王遜位退休。

**abduct**〔æb'dʌkt , əb- 〕*v.* 綁架

—— carry off by force; kidnap

The Greeks attacked Troy to recover Helen, who had been *abducted* by the Trojan prince Paris.

希臘人攻擊特洛伊城，想帶回被特洛伊王子巴里斯綁架的海倫。

**abhor**〔əb'hɔr , æb- 〕*v.* 痛恨；憎惡

—— shrink from; detest; loathe; hate

Janet is doing her best to pass English because she *abhors* the thought of having to repeat it in summer school.

珍妮特憎惡在暑期學校重修英文，所以她盡全力使自己及格。

**abscond**〔æb'skɑnd 〕*v.* 潛逃

—— steal off and hide; depart secretly; flee

A wide search is under way for the manager who *absconded* with $10,000 of his employer's funds.

廣泛的搜查已展開，以逮捕那個帶走雇主一萬元資金潛逃的經理。

**absolve**〔æb'sɑlv , -'zɑlv 〕*v.* 1. 免除（責任）  2. 宣佈赦免罪過

—— 1. set free from some duty or responsibility
　　 2. declare free from guilt or blame

The fact that you were absent when the assignment was given does not *absolve* you from doing the homework.

指定作業時你不在的事實並不能免除你寫作業的責任。

Of the three suspects, two were found guilty and the third was *absolved*. 三個嫌疑犯當中，兩個被判有罪，第三個則無罪釋放。

**abstain**〔əb'sten , æb- 〕*v.* 節制；戒絕

—— withhold oneself from doing something; refrain

My dentist said I would have fewer cavities if I had *abstained* from eating candy. 牙醫說如果我不吃糖，蛀牙就會少一點。

**avert** 〔 ə'vɜt 〕 *v.* 避免

—— turn away; ward off; prevent

The mayor promised to do everything in his power to *avert* a strike by newspaper employees.

市長保證會盡他所有的力量防止報社人員罷工。

**abnormal**[6] 〔 æb'nɔrml̩ 〕 *adj.* 反常的

—— deviating from the normal; unusual; irregular

【記憶技巧】
*ab-* 為表「偏離；離開」的字首。

We had three absences today, which is *abnormal*. Usually, everyone is present.

今天很反常的有三個人缺席，通常每一個人都會出席。

**abrupt**[5] 〔 ə'brʌpt 〕 *adj.* 突然的；意外的

—— broken off; sudden; unexpected

Today's art lesson came to an *abrupt* end when the gongs sounded for a fire drill.

今天的美術課因火災演習的鈴聲大作而突然結束。

**absorbing** 〔 əb'sɔrbɪŋ 〕 *adj.* 極有趣的

—— fully taking away one's attention; extremely interesting; engrossing

That was an *absorbing* book. It held my interest from beginning to end.

這是一本極有趣的書，從頭到尾都讓我感到興致勃勃。

**averse** 〔 ə'vɜs 〕 *adj.* 反對的

—— literally, "turned from"; opposed; disinclined; unwilling

I am in favor of the dance, but I am *averse* to holding it on May 25.

我贊成這次的舞會，但我反對在 5 月 25 日舉行。

Exercise：請由 **Group 1** 中，選出最適當的字，填入空格中。

1. Some children love spinach; others _____ it.

2. An outdoor temperature of 84 degrees is _____ for New York City in January.

3. My father plays golf. What is your father's _____?

4. The people wanted the king to give up his throne, but he refused to _____.

5. Gene said the movie was very interesting, but I didn't find it too _____.

6. It was very fine of Marge to _____ me of blame by admitting her mistake.

7. The kidnapper was arrested when he tried to _____ the child.

8. I nominate Harvey for treasurer. He knows how to keep records and can be trusted not to _____ with our dues.

9. The owner must raise $4,000 in cash at once if he is to _____ bankruptcy.

10. We are _____ to raising the dues. They are too high already.

---

【解答】

1. abhor　2. abnormal　3. avocation　4. abdicate
5. absorbing　6. absolve　7. abduct　8. abscond
9. avert　10. averse

【Group 2】

# Ad — *to*「去」

## adherent〔əd'hɪrənt〕*n.* 擁護者

—— one who sticks to a leader, party, etc.; follower; faithful supporter

You can count on Martha's support in your campaign for reelection. She is one of your most loyal *adherents*.

你可以依賴瑪莎支持你再度競選，她是你最忠實的擁護者之一。

## advent〔'ædvɛnt〕*n.* 來臨

—— a "coming to"; arrival; approach

The Weather Bureau gave adequate warning of the *advent* of the hurricane. 氣象局對颶風的來臨做了充分的警告。

## adversary〔'ædvɚ͵sɛrɪ〕*n.* 對手

—— person "turned toward" or facing another as an opponent; foe; contestant

Before the contest began, the champion shook hands with his *adversary*. 比賽開始前，冠軍選手與他的對手握手。

## adapt[4]〔ə'dæpt〕*v.* 1. 使適應　2. 改編；改裝

—— 1. (literally, "fit to") adjust; suit; fit
2. make suitable for a different use; modify

> 【記憶技巧】
> *ad* (to) + *apt* (fit)
> （去符合一個環境，
> 也就是「適應」）

People who work at night have to *adapt* themselves to sleeping in the daytime. 晚上工作的人得適應白天睡覺。

"Gone With The Wind" was *adapted* for the movies.

「飄」被改編成電影。

# adjoin〔ə'dʒɔɪn〕v. 鄰接

—— be next to; be in contact with

Mexico *adjoins* the United States. 墨西哥與美國鄰接。

# adjourn〔ə'dʒɝn〕v. 延期

—— put off to another day; suspend a meeting to resume at a future time; defer

The judge *adjourned* the court to the following Monday.
法官把開庭的時間延至下星期一。

# addicted〔ə'dɪktɪd〕adj. 上癮的

—— given over (to a habit); habituated

You will not become *addicted* to smoking if you refuse cigarettes when they are offered. 如果有人給香煙時你不抽，就不會上癮了。

# adequate[4]〔'ædəkwɪt〕adj. 足夠的

—— equal to, or sufficient for, a specific need; enough; sufficient

The student who arrived ten minutes late did not have *adequate* time to finish the test. 遲到十分鐘的學生沒有足夠時間寫完試題。

# adjacent〔ə'dʒesṇt〕adj. 鄰近的

—— lying near; neighboring; bordering

The island of Cuba is *adjacent* to Florida.
古巴島接近佛羅里達。

# adverse〔əd'vɝs,'ædvɝs〕adj. 不利的；敵對的

—— in opposition to one's interests; hostile; unfavorable

Because of *adverse* reviews, the producer announced that the play will close with tonight's performance.
因為評論不利，這齣戲的製作人宣布今晚是最後一次的演出。

Exercise：請由 **Group 2** 中，選出最適當的字，填入空格中。

1. With the _____ of autumn, the days become shorter.

2. England was America's _____ in the War of 1812.

3. Is it very expensive to _____ a summer home for year-round living?

4. The child is _____ to sweets; he has an abnormal craving for them.

5. The candidate has few supporters in the rural areas; most of his _____ are in the cities.

---

【解答】

| | | |
|---|---|---|
| 1. advent | 2. adversary | 3. adapt |
| 4. addicted | 5. adherents | |

---

【**Group 3**】

# Ante — *before*「之前」

【**Group 4**】

# Post — *after*「之後」

**antecedents** 〔͵æntə'sidn̩ts 〕 *n. pl.* 祖先
—— ancestors; forefathers

David's *antecedents* came to this country more than a hundred years ago. 大衛的祖先一百多年前來到這個國家。

**anteroom** 〔'æntɪ͵rum 〕 *n.* 接待室

—— room placed before and forming an entrance to another; antechamber; waiting room

If the physician is busy when patients arrive, the nurse asks them to wait in the *anteroom*.

如果病人來的時候醫生很忙，護士就會請他們去接待室等候。

**postmortem** 〔 post'mɔrtəm 〕 *n.* 驗屍

—— thorough examination of a body after death; autopsy

The purpose of a *postmortem* is to discover the cause of death.

驗屍的目的在發現死因。

**postscript** 〔'pos‧skrɪpt , 'post- 〕 *n.* 附筆

—— note added to a letter after it has been written

After signing the letter, I noticed I had omitted an important fact. Therefore, I mentioned it in a *postscript*. 在信上簽了名之後，我發現漏掉了一件要緊的事，於是就把它記在附筆中。

**antedate** 〔'æntɪ͵det , ͵æntɪ'det 〕 *v.* 1. 把日期填早　2. 發生於⋯ 之前；居先

—— 1. assign a date before the true date
　　 2. come before in date; precede

If you used yesterday's date on a check written today, you have *antedated* the check.

如果你在今天的支票上填寫昨天的日期，你就是把支票的日期填早了。

Alaska *antedates* Hawaii as a state, having gained statehood on January 3, 1959, seven months before Hawaii.

阿拉斯加在 1959 年 1 月 3 日成爲美國的一州，比夏威夷早了七個月。

**postdate** 〔͵post'det 〕 *v.* 把日期填遲；發生於⋯之後

—— assign a date after the true date

This is a *postdated* check; it has tomorrow's date on it.

這張支票的日期填遲了，上面的日期是明天的。

## ante meridiem (ˈæntɪ məˈrɪdɪˌɛm , -ˈrɪdɪəm ) adv. 上午；午前
( = a.m. = am = A.M. = AM )

—— before noon

Our classes usually begin at 8 *a.m.* 我們的課程通常在上午八點開始。

## post meridiem (ˌpost məˈrɪdɪˌɛm , -ˈrɪdɪəm ) adv. 下午；午後
( = p.m. = pm = P.M. = PM )

—— after noon

At 4 *p.m.* the chairman announced that the debate was closed.

下午四點時主席宣布辯論結束。

## postgraduate ( postˈgrædʒuɪt , -ˌet ) adj. 大學畢業後的；
研究所的

—— having to do with study after graduation from college

Mary is taking a *postgraduate* course in philosophy.

瑪麗正在唸一門研究所的哲學課程。

Exercise：請由 **Group 3 & 4** 中，選出最適當的字，填入空格中。

1. The records show that most high school graduates continue their education by doing some kind of _____ study.

2. Mr. Sims told me to put tomorrow's date on the letter, but I forgot to _____ it.

3. The _____ showed that the patient had died of natural causes.

4. In some areas, the natives still use the same methods of farming as their _____ did centuries ago.

5. You will not have to add a(n) _____ if you plan your letter carefully.

---
【解答】
1. postgraduate    2. postdate    3. postmortem
4. antecedents    5. postscript
---

## 【Group 5】

# Bi — *two*「二」

## 【Group 6】

# Semi — *half*「一半」

**bicentennial**〔͵baɪsɛn'tɛnɪəl〕*n.* 兩百週年紀念

—— two hundredth anniversary

The *bicentennial* of George Washington's birth was celebrated in 1932. 喬治・華盛頓兩百週年生日紀念於 1932 年舉行。

**semicircle**〔'sɛmə͵sɝkl̩〕*n.* 半圓

—— half of a circle

semicircle

At the end of the lesson, a group gathered about the teacher in a *semicircle* to ask additional questions.

下課後，一群學生聚在老師身旁圍成半圓形，問一些額外的問題。

**bisect**〔baɪ'sɛkt〕*v.* 平分；將…分爲二等分

—— divide into two equal parts

A diameter is a line that *bisects* a circle.

直徑就是將一個圓分爲二等分的直線。

**bicameral**〔baɪ'kæmərəl〕*adj.* 兩院制的

—— consisting of two chambers or legislative houses

The American legislature is *bicameral*; it consists of the House of Representatives and the Senate.
美國的立法制度是兩院制的；包括眾議院及參議院。

## biennial〔baɪˈɛnɪəl〕*adj.* 兩年一次的

—— occurring every two years

A defeated candidate for the House of Representatives must wait two years before running again, because the elections are *biennial*.
一位競選失敗的眾議院候選人須等兩年才能再度競選，因為選舉是兩年一次的。

## bimonthly〔baɪˈmʌnθlɪ〕*adj.* 兩個月一次的

—— occurring every two months

We receive only six bills a year because we are billed on a *bimonthly* basis. 我們一年只收到六次帳單，因為我們是雙月送帳制。

## semiannual〔ˌsɛmɪˈænjʊəl〕*adj.* 每半年一次的

—— occurring every half year, or twice a year; semiyearly

Promotion in our school is *semiannual*; it occurs in January and June. 我們學校每半年升遷一次；各在一月及六月。

## semimonthly〔ˌsɛməˈmʌnθlɪ〕*adj.* 每半個月一次的

—— occurring every half month, or twice a month

Employees paid on a *semimonthly* basis receive two salary checks per month. 半月制付薪的員工一個月會收到兩次薪水支票。

## bilateral〔baɪˈlætərəl〕*adj.* 雙邊的

—— having two sides

French forces joined the Americans in a *bilateral* action against the British at the Battle of Yorktown in 1781.
法軍加入美軍形成雙邊行動，在 1781 年的約克鎮戰役中共同對抗英國。

第三章

**bilingual** 〔 baɪ'lɪŋgwəl 〕 *adj.* 1. 雙語的；能說兩種語言的
　　2. 以兩種語言寫成的
　　── 1. speaking two languages equally well
　　　　2. written in two languages
Montreal has a large number of *bilingual* citizens who speak
English and French.
蒙特婁有很多市民能說英、法兩種語言。
Some schools in Spanish-speaking communities send *bilingual*
notices, written in English and Spanish, to the parents.
一些在西班牙語區內的學校，會寄以英文及西班牙文兩種語言寫成的通知
給學生家長。

**bipartisan** 〔 baɪ'pɑrtəzn̩ 〕 *adj.* 兩黨的
　　── representing two political parties
Congressional committees are *bipartisan*; they consist of both
Democratic and Republican members.
國會的委員會是兩黨制的；包括民主與共和兩黨的黨員。

**semiconscious** 〔ˌsɛmə'kɑnʃəs 〕 *adj.* 半意識的
　　── half conscious; not fully conscious
In the morning, as you begin to awaken, you are in a
*semiconscious* state.
早晨你剛醒來時是處於一種半意識的狀態中。

**semi-detached** 〔ˌsɛmədɪ'tætʃt 〕 *adj.* 雙拼式的；半分離的
　　── partly detached; sharing a wall with an adjoining building on
　　　　one side, but detached on the other
All the houses on the block are attached, except the corner ones,
which are *semi-detached*.
這一街區的房屋都互相毗鄰，只有轉角那些雙拼式的房子例外。

第三章

**semiskilled** 〔,sɛmə'skɪld 〕 *adj.* 半熟練的

—— partly skilled

Workers who enter a *semiskilled* occupation do not have to undergo a long period of training.

進入只需半熟練技巧行業的員工不必受長期的訓練。

---

Exercise：請由 **Group 5 & 6** 中，選出最適當的字，填入空格中。

1. Everyone will be equally close to the fireplace if you arrange the chairs around it in the form of a _____.

2. The inspections are _____; there is one every six months.

3. A state that has both an assembly and a senate has a _____ legislature.

4. Our foreign policy is _____, since it represents the views of both major political parties.

5. Houses that are _____ share a common wall.

---

【解答】

1. semicircle　　2. semiannual　　3. bicameral

4. bipartisan　　5. semi-detached

---

【**Group 7**】

# E, Ex — *out*「向外」

【**Group 8**】

# In, Im — *in, against*「向內；對抗」

**insurgent**〔 ɪn'sɝdʒənt 〕1. *n.* 叛亂者；造反者；叛軍

  2. *adj.* 反叛的

    ── 1. one who rises in revolt against established authority; rebel

      2. rebellious

The king promised to pardon any *insurgent* who would lay down his arms. 國王答應寬恕任何願意放下武器的叛亂者。

General Washington led the *insurgent* forces in the Revolutionary War. 華盛頓將軍在獨立戰爭中領導反叛軍。

**erosion**〔 ɪ'roʒən 〕*n.* 侵蝕

  ── gradual wearing away

Running water is one of the principal causes of soil *erosion*. 流水是土壤侵蝕的主因之一。

**emigrate**[4]〔 'ɛmə,gret 〕*v.* 移出

  ── move out of a country or region to settle in another

In 1889, Charles Steinmetz, an engineer, *emigrated* from Germany.

在 1889 年，工程師查理斯‧史坦米茲移民離開德國。

> **【記憶技巧】**
> *e* (out) + *migr* (move) + *ate* (*v.*)（把東西搬出去，就是「移出」）

**immigrate**[4]〔 'ɪmə,gret 〕*v.* 移入

  ── move into a foreign country or region as a permanent resident

In 1889, Charles Steinmetz *immigrated* to the United States. 在 1889 年，查理斯‧史坦米茲移居美國。

> **【記憶技巧】**
> *im* (into) + *migr* (move) + *ate* (*v.*)（把東西搬進去，就是「移入」）

**evoke**〔 ɪ'vok 〕*v.* 召喚；引起

  ── bring out; call forth; elicit

The suggestion to lengthen the school year has *evoked* considerable opposition. 延長學年的建議引起不少的反對。

第三章

**invoke**〔ɪn'vok〕*v.* 懇求；求助；訴諸於

—— call on for help or protection; appeal to for support

Refusing to answer the question, the witness *invoked* the Fifth Amendment, which protects a person from being compelled to testify against himself. 證人拒絕回答，訴諸於第五條修正案，保護人民不被強迫說出對自己不利的證詞。

**excise**〔ɪk'saɪz〕*v.* 切除

—— cut out; remove by cutting out

With a penknife, he peeled the apple and *excised* the wormy part. 他用一把小刀削去蘋果皮，並且切除有蟲的部份。

**incise**〔ɪn'saɪz〕*v.* 切入；雕刻

—— cut into; carve; engrave

The letters on the monument had been *incised* with a chisel. 紀念碑上的字母是以鑿子刻成的。

**exhibit**[4]〔ɪg'zɪbɪt〕*v.* 展示

—— (literally, "hold out") show; display

The art department is *exhibiting* the outstanding posters produced in its classes. 藝術系正在展示班上學生製作的優良海報。

> 【記憶技巧】
> *ex* (out) + *hibit* (hold)
> (把東西拿出來，就是「展示」)

**inhibit**〔ɪn'hɪbɪt〕*v.* 抑制

—— (literally, "hold in") hold in check; restrain; repress

Ellen told the child not to cry, but he could not *inhibit* his tears. 艾倫跟小孩說不要哭了，但他無法忍住他的眼淚。

**expel**[6]〔ɪk'spɛl〕*v.* 驅逐；開除

—— drive out; force out; compel to leave

> 【記憶技巧】
> *ex* (out) + *pel* (drive) (趕到外面，也就是「驅逐」)

*Expelled* from the university because of poor grades, the student applied for readmission the following term.

因成績太差而被所屬大學開除的那名學生，申請下學期復學。

# impel〔ɪmˊpɛl〕*v.* 驅使；迫使

—— drive on; force; compel

Gregg's low mark in the midterm *impelled* him to study harder for the final.

格瑞格期中考成績太低，迫使他更努力地為期末考研讀。

# enervate〔ˊɛnɚˌvet〕*v.* 使無力

—— (literally, "take out the nerves or strength") lessen the strength of; enfeeble; weaken

Emma was so *enervated* by the broiling sun that she nearly fainted.

艾瑪被炎熱的太陽照得全身無力，幾乎昏倒。

# implicate〔ˊɪmplɪˌket〕*v.* 牽連

—— (literally, "fold in or involve") show to be part of or connected with; involve

The accused is not the only guilty party; two others are *implicated*.

被告並非是唯一有罪者；其他兩個人也牽連在內。

# impugn〔ɪmˊpjun〕*v.* 質疑；攻擊

—— (literally, "fight against") call into question; assail by words or arguments; attack as false; contradict

The treasurer should not have been offended when asked for a financial report.  No one was *impugning* his honesty.

別人向他要財務報告時，那位會計員不該生氣的，沒有人質疑他的誠實。

# incarcerate〔ɪnˊkɑrsəˌret〕*v.* 監禁

—— put into prison; imprison; confine

On July 14, 1789, the people of Paris freed the prisoners *incarcerated* in the Bastille.

1789 年 7 月 14 日，巴黎市民釋放了監禁於巴士底監獄的囚犯。

## inscribe〔ɪn'skraɪb〕*v.* 銘刻；書寫

—— (literally, "write on") write, engrave, or print to create a lasting record

The name of the winner will be *inscribed* on the medal.

得獎者的名字將被刻在獎牌上。

## eminent〔'ɛmənənt〕*adj.* 傑出的；卓越的

—— standing out; conspicuous; distinguished; noteworthy

Steinmetz's discoveries in the field of electricity made him one of the *eminent* scientists of the twentieth century.

史坦米茲在電學上的發現，使他成為二十世紀傑出的科學家之一。

## imminent〔'ɪmənənt〕*adj.* 迫近的

—— hanging threateningly over one's head; about to occur; impending

At the first flash of lightning, the beach crowd scurried for shelter from the *imminent* storm. 第一道閃電出現的時候，海灘的人潮急忙地跑著找地方，以躲避即將來臨的暴風雨。

## exclusive[6]〔ɪk'sklusɪv〕*adj.* 1. 排外的　2. 專用的；獨佔的；獨家的

—— 1. shutting out, or tending to shut out, others
2. not shared with others; single; sole

An *exclusive* club does not readily accept newcomers.

一個排外性的俱樂部不易接納新會員。

Before the game, each team had *exclusive* use of the field for a ten-minute practice period.

比賽前每一支隊伍都可單獨使用場地練習十分鐘。

**inclusive**[6]〔 ɪn'klusɪv 〕 *adj.* 包括的；包括首尾兩天的

—— (literally, "shutting in") including the limits (dates, numbers, etc.) mentioned

The film will be shown from August 22 to 24 *inclusive*, for a total of three days.

這部片子將從 8 月 22 日放映至 24 日，前後算在內共計三天。

Exercise：請由 **Group 7 & 8** 中，選出最適當的字，填入空格中。

1. This afternoon the swimming team has _____ use of the pool. No one else will be admitted.

2. No one can _____ the settler's claim to the property, since he holds the deed to the land.

3. Over the centuries, the Colorado River has carved its bed out of solid rock by the process of _____.

4. A lack of opportunity compelled thousands of able-bodied men to _____ from their native land.

5. Proposals to increase taxes usually _____ strong resistance.

6. The nation faced with famine is expected to _____ the help of its more fortunate neighbors.

7. On the front page, I am going to _____ these words: "To Dad on his fortieth birthday.  Love, Ruth."

8. Learning that his arrest was _____, the insurgent leader went into hiding.

9. The judge asked the guards to _____ the spectators who were creating a disturbance.

10. Jennifer just had to see what was in the package. She could not
_____ her curiosity.

> 【解答】
>
> 1. exclusive  2. impugn  3. erosion  4. emigrate
> 5. evoke  6. invoke  7. inscribe  8. imminent
> 9. expel  10. inhibit

## 【Group 9】

# Extra — *outside*「在外」

## 【Group 10】

# Intra — *within*「在內」

**extracurricular**[6] 〔͵ɛkstrəkə'rɪkjələ 〕

*adj.* 課外的

—— outside the regular curriculum, or
course of study

> 【記憶技巧】
> *extra + curricular*（課
> 程的）（在課程之外，即
> 「課外的」）

Why don't you join an *extracurricular* activity, such as a club, the
school newspaper, or a team?
你何不加入一種課外活動呢？例如社團、校刊，或是球隊。

**extraneous**〔 ɪk'strenɪəs ͵ ɛk- 〕*adj.* 外來的；（與主題）無關的

—— coming from or existing outside; foreign; not essential

You said you would stick to the topic, but you keep introducing
*extraneous* issues. 你說你將不離主題，可是卻一直提出不相干的議題。

**extravagant**〔 ɪk'strævəgənt 〕*adj.* 1. 揮霍的  2. 過度的

—— 1. spending lavishly; wasteful
  2. outside the bounds of reason; excessive

In a few months, the *extravagant* heir spent the fortune of a lifetime. 幾個月內那個揮霍無度的繼承人花掉了一生的財富。
Reliable salesmen do not make *extravagant* claims for their product. 可靠的推銷員不會過度誇張他們的產品。

## intramural〔͵ɪntrə′mjurəl 〕*adj.* 校內的

—— within the walls or boundaries (of a school, college, etc.); confined to members (of a school, college, etc.)

The *intramural* program, in which one class competes with another, gives you a greater chance to participate than the interscholastic program between teams of competing schools.
校內班際間的比賽，比校際間的比賽更能提供你參與的機會。

## intraparty〔′ɪntrə′pɑrtɪ 〕*adj.* 黨內的

—— within a party

The Democrats are trying to heal *intraparty* strife so as to present a united front in the coming election.
民主黨員設法和解黨內的紛爭，以求在未來的選舉中呈現統一的陣線。

## intrastate〔͵ɪntrə′stet 〕*adj.* 州內的

—— within a state

Commerce between the states is regulated by the Interstate Commerce Commission, but *intrastate* commerce is supervised by the states themselves.
州際間的貿易由州際貿易委員會管理，而各州內部的貿易則由各州督導。

## intravenous〔͵ɪntrə′vinəs 〕*adj.* 靜脈的；靜脈注射的

—— within or by way of the veins

Patients are nourished by *intravenous* feeding when too ill to take food by mouth.
當病人不能由口進食時，需藉靜脈注射給食來提供養分。

第三章

Exercise：請由 **Group 9 & 10** 中，選出最適當的字，填入空格中。

1. The candidate's claim that he would win by a landslide was certainly _____, as he was nearly defeated.

2. An air conditioner cools a room and helps to shut out _____ noises.

3. The theft must be regarded as an _____ matter, unless the stolen goods have been transported across state lines.

4. Some educators want to concentrate on _____ sports and do away with interscholastic contests.

5. Though fencing is not in our curriculum, it is offered as an _____ activity.

```
【解答】
1. extravagant      2. extraneous       3. intrastate
4. intramural       5. extracurricular
```

## 【Group 11】

# Contra, Contro, Counter — *against*「對抗」

**con**〔kɑn〕1. *adj.* 反對的　2. *n.* 反對的理由
—— (short for contra)　1. against; on the negative side
　　　2. opposing argument; reason against

Are you on the pro or *con* side of this argument?
你是贊成還是反對這個論點？
Before taking an important step, carefully study the pros and *cons* of the matter.
在對這件事採取重要措施前，先仔細研究利弊得失。

**contraband** 〔ˈkɑntrəˌbænd 〕*n.* 走私品；違禁品

—— merchandise imported or exported contrary to law; smuggled goods

Customs officials examined the luggage of the suspected smuggler but found no *contraband*.

海關人員仔細檢查走私嫌疑犯的行李，卻未發現任何違禁品。

**controversy**[6] 〔ˈkɑntrəˌvɝsɪ 〕*n.* 爭論

—— (literally, "a turning against") dispute; debate; quarrel

American *controversy* with Great Britain over the Oregon Territory nearly led to war.

美國與英國有關奧勒岡領土的爭論幾乎導致戰爭。

**contravene** 〔ˌkɑntrəˈvin 〕*v.* 違反

—— go or act contrary to; violate; disregard; infringe

By invading the neutral nation, the dictator *contravened* his earlier pledge to guarantee its independence.

獨裁者入侵中立國，違反先前保證其獨立的約定。

**countermand** 〔ˌkaʊntɚˈmænd 〕*v.* 取消；撤回（命令）

—— cancel (an order) by issuing a contrary order

The monitor ordered the student to go to the end of the line, but the teacher *countermanded* the order.

班長叫那個學生到行列的最後頭，老師卻取消那個命令。

**counter**[4] 〔ˈkaʊntɚ 〕*adv.* 相反地；背道而馳地　*adj.* 相反的

—— (followed by *to*) contrary; in the opposite direction

The student's plan to drop out of school ran *counter* to his parents' wishes.

那個學生輟學的計畫與他父母的希望背道而馳。

**incontrovertible** 〔ˌɪnkɑntrəˈvɝtəbl̩〕 *adj.* 不容置疑的
—— not able to be "turned against" or disputed; unquestionable
certain; indisputable

The suspects' fingerprints on the safe were considered
*incontrovertible* evidence that he had participated in the robbery.
嫌疑犯留在保險箱上的指紋，成為他參與搶劫不容置疑的證據。

Exercise：請由 **Group 11** 中，選出最適當的字，填入空格中。

1. Until our recent _____, Peggy and I were the best of friends.

2. A person's birth certificate is _____ proof of his age.

3. Vessels carrying _____ are subject to seizure.

4. A superior officer has the power to _____ orders issued by a
   subordinate.

5. I cannot support you in an activity that you undertook _____
   to my advice.

```
【解答】
1. controversy    2. incontrovertible    3. contraband
4. countermand    5. counter
```

【**Group 12**】

# Inter — *between*「在～之間」

**interlude** 〔ˈɪntɚˌlud〕 *n.* （兩件事之間的）空檔時間；穿插的事
—— anything filling the time between two events; interval
Between World War II and the Korean War, there was a five year
*interlude* of peace. 二次世界大戰與韓戰之間，有一段歷時五年的和平。

## intermediary〔ˌɪntɚˈmidɪˌɛrɪ〕*n.* 調停者；中間人

—— go-between; mediator

For his role as *intermediary* in helping to end the Russo-Japanese War, Theodore Roosevelt won the Nobel Peace Prize.

狄奧多‧羅斯福因他在日俄戰爭中擔任調停者，獲得諾貝爾和平獎。

## intermission〔ˌɪntɚˈmɪʃən〕*n.* 休息時間；中止

—— pause between periods of activity; interval; interruption

During the *intermission* between the first and second acts, you will have a chance to purchase refreshments.

在第一幕與第二幕之間的休息時間，你有機會去買點心。

## intercede〔ˌɪntɚˈsid〕*v.* 調停；說情

—— (literally, "go between") interfere to reconcile differences; mediate; plead in another's behalf; intervene

My brother would have lost the argument if Dad hadn't *interceded* for him.

如果當時父親不替哥哥求情，他會輸掉這場爭論。

第三章

## intercept〔ˌɪntɚˈsɛpt〕*v.* 中途攔截

—— (literally, "catch between") stop or seize on the way from one place to another

We gained possession of the ball when Russ *intercepted* a forward pass. 羅斯攔截直傳而過的球時，我們便拿到球了。

## intersect〔ˌɪntɚˈsɛkt〕*v.* 和⋯相交；貫穿

—— (literally, "cut between") cut by passing through or across; divide; cross

The roads *intersect* near the bridge.
這些道路在那座橋附近相交。

**intervene**[6] 〔͵ɪntə'vin 〕 *v.* 1. 介入；調停 2. 介於其間

—— 1. come in to settle a quarrel; intercede; mediate

2. come between

Let the boys settle the dispute by themselves; don't *intervene*.

讓男孩們自行解決爭端；不要介入。

The summer vacation *intervenes* between the close of one school year and the beginning of the next.

暑假介於一學年的結束與下一學年的開始。

**interlinear** 〔͵ɪntə'lɪnɪə 〕 *adj.* 寫在行間的

—— inserted between lines already printed or written

It is difficult to make *interlinear* notes if the space between the lines is very small.

如果各行之間的空間很小，就很難在行間加註了。

**interurban** 〔͵ɪntə'ɜˋbən 〕 *adj.* 城市與城市之間的；鎮與鎮之間的

—— between cities or towns

The only way to get to the next city is by automobile or taxi; there is no *interurban* bus.

到達下一個城市唯一的方法是開車或搭計程車，兩市之間沒有市際公車。

Exercise：請由 **Group 12** 中，選出最適當的字，填入空格中。

1. A warning signal must be posted wherever railroad tracks _____ a highway.

2. Though he has been asked repeatedly to be an _____ in the labor dispute, the mayor so far has refused to intercede.

3. Radio stations sometimes offer a brief _____ of music between the end of one program and the start of another.

4. A special task force is trying to _____ the enemy column advancing on the capital city.

5. Construction funds have been allocated for a four-lane _____ highway linking the three cities.

> 【解答】
>
> 1. intersect     2. intermediary     3. interlude
> 4. intercept     5. interurban

## 【Group 13】

# In, Il, Im, Ir — *not, un*「不;非」

**impunity**〔ɪmˊpjunətɪ〕*n.* 不受處罰

—— state of being not punished; freedom from punishment, harm, loss, etc.

As a result of stricter enforcement, speeders are no longer able to break the law with *impunity*.

由於更嚴格執行法律的結果,超速者已不可能違法而不受罰。

**ingratitude**〔ɪnˊgrætəˌtjud〕*n.* 忘恩負義

—— state of being not grateful; ungratefulness; lack of gratitude

Alice refused to let me see her notes, despite the fact that I have always lent her mine. Did you ever hear of such *ingratitude*?

愛麗絲拒絕讓我看她的筆記,儘管我總是把我的借給她。你聽過如此忘恩負義的事嗎?

**illegible**〔ɪˊlɛdʒəbl̩, ɪlˊlɛdʒ-〕*adj.* 難讀的;難以辨識的

—— not legible; not able to be read

I could read most of the signatures, but a few were *illegible*.

我可以認出大部份的簽名,但有一些難以辨識。

**illiterate** 〔 ɪˈlɪtərɪt , ɪˈlɪtrɪt 〕 *adj.* 不識字的

—— not literate; unable to read and write; uneducated

The new nation undertook to teach its *illiterate* citizens to read and write. 那個新成立的國家著手教導不識字的國民讀和寫。

**illogical** 〔 ɪˈlɑdʒɪk! , ɪlˈlɑdʒɪk! 〕 *adj.* 不合邏輯的；不合常理的

—— not logical; not observing the rules of *logic* (correct reasoning)

It is *illogical* to vote for a candidate whom you have no faith in. 將選票投給一位你沒信心的候選人是不合常理的。

**immaculate** 〔 ɪˈmækjəlɪt 〕 *adj.* 無污點的；潔淨的

—— not spotted; absolutely clean; stainless

Nearly every soap manufacturer claims his product will make dirty linens *immaculate*.
幾乎每一個肥皂製造商都宣稱他的產品可以洗淨骯髒的亞麻布製品。

**immature** 〔 ˌɪməˈtjʊr 〕 *adj.* 不成熟的

—— not mature; not fully grown or developed

Don't use such baby talk! People will think you are mentally *immature*.
別說這麼孩子氣的話！別人會以為你心智未成熟。

**inaccessible** 〔 ˌɪnækˈsɛsəb! , ˌɪnæk- 〕 *adj.* 不能到達的

—— not accessible; not able to be reached; hard to get to

For most of the year, the Eskimo settlements in northern Quebec are *inaccessible*, except by air. 一年中大部份的時間，除了搭飛機外，是到不了北魁北克的愛斯基摩居留地的。

**incessant** 〔 ɪnˈsɛsənt 〕 *adj.* 不斷的

—— not ceasing; continuing without interruption

It is almost impossible to cross our street during the rush hour because of the *incessant* flow of traffic.
尖峰時間車輛川流不息，很難越過我們那條街。

## inflexible〔ɪnˈflɛksəbl̩〕*adj.* 強硬的；不屈的
—— not flexible; not easily bent; firm; unyielding
No compromise is possible when both sides remain *inflexible*.
當雙方態度都很強硬時，是不可能達成協議的。

## inhospitable〔ɪnˈhɑspɪtəbl̩〕*adj.* 不好客的；不親切的；冷淡的
—— not hospitable; not showing kindness to guests and strangers; unfriendly
When the visitors come to our school, we should make them feel at home; otherwise they will think we are *inhospitable*.
當訪客來到我們學校時，應該讓他們有賓至如歸的感覺，否則他們會認為我們待客不親切。

## insoluble〔ɪnˈsɑljəbl̩〕*adj.* 1. 不能解決的　2. 不能溶解的
—— 1. not soluble; incapable of being solved; unsolvable
2. not capable of being dissolved
Scientists are finding solutions to many problems that up to now were *insoluble*. 科學家正在為許多至今尚無解答的問題尋找答案。
Salt dissolves in water, but sand is *insoluble*.
鹽在水中會溶解，而沙子就不能溶解。

## irreconcilable〔ɪˈrɛkənˌsaɪləbl̩, ɪrˈrɛk-〕*adj.* 不能和解的；互相對立的
—— not reconcilable; not able to be brought into friendly accord
After Romeo and Juliet died, their families, who had been *irreconcilable* enemies, became friends.
羅密歐與茱麗葉死後，他們原本相對立的家族，變成了朋友。

**irrelevant** 〔 ɪˈrɛləvənt 〕 *adj.* 不相關的；不切題的

—— not relevant; not applicable; off the topic; extraneous

Stick to the topic; don't make *irrelevant* remarks.

堅守主題；不要說一些不相關的話。

**irrevocable** 〔 ɪˈrɛvəkəbḷ, ɪrˈrɛv- 〕 *adj.* 不能撤銷的；無法挽回的

—— not revocable; incapable of being recalled; past recall

When the umpire says you are out, it is useless to argue because his decision is *irrevocable*.

裁判說你出局時，爭辯是沒有用的，因為他的決定不可能撤銷。

**Exercise：請由 Group 13 中，選出最適當的字，填入空格中。**

1. Half-frozen, the traveler knocked at a strange door, hoping the inhabitants would not be so _____ as to turn him away from their fire.

2. You can't neglect your work with _____ in Mr. McConnell's class because he checks the homework every day.

3. By tracking down every clue, the detective finally succeeded in clearing up the seemingly _____ mystery.

4. On some of the very old tombstones in Boston's Granary Burying Ground, the inscriptions are almost _____.

5. Before the bridge was built, the island was _____ from the mainland, except by ferry.

---

【解答】
| | | |
|---|---|---|
| 1. inhospitable | 2. impunity | 3. insoluble |
| 4. illegible | 5. inaccessible | |

第三章

【Group 14】

# Bene — *good*「好」

【Group 15】

# Mal — *evil*「惡」

**benediction**〔͵bɛnə′dɪkʃən〕*n.* 祝福

—— (literally, "good saying") blessing; good wishes

Before beginning his difficult journey, the young man visited his parents to receive their *benediction*.

在他艱難的旅程開始前，那個年輕人探望他的父母以接受他們的祝福。

**malediction**〔͵mælə′dɪkʃən〕*n.* 詛咒

—— (literally, "evil saying") curse

With her dying breath, Queen Dido pronounced a *malediction* on Aeneas and all his descendants.

黛朵女王以其死前最後一口氣詛咒阿尼厄斯及其子孫。

**benefactor**〔′bɛnə͵fæktɚ, ͵bɛnə′fæktɚ〕*n.* 捐贈人；恩人

—— (literally, "one who does good") person who gives kindly aid, money, or a similar benefit

The museum could not have been built without the gift of a million dollars by a wealthy *benefactor*.

要不是一位富有的捐贈人捐了一百萬元，博物館也蓋不起來。

**malefactor**〔′mælə͵fæktɚ〕*n.* 罪犯

—— (literally, "one who does evil") offender; evildoer; criminal

Shortly after the crime, the *malefactor* was apprehended and turned over to the police.

犯罪後不久，那個罪犯就被逮捕而且移交警方。

**beneficiary**〔͵bɛnə'fɪʃərɪ , -'fɪʃɪ͵ɛrɪ 〕 *n.* 受益者

—— person receiving some good, advantage, or benefit

The sick and the needy will be the *beneficiaries* of your gift to the community fund. 病人與貧民將成爲你對社區基金贈與的受益者。

**malice**〔'mælɪs 〕 *n.* 惡意

—— ill will; intention or desire to harm another; enmity; malevolence

I suspect Ronnie tripped me so that I wouldn't be able to play tomorrow. He did it not as a joke but out of *malice*. 我懷疑羅尼爲了讓我明天無法比賽而絆倒我，他這麼做並非開玩笑，而是出自惡意。

**malnutrition**〔͵mælnju'trɪʃən 〕 *n.* 營養不良

—— bad or faulty nutrition; poor nourishment

The lack of milk and fresh vegetables in the child's diet was responsible for his *malnutrition*.
這個小孩飲食中缺乏牛奶及新鮮蔬菜造成他營養不良。

**maltreat**〔 mæl'trit 〕 *v.* 虐待

—— treat badly or roughly; mistreat; abuse

Two news photographers were attacked by the mob, and their cameras were smashed. It is disgraceful that they were so *maltreated*. 兩個新聞攝影者受到暴徒攻擊，他們的照相機也被砸碎。讓他們遭受如此虐待，實在可恥。

**beneficial**[5]〔͵bɛnə'fɪʃəl 〕 *adj.* 有益的

—— productive of good; helpful; advantageous

【記憶技巧】
*bene* (good) + *fic* (do) + *ial* (*adj.*)

Rest is usually *beneficial* to a person suffering from a bad cold.
休息對罹患重感冒的人經常是很有幫助的。

# benevolent〔bə′nɛvələnt〕 *adj.* 慈善的

—— (literally, "wishing well") disposed to promote the welfare of others; kind; charitable

A *benevolent* employer has a sincere interest in the welfare of his employees. 一個慈善的雇主會真誠地關懷員工的福利。

# malevolent〔mə′lɛvələnt〕 *adj.* 有惡意的；心懷不軌的

—— (literally, "wishing ill") showing ill will; spiteful

I have heard some *malevolent* misrepresentation of her. 我聽到有些人惡意曲解她的話。

# maladjusted〔‚mælə′dʒʌstɪd〕 *adj.* 不能適應環境的；失調的

—— badly adjusted; out of harmony with one's environment

Carlo was *maladjusted* in the early grades, not because of poor intelligence but because he couldn't speak English.
卡蘿在前幾個年級時不能適應環境，並非由於他智力差，而是因為他不會說英語。

Exercise：請由 **Group 14 & 15** 中，選出最適當的字，填入空格中。

1. It is uncommon for a _____ child to come from a home where there are warm family relationships.

2. The hero of Charles Dickens' novel *Great Expectations* received considerable financial aid from an unknown _____.

3. Mrs. Adams will inherit a fortune, since she is named as the exclusive _____ in her wealthy uncle's will.

4. Paul couldn't understand why anyone should bear him so much _____ as to tear his notes to bits.

第三章

5. Philip Nolan, in Edward Everett Hale's short story *The Man Without a Country*, is punished for uttering a _____ on the United States.

┌ 【解答】 ─────────────────────────────────────┐
1. malevolent    2. benefactor    3. beneficiary
4. malice       5. malediction
└────────────────────────────────────────────────┘

## 【Group 16】

# De — *down, opposite of*「向下；相反」

**demolish**〔dɪ'mɑlɪʃ〕*v.* 拆除；破壞

—— pull or tear down; destroy

A wrecking crew is *demolishing* the old building.
拆除隊正在拆除這幢老建築物。

**demote**〔dɪ'mot〕*v.* 降級

—— move down in grade or rank

For being absent without leave, the corporal was *demoted* to private. 這位下士因不假外出而被降爲上等兵。

**depreciate**〔dɪ'priʃɪ,et〕*v.* 1. 貶值；減價    2. 輕視

—— 1. go down in price or value
     2. speak slightingly of; belittle; disparage

Automobiles *depreciate* rapidly; a $2,500 car is worth less than $2,000 within a year of purchase.
汽車貶值很快；一輛兩千五百元的車買不到一年就不值兩千元了。
The building superintendent feels *depreciated* if you refer to him as the "janitor."
如果你叫這幢建築物的管理員「工友」，他就會覺得被輕視了。

第三章

**despise**[5]〔 dɪ'spaɪz 〕*v.* 輕視

—— look down on; scorn; feel contempt for

> 【記憶技巧】
> *de* (down) + *spise* (see)
> （把別人看得很低，即
> 「輕視」）

Students who tell lies are *despised* by their classmates. 說謊的學生會被同班同學輕視。

**deviate**〔 'divɪ,et 〕*v.* 脫離（常軌）；違反

—— turn aside, or down (from a route or rule); stray

Mr. Parker always notifies the parents when a student neglects his homework, and he will not *deviate* from this rule in your case. 每次學生不寫家庭作業時，派克先生都會通知他的父母，當然你這次他也不會違反原則。

**devour**[5]〔 dɪ'vaʊr 〕*v.* 狼吞虎嚥；吞食

—— (literally, "gulp down") eat greedily; eat like an animal

> 【記憶技巧】
> *de* (down) + *vour*
> (swallow)（把東西直接吞
> 下去，就是「狼吞虎嚥」）

The children must have been starved when they came in for dinner because they *devoured* their food. 孩子們在進來吃晚餐時一定餓壞了，因為他們狼吞虎嚥地把食物吃掉。

**decadent**〔 'dɛkədənt 〕*adj.* 頹廢的；式微的；衰弱的

—— (literally, "falling down") deteriorating; growing worse; declining

The *decadent* downtown section was once a flourishing business district. 式微的鬧區地段一度曾是繁華的商業區。

**deciduous**〔 dɪ'sɪdʒʊəs 〕*adj.* 落葉性的

—— having leaves that fall down at the end of the growing season; shedding leaves

Maple, elm, birch, and other *deciduous* trees lose their leaves in the fall. 楓樹、榆樹、樺樹，及其他落葉性的樹木，在秋天會掉葉子。

**demented**〔dɪ'mɛntɪd〕*adj.* 瘋狂的

—— out of (down from) one's mind; mad; insane; deranged

Whoever did this must have been *demented*; no sane person would have acted in such a way.

凡是做這件事的人一定是瘋了，沒有任何正常人會這麼做。

**dependent**⁴〔dɪ'pɛndənt〕*adj.* 依賴的

—— (literally, "hanging down from") unable to exist without the support of another

Children are *dependent* on their parents until they are able to earn their own living. 小孩在他們能獨立謀生前都得依賴父母。

Exercise：請由 **Group 16** 中，選出最適當的字，填入空格中。

1. The bus driver cannot drop you off at your front door because he is not permitted to _____ from his route.

2. Streets lined with _____ trees are strewn with fallen leaves each autumn.

3. The patient's speech was not rational but like that of a _____ person.

4. Retired people like to have an income of their own so as not to be _____ on relatives.

5. The Romans were well past the peak of their glory and had become a _____ people by 400 A.D.

--------【解答】--------
| | | |
|---|---|---|
| 1. deviate | 2. deciduous | 3. demented |
| 4. dependent | 5. decadent | |

第三章

【Group 17】

# Dis — *opposite of*「相反」

**discrepancy**〔 dɪ'skrɛpənsɪ 〕*n.* 矛盾；不一致；差異
—— disagreement; difference; inconsistency; variation
Jack should have had $8 in his wallet, but he had only $6. He could not account for the *discrepancy*.
傑克皮夾裡應該有八塊錢，但卻只有六塊，他無法解釋這矛盾的地方。

**disrepair**〔 ˌdɪsrɪ'pɛr 〕*n.* 失修；破敗
—— opposite of good condition or repair; bad condition
The bicycle I lent Tom had been in good condition, but he returned it in *disrepair*.
我借給湯姆用的腳踏車是好的，但是他卻還我一輛破損待修的車子。

**discredit**〔 dɪs'krɛdɪt 〕*v.* 不相信
—— disbelieve; refuse to trust
The parents *discredited* the child's story, since he was in the habit of telling falsehoods. 父母親不相信那小孩說的話，因為他有說謊的習慣。

**disintegrate**〔 dɪs'ɪntə,gret 〕*v.* 使瓦解；使崩潰
—— do the opposite of "integrate" (make into a whole); break into bits

The explosion *disintegrated* an entire wing of the factory.
那次爆炸瓦解了工廠的一整邊。

**dissent**〔 dɪ'sɛnt 〕*v.* 不同意
—— feel differently; differ in opinion; disagree
When the matter was put to a vote, 29 agreed and 4 *dissented*.
當這件事訴諸於表決時，二十九票贊成，四票反對。

**distract**[6]〔 dɪ'strækt 〕 *v.* 使分心;轉移

—— draw away (the mind or attention);
divert

Passengers should do nothing to *distract*
the driver's attention from the road.
乘客不應該做任何使駕駛人分心的事。

【記憶技巧】
*dis* (apart) + *tract*
(draw)(拉往別的方
向,也就是「使分心」)

**discontent**〔 ˌdɪskən'tɛnt 〕 *adj.* 不滿意的

—— (usually followed by *with*) opposite of "content"; dissatisfied;
discontented

Dan was *discontent* with his Spanish mark; he had expected at
least 10 points more.
丹對他的西班牙文成績感到不滿,他所預期的分數至少還要再多十分。

**dispassionate**〔 dɪs'pæʃənɪt 〕 *adj.* 冷靜的;公平的

—— opposite of "passionate" (showing strong feeling); calm;
composed; impartial

For a *dispassionate* account of how the fight started, ask a neutral
observer —— not a participant.
關於這場爭鬥怎麼開始的,想得到公平冷靜的解說,得去問中立的旁觀
者,而不能問當事人。

**dissident**[6]〔'dɪsədənt 〕 *adj.* 意見不同的;有異議的
*n.* 意見不同者

—— (literally, "sitting apart") not
agreeing; dissenting

The compromise was welcomed by all
the strikers except a small *dissident* group who felt that the raises
were too small. 除了少數人認為薪水加得太少而持有異議外,所有的罷
工者都歡迎這次的和解。

【記憶技巧】
*dis* (apart) + *sid* (sit) +
*ent* ( 人 )(分開坐的人,
表示「意見不同者」)

**Exercise：請由 Group 17 中，選出最適當的字，填入空格中。**

1. The leader conferred with several _____ members of his party in an attempt to win them over to his views.

2. Add your marks for the different parts of the test to see if they equal your total mark. If there is a _____, notify the teacher.

3. The negligent owner allowed his property to fall into _____.

4. I had no reason to _____ John's story, since he had always told me the truth.

5. Turn off the television set while you are doing homework, or it will _____ your attention.

> 【解答】
> 1. dissident      2. discrepancy      3. disrepair
> 4. discredit      5. distract

【**Group 18**】

# Se — *apart*「分離」

**secession**〔 si'sɛʃən 〕*n.* 脫離；退出

—— (literally, "a going apart") withdrawal from an organization or federation

South Carolina's *secession* was imitated by ten other states and led to the formation of the Confederacy.

南卡羅萊納州退出聯邦為其他十州所仿效，導致南部聯邦的形成。

**sedition** 〔 sɪ'dɪʃən 〕 *n.* 煽動叛亂

—— going apart from, or against, an established government; action, speech, or writing to overthrow the government

The signers of the Declaration of Independence, if captured by the enemy, would probably have been tried for *sedition*.

獨立宣言的簽署者如果被敵人抓到，可能會因煽動叛亂罪名而被審判。

**secede** 〔 sɪ'sid 〕 *v.* 退出；脫離

—— (literally, "go apart") withdraw from an organization or federation

When Abraham Lincoln was elected President in 1860, South Carolina *seceded* from the Union.

當亞伯拉罕・林肯在 1860 年當選為總統時，南卡羅萊納州便退出聯邦。

**seclude** 〔 sɪ'klud 〕 *v.* 隔絕

—— keep apart from others; place in solitude; isolate

Ann was so upset by her failure in math that she *secluded* herself and refused to see anyone.

安因為數學考不及格而心煩，所以她把自己隔絕起來，拒絕見任何人。

**segregate** 〔'sɛgrɪˌget 〕 *v.* 分離

—— (literally, "set apart from the herd") separate from the main body

In most high schools, boys and girls attend the same classes, except in health education, where they are *segregated*. 大部份的高中生都是男女生一起上課，只有上衛教課的時候才把他們分開。

**secure**[5] 〔 sɪ'kjur 〕 *adj.* 1. 安全的　2. 放心的

—— 1. safe against loss, attack, or danger
　　2. apart, or free, from care, fear, or worry; confident

> 【記憶技巧】
> *se* (free from) + *cure* (care) ( 沒有憂慮的，表示「安全的」)

Land in a growing city is a *secure* investment.
在一個逐漸成長的都市裡，土地是一種安全的投資。
Are you worried about passing the midterm exam, or do you feel
*secure*? 你在擔心如何通過期中考，還是你覺得很放心？

Exercise：請由 **Group 18** 中，選出最適當的字，填入空格中。

1. The Armed Forces are forbidden by law to _____ servicemen
   on the basis of their ethnicity or religion.

2. In a dictatorship, anyone who criticizes the head of state may be
   charged with _____.

3. Three of the teams have threatened to _____ from the league
   unless two umpires are assigned to each game.

4. As the storm approached, coastal residents were evacuated to
   more _____ quarters in the interior.

5. Some students prefer to study for a test with friends; others like
   to _____ themselves with their books.

--- 【解答】 ---------------------------------
1. segregate      2. sedition       3. secede
4. secure         5. seclude

【**Group 19**】

# Circum — *round*「周圍」

**circumference**〔səˈkʌmfərəns〕*n.* 圓周；物體的周邊
—— distance around a circle or rounded body; perimeter

Circumference

The *circumference* of a circle equals π times the diameter.
圓周等於 π 乘以直徑。

## circumlocution〔͵sɝkəmloˈkjuʃən〕*n.* 迂迴的說法；婉轉語；繞圈子的話

—— roundabout way of speaking; use of an excessive number of words to express an idea

The *circumlocution* "the game ended with a score that was not in our favor" should be replaced by "we lost the game."
「這場比賽在比數對我們不利的情況下結束」是繞圈子的話，應該說「我們輸了這場比賽」。

## circumnavigate〔͵sɝkəmˈnævə͵get〕*n.* 環航

—— sail around

Ferdinand Magellan's expedition was the first to *circumnavigate* the globe. 斐迪南・麥哲倫的遠征是第一次環繞世界的航行。

## circumscribe〔͵sɝkəmˈskraɪb〕*v.* 1. 限制　2. 在…上面劃圈

—— 1. limit; restrict　　2. draw a line around

The patient was placed on a very *circumscribed* diet; he was forbidden to have coffee, spices, or raw fruits or vegetables.
這病患的飲食極受限制，他不能喝咖啡、吃香料，或生的水果或蔬菜。
The principal has requested all teachers to *circumscribe* failures in red on the report cards.
校長要求所有老師把成績單上不及格者用紅筆圈起來。

## circumvent〔͵sɝkəmˈvɛnt〕*v.* 逃避；規避；環繞

—— go around; get the better of; frustrate

To *circumvent* local sales taxes, shoppers often buy in neighboring communities that do not have such taxes.
爲了逃避當地的貨物稅，購物者經常在鄰近不徵此稅的社區買東西。

**circumspect**〔ˈsɜˈkəmˌspɛkt〕 *adj.* 慎重的；謹慎小心的

—— looking around and paying attention to all possible consequences before acting; cautious; prudent

Don't jump to a conclusion before considering all the facts. Be *circumspect*. 在所有的事未考慮好之前，不要遽下結論，要慎重點。

Exercise：請由 **Group 19** 中，選出最適當的字，填入空格中。

1. A physician may decide to ———— the physical activities and diet of a heart disease patient.

2. Obey the regulations; don't try to ———— them.

3. If you had been ————, you would have tested the used phonograph before buying it.

4. The ———— of the earth at its equator is nearly 25,000 miles.

5. The rowers expected to ———— the island in a couple of hours, but by evening they were less than halfway around.

> ---【解答】------------------------------
> 1. circumscribe　2. circumvent　3. circumspect
> 4. circumference　5. circumnavigate

第三章

## 【Group 20】

# Con, Co, Col, Cor — *together*「一起」

**collusion**〔kəˈluʒən, -ˈljuʒən〕 *n.* 勾結；串通

—— (literally, "playing together") secret agreement for a fraudulent purpose; conspiracy; plot

It was not known whether the price increases resulted from higher costs or from *collusion* among the producers.
不知道價格的上漲是起因於成本的提高，還是製造者之間的勾結。

## concord 〔'kɑnkɔrd 〕 *n.* 和諧

—— state of being together in heart or mind; agreement; harmony

Neighbors cannot live in *concord* if their children keep fighting with one another.
如果孩子們總是打來打去的，鄰居間就無法和諧相處。

## coalesce 〔,koə'lɛs 〕 *v.* 聯合；合併

—— grow together; unite into one; combine

During the Revolutionary War, the thirteen colonies *coalesced* into one nation. 獨立戰爭期間，十三個殖民地聯合成一個國家。

## collaborate 〔 kə'læbə,ret 〕 *v.* 合作

—— work together

Tom is *collaborating* on the work with his friend.
湯姆與他的朋友一起做那件工作。

## convene 〔 kən'vin 〕 *v.* 集合

—— come together in a body; meet; assemble

The House and the Senate will *convene* at noon to hear an address by the President. 眾議院與參議院將在中午集合聽總統發表演說。

## correspond[4] 〔,kɔrə'spɑnd 〕 *v.* 符合；通信

—— (literally, "answer together") agree; be in harmony; match; tally

Jack's account of how the fight started did not *correspond* with the other boy's version. 傑克描述這場架的起因與另外一個男孩的說法不符。

> 【記憶技巧】
> *cor* (together) + *respond* (answer) ( 相互回信，表示「通信」)

**coherent**[6] ﹝ koˈhɪrənt ﹞ *adj.* 有條理的；前後一致的

—— sticking together; logically connected

【記憶技巧】
*co* (together) + *her* (stick) + *ent* (*adj.*)（前後黏在一起，表示「前後一致的」）

In *coherent* writing, every sentence is connected in thought to the previous sentence. 有條理的寫作，每一個句子的想法都與上一個句子相連結。

**congenital** ﹝ kənˈdʒɛnətḷ ﹞ *adj.* 先天性的

—— (literally, "born with") existing at birth; inborn

Helen Keller's deafness and blindness were not *congenital* defects but were acquired after birth.

海倫‧凱勒的聾與盲不是先天的缺陷，而是後天造成的。

Exercise：請由 **Group 20** 中，選出最適當的字，填入空格中。

1. Though elected in November, the new Congress does not _____ until the following January.

2. If your seat number does not _____ to your ticket number, the usher may ask you to move.

3. When Billy Budd, the peacemaker, was aboard, there was perfect _____ among the sailors.

4. Do you want to _____ with me in the experiment, or do you prefer to work alone?

5. Just above St. Louis, the Missouri and Mississippi Rivers _____ into a single waterway.

【解答】
1. convene　　2. correspond　　3. concord
4. collaborate　　5. coalesce

【Group 21】

# Ob — *against, over*「對抗;超越」

**obstacle**[4]〔ˈɑbstəkl̩〕 *n.* 障礙;阻礙

—— something standing in the way; hindrance; obstruction; impediment

If we beat Central High tomorrow, we shall have removed the last *obstacle* between us and the championship.

如果我們明天擊敗中央中學,便掃除掉我們與冠軍之間的最後障礙。

**obliterate**〔 əˈblɪtəˌret 〕 *v.* 消除;擦掉

—— (literally, "cover over letters"); erase; blot out; destroy; remove all traces of

Today's rain has completely *obliterated* yesterday's snow; not a trace remains.

今天下的雨把昨天的積雪完全除去,一點也不留。

**obsess**〔 əbˈsɛs 〕 *v.* 困擾;縈繞於心

—— (literally, "sit over") trouble the mind of; haunt

The notion that she had forgotten to lock the front door *obsessed* Mother all through the movie.

在看電影的時候,忘了鎖前門的想法一直縈繞著媽媽。

**obstruct**〔 əbˈstrʌkt 〕 *v.* 阻礙

—— be in the way of; hinder; impede; block

The disabled vehicles *obstructed* traffic until removed by a tow truck.

拋錨的車子直到被拖車拖走後才不阻礙交通。

# obtrude〔əb'trud〕*v.* 強加;逼人接受;闖入

—— (literally, "thrust against") thrust forward without being asked; intrude

It is unwise for an outsider to *obtrude* his opinions into a family quarrel. 局外人硬要把自己的想法加入一件家庭爭論中是不智的。

# obviate〔'ɑbvɪ,et〕*v.* 排除;避免

—— (literally, "get in the way of") meet and dispose of; make unnecessary

By removing her hat, the lady in front *obviated* the need for me to change my seat. 前座的小姐脫掉她的帽子,使我不必換座位。

Exercise:請由 **Group 21** 中,選出最適當的字,填入空格中。

1. A dropout will discover that the lack of a high school diploma is a serious _____ to good employment.

2. The picketers sat on the front steps in an attempt to _____ the entrance.

3. To _____ waiting in line at the box office, order your tickets by mail.

4. Despite the fact that Harry is a careful driver, the possibility of his having an accident continues to _____ his mother.

5. Though I tried to forget the incident, I couldn't _____ it from my mind.

【解答】
| 1. obstacle | 2. obstruct | 3. obviate |
|-------------|-------------|------------|
| 4. obsess   | 5. obliterate |          |

## 【Group 22】

# Per — *through*, *thoroughly*「貫穿；徹底地」

**perforate**〔'pɝfə,ret〕*v.* 刺穿；打孔

—— (literally, "bore through") make a hole or holes through; pierce; puncture

The physician said the tack had gone through Betty's shoe and sock without *perforating* her skin.

醫生說大頭針穿過貝蒂的鞋襪，但未刺傷她的皮膚。

**permeate**〔'pɝmɪ,et〕*v.* 瀰漫；滲過

—— pass through; penetrate; spread through

At breakfast the aroma of freshly brewed coffee *permeates* the kitchen and dining room.

吃早餐時剛泡好咖啡的香味瀰漫整個廚房與飯廳。

**perplex**〔pɚ'plɛks〕*v.* 使困惑

—— confuse thoroughly; puzzle; bewilder

I need help with the fourth problem; it *perplexes* me.

我需要人幫我解第四題；它使我困惑。

**persist**[5]〔pɚ'zɪst , pɚ'sɪst〕*v.* 1. 堅持　2. 持續

—— (literally, "stand to the end")

　　1. continue in spite of opposition; refuse to stop; persevere

　　2. continue to exist; last; endure

> 【記憶技巧】
> *per* (thoroughly) + *sist* (stand)（一直站著，就是「堅持」）

The teacher told Eric to stop whispering. When he *persisted* she sent him to the dean. 老師叫艾立克不要說悄悄話。當他依舊我行我素時，老師就送他到教務處。

第三章

The rain was supposed to end in the morning, but it *persisted*
through the afternoon and evening.
雨應該在早上停的，卻持續下了一個下午及晚上。

# perturb〔pɚ'tɝb〕*v.* 使不安；擾亂

—— disturb thoroughly or considerably; make uneasy; agitate;
upset

Maggie's parents were *perturbed* when they learned she had failed
two subjects. 瑪姬的父母知道她兩科不及格時感到很不安。

# perennial〔pə'rɛnɪəl〕1. *adj.* 永久的　2. *n.* 多年生植物

—— 1. continuing through the years; enduring; unceasing
　　2. plant that lives through the years

Authors have come and gone, but Shakespeare has remained a
*perennial* favorite.
作家們曇花一現般地來了又走，只有莎士比亞成為人們永久的喜好。
*Perennials* like the azalea and forsythia bloom year after year.
多年生的植物，如杜鵑、連翹，一年接一年地開花。

# pertinent〔'pɝtn̩ənt〕*adj.* 有關的；貼切的

—— (literally, "reaching through to") connected with the matter
under consideration; to the point; related; relevant

Stick to the point; don't give information that is not *pertinent*.
堅守主題；不要扯一些不相關的事。

## Exercise：請由 **Group 22** 中，選出最適當的字，填入空格中。

1. The farmers' claim of being underpaid for their produce is by
no means new; it has been their _____ complaint.

2. Why do you _____ in asking for my notes when I have told
you I don't have any?

3. Train conductors use hole punchers to _____ passenger tickets.

4. We thought the bad news would upset Tom, but it didn't seem to _____ him.

5. Road signs that _____ residents of this community are even more confusing to out-of-town visitors.

> 【解答】
>
> 1. perennial  2. persist  3. perforate
> 4. perturb  5. perplex

## 【Group 23】

# Pre — *before* 「先前」

**preface**[6] (ˈprɛfɪs) *n.* 序言
—— foreword; preliminary remarks;
author's introduction to a book

> 【記憶技巧】
> *pre* (before) + *face*
> (speak) (一本書開頭
> 的話，就是「序言」)

The *preface* usually provides information
that the reader should know before beginning the book.
序言常提供讀者一些閱讀前必須知道的事項。

**preview**[5] (ˈpriˌvju , priˈvju) *n.* 預演；預展；預告片
—— view of something before it is shown
to the public

> 【記憶技巧】
> *pre* (before) + *view*
> (see) (之前先看的，
> 就是「預告片」)

Last night my parents attended a *preview*
of a play scheduled to open next Tuesday.
昨天晚上我父母親去看了一齣定於下星期二演出戲劇的預演。

**precede**[6] 〔 pri'sid , prɪ- 〕*v.* 在⋯之前

—— go before; come before

Did your report follow or *precede* Jane's?
你的報告在珍之後還是之前？

> 【記憶技巧】
> *pre* (before) + *cede*
> (go)（走在前面，表示
> 「在⋯之前」）

**preclude**〔 prɪ'klud 〕*v.* 阻止；妨礙

—— put a barrier before; impede; prevent; make impossible

A prior engagement *precludes* my coming to your party.
先前的一個約會使我不能參加你的宴會。

**preconceive**〔 ˌprikən'siv 〕*v.* 預先形成；預想

—— form an opinion of beforehand without adequate evidence

My *preconceived* dislike for the book disappeared when I read a
few chapters. 先前對這本書的厭惡在我讀了幾章以後就消失了。

**prefabricate**〔 pri'fæbrəˌket 〕*v.* 預先建造組合

—— construct beforehand

*Prefabricated* homes are quickly erected by putting together large
sections previously constructed at a factory. 組合式房屋只要把事先
在工廠做好的大組件拼裝起來，就可以很快地蓋好。

**premeditate**〔 prɪ'mɛdəˌtet 〕*v.* 預謀；預先考量

—— consider beforehand

The jury decided that the blow was struck in a moment of panic
and had not been *premeditated*.
陪審團判決那一拳是在恐慌下擊出的，並非預謀。

**presume**[6]〔 prɪ'zum 〕*v.* 假定；推測

—— (literally, "take beforehand")
take for granted without proof;
assume; suppose

> 【記憶技巧】
> *pre* (before) + *sume*
> (take)（「假定」就是事
> 先採取一個想法）

第三章

Nineteen of the sailors have been rescued. One is missing and *presumed* dead.

十九個船員獲救，有一個失踪，且被認爲死亡。

# precocious 〔 prɪˋkoʃəs 〕 *adj.* 早熟的

—— (literally, "cooked or ripened before its time") showing mature characteristics at an early age

If Nancy's three-year-old brother can read, he must be a *precocious* child.

如果南西三歲大的弟弟會讀書，那他一定是個早熟的小孩。

## Exercise：請由 **Group 23** 中，選出最適當的字，填入空格中。

1. The _____ lad showed a skill that was unusual for one so young.

2. Joel's numerous absences _____ his passing the first quarter.

3. I _____ the directions to Barbara's house are correct, since she gave them to me herself.

4. A group of distinguished specialists saw a _____ of the exhibit before it was opened to the public.

5. Your certainty of failure is _____; the marks have not yet been announced.

```
----- 【解答】--------------------------------
  1. precocious      2. preclude       3. presume
  4. preview         5. preconceived
---------------------------------------------
```

【Group 24】

# Pro —— *forward*「向前」

**proponent**〔 prə'ponənt 〕*n.* 提議者；支持者

—— person who puts forth a proposal or argues in favor of
something; advocate; supporter

At the budget hearing, both the *proponents* and the opponents of
the tax increase will be able to present their views.

預算聽證會時，加稅的贊成者與反對者都可以提出他們的看法。

**prospect**[5]〔'praspɛkt 〕*n.* 期望；可能性

—— thing looked forward to;
expectation; vision

To a freshman, graduation is a distant

【記憶技巧】
*pro* (forward) + *spect*
(look at)（向前看，表
示心中充滿「期望」）

but pleasant *prospect.* 對新鮮人而言，畢業是遙遠但愉快的期望。

**procrastinate**〔 pro'kræstə,net 〕*v.* 拖延

—— (literally, "move forward to tomorrow") put things off from
day to day; delay

Start working on the assignment without delay. It doesn't pay to
*procrastinate.* 馬上寫功課，不要耽擱，拖延是沒有好處的。

**project**[2]〔 prə'dʒɛkt 〕*v.* 投射；發射 〔'pradʒɛkt 〕*n.* 計劃

—— throw or cast forward

The apparatus *projects* missiles into space.

那項裝置把飛彈發射至空中。

【記憶技巧】
*pro* (forward) + *ject*
(throw)（往前丟，就
是「投射；發射」）

**propel**[6]〔 prə'pɛl 〕*v.* 推進；驅使

—— impel forward; drive onward; force
ahead

【記憶技巧】
*pro* (forward) + *pel*
(drive)（驅策往前，
也就是「推進」）

第三章

Jet-*propelled* planes travel at very high speeds.
噴射推進式的飛機速度很快。

## protract〔pro'trækt〕*v.* 延長

—— (literally, "drag forward") draw out; lengthen; extend;
prolong

Our cousins stayed with us only for the weekend but promised to
return in July for a *protracted* visit.
我們的表兄弟只跟我們住了一個週末，但他們答應七月再來住久一點。

## protrude〔pro'trud〕*v.* 伸出；突出

—— thrust forth; stick out

Keep your feet under your desk; do not let them *protrude* into the
aisle. 把你的腳放在書桌下，不要伸到走道上。

## provoke[6]〔prə'vok〕*v.* 1. 激怒　2. 引起

—— 1. make angry; incense
2. call forth; bring on; cause

> 【記憶技巧】
> *pro* (forth) + *voke* (call)
> （把前面的人叫住，打算
> 「激怒」他）

There would have been no fight if you
hadn't *provoked* your brother by calling him names.
要不是你罵你弟弟而激怒他，兩個人就不會打起來了。
Jeff's account of his experiences on a farm *provoked* much
laughter. 傑夫描述他在農場時的經驗，引人大笑。

## proficient〔prə'fɪʃənt〕*adj.* 精通的；擅長的

—— (literally, "going forward") well advanced in any subject or
occupation; skilled; adept; expert

When I fell behind in French, the teacher asked one of the more
*proficient* students to help me.
我的法文落後時，老師叫一位比較精通法文的學生來幫我忙。

# profuse 〔 prə'fjus 〕 *adj.* 豐富的；大量的；揮霍的

—— pouring forth freely; exceedingly generous; extravagant

Despite a large income, the actor has saved very little because he is a *profuse* spender.

儘管收入很多，這個演員卻沒什麼積蓄，因為他揮霍無度。

# prominent[4] 〔'prɑmənənt 〕 *adj.* 傑出的

—— (literally, "jutting forward")
standing out; notable; important

The Mayor, the Governor, and several other *prominent* citizens attended the preview.

市長、州長，以及其他幾位傑出的市民，都參加了這次的試演。

【記憶技巧】
*pro* (forth) + *min* (jut 突出) + *ent* (*adj.*) ( 卓越人士的表現都很傑出 )

Exercise：請由 **Group 24** 中，選出最適當的字，填入空格中。

1. The _____ of a sizable raise impelled the new employee to do his best.

2. The Senator's enthusiastic supporters are _____ in their praises of his record.

3. George Stephenson was the first to use steam power to _____ a locomotive.

4. You must not expect an apprentice to be as _____ as a master craftsman.

5. The proposal to demolish the historic building is sure to _____ a storm of protest.

【解答】
| | | |
|---|---|---|
| 1. prospect | 2. profuse | 3. propel |
| 4. proficient | 5. provoke | |

第三章

## 第二部份：拉丁字根

### 【Group 1】

# Am, Amor — *love, liking*「愛；喜歡」

**amateur**[4]〔'æmə,tʃur〕*n.* 1. 業餘愛好者
2. 生手；不熟練者

Group 1~20

—— (literally, "lover")

1. person who follows a particular
   pursuit because he likes it,
   rather than as a profession

【記憶技巧】
***amat*** (love) + ***eur*** ( 人 ) ( 只是愛好者，沒有將嗜好當成職業，所以是「業餘愛好者」)

2. one who performs rather poorly; inexperienced person

The performance was staged by a group of *amateurs* who have been studying dramatics as a hobby.
這場表演由一群以研究演技爲嗜好的業餘愛好者演出。
When it comes to baking a cake, Mother's the expert; I'm only an *amateur.* 一提到做蛋糕，媽媽是專家，我只是生手而已。

**amity**〔'æmətɪ〕*n.* 友好

—— friendship; goodwill; friendly relations

We must look ahead to the time when the dispute is over and *amity* is restored. 我們必須期待爭端結束，重歸友好那一刻的來臨。

**amiable**[6]〔'æmɪəbḷ〕*adj.* 和藹可親的；友善的

—— friendly and pleasant

【記憶技巧】
***ami*** (love) + ***ible*** (adj.)

Cindy is an *amiable* person; everybody
likes her. 辛蒂是個和藹可親的人，每一個人都喜歡她。

**amicable**〔'æmɪkəbḷ〕*adj.* 友好的；和平的

—— characterized by friendliness rather than antagonism; friendly; neighborly; not quarrelsome

Let us try to settle our differences in an *amicable* manner.
讓我們試著以和平的態度解決爭端。

**amorous**〔'æmərəs〕*adj.* 戀愛的；多情的

—— having to do with love; loving; inclined to love

In the famous balcony scene, the *amorous* Romeo expresses undying love for Juliet.

在著名的陽台示愛那一幕中，多情的羅密歐向茱麗葉表達他無盡的愛意。

**enamored**〔ɪn'æmə-d〕*adj.* 喜愛的；迷戀的

—— (usually followed by *of*) inflamed with love; charmed; captivated

John Rolfe, an English settler, became *enamored* of the Indian princess Pocahontas and married her. 約翰・羅夫，一位英國移民，愛上了印第安公主寶嘉康蒂並且與她結婚。

## 【Group 2】

# Anim — *mind, will*「精神；意志」

**animosity**〔ˌænə'mɑsətɪ〕*n.* 仇恨；敵意

—— ill will (usually leading to active opposition); violent hatred

Someday the *animosity* that led to the war will be replaced by amity. 總有一天導致戰爭的仇恨會被友好關係所取代。

**animus**〔'ænəməs〕*n.* 惡意；敵意

—— ill will (usually controlled)

Though David defeated me in the election I bear no *animus* toward him; we are good friends.

雖然大衛在選舉中擊敗我，我對他不存絲毫敵意，我們是好朋友。

**equanimity**〔ˌikwə'nɪmətɪ , ˌɛkwə-〕*n.* 鎮靜；沉著；平靜

—— evenness of mind or temper; emotional balance; composure; calmness

第三章

If you become extremely upset when you lose a game, it is a sign that you lack *equanimity*.

如果你輸了一場比賽，就變得很不高興，那表示你缺乏沉著鎮定。

# unanimity〔͵junə'nɪmətɪ〕*n.* 全體一致

—— oneness of mind; complete agreement

In almost every discussion there is bound to be some disagreement. Don't expect *unanimity*.

幾乎每一次討論都一定會有一些意見不合，別期待全體一致、毫無異議。

# magnanimous〔mæg'nænəməs〕*adj.* 寬宏大量的

—— showing greatness or nobility of mind; above what is low or petty; forgiving; generous

The first time I was late, Miss O'Neill excused me with the warning that she would not be so *magnanimous* the next time.

我第一次遲到時，歐尼爾小姐原諒我，但她警告下一次她就不會這麼寬宏大量了。

# unanimous[6]〔ju'nænəməs〕*adj.* 全體一致的

—— of one mind; in complete accord

Except for one student, who voted "no," the class was *unanimous* in wanting the party.

除了一個學生投反對票外，全班一致希望開個派對。

> 【記憶技巧】
> *un* (one) + *anim* (mind) + *ous* (*adj.*)（萬眾一心，表示「全體一致的」）

**Exercise：**請由 **Group 1 & 2** 中，選出最適當的字，填入空格中。

1. After his first success as a lover on screen, the actor was cast only in _____ roles.

2. The prospect of financial reward has induced many a(n) _____ to turn professional.

3. Don't brood over your defeat. Accept it with _____.

4. It is hard for a conceited person to like anyone because he is so _____ of himself.

5. The 9-0 verdict against the defendant shows that the judges were _____.

> 【解答】
> 1. amorous    2. amateur    3. equanimity
> 4. enamored   5. unanimous

## 【Group 3】

# Fin — *end, boundary*「結束；界限」

**affinity** 〔 ə′fɪnətɪ 〕 *n.* 關係密切；喜愛；吸引力

—— (literally, condition of being "near the boundary" or "a neighbor") kinship; sympathy; liking; attraction

Because they share the same language and ideals, Americans and Englishmen have an *affinity* for one another.
因為擁有共同的語言與理想，美國人與英國人之間關係很密切。

**finale** 〔 fɪ′nɑlɪ 〕 *n.* 終場；最後一幕；終曲

—— end or final part of a musical composition, opera, play, etc.

Every skit in our class show was loudly applauded, from the opening act to the *finale*. 班上戲劇表演中每個幽默諷刺處都受到熱烈的掌聲，從第一幕到終場都是如此。

第三章

**finis** 〔ˈfaɪnɪs 〕 *n.* 完結篇；劇終

—— end; conclusion

The story is far from complete because the *finis* is not yet written.

那個故事離完成還遠得很，因爲結尾還沒寫。

**confine**[4] 〔 kənˈfaɪn 〕 *v.* 限制

—— keep within limits; restrict

I will *confine* my remarks to the causes of the War of 1812; the next speaker will discuss its results.

我所談的只限於 1812 年戰爭的起因，下一位演說者將會討論它的結果。

**definitive** 〔 dɪˈfɪnətɪv 〕 *adj.* 決定性的；最終的；不可更改的

—— serving to end an unsettled matter; conclusive; final

Remember that your answer will be treated as *definitive*. You will not be permitted to change it.

記住你的答案將具有決定性，不准更改。

## 【Group 4】

# Flu, Fluc, Flux —— *flow*「流」

**fluid**[6] 〔ˈfluɪd 〕 1. *n.* 液體；流體　2. *adj.* 不固定的；易變的

—— 1. substance that flows
　　 2. not rigid; changing easily

【記憶技巧】
*flu* (flow) + *id*

Air, water, molasses, and milk are all *fluids*.

空氣、水、糖蜜及牛奶都是流體。

During November, the military situation remained *fluid*, with advances and retreats by both sides.

十一月的時候，戰況不大穩定，雙方皆有前進及後退。

第三章

**flux**〔flʌks〕*n.* 不斷變化；不斷波動
—— continuous flow or changing; unceasing change
When prices are in a state of *flux*, many buyers delay purchases until conditions are more settled.
物價波動時，許多購買者皆延遲採購，直到狀況穩定一點時為止。

**influx**〔ˈɪnˌflʌks〕*n.* 流入；注入
—— inflow; inpouring
The discovery of gold in California in 1848 caused a large *influx* of settlers from the East.
加州在 1848 年發現黃金以後，引來大批東部移民的流入。

**fluctuate**〔ˈflʌktʃʊˌet〕*v.* 波動；升降
—— flow like a wave; move up and down; change often and irregularly; be unsteady
Recently the price of a pound of tomatoes has *fluctuated* from a high of 45 ¢ to a low of 29 ¢ .
近來一磅蕃茄的價格在最高價四十五分與最低價二十九分之間波動著。

**fluent**[4]〔ˈfluənt〕*adj.* 流利的
—— ready with a flow of words; speaking or writing easily
Do you have to grope for words, or are you a *fluent* speaker?
你得思索如何用字，還是你是一位流利的演說者？

> 【記憶技巧】
> *flu* (flow) + *ent* (adj.)
> （說話像水流一樣順暢，
> 表示「流利的」）

Exercise：請由 **Group 3 & 4** 中，選出最適當的字，填入空格中。

1. A diplomat should be ——————— in the language of the country where he represents us.

2. During the late spring, beach resorts ready themselves for the expected _____ of summer visitors.

3. The entire cast appeared on stage after the _____ to acknowledge the applause.

4. Unlike a lower court ruling, which may be reversed on appeal, a Supreme Court decision is _____.

5. There is a(n) _____ among classmates that is often as strong as loyalty to one's family.

---
【解答】

| | | |
|---|---|---|
| 1. fluent | 2. influx | 3. finale |
| 4. definitive | 5. affinity | |
---

## 【Group 5】

# Gen, Gener, Genit — *birth*, *class*「生；種類」

**genre**〔'ʒɑnrə〕*n.*（文藝作品之）類型；體裁

—— kind; sort; category

Poe was the originator of a *genre* of detective story.

愛倫坡是偵探小說類型的創始者。

**progenitor**〔pro'dʒɛnətə〕*n.* 祖先

—— ancestor to whom a group traces its birth; forefather

The Bible states that Adam was the *progenitor* of the human race.

聖經上說亞當是人類的始祖。

**degenerate**〔dɪ'dʒɛnə,ret〕*v.* 墮落；退步

—— sink to a lower class or standard; grow worse; deteriorate

But for the skill of the presiding officer, the debate would have *degenerated* into an exchange of insults.

要不是主持官員巧妙的排解，這場辯論會將淪爲交相辱罵。

**engender**〔ɪn'dʒɛndɚ, ɛn-〕*v.* 產生

—— cause to be born again; put new life into; reform completely

Name-calling *engenders* hatred. 誹謗產生怨恨。

**regenerate**〔rɪ'dʒɛnə,ret〕*v.* 使重獲新生

—— give birth to; create; generate; produce; cause

The new manager *regenerated* the losing team and made it a strong contender for first place.

新來的經理再造這支打輸的球隊，使它變成有力的冠軍爭奪者。

## 【Group 6】

# Greg —— *gather*「聚集」

**aggregation**〔,ægrɪ'geʃən〕*n.* 聚集；集合體

—— gathering of individuals into a body or group; assemblage

At the airport, the homecoming champions were welcomed by a huge *aggregation* of admirers.

凱旋歸國的冠軍得主們在機場受到一大群仰慕者的歡迎。

**congregation**〔,kɑŋgrɪ'geʃən〕*n.* 集合；（聚集做禮拜的）會衆

—— "flock" or gathering of people for religious worship

The minister addressed the *congregation* on the meaning of brotherhood.

牧師以四海皆兄弟的意義爲主題，向聚會的群衆發表演說。

**segregation**〔͵sɛgrɪ'geʃən 〕*n.* 隔離
—— separation from the "flock" or main body; setting apart;
isolation
The warden believes in *segregation* of first offenders from
hardened criminals. 典獄長認爲得隔離初犯者與累犯者。

**aggregate**〔'ægrɪgɪt , -͵get 〕*adj.* 集合的；集體的
—— gathered together in one mass, total; collective
The *aggregate* strength of the allies was impressive, though
individually some were quite weak.
聯盟者集體的力量是可觀的，雖然個別來說有些相當微弱。

**gregarious**〔 grɪ'gɛrɪəs 〕*adj.* 群居的；喜好群居的
—— inclined to associate with the "flock" or group; fond of being
with others
Except for hermits and recluses, who shun company, most people
are *gregarious*.
除規避人群的隱士及遁世者外，大部份人都是喜好群居的。

Exercise：請由 **Group 5 & 6** 中，選出最適當的字，填入空格中。

1. New housing developments, shopping centers, and schools can
   _____ decadent neighborhoods.

2. The _____ rose and sang a hymn.

3. Unless healed soon, these animosities are sure to _____
   armed conflict.

4. Keep a record of the points scored by each player, as well as
   the team's _____ score.

5. A very young child prefers to play by himself, but as he grows
older he becomes _____.

---

【解答】
1. regenerate    2. congregation    3. engender
4. aggregate    5. gregarious

---

【Group 7】

# Here, Hes — *stick*「附著」

**coherence**〔koˈhɪrəns〕*n.* 連貫性；一致性

—— state of sticking together; consistency; logical connection

If the relationship between the first sentence and what follows is
not clear, the paragraph lacks *coherence*.

如果第一句與下一句之間的關係並不清楚，那麼這一段就缺乏連貫性。

**cohesion**〔koˈhiʒən〕*n.* 團結；凝聚力

—— act or state of sticking together; union; unity

There can be no real *cohesion* in an alliance if the parties have
little in common. 如果一個聯盟的參與者之間沒什麼共同性，那麼就
沒有真正的凝聚力可言。

**adhere**〔ədˈhɪr , æd-〕*v.* 黏著；擁護；堅信

—— stick; hold fast; cling; be attached

Apply the sticker according to the directions, or it will not *adhere*.
按照說明使用貼紙，否則它就黏不起來了。

**cohere**〔koˈhɪr〕*v.* 連貫；前後一致；黏著

—— stick together; hold together firmly

第三章

I glued together the fragments of the vase, but they did not *cohere*.
我把花瓶的碎片黏在一起，但卻合不起來。

**inherent**[6] 〔 ɪnˈhɪrənt 〕 *adj.* 天生的；固有的

—— (literally, "sticking in")
deeply infixed; intrinsic;
essential

> 【記憶技巧】
> *in* (in) + *here* (stick) + (*e*)*nt*
> (*adj.*)（黏在身上的）

Because of her *inherent* carelessness, I doubt my sister can ever be
a good driver. 由於天生的粗心大意，我懷疑妹妹無法成爲一位好駕駛。

## 【Group 8】

# Lateral — *side*「邊」

**quadrilateral**〔͵kwɑdrəˈlætərəl , -ˈlætrəl 〕 *n.* 四邊形

—— plane figure having four sides and four angles

A square is a *quadrilateral*. 正方形是四邊形的一種。

QUADRILATERALS

**collateral**〔 kəˈlætərəl 〕 *adj.* 附帶的；並行的

—— situated at the side; accompanying; parallel; additional;
supplementary

After voting for the road building program, the legislature took up
the *collateral* issue of how to raise the necessary funds.
道路建築計畫投票通過後，立法院繼續討論如何籌措必須資金的附帶事項。

**equilateral**〔͵ikwəˈlætərəl 〕 *adj.* 等邊的

—— having all sides equal

If one side of an *equilateral* triangle measures three feet, the other
two must also be three feet each.
如果等邊三角形的一邊是三呎長，那麼其他兩邊也一定是三呎長。

**lateral** 〔'lætərəl 〕 *adj.* 側面的

—— of or pertaining to the side

The building plan shows both a front and a *lateral* view of the proposed structure. 建築設計圖顯示出計畫中建物的正面與側面圖。

**multilateral** 〔ˌmʌltɪ'lætərəl 〕 *adj.* 多邊的

—— having many sides

The participants hope to reach a *multilateral* agreement on banning nuclear tests in their respective countries.
這些參與者希望能達成多邊的協議，禁止在各自的國家進行核子試驗。

**unilateral** 〔ˌjunɪ'lætərəl 〕 *adj.* 片面的

—— one-sided; undertaken by one side only

Don't judge the matter by my opponent's *unilateral* statement.
不要只聽我對手的片面之辭就評斷那件事。

Exercise：請由 **Group 7 & 8** 中，選出最適當的字，填入空格中。

1. Most city blocks are shaped like a(n) _____.

2. Are you speaking for all the members of your club or giving only your _____ views?

3. Some believe that might is right, but I do not _____ to that doctrine.

4. When we were studying *Johnny Tremain*, our teacher assigned _____ reading on the Revolutionary War.

5. The politician's _____ personality as champion of justice, defender of the poor, supporter of education, and friend of business won him many adherents.

第三章

## 【Group 9】

# Litera — *letter*「字」

**alliteration**〔 ə,lɪtə'reʃən 〕*n.* 頭韻（即一群字的起頭字母）

—— repetition of the same letter or consonant at the beginning of consecutive words

Note the ***alliteration*** in the line "*S*ing a *s*ong of *s*ixpence."

注意這行中的頭韻 "Sing a song of sixpence."。

**literacy**[6]〔'lɪtərəsɪ 〕*n.* 讀寫的能力

—— state of being lettered or educated; ability to read and write

When registering as a new voter, take along your diploma as proof of ***literacy***.

當你要登記成爲有投票權的人時，帶著你的文憑以證明你有讀寫的能力。

**literal**[6]〔'lɪtərəl 〕*adj.* 照字面意義的

—— following the letters or exact words of the original

We translate "laissez-faire" as "absence of government interference," but its ***literal*** meaning is "let do."

我們把 "laissez–faire" 翻譯成「政府的不干涉主義」，但它字面上的意義是「讓他做吧」。

**literary**[4]〔'lɪtə,rɛrɪ 〕*adj.* 文學的

—— having to do with letters or literature

Mark Twain is one of the greatest figures in our ***literary*** history. 馬克・吐溫是我們的文學史上最偉大的人物之一。

【記憶技巧】
***liter*** (letter 突出) + ***ary*** (*adj.*) ( 有關文字的，就是「文學的」)

**literate**[6] 〔ˈlɪtərɪt 〕*adj.* 能讀寫的；識字的

—— lettered; able to read and write; educated

The school's main goal in working with adults who can neither read nor write is to make them *literate*.

這所學校對於不能讀寫的成人，主要的工作目標是使他們可以閱讀和寫字。

## 【Group 10】

# Luc, Lum — *light*「光」

**luminary**〔ˈlumə͵nɛrɪ 〕*n.* 名人

—— one who is a source of light or inspiration to others; famous person

A number of *luminaries*, including a Nobel prize winner and two leading authors, will be present.

很多名人，包括一位諾貝爾獎得主及二位首屈一指的作家，都將出席。

**elucidate**〔 ɪˈlusə͵det , ɪˈlju- 〕*v.* 說明

—— throw light upon; make clear; explain

I asked the teacher to *elucidate* a point that was not clear to me.

我請老師說明一點我不大明白的地方。

**lucid**〔ˈlusɪd 〕*adj.* 清澈的；明白的；易懂的

—— (literally, "containing light") clear; easy to understand

To obviate misunderstanding, state the directions in the most *lucid* way possible.

為了避免誤解，儘可能明白地說明。

**luminous**〔ˈlumənəs 〕*adj.* 發亮的

—— emitting light; shining; brilliant

第三章

With this watch you can tell time in the dark because its hands and dial are *luminous*.

用這支錶你可以在黑暗中看時間，因為它的指針和錶面都是會發亮的。

## translucent〔 træns'lusn̩t 〕 *adj.* 半透明的

—— letting light through

Lamp shades are *translucent* but not transparent.

燈罩是半透明而不是全部透明的。

Exercise：請由 **Group 9 & 10** 中，選出最適當的字，填入空格中。

1. You need not prove that you can read and write. No one doubts your _____.

2. _____ paint is used for road signs so that they may be visible to night drivers.

3. Gary tried to _____ the matter, but he only made us more confused.

4. A host of admirers surrounded the sports _____ to ask for his autograph.

5. Did you know that the _____ meaning of Philip is "lover of horses"?

---

【解答】

| | | |
|---|---|---|
| 1. literacy | 2. Luminous | 3. elucidate |
| 4. luminary | 5. literal | |

## 【Group 11】

# Man, Manu — *hand*「手」

**manacle**〔'mænəkḷ〕*n.* 手銬；束縛
—— handcuff

The *manacles* were removed from the prisoner's wrists.
手銬從犯人的手腕上除去了。

**mandate**〔'mændet〕*n.* 1. 命令；指示　2. 託管地
—— (literally, something "given into one's hand")
　　1. authoritative command; order
　　2. territory entrusted to the administration of another country

The walkout was a clear violation of the court's *mandate* against
a strike.　這罷工很顯然違反了法院不許罷工的命令。
After World War I, Syria became a French *mandate*.
第一次世界大戰後，敘利亞成了法國的託管地。

**manual**⁴〔'mænjʊəl〕1. *n.* 手冊　2. *adj.* 用手操作的
—— 1. small, helpful book capable of being carried in the hand;
　　　handbook
　　2. relating to, or done with, the hands

Each student has a learner's permit and a copy of the "Driver's
*Manual*."
每一個學生都有學習許可證，還有一份駕駛手冊。
Milking, formerly a *manual* operation, is now done by machine.
先前擠乳是用手操作的，現在則是用機器。

**manuscript**⁶〔'mænjə,skrɪpt〕*n.* 手稿
—— document written by hand, or
　　typewritten

> 【記憶技巧】
> *manu* (hand) + *script*
> (write)（用手寫的紙
> 張，也就是「手稿」)

第三章

The author's *manuscript* is now at the printer.
作者的手稿現在正在排印中。

## emancipate〔ɪ'mænsə,pet〕*v.* 解放；使不受束縛

—— (literally, "take from the hand" or power of another) release from bondage; set free; liberate

The washing machine has *emancipated* housewives from a great deal of drudgery.
洗衣機已經使家庭主婦們擺脫了一大堆辛苦的工作。

## manipulate[6]〔mə'nɪpjə,let〕*v.* 操縱

—— operate with the hands; handle or manage skillfully

In today's lesson I learned how to *manipulate* the steering wheel.
在今天的課程中，我學到了如何去操縱方向盤。

> 【記憶技巧】
> *mani* (hand) + *pul* (pull) + *ate* (*v.*) (「操縱」要用手去拉動控制)

## 【Group 12】

# Pend, Pens —— *hang*「懸掛」

## appendix〔ə'pɛndɪks〕*n.* 附錄

—— (literally, something "hung on") matter added to the end of a book or document

A school edition of a novel usually has an *appendix* containing explanatory notes.
用作教科書的小說版本通常有個附錄，裡面有解釋說明的注釋。

## pendant〔'pɛndənt〕*n.* ( 項鍊、手鐲上的 ) 垂飾

—— hanging ornament

第三章

The *pendant* dangling from the chain around her neck looked like a medal, but it was really a watch. 掛在她脖上的一條項鍊，有個垂飾搖搖晃晃看起來像獎章，但事實上是一支手錶。

## suspense[6] 〔 sə'spɛns 〕 *n.* 懸疑；焦慮

—— condition of being left "hanging" or in doubt; mental uncertainty; anxiety

If you have seen the marks, please tell me whether I passed or failed; don't keep me in *suspense*!
如果你看了分數，請告訴我過了還是沒過，別讓我處在焦慮中！

## append 〔 ə'pɛnd 〕 *v.* 附加

—— (literally, "hang on") attach; add as a supplement

If you hand in your report late, *append* a note explaining the reason for the delay.
如果你的報告遲交了，要附加一張紙條解釋你遲交的原因。

## suspend[5] 〔 sə'spɛnd 〕 *v.* 1. 懸掛　2. 暫停

—— 1. hang attaching to something
　　 2. stop temporarily; make inoperative
　　　 for a while

> 【記憶技巧】
> *sus* (under) + *pend*
> (hand) ( 布幕垂吊而
> 下，表示演出「暫停」)

She wore a green pendant *suspended* from a silver chain.
她戴了一個綠色垂飾，是掛在銀鍊上的。
Train service will be *suspended* from midnight to 4 a.m. to permit repairs. 火車服務從午夜到清晨四點停止，以便維修。

## impending 〔 ɪm'pɛndɪŋ 〕 *adj.* 即將發生的；迫近的

—— overhanging; threatening to occur soon; imminent

At the first flash of lightning, people scurried for shelter from the *impending* storm.
第一次閃電時，人們就趕快跑到蔽護處以防迫近的暴風雨。

**pending** 〔'pɛndɪŋ〕1. *adj.* 待解決的　2. *prep.* 直到
—— (literally, "hanging")
　　1. waiting to be settled; not yet decided
　　2. until

Has a decision been reached on a date for the game, or is the matter still *pending*?
比賽日期決定了嗎，還是尚未解決？

Barbara agreed to conduct the meeting *pending* the election of a permanent chairman.
芭芭拉同意主持那個議會直到選舉出固定的主席。

Exercise：請由 **Group 11 & 12** 中，選出最適當的字，填入空格中。

1. Can you operate this gadget?  I don't know how to ＿＿＿＿ it.

2. As the enemy approached, the defenders readied themselves for the ＿＿＿＿ attack.

3. Because of the labor dispute, the city's daily newspapers had to ＿＿＿＿ publication.

4. The Abolitionists wanted President Lincoln to ＿＿＿＿ all the slaves.

5. The retiring manager has agreed to stay on, ＿＿＿＿ the choice of a new manager.

---

【解答】
1. manipulate　2. impending　3. suspend
4. emancipate　5. pending

---

【Group 13】

# Pon, Pos — *put*「放置」

**depose**〔dɪ'poz〕*v.* 免職；罷黜；廢（王位）

—— (literally, "put down") put out of office; dethrone

Did the king abdicate or was he *deposed*?

那個國王是自己放棄王位還是被廢的？

**impose**[5]〔ɪm'poz〕*v.* 強加

—— put on as a burden, duty, tax, etc.;
inflict

> 【記憶技巧】
> *im* (on) + *pose*
> (place)（把東西放在
> 上面，表示「強加」）

Cleaning up after the job is the repairman's
responsibility. Don't let him *impose* it on you.

工作之後，清理收拾是修理工人的責任，別讓他加在你身上。

**postpone**[3]〔post'pon〕*v.* 拖延

—— (literally, "put after") put off; defer;
delay

> 【記憶技巧】
> *post* (after) + *pone*
> (put)（將時間往後
> 挪，就是「延期」）

Mr. Marx has *postponed* the test until
tomorrow to give us an extra day to study.

馬克斯先生已將考試延至明天，好讓我們多一天唸書的時間。

**superimpose**〔,supɚɪm'poz〕*v.* 添加

—— put on top of or over; attach as an addition

Today's snowfall *superimposed* a fresh two inches on yesterday's
accumulation. 今天的雪又新添加了兩吋在昨天的積雪上。

**transpose**〔træns'poz〕*v.* 調換

—— (literally, "put across") change the relative order of;
interchange

There is a misspelled word on your paper, "strenght." Correct it by *transposing* the last two letters.

你的考卷上有個拼錯的字 "strenght"，把最後兩個字母調換過來改正它。

## 【Group 14】

# Scrib, Script — *write*「寫」

**inscription**〔ɪnˈskrɪpʃən〕*n.* 銘刻；題字

—— something inscribed (written) on a monument, coin, etc.

The *inscription* on Paul's medal reads "For Excellence in English."

保羅獎牌上所題的字是「英文特優」。

**scribe**〔skraɪb〕*n.* 抄寫員；作家；記者

—— person who writes; author; journalist

Both candidates used professional *scribes* to prepare their campaign speeches.

兩個候選人都用了專業的作家來準備他們的競選演講。

**script**[6]〔skrɪpt〕*n.* 劇本；原稿

—— written text of a play, speech, etc.

How much time did the actors have to memorize the *script*?

演員花了多少時間來記住劇本？

> 【記憶技巧】
> *script* (write)（最初
> 寫下來的東西，也就
> 是「原稿」）

**subscriber**〔səbˈskraɪbɚ〕*n.* 訂閱者；用戶；簽署者

—— one who writes his name at the end of a document, thereby indicating his approval

The petition to nominate Sue for president of the freshman class already has forty-three *subscribers*.

提名蘇為大一班級主席的請願已有四十三人附議了。

**conscript**〔 kən'skrɪpt 〕 *v.* 徵召

—— enroll (write down) into military service by compulsion; draft

When there are not enough volunteers for the armed forces, the government *conscripts* additional men.

當三軍的志願入伍者不夠時，政府就會徵召額外的士兵。

**prescribe**[6]〔 prɪ'skraɪb 〕 *v.* 1. 規定　2. 開藥方

—— (literally, "write before")

1. order; dictate; direct

2. order as a remedy

The law *prescribes* that aliens may not vote. 法律規定外國人不可以投票。

【記憶技巧】
*pre* (before) + *scribe* (write)（病人拿藥前，醫生會寫下藥名）

Her physician *prescribed* some pills, a light diet, and plenty of rest.

她的醫生開了一些藥丸，要她飲食清淡，並且多休息。

Exercise：請由 **Group 13 & 14** 中，選出最適當的字，填入空格中。

1. At one point in his address, the President inserted some remarks that were not in the _____ previously released to the press.

2. The insurgents aim to _____ the king and establish a republic.

3. According to the _____ on its cornerstone, this school was erected in 1929.

4. With war impending, the nation hastened to _____ all able-bodied men.

5. If Dad should _____ his mortgage payment, the bank may superimpose a late fee.

┌--- 【解答】 ------------------------------------┐
│ 1. script       2. depose      3. inscription │
│ 4. conscript    5. postpone                   │
└------------------------------------------------┘

## 【Group 15】

# Simil, Simul — *similar*「相似」

**similarity**[3]〔‚sɪmə'lærətɪ〕*n.* 類似

—— likeness; resemblance

The two pills are alike in color and shape, but there the *similarity* ends. 這兩顆藥丸的顏色和形狀都很相像，但類似的地方也僅止於此。

**simile**〔'sɪmə‚li〕*n.* 明喻

—— comparison of two different things introduced by "like" or "as"

"He is as brave as a lion." is a *simile.*
「他勇猛如獅。」是一句明喻。

**assimilate**〔ə'sɪml‚et〕*v.* 1.同化；融合；使（語音）同化
2. 吸收

—— 1. make similar or alike

—— 2. take in and incorporate as one's own; absorb

The letter *n* in the prefix *in* is often *assimilated* with the following letter. For example, "in" plus "legible" becomes "i*l*legible."
字首 in 的 n，常被下一個字母同化。例如 in 加上 legible 變成 i*l*legible。
A bright student *assimilates* knowledge rapidly.
聰明的學生能很快地吸收知識。

**simulate**〔'sɪmjə‚let〕*v.* 模擬；模仿；假裝；扮演

—— give the appearance of; feign; imitate

Nancy was the star of the show; she *simulated* the bewildered mother very effectively.

南西是那齣戲的主角,她扮演那昏亂的母親給人印象非常深刻。

**dissimilar** ( dɪ'sɪmələ ) *adj.* 不相似的;不同的

—— not similar; unlike; different

These gloves are not a pair; they are quite *dissimilar*.

這兩隻手套不是成對的,它們相當不同。

**simultaneous**[6] (ˌsɪml̩'tenɪəs ) *adj.* 同時的;同時發生的

—— existing or happening at the same time; concurrent

> 【記憶技巧】
> *simul* (same) + *taneous* (*adj.*)

The flash of an explosion reaches us before the sound, though the two are *simultaneous*.

爆炸後,我們先看到閃光然後才聽到聲音,雖然它們是同時發生的。

## 【Group 16】

# Sol, Soli — *single*「單一」

**soliloquy** ( sə'lɪləkwɪ ) *n.* 獨白

—— speech made to oneself when alone

What an actor says in a *soliloquy* is heard by no one except the audience. 演員的獨白只能被觀眾聽到。

**solitude**[6] ( 'salə,tjud ) *n.* 孤獨

—— condition of being alone; loneliness; seclusion

> 【記憶技巧】
> *sol* (alone) + *itude* ( 表性質的字尾 )

Though I like company, there are times when I prefer *solitude*.

雖然我喜歡同伴,但有時我卻比較喜歡孤獨。

**solo**[5] 〔'solo 〕 *n.* 獨唱；獨奏

── musical composition (*or* anything) performed by a single person

Instead of singing a *solo*, Brenda would prefer to join with me in a duet. 布蘭達比較喜歡和我一起二重唱，而比較不喜歡獨唱。

**desolate** 1. 〔'dɛslˌet 〕 *v.* 使荒蕪　2. 〔'dɛslɪt 〕 *adj.* 荒涼的

── 1. make lonely; deprive of inhabitants; lay waste
　　2. left alone; deserted; forlorn

After the war, the villagers hope to return to their *desolated* homes. 戰爭結束後，村民們希望能夠回到他們荒蕪的家園。

At 5:30 a.m. the normally crowded intersection looks *desolate*. 在清晨五點三十分，平時擁擠的十字路口看起來很荒涼。

**sole**[5] 〔 sol 〕 *adj.* 唯一的；單獨的

── one and only; single

Franklin D. Roosevelt was the *sole* candidate to be elected President for a fourth term.

富蘭克林‧迪‧羅斯福是第四任總統唯一的候選人。

Franklin D. Roosevelt

**solitary**[5] 〔'sɑləˌtɛrɪ 〕 *adj.* 孤獨的

── being or living alone; without companions

A hermit leads a *solitary* existence. 隱士都過著孤獨的生活。

Exercise：請由 **Group 15 & 16** 中，選出最適當的字，填入空格中。

1. Did you know you were using a(n) _____ when you said I was as sly as a fox?

2. After the chorus sang the first number, Stanley played a violin _____.

3. The closing of the huge factory did not _____ the area, as few of the workers moved away.

4. Don't compare Jane with Peggy; the two are entirely _____.

5. If you announce the results at that speed, the class will be unable to _____ them.

> 【解答】
>
> 1. simile    2. solo    3. desolate
> 4. dissimilar    5. assimilate

## 【Group 17】

## Solv, Solu, Solut — *loosen*「鬆開」

**dissolution**〔͵dɪsə'luʃən〕*n.* (議會、團體等) 解散

—— act of "loosening" or breaking up into component parts; disintegration; ruin; destruction

When President Lincoln took office, the Union faced imminent *dissolution.* 當林肯總統就職,北軍就面臨著迫切的解散問題。

**dissolve**[6]〔dɪ'zɑlv〕*v.* 1. 溶解;解散　2. 使消失;使破滅

—— (literally, "loosen apart")

    1. break up; disintegrate

    2. cause to disappear; end

> 【記憶技巧】
>
> *dis* (apart) + *solve* (loosen) (鬆開成爲個體,也就是「溶解」)

Since the members lack mutual interests, the club will probably *dissolve.*
由於成員們缺乏共同的興趣,那個俱樂部很可能會解散。

After our quarrel, Grace and I *dissolved* our friendship.
爭吵後,葛麗絲和我結束了友誼。

**resolution**[4] 〔͵rɛzə'ljuʃən 〕 *n.* 解決；解答；決心

—— (literally, "act of unloosening") solving; solution; answer

The *resolution* of our air and water pollution problems will be difficult and costly.
要解決我們空氣和水源的污染問題，將會很困難而且耗資很大。

**resolve**[4] 〔rɪ'zɑlv 〕 *v.* 解決；解釋；決定；決心

—— (literally, "unloosen") break up; solve; explain; unravel

A witness provided the clue that *resolved* the mystery. 一個目擊者提供線索揭開了那個秘密。

> 【記憶技巧】
> *re* (back) + *solve* (loosen) ( 把緊張情緒放鬆，表示「決定」好了 )

**absolute**[4] 〔'æbsə͵lut 〕 *adj.* 絕對的；完全的；專制的

—— free ("loosened") from control or restriction; autocratic; despotic

A democratic ruler is restricted by a constitution, a legislature, and courts, but a dictator has *absolute* power. 一個民主的統治者會被憲法、議會，和法院所限制，但是一個獨裁者卻擁有無限的權力。

**soluble** 〔'sɑljəbḷ 〕 *adj.* 1. 可溶解的　2. 可解決的

—— (literally, "able to be loosened")
1. capable of being dissolved or made into a liquid
2. solvable

Sugar is *soluble* in water. 糖溶於水。
Someone would have found the answer by now if the problem were *soluble*.
如果那個問題是可以解決的，至今應該有人已經找到了答案。

**solvent** 〔'sɑlvənt 〕 1. *n.* 溶劑　2. *adj.* 有償債能力的

—— 1. substance, usually liquid, able to dissolve ("loosen") another substance, known as the solute
2. able to pay all one's legal debts

第三章

In a saltwater solution, the water is the *solvent* and the salt is the solute. 在食鹽溶液中，水是溶劑，鹽是溶質。

The examiners found the bank *solvent,* much to the relief of its depositors.

審察員判定那個銀行有償付能力，使得存款人大大的鬆了一口氣。

## 【Group 18】

# Und, Unda — *wave, flow*「波浪；流」

**abound**[6]〔ə'baʊnd〕*v.* 充滿；大量存在

—— (literally, "rise in waves" *or* "overflow")

    1. (with "in" *or* "with") be well supplied; teem

    2. be plentiful; be present in great quantity

Our nation *abounds* in opportunities for well-educated young men and women.

我們國家有很多機會給那些受過良好教育的年輕男女。

Fish *abound* in the waters off Newfoundland.

紐芬蘭的外海中有很多魚。

**inundate**〔'ɪnʌn‚det , ɪn'ʌndet〕*v.* 如洪水般湧進；氾濫

—— flood; overflow; deluge; overwhelm

On Election Night, the victor's offices were *inundated* by congratulatory messages.

在選舉之夜，勝利者的辦公室湧進了無數的賀電。

**redound**〔rɪ'daʊnd〕*v.* 有助於；報償；報應

—— contribute; flow back as a result

Our team's sportsmanlike conduct *redounds* to the credit of the school. 我們球隊有運動家精神的表現有助於提高學校的榮譽。

**abundant**[5] 〔 ə'bʌndənt 〕 *adj.* 豐富的；充足的

—— (literally, "rising in waves") more than sufficient; plentiful

Before Christmas, the stores have *abundant* supplies of toys.

在聖誕節前，商店有充足的玩具供應。

**redundant**[6] 〔 rɪ'dʌndənt 〕 *adj.* 多餘的

—— (literally, "flowing back") exceeding what is necessary; superfluous; surplus

【記憶技巧】
*re* (again) + *dund* (wave) + *ant* (*adj.*) ( 浪再度回來，表示「多餘的」)

Remove the last word of the following sentence because it is *redundant*: "My report is longer than Bob's report."

去掉下面句子的最後一個字，因爲它是多餘的："My report is longer than Bob's report."。

Exercise：請由 **Group 17 & 18** 中，選出最適當的字，填入空格中。

1. Mutual suspicion and jealousy led to the eventual _____ of the alliance.

2. The blue whale, once _____ in Antarctic waters, is becoming more and more scarce.

3. The firm is in no danger of bankruptcy; it is completely _____.

4. Several offshore areas _____ in oil.

5. Either of the signers can _____ the agreement by giving thirty days' written notice to the other.

【解答】
1. dissolution  2. abundant  3. solvent
4. abound  5. dissolve

## 【Group 19】

# Ver, Vera, Veri — *true*, *truth*「真的；真實」

**veracity**〔vəˈræsətɪ〕*n.* 誠實

—— truthfulness (of persons)

Since you have lied to us in the past, you should not wonder that we doubt your *veracity*.

既然你以前向我們撒過謊，你不應該奇怪我們會懷疑你的誠實。

**verdict**〔ˈvɜdɪkt〕*n.* 判決；判斷

—— (literally, something "truly said") decision of a jury; opinion; judgment

We would like to know your *verdict* in the matter.

我們想要知道你對此事的判斷。

**verity**〔ˈvɛrətɪ〕*n.* 真實性

—— truth (of things); something true; true statement

That smoking is injurious to health is a scientifically established *verity*. 吸煙有害健康是科學上既定的事實。

**aver**〔əˈvɜ〕*v.* 斷言

—— state to be true; affirm confidently; assert

Two eyewitnesses *averred* they had seen the defendant at the scene. 兩個目擊者斷言他們在現場看到那個被告。

**verify**〔ˈvɛrəˌfaɪ〕*v.* 證實

—— prove to be true; confirm; substantiate; corroborate

So far, the charges have been neither disproved nor *verified*.

至今，那些控告既沒找到反證，也沒被證實。

**veritable**〔'vɛrətəbḷ〕 *adj.* 眞正的

——— true; actual; genuine; real; authentic

As the pretended heirs of Peter Wilks were disposing of his fortune, the *veritable* heirs arrived. 當冒充的彼德‧威爾克斯繼承人正在處置他的財產時，眞正的繼承人來了。

## 【Group 20】

# Vid, Vis — *see*「看」

**visibility**〔ˌvɪzə'bɪlətɪ〕 *n.* 能見度

——— degree of clearness of the atmosphere, with reference to the distance at which objects can be clearly seen

With the fog rolling in and *visibility* approaching zero, it was virtually impossible for planes to land.
霧滾滾而來而且能見度幾近於零的情況下，飛機實在不可能降落。

**envision**〔ɛn'vɪʒən〕 *v.* 想像（未來）

——— foresee; envisage; have a mental picture of (something not yet a reality)

Her dance teacher *envisions* Mary as a prima ballerina.
舞蹈老師想像瑪麗將來成爲首席芭蕾舞星。

**improvise**〔ˌɪmprə'vaɪz〕 *v.* 即興演出；即席而做

——— (literally, "do something without having prepared or seen it beforehand") compose, recite, or sing on the spur of the moment

Did the entertainer prepare his jokes before the program, or *improvise* them as he went along?
那位藝人是在節目前準備他的笑話，還是當他進行時才即席而做的？

第三章

**revise**[4] 〔 rɪ'vaɪz 〕 *v.* 修訂;再檢查

—— look at again to correct errors and make improvements; examine and improve

Before handing in your composition, be sure to *revise* it carefully. 在你交作文以前,一定要再仔細檢查一遍。

**invisible** 〔 ɪn'vɪzəbl̩ 〕 *adj.* 看不見的

—— not able to be seen

The microscope enables us to see organisms *invisible* to the naked eye. 顯微鏡使我們能看到用肉眼看不見的有機組織。

**video**[2] 〔'vɪdɪ,o 〕 *adj.* 影像的;電視的   *n.* 影片

—— having to do with the transmission or reception of what is seen

The audio (sound) and *video* signals of a television program can be recorded. 電視節目的聲音與影像可被錄下來。

**visual**[4] 〔'vɪʒʊəl 〕 *adj.* 可見的

—— having to do with sight

Radar tells us of an approaching object long before *visual* contact is possible. 雷達早在視覺接觸前就告訴我們有個正在接近的物體。

Exercise:請由 **Group 19 & 20** 中,選出最適當的字,填入空格中。

1. I am not much of a student, but Norman is a(n) _____ scholar.

2. Since words alone may fail to convey an idea, teachers often use _____ aids, such as pictures, charts, and films.

第三章

3. La Guardia Airport reports a temperature of 68° and _____ up to three miles.

4. Since the speaker had not prepared his talk, he had to _____ one.

5. You may believe this statement; it comes from a person of unquestionable _____.

---
【解答】
1. veritable      2. visual      3. visibility
4. improvise     5. veracity
---

# REVIEW ★

Exercise 1：選出正確答案

( ) 1. Congressional elections are a _____ affair; they are held every two years.

     (A) semiannual          (B) biennial

( ) 2. You may vote "yes" or "no" or, if you wish, you may _____.

     (A) abstain              (B) adjoin

( ) 3. Many boys at one time or another want to become firemen, but few of them actually enter that _____.

     (A) avocation          (B) vocation

( ) 4. The flight was delayed because of _____ weather.

     (A) adverse            (B) averse

第三章

(   ) 5. The American Revolution (1775) ＿＿＿＿ the French
Revolution (1789) by fourteen years.
(A) postdated              (B) antedated

(   ) 6. An imminent event belongs to the ＿＿＿＿.
(A) recent past            (B) present
(C) near future            (D) dim past
(E) distant future

(   ) 7. Bob is not exclusive; he ＿＿＿＿.
(A) tries hard             (B) makes friends easily
(C) comes on time          (D) keeps to himself
(E) prepares his homework

(   ) 8. Captain John Smith was spared when Pocahontas ＿＿＿＿
in his behalf.
(A) intervened             (B) contravened
(C) intersected            (D) implicated
(E) intercepted

(   ) 9. In an intraparty dispute, none of the participants are
＿＿＿＿.
(A) members                (B) entirely right
(C) stubborn               (D) all wrong
(E) outsiders

(   ) 10. There was no intermission in the fighting except for one
＿＿＿＿.
(A) U.N. protest           (B) minor skirmish
(C) surprise attack        (D) three-day truce
(E) shipment by the Allies

第三章

( ) 11. The overeager student shouted out the answer, unable to inhibit his _____.

(A) disappointment      (B) apprehension

(C) enthusiasm      (D) anger

(E) curiosity

( ) 12. The patient was in the hospital from November 23 to December 3, inclusive, a period of _____ days.

(A) twelve      (B) nine

(C) ten      (D) thirteen

(E) eleven

( ) 13. In next week's debate, Sheila will argue on the con, or _____, side of the question.

(A) negative      (B) extraneous

(C) intrinsic      (D) controversial

(E) positive

( ) 14. Quarrelsome neighbors rarely _____ one another's views.

(A) countermand      (B) censure

(C) advocate      (D) invoke

(E) contradict

( ) 15. A number of members asked me to intercede, but I refused to act as a(n) _____.

(A) understudy      (B) insurgent

(C) adversary      (D) go-between

(E) adherent

第三章

Exercise 2：下列各題中，選出與斜體字意義最相近的答案。

( 　 ) 1. painful *interlude*

    (A) delay                      (B) dispute

    (C) interval                  (D) intermediary

( 　 ) 2. deeply *implicated*

    (A) sorry                      (B) involved

    (C) indebted                 (D) hurt

( 　 ) 3. *counter* to expectation

    (A) look forward            (B) respond

    (C) appeal                   (D) contrary

( 　 ) 4. *exclusive* owner

    (A) sole                       (B) wealthy

    (C) rightful                  (D) principal

( 　 ) 5. neatly *excised*

    (A) inserted                 (B) removed

    (C) inscribed                (D) repaired

( 　 ) 6. *evoked* protests

    (A) disregarded            (B) contradicted

    (C) elicited                 (D) banned

( 　 ) 7. *intrinsic* character

    (A) inclusive               (B) extraneous

    (C) unusual                (D) essential

( 　 ) 8. *uninhibited* response

    (A) untruthful              (B) angry

    (C) unrestrained           (D) thoughtful

第三章

( ) 9. *impending* downfall

    (A) recent                (B) imminent

    (C) noteworthy        (D) disastrous

( ) 10. feel *impelled*

    (A) forced              (B) intercepted

    (C) explained         (D) expelled

( ) 11. *immaculate* record

    (A) imperfect         (B) dispassionate

    (C) faultless          (D) unbeatable

( ) 12. *irrevocable* mistake

    (A) minor               (B) natural

    (C) unforgivable      (D) past recall

( ) 13. easily *distracted*

    (A) upset               (B) diverted

    (C) abused            (D) averted

( ) 14. *incessant* chatter

    (A) worthless         (B) noisy

    (C) unceasing       (D) illogical

( ) 15. *benevolent* despot

    (A) lavish              (B) inhospitable

    (C) wise                (D) kind

( ) 16. without *deviating*

    (A) straying          (B) seceding

    (C) stopping         (D) hurrying

第三章

(　) 17. wide *discrepancy*
    (A) reduction        (B) variation
    (C) increase        (D) agreement

(　) 18. *inflexible* stand
    (A) immature        (B) pliable
    (C) obstinate        (D) defenseless

(　) 19. completely *deranged*
    (A) enervated        (B) demolished
    (C) unnerved        (D) demented

(　) 20. never *secure*
    (A) in danger        (B) separate
    (C) safe        (D) obtained

(　) 21. quite *unperturbed*
    (A) agitated        (B) upset
    (C) unrelated        (D) calm

(　) 22. act in *collusion*
    (A) discord        (B) conspiracy
    (C) expectation        (D) harmony

(　) 23. further *procrastination*
    (A) progress        (B) haste
    (C) complaint        (D) delay

(　) 24. *precludes* my joining
    (A) comes before        (B) postpones
    (C) prevents        (D) makes possible

第二章

( ) 25. *provoked* the voters

    (A) incensed                 (B) perplexed

    (C) obsessed                (D) impeded

( ) 26. *circumvented* our plan

    (A) deferred                (B) frustrated

    (C) projected               (D) advocated

( ) 27. *presumed* guilt

    (A) limited                 (B) supposed

    (C) obvious                (D) proved

( ) 28. *obviated* the repetition

    (A) made unnecessary     (B) prolonged

    (C) erased                (D) hindered

( ) 29. *incoherent* statements

    (A) profuse                (B) relevant

    (C) sticking together       (D) illogical

( ) 30. *prominent* advocate

    (A) adept                 (B) notable

    (C) prudent                (D) extravagant

( ) 31. without *fluctuation*

    (A) procrastination       (B) honesty

    (C) frequent change       (D) foresight

( ) 32. different *genre*

    (A) plan                 (B) category

    (C) reason                (D) manner

第三章

( ) 33. *magnanimous* offer
 (A) generous      (B) stingy
 (C) decisive      (D) dishonest

( ) 34. *enmity* toward none
 (A) ingratitude     (B) impunity
 (C) amity       (D) animus

( ) 35. *lucid* explanation
 (A) lengthy      (B) clear
 (C) complicated     (D) vague

( ) 36. noisy *aggregation*
 (A) protest      (B) welcome
 (C) assemblage     (D) isolation

( ) 37. perfect *equanimity*
 (A) fairness      (B) explanation
 (C) solution      (D) composure

( ) 38. *lateral* branch
 (A) essential      (D) fixed
 (C) side       (D) original

( ) 39. always *amiable*
 (A) late       (B) good-natured
 (C) petty       (D) quarrelsome

( ) 40. *tentative* solution
 (A) provisional     (B) definitive
 (C) amicable      (D) convincing

第三章

Exercise 3：下列各題中，選出意義與其他四者無關的答案。

( ) 1. (A) liberated　　(B) freed　　(C) emancipated
　　　　(D) released　　(E) manacled

( ) 2. (A) prescribe　　(B) order　　(C) heal
　　　　(D) dictate　　(E) direct

( ) 3. (A) absolute　　(B) controlled　　(C) despotic
　　　　(D) tyrannical　　(E) autocratic

( ) 4. (A) literal　　(B) manual　　(C) dental
　　　　(D) nasal　　(E) facial

( ) 5. (A) remote　　(B) imminent　　(C) approaching
　　　　(D) impending　　(E) close

( ) 6. (A) writer　　(B) author　　(C) journalist
　　　　(D) appendix　　(E) scribe

( ) 7. (A) conscripted　　(B) imitated　　(C) feigned
　　　　(D) pretended　　(E) simulated

( ) 8. (A) deserted　　(B) alone　　(C) forlorn
　　　　(D) dissimilar　　(E) desolate

( ) 9. (A) solitude　　(B) resolution　　(C) aloneness
　　　　(D) isolation　　(E) seclusion

( ) 10. (A) mandate　　(B) dictate　　(C) order
　　　　(D) command　　(E) verdict

第三章

Exercise 4：配合題：從 **A～J** 中選出意義相反的答案，填在空格中。

| COLUMN I | COLUMN II |
|---|---|
| (　) 1. detached | (A) simultaneous |
| (　) 2. occurring sooner or later | (B) unverified |
| (　) 3. able to pay all one's legal debts | (C) resolved |
| (　) 4. corroborated | (D) suspense |
| (　) 5. not interchanged | (E) solitary |
| (　) 6. unsolved | (F) soluble |
| (　) 7. with companions | (G) appended |
| (　) 8. incapable of being dissolved | (H) superimposed |
| (　) 9. absence of anxiety | (I) insolvent |
| (　) 10. placed underneath | (J) transposed |

【解答】

| | | | | | | | |
|---|---|---|---|---|---|---|---|
| **Ex 1.** | 1. B | 2. A | 3. B | 4. A | 5. B | 6. C | 7. B | 8. A |
| | 9. E | 10. D | 11. C | 12. E | 13. A | 14. C | 15. D | |
| **Ex 2.** | 1. C | 2. B | 3. D | 4. A | 5. B | 6. C | 7. D | 8. C |
| | 9. B | 10. A | 11. C | 12. D | 13. B | 14. C | 15. D | 16. A |
| | 17. B | 18. C | 19. D | 20. C | 21. D | 22. B | 23. D | 24. C |
| | 25. A | 26. B | 27. B | 28. A | 29. D | 30. B | 31. C | 32. B |
| | 33. A | 34. D | 35. B | 36. C | 37. D | 38. C | 39. B | 40. A |
| **Ex 3.** | 1. E | 2. C | 3. B | 4. A | 5. A | 6. D | 7. A | 8. D |
| | 9. B | 10. E | | | | | | |
| **Ex 4.** | 1. G | 2. A | 3. I | 4. B | 5. J | 6. C | 7. E | 8. F |
| | 9. D | 10. H | | | | | | |

第三章

# 第四章
# 認識盎格魯‧撒克遜字首以增加字彙

## 什麼是字首

字首是放在字或字根前，以形成新字的字。

| PREFIX | WORD OR ROOT | NEW WORD |
|---|---|---|
| FORE (Anglo-Saxon prefix meaning "beforehand") | + SEE | = FORESEE (= "see beforehand") |
| DIS (Latin prefix meaning "apart") | + SECT (root meaning "cut") | = DISSECT (= "cut apart") |
| HYPER (Greek prefix meaning "over") | + CRITICAL | = HYPERCRITICAL (= "overcritical") |

## 爲什麼要讀字首

　　了解字首和其意義，能幫助你增加字彙。以特定字首開頭的英文字爲數很多，而且一直在增加。你一旦知道某個特定字首的意思，就容易了解任何用那個字首開頭的字。例如你學會拉丁字首的 bi 意思是 two，那麼看到 bipartisan（兩黨的），bilingual（能說兩種語言的），bisect（平分），就比較快了解意思。

## 本章目的

　　1. 使你熟悉重要的盎格魯‧撒克遜字首。
　　2. 幫助你熟記用這些字首開頭的常用單字。

第四章

【Group 1】

# Fore — *before*「在前」

Group 1～20

**forearm**〔'for͵ɑrm〕*n.* 前臂
—— (literally, "front part of the arm") part of the arm from the
wrist to the elbow
Henry protected his face from George's blows by raising his
*forearms*. 亨利舉起前臂以防喬治打他的臉。

**forebear**〔'for͵bɛr〕*n.* 祖先
—— (literally, "one who has been or existed before") ancestor;
forefather
John F. Kennedy's *forebears* migrated to America from Ireland.
約翰‧甘迺迪的祖先從愛爾蘭移民到美國。

**foreboding**〔'for͵bodɪŋ〕*n.* (不祥的)預感
—— feeling beforehand of coming trouble; misgiving;
presentiment
The day before the accident, I had a *foreboding* that something
would go wrong. 意外的前一天，我就有預感壞事會發生。

**forecast**[4]〔'for͵kæst〕*n.* 預報；預測
—— estimate beforehand of a future
happening; prediction; prophecy
Have you listened to the weather *forecast*
for tomorrow? 你聽了明天的氣象預報嗎？

> 【記憶技巧】
> *fore* (before) + *cast*
> (throw) (事先放出消
> 息，就是「預測」)

**forefront**〔'for͵frʌnt〕*n.* 最前線；最前面
—— (literally, "front part of the front") foremost place or part;
vanguard

第四章

In combat the officer was always in the *forefront* of the attack, leading his men on to victory.

交戰時長官總是站在進攻的最前線，領導他的士兵贏得勝利。

**foresight** 〔'for͵saɪt 〕 *n.* 先見（之明）；遠見

—— power of seeing beforehand what is likely to happen; prudence

*Foresight* is better than hindsight. 有先見之明比事後聰明好。

**foreword** 〔'for͵wɝd 〕 *n.* 前言

—— front matter preceding the text of a book; preface; introduction

Before Chapter I, there is a brief *foreword* in which the author explains why he wrote the book.

在第一章前，都有一篇作者解釋為何寫這本書的簡短前言。

**foreshadow** 〔 for'ʃædo 〕 *v.* 是…的預兆；預示

—— indicate beforehand

Our defeat in the championship game was *foreshadowed* by injuries to two of our star players in a previous game.

我們冠軍賽會失敗，早就由我們兩個明星球員在前場比賽中受傷顯示出來了。

**foregoing** 〔 for'goɪŋ 〕 *adj.* 先前的；前面的

—— going before; preceding

Carefully review the *foregoing* chapter before reading any further.

在更進一步閱讀以前，先仔細複習一下前面的一章。

**foremost** 〔'for͵most 〕 *adj.* 最先的；主要的

—— standing at the front; first; most advanced; leading; principal; chief

Did you know that Benjamin Franklin was one of the *foremost* inventors of the eighteenth century?

你知道班傑明・富蘭克林是十八世紀最重要的發明家之一嗎？

Exercise：請由 **Group 1** 中，選出最適當的字，填入空格中。

1. When asked if he thought we would win, the coach refused to make a _____.

2. Don't cram for a test the night before; be sensible and spread your review over several of the _____ days.

3. My sister's long gloves cover the hand, the wrist, and the

   _____.

4. I should have had the _____ to buy a warm coat before it got too cold; now all the best ones have been sold.

5. As he set out on his last mission, the hero had a _____ that he might not return.

> 【解答】
> 1. forecast　　　2. foregoing　　　3. forearm
> 4. foresight　　　5. foreboding

**【Group 2】**

# Mis — *bad(ly)*, *wrong(ly)*
## 「壞的（地）；錯的（地）」

**misbelief**〔͵mɪsbə'lif〕*n.* 錯誤的見解

—— wrong or erroneous belief

People thought the earth was flat until Columbus corrected that *misbelief.* 人們認爲地球是平的，直到哥倫布糾正了那錯誤的觀念。

**misdeed**〔 mɪs'did 〕*n.* 惡行；罪行

—— bad act; wicked deed

The wrongdoer was punished for his *misdeed* by a fine and imprisonment. 犯罪者因惡行而入獄並懲處罰金。

**misgiving**〔 mɪs'gɪvɪŋ 〕*n.* 不安；疑慮

—— uneasy feeling; feeling of doubt or suspicion; foreboding; lack of confidence

Dad has no *misgivings* when Mother takes the wheel, because she is an excellent driver.

當母親開車時，父親不會覺得不安，因爲她很會開車。

**mishap**〔 'mɪsˌhæp 〕*n.* 不幸事故；災難

—— bad happening; misfortune; unlucky accident; mischance

Right after the collision, each driver blamed the other for the *mishap.* 相撞之後，兩個駕駛人都互相指責這次的不幸事故是因爲對方。

**misstep**〔 mɪs'stɛp 〕*n.* 失足；錯誤；失策

—— wrong step; slip in conduct or judgment; blunder

Quitting school is a *misstep* that you may regret for the rest of your life. 休學會是你餘生都遺憾的過失。

**misfire**〔 mɪs'faɪr 〕*v.* ( 槍彈 ) 射不出

—— (literally, "fire wrongly") to fail to be fired or exploded properly

The bear escaped when the hunter's rifle *misfired.*
當獵人的來福槍射不出子彈時，熊就逃跑了。

# mislay〔 mɪsˈle 〕*v.* 把…放錯位置；遺失

—— to put or lay in an unremembered place; lose

Yesterday I *mislaid* my biology book, and it took me about a half hour to find it.

昨天我把生物學的書放錯位置，使得我花了大約半小時才找到它。

# mislead[4]〔 mɪsˈlid 〕*v.* 誤導；使誤解

—— to lead astray (in the wrong direction); deceive; delude; beguile

Some traffic signs are so confusing that they *mislead* the traveler.

有些交通標誌非常混淆，常使旅行者走錯路。

Exercise：請由 **Group 2** 中，選出最適當的字，填入空格中。

1. Luckily, no one was seriously hurt in the airplane _____.

2. Where is your report card? Did you lose it or _____ it?

3. I hated to lend Marie my notes because of a _____ that she might not return them in time.

4. A soldier would be in serious jeopardy if his weapon should _____.

5. It is against the law to put out advertisements that _____ the public.

## 【Group 3】

# Out — *beyond, more than*「超過；比～更」

**outlook**⁶〔'aʊtˌlʊk〕*n.* 展望；看法

—— a looking beyond; prospect for the future

The *outlook* for unskilled laborers is not bright, as their jobs are gradually being taken over by machines.

無技能的勞工的展望並不好，因為他們的工作會漸漸被機器所取代。

**output**⁵〔'aʊtˌpʊt〕*n.* 產量；產品

—— (literally, what is "put out") a yield or product; an amount produced

The *output* of the average American factory worker is steadily increasing. 一般美國工廠工人的生產量在穩定成長中。

**outgrow**〔aʊt'gro〕*v.* 個子長得穿不下；長大成熟而不再

—— to grow beyond or too large for

The jacket Dad bought me last year is too small. I have *outgrown* it. 去年父親買給我的夾克太小了。我已經長得太大，穿不下了。

**outlast**〔aʊt'læst〕*v.* 比⋯持久；較⋯耐用

—— to last longer than; outlive; survive

Our kitchen table is more solidly constructed than the chairs and will probably *outlast* them.

我們廚房的桌子比椅子造得更穩固，很可能較椅子耐用。

**outrun**〔aʊt'rʌn〕*v.* 跑得比⋯快

—— to run faster than

We scored a touchdown when Joe caught a forward pass and *outran* his pursuers.

當喬接到前方傳來的球，跑得比追者快時，我們的橄欖球觸地得分。

第四章

**outwit**〔 aʊt′wɪt 〕*v.* 以機智勝過

——to get the better of by being more clever

In his detective stories, Jim manages to *outwit* the cleverest criminals. 在他的偵探小說中，吉姆設法以機智取勝最聰明的罪犯。

**outlandish**〔 aʊt′lændɪʃ 〕*adj.* 稀奇古怪的；怪異的

——looking or sounding as if it belongs to a (foreign) land beyond ours; strange; fantastic

A masquerade is always interesting because people come in such *outlandish* costumes.
化裝舞會一向很有趣，因爲人們都穿著稀奇古怪的服裝來。

**outspoken**〔′aʊt′spokən 〕*adj.* 直言不諱的；直率的

——speaking out freely or boldly; frank; not reserved

Mary sometimes hurts others when she criticizes their work because she is too *outspoken*.
因爲瑪麗太直言不諱，因此當她批評別人的工作時，有時會傷害到他們。

Exercise：請由 **Group 3** 中，選出最適當的字，填入空格中。

1. I know I shall get the truth when I ask Alice because she is very _____.

2. Where did you get that _____ hat? I never saw anything like it before.

3. My little brother has the thumb-sucking habit, but Mother hopes he will _____ it when he begins school.

4. These sneakers are the best I have ever had. They will _____ any other brand by at least a month.

5. Our prospects for retaining the championship are good, but the
_____ may change if one of our key players is hurt or
becomes ill.

---

【解答】

1. outspoken    2. outlandish    3. outgrow
4. outlast      5. outlook

---

## 【Group 4】

# Over — *too, over*「太；超過」

**overdose**〔'ovɚ,dos〕*n.* 服藥過量

—— quantity of medicine beyond what is to be taken
at one time or in a given period; too big a dose

Do not take more of the medicine than the doctor ordered; an
*overdose* may be dangerous.

服藥不要超過醫生所指示的量，因爲服藥過量可能很危險。

**oversupply**〔'ovɚsə,plaɪ〕*n.* 供應過量

—— too great a supply; an excessive supply

We have a shortage of skilled technicians but an *oversupply* of
unskilled workers.

我們缺少技術人員，卻有過量沒技能的工人。

**overburden**〔'ovɚ'bɝdn̩〕*v.* 使負擔過重

—— to place too heavy a load on; burden excessively; overtax

It would *overburden* me to have my piano lesson on Thursday
because I have so much homework on that day.

如果星期四有鋼琴課會使我負擔過重，因爲那天我已有了太多的功課。

**overestimate** 〔'ovɚ'ɛstə,met 〕*v.* 高估

—— to make too high an estimate (rough calculation) of the worth
or size of something or someone; overvalue

Joe *overestimated* the capacity of the bus when he thought it could
hold 60; it has room for only 48. 喬高估了公車的容載量，他以為能載
六十人，實際上它的空間只能容納四十八人。

**overshadow** 〔,ovɚ'ʃædo 〕*v.* 使蒙上陰影；使黯然失色

—— to cast a shadow over; be more important than; outweigh

Their gaieties were *overshadowed* by the sad news.
這不幸的消息使他們的歡樂蒙上了陰影。

**overwhelm** [5] 〔,ovɚ'hwɛlm 〕*v.* 壓倒；使無法對付

—— to cover over completely; overpower; overthrow; crush

The department store guards were nearly *overwhelmed* by the
crowds of shoppers waiting for the sale to begin.
百貨公司的警衛幾乎無法應付成群等待大拍賣開始的購物者。

**overbearing** 〔,ovɚ'bɛrɪŋ 〕*adj.* 專橫的；傲慢的

—— domineering over others; inclined to dictate

When the monitor gave too many orders, the teacher scolded him
for being *overbearing*. 當班長下太多命令時，老師責備他太專橫了。

**overconfident** 〔'ovɚ'kɑnfədənt 〕*adj.* 過於自信的

—— too sure of oneself; excessively confident

I was so sure of passing that I wasn't going to study, but Dad
advised me not to be *overconfident*.
我確信不用讀書就可及格，但父親勸我別太自信。

**overgenerous** 〔'ovɚ'dʒɛnərəs 〕*adj.* 過於慷慨的

—— too liberal in giving; excessively openhanded

第
四
章

Because the service was poor, Mother thought Dad was *overgenerous* in leaving the waiter a 15% tip.

因爲服務差，母親認爲父親給服務生百分之十五的小費太過大方。

Exercise：請由 **Group 4** 中，選出最適當的字，填入空格中。

1. There will be too much food left over if you seriously _____ the number who will attend the party.

2. The teacher won't let monitors carry more than twelve books at a time because he doesn't want them to _____ themselves.

3. Why did you buy more ping-pong balls? Don't you know we have an _____?

4. I think my English teacher was _____ when he gave me a 99 because I didn't deserve such a high mark.

5. At first the sergeant was very domineering, but as he got to know the men he became less _____.

```
【解答】
1. overestimate    2. overburden    3. oversupply
4. overgenerous    5. overbearing
```

【**Group 5**】

# Un — *not*「非」

**unconcern**〔͵ʌnkən'sɝn〕*n.* 不關心；不感興趣

—— lack of concern, anxiety, or interest; indifference

The audience was breathless with anxiety during the daring
tightrope act, though the acrobats themselves performed with
seeming ***unconcern*** for their own safety.
在大膽的走鋼索表演中，觀眾都因焦慮而摒住氣息，雖然那些走鋼索的人
表現得毫不在意他們自己的安全。

**undeceive**〔͵ʌndɪ'siv〕*v.* 使醒悟；使不受騙

—— free from deception or mistaken ideas; set straight

If you think I can get Mr. Black to hire you because he is my
cousin, let me ***undeceive*** you. I have no influence with him.
如果你認為我能使布雷克先生雇用你，是因為他是我堂兄弟的話，讓我
老實告訴你，我對他沒有影響力。

**unnerve**〔ʌn'nɝv〕*v.* 使失去勇氣；使緊張不安

—— deprive of nerve or courage; cause to lose self-control; unsettle

The unsportsmanlike noises of the fans so ***unnerved*** our star player
that he missed two foul shots in a row. 沒運動風度的球迷發出的鬧
聲，使我們的明星球員緊張不安，結果接連兩次罰球都沒進。

**unscramble**〔ʌn'skræmbl̩〕*v.* 整理；使不再混亂

—— do the opposite of scramble; restore to intelligible form

The previous secretary had mixed up the files so badly that it took
my sister about a week to ***unscramble*** them.
先前的祕書把檔案混得很亂，使我姊姊花了大約一星期才把它們整理好。

**unshackle**〔ʌn'ʃækl̩〕*v.* 除去⋯的枷鎖；使⋯恢復自由

—— release from a shackle (anything that confines the legs or
　arms); set free from restraint

When mutinous sailors were put in irons in the olden days, nobody
was allowed to ***unshackle*** them.
以前當叛變的水手被戴上腳鐐手銬時，任何人都不准除去他們的枷鎖。

**unabridged** 〔ˌʌnəˈbrɪdʒd 〕 *adj.* （書或文章）未刪節的；完整的

—— not abridged; not made shorter; complete

Though an abridged dictionary is convenient to use, it contains far fewer definitions than an *unabridged* dictionary. 雖然一本刪節版的字典方便使用，但它所含字辭的定義卻比未刪節的字典少得多。

**unbiased** 〔 ʌnˈbaɪəst 〕 *adj.* 無偏見的；公平的

—— not biased; not prejudiced in favor of or against; fair

Don't ask the mother of a contestant to serve as a judge because it may be hard for her to remain *unbiased*.
別要選手的母親作裁判，因為她可能很難保持公平。

**unquenchable** 〔 ʌnˈkwɛntʃəbḷ 〕 *adj.* 無法抑制的；不能消除的

—— not quenchable; not capable of being satisfied; inextinguishable

Many teenagers have an *unquenchable* thirst for adventure stories; they read one after another. 許多青少年對於冒險故事有一種難以抑制的渴望，他們會一本接一本地讀。

**unwary** 〔 ʌnˈwɛrɪ 〕 *adj.* 不小心的

—— not wary; not alert; heedless

An *unwary* pedestrian is much more likely to be struck by a car than one who looks both ways and crosses with the light.
一個不小心的行人比一個過馬路時會看雙向車輛，並遵守交通燈號的人，更有可能被車撞到。

Exercise：請由 **Group 5** 中，選出最適當的字，填入空格中。

1. If you are behind Harvey on the line at the water fountain, just be patient; he has an almost _____ thirst.

2. The guards were warned that their prisoner would try to escape if they were the least bit _____.

3. I visited Grandma every day when she was in the hospital! I can't understand why you are accusing me of _____ about her health!

4. When looking up a difficult technical word, it's a good idea to consult an _____ dictionary.

5. Both the strikers and their employers want the mayor to arbitrate their dispute because they consider him _____.

【解答】
1. unquenchable　2. unwary　3. unconcern
4. unabridged　5. unbiased

## 【Group 6】

# Under — *beneath, insufficient(ly)*
# 「在下；不足的（地）」

**underbrush** 〔'ʌndɚ͵brʌʃ 〕 *n.* 矮樹叢

—— shrubs, bushes, etc., growing beneath large trees in a forest; undergrowth

On its way through the dense jungle, the patrol had to be constantly wary of enemy soldiers concealed in the *underbrush*.
在穿過濃密叢林的路上，巡邏隊必須不斷提防著隱藏在矮樹叢中的敵軍。

**undergraduate**[5] 〔͵ʌndɚ'grædʒʊɪt 〕 *n.* 大學生

—— (literally, "lower than a graduate") a student in a college or university who has not yet earned his first degree

Most *undergraduates* take four years to earn a degree, but some achieve it sooner by attending summer sessions.

大多數的大學生須花四年獲得學位，但有一些學生參加暑期班就可更快獲得。

## underpayment 〔ˈʌndəˈpemənt 〕 *n.* 繳付不足；付款不足

—— insufficient payment

If too little is deducted from Dad's weekly wages for income tax, it results in an *underpayment* at the end of the year. 如果父親每週的工資扣繳所得稅的金額太少，年底就會發生不夠繳付的結果。

## undersigned 〔ˌʌndəˈsaɪnd 〕 *n.* 署名者

—— person or persons who sign at the end of (literally, "under") a letter or document

Among the *undersigned* in the petition to the governor were some of the most prominent persons in the state.

向州長提出請願書的一些署名者中，有一些是州內最傑出的人士。

## understatement 〔ˈʌndəˌstetmənt 〕 *n.* 輕描淡寫

—— a statement below the truth; a restrained statement in mocking contrast to what might be said

Frank's remark that he was "slightly bruised" in the accident is an *understatement*; he suffered two fractured ribs.

法蘭克說他在車禍中「輕微瘀傷」是輕描淡寫，其實他斷了兩根肋骨。

## understudy 〔ˈʌndəˌstʌdɪ 〕 *n.* 候補演員

—— one who "studies under" and learns the part of a regular performer so as to be his substitute if necessary

While the star is recuperating from her illness, her role will be played by her *understudy*.

當明星正在休養恢復健康時，她的角色由候補演員代替。

第四章

**underscore** 〔͵ʌndɚˈskɔr 〕 *v.* 在…劃底線；強調

—— draw a line beneath; emphasize

When we take notes, our teacher wants us to *underscore* items that are especially important.

當我們記重點時，我們老師要我們在特別重要的項目下劃線。

**undersell** 〔͵ʌndɚˈsɛl 〕 *v.* 以比…低的價格出售

—— sell at a lower price than

When discount houses tried to *undersell* department stores, the latter reduced prices too, and adopted the slogan "We will not be *undersold.*"

當廉價商店嘗試將售價低於百貨公司時，百貨公司也降了價，同時採用了「別人不會比我們便宜」的口號。

**underdeveloped** 〔͵ʌndɚdɪˈvɛləpt 〕 *adj.* 低度開發的

—— insufficiently developed because of a lack of capital and trained personnel for exploiting natural resources

Our country has spent billions of dollars to help the *underdeveloped* nations improve their standard of living.

我們國家已花了好幾十億元去幫助低開發國家，改善他們的生活水準。

**underprivileged** 〔ˈʌndɚˈprɪvəlɪdʒd 〕 *adj.* 貧困的；條件較多數人差的；弱勢的

—— insufficiently privileged; deprived through social or economic oppression of some of the fundamental rights supposed to belong to all

The *underprivileged* child from the crowded slum tenement has many more problems to overcome than the child from the middle-class home.

來自擁擠貧民窟廉價公寓中貧困的孩子，比來自中產階級家庭的孩子，有更多的問題要克服。

第四章

Exercise：請由 **Group 6** 中，選出最適當的字，填入空格中。

1. The advanced course is for students with a bachelor's degree, but I understand that an outstanding _____ may enroll if the instructor approves.

2. Though an _____ must master long and difficult roles, he has no assurance that he will ever be called on to perform.

3. Arline told me she "passed," but that's an _____; the fact is that she got the highest mark in the class.

4. Mike's tee shot disappeared after hitting one of the trees, and he had to hunt for the ball in the _____.

5. Because they buy in larger quantities at lower prices, chain stores are usually able to _____ small merchants.

> 【解答】
> 1. undergraduate    2. understudy
> 3. understatement    4. underbrush    5. undersell

【**Group 7**】

# Up — *up, upward*「上；向上」

**upheaval**〔ʌpˈhivḷ〕*n.* 動亂

—— violent heaving up; commotion; extreme agitation

The prime minister's proposal for new taxes created such an *upheaval* that his government fell.

首相新稅制的計畫造成如此大的混亂，以致於他的政府倒閣。

**upkeep**〔ˈʌpˌkip〕*n.* 保養；維修；保養費；維修費

—— maintenance ("keeping up"); cost of operating and repairing

Our neighbor traded in his old car because the ***upkeep*** had become too high.

我們的鄰居用舊車折價買了輛新車，因為汽車保養費已變得太昂貴了。

**upstart**〔ˈʌpˌstɑrt〕*n.* 暴發戶；新貴；突然發跡的人

—— person who has suddenly risen to wealth and power, especially if he is conceited and unpleasant

When the new representative entered the legislature, some older members received him coldly because they regarded him as an ***upstart.*** 當新的代表進入議會，一些老議員們表現冷淡，因為他們認為他是一個突然發跡的人。

**upturn**〔ˈʌpˌtɜn〕*n.* 好轉；上揚

—— upward turn toward better conditions

Most merchants report a slowdown in sales for October, but confidently expect an ***upturn*** with the approach of Christmas.

大多數商人說十月份的銷售量衰退，但很有自信地預料情況將會隨著聖誕節的來臨而好轉。

**update**[5]〔ʌpˈdet〕*v.* 使成為最新

—— bring up to date

Our world geography teacher has just received an ***updated*** map that shows the latest national boundaries.

我們的世界地理老師剛收到一份最新的地圖，它顯示了最新的國家邊界。

**upgrade**[6]〔ˈʌpˈgred〕*v.* 使升級；提升；改善

—— raise the grade or quality of; improve

To qualify for better jobs, many employees attend evening courses where they can ***upgrade*** their skills. 為了能勝任更好的工作，許多員工參加晚間的課程來提升他們的工作技能。

**uproot** 〔ʌpˈrut〕 *v.* 根除；徹底消滅

—— pull up by the roots; remove completely; eradicate; destroy

The love of liberty is so firmly embedded in men's hearts that no tyrant can hope to *uproot* it.

對自由的熱愛如此深植人心，以致於沒有任何暴君能根絕它。

**upcoming** 〔ˈʌpˌkʌmɪŋ〕 *adj.* 即將來臨的

—— coming up; being in the near future; forthcoming; approaching

The management will be glad to mail you its leaflet, which contains news of *upcoming* films.

公司會很樂意寄給你它的傳單，裡面包括了最近的電影訊息。

**upright**[5] 〔ˈʌpˌraɪt〕 *adj.* 直立的

—— standing up straight on the feet; erect

When knocked off his feet, the boxer waited till the count of nine before returning to an *upright* position.

當拳擊手被擊倒時，直到數到九時，才又站了起來。

Exercise：請由 **Group 7** 中，選出最適當的字，填入空格中。

1. Some believe that today's victory, the first in four weeks, marks an _____ in the team's fortune.

2. To improve his book, the author will have to _____ the last chapter, to include the events of the past ten years.

3. It is easier to destroy weeds with a chemical spray than to _____ them by hand.

4. What is the name of the city department responsible for the _____ of our roads?

第四章

5. The manufacturer has done everything possible to _____ his product, with the result that it is now of excellent quality.

---
【解答】
1. upturn　　　2. update　　　3. uproot
4. upkeep　　　5. upgrade
---

## 【Group 8】

# With — *back, away, against*
# 「向後；離開；對抗」

**withdraw**⁴〔 wɪð'drɔ 〕*v.* 撤退；撤銷；提（款）

—— take or draw back or away

【記憶技巧】
*with* (back) + *draw*（拉）

Tom is my principal backer; if he *withdraws* his support, I don't see how I can be elected. 湯姆是我主要的支持者，如果他撤銷他的援助，我不知道我如何才能被選上。

**withdrawal**〔 wɪð'drɔəl 〕*n.* 退出；提款

—— act of taking back or drawing out from a place of deposit

My uncle paid for his vacation trip by making a *withdrawal* from his bank account.
我叔叔從銀行帳戶裡提款出來，以支付他的假期旅費。

**withdrawn**〔 wɪð'drɔn 〕*adj.* 沉默寡言的；性格內向的

—— drawn back or removed from easy approach; socially detached; unresponsive; introverted

We talked to the neighbor's youngster and tried to be friendly, but he didn't say anything; he seemed to be *withdrawn*. 我們和鄰居少年說話，想表現得很友善，但他一句話也沒說，似乎很內向。

第四章

**withhold** 〔 wɪð'hold 〕 *v.* 拒絕給予；扣留；保留

—— hold back; keep from giving; restrain

Please don't interrupt me. If you have something to say, *withhold* your comment until I have finished speaking.

請別打岔。如果你有話要說，先保留一下你的意見等我說完。

**withholding tax** 〔 wɪð'holdɪŋ 'tæks 〕 *n.* 雇主替政府從職員薪資扣繳的所得稅

—— sum withheld or deducted from wages for tax purposes

Your employer is required to deduct a certain amount from your salary as a *withholding tax* payable to the federal government.

你的老闆必須從你的薪資中扣繳一定的稅額，再繳交給聯邦政府。

**withstand**[6] 〔 wɪθ'stænd 〕 *v.* 抵抗

—— stand up against; hold out; resist; endure

The walls of a dam must be strong enough to *withstand* tremendous water pressure.

水壩的牆必須夠堅固，以抵抗巨大的水壓。

> 【記憶技巧】
> *with* (against) +
> *stand* ( 站著反對，
> 就是「抵抗」)

**notwithstanding** 〔'natwɪθ'stændɪŋ 〕 *prep.* 儘管

—— (literally, "not standing against") in spite of; despite

*Notwithstanding* their advantage of height, the visiting players were unable to beat our basketball team.

儘管來訪球員有個子高的優勢，但他們仍然無法打敗我們的籃球隊。

Exercise：請由 **Group 8** 中，選出最適當的字，填入空格中。

1. You can make a deposit or a _____ by mail, without going to the bank.

第四章

2. The head of a family pays a smaller ＿＿＿＿ than a single employee earning the same salary.

3. The mayor has approved plans for constructing the new roadway, ＿＿＿＿ the protests from residents of the area.

4. As a result of a disagreement with his partners, the lawyer announced that he would ＿＿＿＿ from the firm and open an office of his own.

5. The training that astronauts receive teaches them how to ＿＿＿＿ the hazards of space exploration.

【解答】
1. withdrawal  2. withholding tax
3. notwithstanding  4. withdraw  5. withstand

## REVIEW ★

Exercise 1：寫出與題前解釋意義相同，且字首為 **fore, mis, out** 或 **over** 的單字。

( ) 1. seen beforehand ＿＿＿foreseen＿＿＿

( ) 2. badly matched ＿＿＿＿＿＿

( ) 3. grown to excess ＿＿＿＿＿＿

( ) 4. use wrongly ＿＿＿＿＿＿

( ) 5. cooked too much ＿＿＿＿＿＿

( ) 6. person beyond the law ＿＿＿＿＿＿

第四章

( ) 7. wrong interpretation _____

( ) 8. doom beforehand _____

( ) 9. ride faster than _____

( ) 10. inform incorrectly _____

( ) 11. too cautious _____

( ) 12. bad calculation _____

( ) 13. front feet (of a four-legged animal)

_____

( ) 14. too simplified _____

( ) 15. swim better than _____

( ) 16. govern badly _____

( ) 17. stay too long _____

( ) 18. one who runs before _____

( ) 19. wrong statement _____

( ) 20. shout louder than _____

Exercise 2：寫出與題前解釋意義相同，且字首為 **un, under, up** 或 **with** 的單字。

( ) 1. lying beneath _____

( ) 2. not able to be avoided _____

( ) 3. hold back _____

(　) 4. insufficiently paid　　　　＿＿＿＿＿＿＿＿

(　) 5. act or instance of rising up　＿＿＿＿＿＿＿＿

(　) 6. do the opposite of *lock*　　＿＿＿＿＿＿＿＿

(　) 7. lower (criminal) part of the world

　　＿＿＿＿＿＿＿＿

(　) 8. stand up against　　　　　＿＿＿＿＿＿＿＿

(　) 9. one who holds up, supports, or defends

　　＿＿＿＿＿＿＿＿

(　) 10. sum taken (drawn) back from a bank account

　　＿＿＿＿＿＿＿＿

(　) 11. not sociable　　　　　　＿＿＿＿＿＿＿＿

(　) 12. upward stroke　　　　　＿＿＿＿＿＿＿＿

(　) 13. charge lower than the proper price

　　＿＿＿＿＿＿＿＿

(　) 14. draw back or away　　　＿＿＿＿＿＿＿＿

(　) 15. lack of reality　　　　　＿＿＿＿＿＿＿＿

(　) 16. stretched upward　　　　＿＿＿＿＿＿＿＿

(　) 17. one who holds back　　　＿＿＿＿＿＿＿＿

(　) 18. released from a leash　　＿＿＿＿＿＿＿＿

(　) 19. beneath the surface of the sea　＿＿＿＿＿＿＿＿

(　) 20. upward thrust　　　　　＿＿＿＿＿＿＿＿

第四章

# Exercise 3：下列各題中，選出意義與其他三者無關的答案。

( ) 1. (A) careful　(B) alert　(C) wary　(D) upstart

( ) 2. (A) approaching　(B) foreshadowing
(C) forthcoming　(D) upcoming

( ) 3. (A) undeceived　(B) beguiled
(C) misled　(D) misinformed

( ) 4. (A) biased　(B) underprivileged
(C) prejudiced　(D) unfair

( ) 5. (A) unmask　(B) ungag　(C) expose　(D) unveil

( ) 6. (A) abridged　(B) incomplete　(C) uncut　(D) shortened

( ) 7 (A) released　(B) shackled　(C) restrained　(D) confined

( ) 8. (A) withdrawn　(B) unresponsive
(C) underdeveloped　(D) unsociable

( ) 9. (A) destroy　(B) eradicate
(C) uproot　(D) unscramble

( ) 10. (A) underscore　(B) underline
(C) understudy　(D) emphasize

( ) 11. (A) ancestor　(B) forefather
(C) descendant　(D) forebear

( ) 12. (A) outlived　(B) survived　(C) outlasted　(D) outwitted

( ) 13. (A) principal　(B) foremost　(C) latest　(D) chief

( ) 14. (A) misgiving　(B) blunder
(C) foreboding　(D) presentiment

( ) 15. (A) overcast　(B) overburden　(C) overload　(D) overtax

( ) 16. (A) luck　　　　　　　　(B) foresight
　　　　(C) prudence　　　　　　(D) forethought

( ) 17. (A) output　　(B) yield　　(C) surrender　(D) product

( ) 18. (A) misfortune　　　　　(B) mishap
　　　　(C) mischance　　　　　(D) mistrust

( ) 19. (A) overbearing　　　　(B) beguiling
　　　　(C) deluding　　　　　　(D) misleading

( ) 20. (A) prediction　　　　　(B) prophecy
　　　　(C) forecast　　　　　　(D) fortune

----【解答】------------------------------------

**Ex 1.**　1. foreseen　　　　2. mismatched　　　3. outgrown
　　　　4. misuse　　　　　5. overcooked　　　6. outlaw
　　　　7. misinterpretation　8. foredoom　　　9. outride
　　　　10. misinform　　　11. overcautious　　12. miscalculation
　　　　13. forefeet　　　　14. oversimplified　15. outswim
　　　　16. misgovern　　　17. outstay　　　　18. forerunner
　　　　19. misstatement　　20. outshout

**Ex 2.**　1. underlying　　　2. unavoidable　　3. withhold
　　　　4. underpaid　　　5. uprising　　　　6. unlock
　　　　7. underworld　　　8. withstand　　　9. upholder
　　　　10. withdrawal　　11. unsociable　　12. upstroke
　　　　13. undercharge　14. withdraw　　　15. unreality
　　　　16. upstretched　17. withholder　　18. unleashed
　　　　19. undersea　　　20. upthrust

**Ex 3.**　1. D　　2. B　　3. A　　4. B　　5. B　　6. C　　7. A　　8. C
　　　　9. D　10. C　11. C　12. D　13. C　14. B　15. A　16. A
　　　　17. C　18. D　19. A　20. D

第
四
章

# 第五章
# 出自希臘羅馬神話的字彙

> 　　本章會教你用來自古希臘羅馬的重要字彙。希臘人創造了美麗的神話，後來由羅馬人改寫，其影響深遠。而源於那些神話的字，是受過良好教育的人應該知道的。以下所討論的字，除 Draconian, laconic, Lucullan, philippic, Pyrrhic, solon, thespian 是基於史實，其餘都源自神話。

**Adonis** 〔 əˈdɑnɪs 〕 *n.* 美男子

—— very handsome young man

　　( *Adonis* 是愛神阿芙羅黛蒂所愛的英俊男子 )

Peter, who was chosen the handsomest boy in the senior class, is quite an *Adonis*.

彼得真是一個美男子，他在高年級班上被選爲最英俊的男孩。

Adonis

**aegis** 〔ˈidʒɪs 〕 *n.* 庇護；支持

—— 1. shield or protection

　　2. auspices or sponsorship

aegis

　　( *aegis* 是保護宙斯的盾牌 )

An international force under the *aegis* of the United Nations has been dispatched to the troubled area.

國際部隊在聯合國的支持下，已被派遣到變亂的地區。

**amazon** 〔ˈæməˌzɑn 〕 *n.* 有男子氣概的女人；女中豪傑

—— tall, strong, masculine woman

　　( *Amazon* 是神話中一支高大、強壯、有男子氣概的女戰士族 )

Pioneer women were veritable *amazons*, performing heavy household chores in addition to toiling in the fields beside their menfolk. 拓荒的女性確實很有男子氣概，要做家中粗重的工作，還要和男人在田裡辛勞工作。

# ambrosial〔 æm'broʒɪəl 〕*adj.* 非常美味的

—— exceptionally pleasing to taste or smell; extremely delicious; excellent

（ *ambrosia* 是神享用的美味可口食物）

The *ambrosial* aroma of the roast whetted our appetites.
烤肉的美味香氣刺激了我們的食慾。

# atlas〔'ætləs 〕*n.* 地圖集；地圖

—— book of maps

Atlas

（ *Atlas* 是以雙肩揹負天的巨人，而昔日地圖集卷首有 Atlas 肩負地球的圖畫）

For reliable information about present national boundaries, consult an up-to-date *atlas*.
要得到現今國家邊界的可靠資訊，查閱一下最新的地圖。

# auroral〔 ɔ'rorəl 〕*adj.* 1. 曙光的　2. 玫瑰色的

—— 1. pertaining to or resembling the dawn

2. rosy

（ *Aurora* 是曙光女神）

The darkness waned and a faint *auroral* glow began to appear in the east.
黑暗接近尾聲，而一道微弱的曙光開始從東方出現。

# bacchanalian〔ˌbækə'nelɪən 〕*adj.* 飲酒狂歡的

—— jovial or wild with drunkenness

（ *Bacchus* 是酒神）

Bacchus

At 2 A.M. the neighbors called the police to quell the *bacchanalian* revelry in the upstairs apartment.

清晨兩點，鄰居們叫警察來制止公寓樓上的飲酒狂歡。

# chimerical〔kə'mɪrɪk!〕adj. 荒誕不經的；幻想的

—— fantastic; unreal; impossible; absurd

（*Chimera* 是獅頭、羊身、蛇尾能吐火的怪獸）

Chimera

At first, Robert Fulton's plans for his steamboat were derided as *chimerical* nonsense.

起初，羅伯特‧富爾頓的汽船計畫被嘲笑爲荒誕無聊的事。

# Draconian〔drə'konɪən〕adj. 嚴苛的

—— cruel; harsh; severe

（*Draco* 是希臘立法者，草擬了嚴峻的法典）

The dictator took *Draconian* measures against those he suspected of plotting a rebellion.

獨裁者以嚴苛的手段來對付那些他懷疑陰謀反叛的人。

# Elysian〔ɪ'lɪʒɪən〕adj. 極樂的；快樂的

—— delightful; blissful; heavenly

（*Elysium* 是神話中勇敢及善良的人死後安居的樂土）

Students studying for final examinations yearn for the *Elysian* idleness of the summer vacation.

正在讀書準備期末考的學生，渴望著閒逸快樂的暑假。

# hector〔'hɛktɚ〕v. 1. 欺凌；威嚇　2. 咆哮

—— 1. bully; intimidate with threats　2. bluster

（*Hector* 是特洛伊人中最勇敢者）

Hector

The picketers did not allow themselves to be provoked, despite the unruly crowds that gathered to *hector* them. 罷工時的糾察隊員不允許自己被激怒，即使那些蠻橫的群衆集結去威嚇他們。

# Herculean〔ˌhɝkjə'liən〕*adj.* 1. 非常困難的　2. 需要大力氣的

—— 1. very difficult

2. having or requiring the strength of Hercules

（*Hercules* 是一位有超人力量的英雄）

Hercules

Among the *Herculean* tasks confronting large cities are slum
clearance and traffic control.

大城市所面臨極困難的工作中，包含清除貧民窟和管制交通。

# hermetic〔hɝ'mɛtɪk〕*adj.* 密封的

—— airtight

（*Hermes* 除商業、辯才等其他的象徵外，還是魔法之神）

Dad had to break the *hermetic* seal to get a pill from the new
bottle. 父親必須打開密封的封口，從新瓶中拿出一顆藥丸。

# iridescent〔ˌɪrə'dɛsn̩t〕*adj.* 彩虹色的

—— having colors like the rainbow

（*Iris* 是彩虹女神）

Iris

Children enjoy blowing *iridescent* soap bubbles from pipes.

孩子們喜歡從管中吹出彩虹色的肥皂泡泡。

# jovial〔'dʒovɪəl〕*adj.* 快樂的

—— jolly; merry; good-humored

（*Jove* 又稱 *Jupiter* 即木星，傳說在其影響力下出生者天性愉快）

Our *jovial* host entertained us with several amusing anecdotes
about his employer.

我們快樂的主人用幾則有關他老闆的趣聞來娛樂我們。

# labyrinthine〔ˌlæbə'rɪnθɪn〕*adj.* 1. 像迷宮的　2. 複雜的

—— 1. full of confusing passageways; intricate

2. complicated, like the Labyrinth

（*Labyrinth* 是建築在克里特的迷宮）

Out-of-towners may easily lose their way in New York City's
*labyrinthine* subway passages.
外地人可能很容易就在紐約市如迷宮般的地鐵線中迷失。

**laconic** 〔 lə'kɑnɪk 〕 *adj.* 簡明的
—— using words sparingly; terse; concise
　　（ *Lakonikos* 是斯巴達人之意，而斯巴達人以簡明出名 ）
All I received in response to my request was the *laconic* reply
"Wait." 我的要求所獲得的反應只是簡明的回答：「等。」

**lethargic** 〔 lɪ'θɑrdʒɪk 〕 *adj.* 昏睡的；無精打采的；懶洋洋的
—— unnaturally drowsy; sluggish; dull
　　（ *Lethe* 是陰間的一條河，如果人飲其水就會忘掉過去的一切 ）
For several hours after the operation the patient was *lethargic*
because of the anesthetic. 手術後幾小時，病人因麻醉藥而昏睡著。

**Lucullan** 〔 lu'kʌlən 〕 *adj.* ( 食物 ) 豐盛的；豪華的；奢華的
—— sumptuous; luxurious
　　（ *Lucullus* 是一位舉辦豪華宴會的羅馬人 ）
Thanksgiving dinner at Grandmother's is a virtual *Lucullan* feast.
祖母家的感恩節晚餐眞的是豪奢的盛宴。

**martial**[5] 〔 'mɑrʃəl 〕 *adj.* 好戰的
—— pertaining to war; warlike
　　（ *Mars* 是戰神 ）

> 【記憶技巧】
> martial 這個字源自
> Mars ( 戰神 )。

The Helvetians were a *martial* people who tried to conquer
southern Gaul. 赫爾維希亞人是一個好戰的民族，嘗試征服南方的高盧。

**mentor** 〔 'mɛntor 〕 *n.* 1. 顧問；良師　2. 體育教練
—— 1. wise and trusted adviser
　　　2. athletic coach

第五章

（ *Mentor* 是奧德賽斯的忠實朋友，而且奧德賽斯還委託 Mentor 教導他的兒子）

The retiring foreman was persuaded to stay on for a month as *mentor* to his successor.

退休的領班被勸留下一個月，做繼任者的顧問。

**mercurial**〔 mɝˈkjʊrɪəl 〕*adj.* 1. 活潑的；敏捷的　2. 易變的；反覆無常的　3. 含汞的

—— 1. quick; vivacious　2. changeable　3. containing mercury

（ *Mercury* 是眾神的使者，也是商業、魔法、辯才之神，另外還是旅行者、歹徒、小偷的守護神。它的名字代表一個行星（水星），也代表一種金屬，即水銀）

The older partner is rather dull and morose, but the younger has a *mercurial* temperament that appeals to customers. 較年長的合夥人相當遲鈍難侍候，但那個較年輕的個性卻相當活潑，常討顧客們歡心。

**myrmidon**〔ˈmɝməˌdɑn 〕*n.* 部下；忠實的追隨者

—— obedient and unquestioning follower

（ *Myrmidons* 是一支驍勇善戰的部族，曾伴隨阿奇里斯參加特洛伊戰爭）

The dictator surrounded himself with *myrmidons* who would loyally and pitilessly execute all orders.

那個獨裁者有一些能忠實地、毫不留情執行命令的部下在他周圍。

**nemesis**〔ˈnɛməsɪs 〕*n.* 1. 天譴；報應　2. 強敵

—— 1. due punishment for evil deeds
　　2. one who inflicts such punishment
　　（ *Nemesis* 是復仇女神）

Nemesis

Napoleon crushed many opponents, but Wellington proved to be his *nemesis*. 拿破崙征服了許多對手，但威靈頓最後成為他的強敵。

**odyssey**〔'ɑdəsɪ〕*n.* 長期的旅行

—— any long series of wanderings or travels

（*Odyssey* 是有關奧德賽在特洛伊戰爭後，十年流浪返鄉的史詩）

Your travel agent will gladly plan a year's *odyssey* to places of interest around the world. 你的旅行代辦人將會很樂意為你計劃一年的旅行，到世界各地有趣的地方。

**paean**〔'piən〕*n.* 頌歌

—— song or hymn of praise, joy, or triumph

（*paean* 是讚美阿波羅的頌歌）

When the victory was announced, people danced in the streets and sang *paeans* of joy.

當宣布勝利後，人們在街上跳著舞，並唱著歡樂的頌歌。

**palladium**〔pə'ledɪəm〕*n.* 守護神；保障

Palladium

—— safeguard or protection

（*Palladium* 是佩拉斯・雅典娜 —— 特洛伊城保護女神的雕像）

The little girl habitually fell asleep clutching a battered doll, her *palladium*. 那小女孩習慣抱一個破舊的娃娃入睡，那是她的守護神。

**panic**[3]〔'pænɪk〕*n.* 驚慌

—— unreasoning, sudden fright that grips a multitude

（*Pan* 是恐慌之神）

A *panic* ensued when someone in the crowded auditorium yelled "Fire!" 當有人在擁擠的大禮堂中大喊「失火！」時，一陣驚慌隨之而起。

**philippic**〔fə'lɪpɪk〕*n.* 漫罵演說；猛烈的抨擊

—— bitter denunciation

（*Philippics* 是狄摩西尼斯所發表攻擊馬其頓菲利普王的演說）

In an hour-long *philippic*, the legislator denounced the lobbyists opposing his bill.

在一小時的漫罵演說中，立法者抨擊遊說者反對他的法案。

第五章

**plutocratic**〔͵plutə'krætɪk〕*adj.* 富豪的；財閥的
—— having great influence because of one's wealth
（*Plutus* 是財富之神）
A handful of *plutocratic* investors, each owning more than a
thousand shares, determined the policies of the corporation. 少數有
錢的投資者，他們每一個人都擁有超過一千股，決定著公司政策的方針。

**procrustean**〔pro'krʌstɪən〕*adj.* 用暴力使人合乎規定的；
強求一致的
—— cruel or inflexible in enforcing conformity
（*Procrustes* 是一個強盜，抓到受害者後會拉長他們的身體或砍掉
腿以配合他床舖的長度）
The martinet governed his classroom with *procrustean* discipline,
assigning a week's detention to all offenders, no matter what the
offense. 訓練嚴格的軍人以硬性規定來管理他的班級，規定不管觸犯什
麼，只要是違規者都要拘留一星期。

**protean**〔pro'tiən〕*adj.* 1. 變化多端的；反覆無常的
2. 變化自如的
—— 1. exceedingly variable
2. readily assuming different forms or shapes
（*Proteus* 是海神，能隨意變換形狀以困惑他的俘虜）

Proteus

The witness's *protean* tactics under cross-examination gave the
impression that he was untrustworthy.
在嚴密詢問下，證人反覆無常的策略給人的印象是他不可靠。

**Pyrrhic**〔'pɪrɪk〕*adj.* 付出慘痛代價的；犧牲重大的
—— ruinous; gained at too great a cost
（*Pyrrhus* 是希臘的一位國王，在打敗羅馬人的戰役中損失慘重）
Our winning the opening game was a *Pyrrhic* victory, as our
leading scorer was seriously injured. 我們贏得公開賽是一場犧牲
重大所獲得的勝利，因為我們主要得分員受了很嚴重的傷。

**saturnine**〔ˈsætəˌnaɪn〕*adj.* 沉默寡言的；陰沉的
—— taciturn; gloomy; morose
（ *Saturn* 是 Jupiter 之父，雖然傳說中他的統治期是黃金時代，可是煉丹家與天文學家把他的名字與鉛金屬相聯結，因而成為笨重與遲鈍的象徵）

My former roommate was a *saturnine* scholar who said very little and smiled rarely.
我之前的室友是一位沉默寡言的學者，他很少說話也很少笑。

**siren**[6]〔ˈsaɪrən〕*n.* 1. 迷人的女人；妖婦　2. 歌聲美妙的女子　3. 汽笛；警報器
—— 1. dangerous, attractive woman
　　2. a woman who sings sweetly
　　3. apparatus for sounding loud warnings

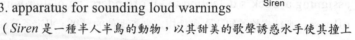
Siren

（ *Siren* 是一種半人半鳥的動物，以其甜美的歌聲誘惑水手使其撞上岩石而死亡）

The enemy employed a red-haired *siren* as a spy.
敵方雇用了一名紅髮美女作間諜。

**solon**〔ˈsolən〕*n.* 1. 議員　2. 賢人
—— 1. legislator　2. wise man
（ *Solon* 為著名的雅典立法者）

Solon

Next week the *solons* will return to the capital for the opening of the legislature. 下星期因為議會開始，議員會回到首都。

**stentorian**〔stɛnˈtorɪən〕*adj.* 大聲的；（嗓音）洪亮的
—— very loud
（ *Stentor* 是傳說中一位大聲的傳令官，其音量相當於五十個人）

Speak softly; you don't need a *stentorian* voice to be heard in this small room.
說話輕柔點；在這小房間裡你不需要這麼大聲就能被聽見。

**Stygian**〔'stɪdʒɪən〕*adj.* 陰森森的；黑暗的

—— infernal; dark; gloomy（*Styx* 是地獄裏的一條河）

A power failure at 11:03 P.M. plunged the city into *Stygian* blackness. 晚上十一時三分停電，使全市陷入陰森森的黑暗中。

**tantalize**〔'tæntl̩ˌaɪz〕*v.* 1. 使可望而不可及　2. 逗弄

—— 1. excite a hope but prevent its fulfillment　2. tease

（*Tantalus* 因為洩漏天機被罰站在陰府裡，雖然又餓又渴，食物和水又近在眼前，但卻怎樣也拿不到）

The considerate hostess removed the strawberry shortcake from the table so as not to *tantalize* her weight-conscious guest. 體貼心細的女主人將草莓奶油甜酥餅從桌上移走，使她擔心體重的客人不會因看著吃不著而難受。

**terpsichorean**〔ˌtɝpsɪkə'riən〕*adj.* 舞蹈的

—— pertaining to dancing

（*Terpsichore* 是傳說中希臘九女神裡主掌舞蹈的）

Terpsichore

The reviewers lauded the ballet troupe for its *terpsichorean* artistry. 評論家稱讚芭蕾舞蹈團員的舞蹈藝術。

**thespian**〔'θɛspɪən〕*adj.* 戲劇的

—— pertaining to drama or acting（*Thespis* 號稱希臘的戲劇之父）

If you enjoy acting in plays, join your school's *thespian* club. 如果你喜歡戲劇表演，就加入你學校的戲劇社。

**titanic**〔taɪ'tænɪk〕*adj.* 巨大的

—— of enormous strength, size, or power

（*Titans* 是被宙斯擊敗的一些不守法又力大無窮的巨人）

Titan

By a *titanic* effort, our football team won the victory. 藉著很大的努力，我們的橄欖球隊贏得勝利。

第五章

# REVIEW ★

Exercise 1：選出正確答案

( ) 1. Photographs of _____ celebrities decorated the walls of the dance studio.
   (A) operatic      (B) invisible      (C) thespian
   (D) sluggish      (E) terpsichorean

( ) 2. The wrestler's _____ maneuvers made it difficult for his opponent to obtain a hold.
   (A) hermetic      (B) protean      (C) titanic
   (D) procrustean      (E) philippic

( ) 3. In a locker-room speech between halves, the _____ reaffirmed his confidence in his _____.
   (A) conductor…myrmidons      (B) amazon…team
   (C) myrmidon…adherents      (D) conductor…mentors
   (E) coach…squad

( ) 4. Many literary works describe a paradise where the _____ dwell in _____ repose.
   (A) heroic…Stygian      (B) nemeses…stygian
   (C) sirens…abject      (D) perfidious…ambrosial
   (E) brave…Elysian

( ) 5. When people become _____, their ability to reason gives way to fear.
   (A) lethargic      (B) saturnine      (C) panicky
   (D) Draconian      (E) plutocratic

第五章

( ) 6. The audience laughed to see the corpulent actor _____ by his puny companion's hectoring.
   (A) convinced     (B) betrayed     (C) tripped
   (D) intimidated     (E) encouraged

( ) 7. The Pyrrhic victory was cause for widespread _____.
   (A) dejection     (B) optimism     (C) paeans
   (D) satisfaction     (E) promotions

( ) 8. Only a person with a _____ voice could have made himself heard above the din of the angry crowd.
   (A) Herculean     (B) stentorian     (C) jovial
   (D) laconic     (E) titanic

( ) 9. Our _____ host always enjoys having friends over to share his Lucullan suppers.
   (A) cursive     (B) martial     (C) fractious
   (D) convivial     (E) sanguine

( ) 10. Psychoanalysis can help a patient recall long-forgotten experiences lost in the _____ recesses of his mind.
   (A) labyrinthine     (B) chimerical     (C) iridescent
   (D) auroral     (E) mercurial

Exercise 2：下列各題中，選出與斜體字意義最相近的答案。

( ) 1. *Ambrosial* fare
   (A) expensive          (B) cut-rate
   (C) railroad          (D) delicious

( ) 2. Unemployed *thespians*
   (A) musicians     (B) actors     (C) dancers     (D) loafers

第
五
章

(   ) 3. *Martial* airs

     (A) matrimonial       (B) tuneful

     (C) military       (D) soothing

(   ) 4. Impassioned *philippic*

     (A) plea       (B) message

     (C) praise       (D) denunciation

(   ) 5. *Plutocratic* associates

     (A) loyal and wealthy       (B) jovial

     (C) carefree       (D) rich and influential

(   ) 6. *Draconian* laws

     (A) democratic       (B) severe

     (C) unpopular       (D) unenforced

(   ) 7. *Hermetic* compartments

     (A) rigid       (B) tiny

     (C) airtight       (D) labyrinthine

(   ) 8. Road *atlas*

     (A) highwayman       (B) map collection

     (C) network       (D) blind alley

(   ) 9. Endless *odyssey*

     (A) story       (B) wanderings

     (C) sufferings       (D) errands

(   ) 10. A new *Adonis*

     (A) lover       (B) movie actor

     (C) myrmidon       (D) handsome youth

第五章

## Exercise 3：類比

( ) 1. SOLON : LAWS
(A) atlas : maps (B) ruler : subjects
(C) philosopher : credentials
(D) craftsman : trade (E) composer : operas

( ) 2. SIREN : BEAUTY
(A) victim : trap (B) temptress : prey
(C) hunter : bait (D) alarm : confidence
(E) worm : fish

( ) 3. TANTALIZE : SATISFY
(A) Elysian : blissful
(B) encomium : commendation
(C) rainbow : iridescent (D) agree : differ
(E) delay : postpone

( ) 4. NEMESIS : EVILDOER
(A) avenger : victim (B) retribution : wrongdoer
(C) punishment : benefactor
(D) justice : donator (E) reward : enemy

( ) 5. AMAZON : STRENGTH
(A) comedienne : humor (B) river : jungle
(C) nurse : invalid (D) warrior : civilian
(E) servant : indifference

( ) 6. PALLADIUM : DANGER
(A) rumor : panic (B) arena : excitement
(C) investigation : truth (D) experience : skill
(E) rain : drought

第五章

(　　) 7. MERCURIAL : VIVACITY

    (A) procrustean : rigidity　　(B) protean : uniformity

    (C) ethereal : earth　　(D) saturnine : hilarity

    (E) ambrosial : dawn

(　　) 8. PAEAN : ECSTASY

    (A) anthem : nation　　(B) suffering : rejoicing

    (C) lament : sorrow　　(D) sadness : joy

    (E) hymn : congregation

(　　) 9. THESPIAN : TERPSICHOREAN

    (A) painting : ballet　　(B) oratory : music

    (C) acting : sculpture　　(D) drama : dancing

    (E) composing : singing

(　　) 10. AURORAL : DAY

    (A) overture : opera　　(B) infantile : human being

    (C) preface : book　　(D) introductory : conclusion

    (E) tadpole : frog

---

**【解答】**

| | | | | | | | | |
|---|---|---|---|---|---|---|---|---|
| **Ex 1.** | 1. E | 2. B | 3. E | 4. E | 5. C | 6. D | 7. A | 8. B |
| | 9. D | 10. A | | | | | | |
| **Ex 2.** | 1. D | 2. B | 3. C | 4. D | 5. D | 6. B | 7. C | 8. B |
| | 9. B | 10. D | | | | | | |
| **Ex 3.** | 1. E | 2. C | 3. D | 4. B | 5. A | 6. E | 7. A | 8. C |
| | 9. D | 10. B | | | | | | |

第五章

# 第六章
# 出自法文的英文字彙

英文在採用有用的法文字時，從沒遲疑過。任何法文辭句只要比類似的英文辭句更能表達思想，就遲早會被併入英文。這過程幾世紀來一直在進行。

本章教你如何用一些更重要的法文字和辭句，它們是有教養的人應該知道的。

## 【Group 1】

## 描述人的字

Group 1～10

**au courant**〔 oku'rã 〕 *adj.* 熟知時事的；趕上時代的
—— well-informed; up-to-date
By reading reviews, you can keep *au courant* with new developments in literature, films, television, and the theater. 你讀評論可熟知文學、電影‧電視，和戲劇等的新發展。

**blasé**〔 blɑ'ze , 'blɑze 〕 *adj.* 厭於享樂的
—— tired of pleasures; bored
Edna has been attending too many parties during the holidays; she appears *blasé*. 愛德娜在假日已經參加了太多派對，她似乎厭倦了享樂。

**chic**〔 ʃik , ʃɪk 〕 *adj.* 時髦的
—— stylish
She looked very *chic* in her new hat. 她戴著新帽子看起來很時髦。

**debonair** [ˌdɛbəˈnɛr] *adj.* 溫文有禮的；風度翩翩的；快樂的

—— affable and courteous; gay; pleasant

The headwaiter was *debonair* with the guests but firm with the waiters. 領班對客人溫文有禮，但是對服務生卻很嚴厲。

**maladroit** [ˌmæləˈdrɔɪt] *adj.* 笨拙的（↔ adroit）

—— unskillful; clumsy

Our new supervisor is clever in matters in which his predecessor was *maladroit*.

我們新的主管在他前任做得笨拙的事上很聰明。

**naive**[5] [nɑˈiv] *adj.* 天眞的；質樸的

—— simple in nature; artless; ingenuous

【記憶技巧】

naive 是法文，所以發音很特別。

You are *naive* if you believe implacable foes can be reconciled easily. 如果你認爲殘忍的敵人能輕易和解，那麼你就太天眞了。

**nonchalant** [ˈnɑnʃələnt] *adj.* 漠不關心的；不在乎的

—— without concern or enthusiasm; indifferent

I am amazed that you can be so *nonchalant* about the coming test when everyone else is so worried.

每個人都擔心即將來臨的考試時，你卻毫不在乎，眞令我驚訝。

Exercise：請由 **Group 1** 中，選出最適當的字，填入空格中。

1. Some advertising is so exaggerated that only a(n) _____ person would believe it

2. If every meal were a banquet, we should all soon become _____, bored with even the most delicious food.

3. Read a good daily newspaper to keep _____ with what is going on in the world.

4. The cuts on the teenager's face showed that he was still _____ in the use of his razor.

5. Unlike his discourteous predecessor, the new service manager is quite _____.

---

【解答】

1. naive          2. blasé          3. au courant
4. maladroit      5. debonair

---

## 【Group 2】

# 表示人的字

**attaché** 〔͵ætə'ʃe , ə'tæʃe〕 *n.*（大使或公使的）隨員；大使館或公使館的館員

—— member of the diplomatic staff of an ambassador or minister

We were unable to see the ambassador, but we spoke to one of the *attachés*.

我們見不到大使，但是跟一位大使的隨員談話。

**bourgeoisie** 〔͵burʒwɑ'zi〕 *n.* 中產階級

—— the middle class

A virile *bourgeoisie* contributes to a nation's prosperity.

強而有力的中產階級促進國家的繁榮。

**chargé d'affaires** 〔ʃɑr'ʒedæ'fɛr〕 *n.* 代理大使

—— temporary substitute for an ambassador

Whom did the President designate as *chargé d'affaires* when he recalled the ambassador? 總統把大使召回後，指派誰爲代理大使？

## connoisseur 〔͵kɑnə'sɜ , -'sjur 〕 *n.* 鑑定家；鑑賞家；行家

—— expert; critical judge

To verify the gem's value, we consulted a *connoisseur* of rare diamonds. 爲了鑑定珠寶的價值，我們請教一位稀有鑽石的鑑定家。

## coterie 〔'kotərɪ 〕 *n.* （有共同興趣、常排外的）小圈子；小集團

—— set or circle of acquaintances; clique

Helen won't bowl with us; she has her own *coterie* of bowling friends. 海倫不會跟我們打保齡球；她自己有一群打保齡球的朋友。

## debutante 〔͵dɛbju'tɑnt , 'dɛbjə͵tænt 〕 *n.* 初次進入社交界的少女

—— girl who has just made her debut (formal entrance into society)

The *debutante's* photograph was at the head of the society page. 那位初次進入社交界的少女的照片登在社會版的最上頭。

## devotee 〔͵dɛvə'ti 〕 *n.* 狂熱者；獻身者；熱愛者

—— ardent adherent; partisan

Samuel Adams was a passionate *devotee* of American independence. 山繆・亞當斯熱情獻身於美國獨立。

Samuel Adams

## elite[6] 〔 ɪ'lit , e'lit 〕 *n.* 精英份子

—— group of superior individuals; aristocracy; choice part

Fred likes to consider himself a member of the intellectual *elite*. 弗瑞德喜歡自認爲是知識精英份子。

## émigré 〔͵emi'gre 〕 *n.* 逃難者；流亡者

—— refugee

A committee was formed to find housing and employment for the anxious *émigrés*.

一個為焦慮的難民找尋住屋及工作機會的委員會成立了。

## entrepreneur〔͵ɑntrəprə'nɝ〕*n.* 企業家

—— one who assumes the risks and management of a business

What *entrepreneur* will invest his capital unless there is some prospect of a profit?

除非有利可圖，否則有那位企業家肯投下他的資本呢？

## envoy〔'ɛnvɔɪ〕*n.* 1. 使者 2. 公使

—— 1. messenger
2. diplomatic agent

The President's *envoy* to the conference has not yet been chosen.

總統參加會議的使者尚未選出。

## fiancé[5]〔͵fiən'se , fi͵ɑn'se , fi'ɑnse〕*n.* 未婚夫

—— person engaged to be married

Madeline introduced Mr. Cole as her *fiancé*.

瑪德蓮介紹她的未婚夫柯爾先生。

## gendarme〔'ʒɑndɑrm〕*n.* 憲兵

—— policeman with military training

The chargé d'affaires requested that extra *gendarmes* be posted outside the embassy.

代理大使要求在大使館外佈署額外的憲兵。

## ingénue〔æʒe'ny〕*n.* 1. 天真無邪的女子

2. 扮演清純少女的女演員

—— 1. naive young woman
2. actress playing the role of a naive young woman

She was as simple and pretty as a film *ingénue*.

她天眞、美麗有如電影中清純玉女的典型。

## maître d'hôtel（ˈmɛtrə doˈtɛl）*n.* 服務生領班

—— headwaiter

The *maître d'hôtel* supervises the waiters.

服務生領班監督服務生。

## martinet（ˌmɑrtn̩ˈɛt , ˈmɑrtn̩ˌɛt）*n.* 厲行嚴格紀律的人

—— person who enforces very strict discipline

Our dean is an understanding counselor, not a *martinet*.

我們的學院院長是一位善解人意的好顧問，而非厲行嚴格紀律者。

## nouveaux riches（ˌnuvoˈriʃ）*n. pl.* 暴發戶

—— persons newly rich

An unexpected inheritance catapulted him into the ranks of the *nouveaux riches*. 一筆意外的遺產使他晉身爲暴發戶之列。

## protégé（ˈprotəˌʒe , ˌprotəˈʒe）*n.* 被保護者

—— person under the care and protection of another

He is a *protégé* of the governor. 他受到州長的保護。

## raconteur（ˌrækɑnˈtɝ）*n.* 擅長講故事的人

—— person who excels in telling stories, anecdotes, etc.

Mark Twain was an excellent *raconteur*.

馬克・吐溫擅長說故事。

Mark Twain

Exercise：請由 **Group 2** 中，選出最適當的字，填入空格中。

1. Rita's engagement was nearly broken when she quarreled with her _____.

2. Between the nobles on one extreme and the peasants on the other, a middle class known as the _____ emerged.

3. Bill can relate an anecdote better than I; he is a fine _____.

4. Though the Allens are friendly to everyone, they have rarely visited with anyone outside their tightly knit _____.

5. Anyone who flees his native land to escape political oppression is a(n) _____.

---

【解答】

1. fiancé　　　2. bourgeoisie　　3. raconteur
4. coterie　　　5. émigré

---

## 【Group 3】

# 與人的特性或情感有關的字

**éclat**〔ɪ'klɑ , e'klɑ〕*n.* 輝煌的成就；喝采

—— brilliancy of achievement

The violinist performed with great *éclat*.

那小提琴家在大聲的喝采中完成演出。

**élan**〔e'lɑ̃〕*n.* 熱心；熱忱；活力

—— enthusiasm; eagerness for action

Because the cast had rehearsed with such *élan*, the director had few apprehensions about the opening-night performance.

因為演員們都很熱心地排演，導演不大擔心首演之夜的演出。

**ennui**〔'ɑnwi , ɑ̃'nyi〕*n.* 無聊；倦怠

—— feeling of weariness and discontent; boredom; tedium

You too would suffer from *ennui* if you had to spend months in a hospital bed.

如果你必須在醫院的病床上躺好幾個月，那麼你也會感到無聊的。

## esprit de corps 〔 ε‚sprɪdəˈkor , -ˈkɔr 〕 *n.* 團隊精神

—— feeling of union and common interest pervading a group; devotion to a group or to its ideals

The employees showed extraordinary *esprit de corps* when they volunteered to work Saturdays for the duration of the crisis.

員工們自願在星期六工作以度過危機期，顯示出無比的團隊精神。

## finesse 〔 fəˈnɛs 〕 *n.* 手法

—— skill

The adroit prosecutor arranged his questions with admirable *finesse*.

那精明的檢察官以令人讚賞的手法安排他的問題。

## legerdemain 〔‚lɛdʒədɪˈmen 〕 *n.* 戲法；詐術

—— sleight of hand; artful trick

By a feat of *legerdemain*, the magician produced a rabbit from his hat. 魔術師利用戲法從帽子裡變出一隻兔子來。

## malaise 〔 mæˈlez 〕 *n.* 不舒服

—— vague feeling of bodily discomfort or illness

After the heavy, late supper, he experienced a feeling of *malaise*.

在吃過油膩、難消化的很晚的晚餐後，他感到不舒服。

## noblesse oblige 〔 noˈblɛsoˈbliʒ , nɔˈblɛsɔˈbliʒ 〕 *n.* 地位高則責任重；貴族義務

—— principle that persons of high rank or birth are obliged to act nobly

In the olden days, kings and other nobles, observing the principle of *noblesse oblige*, fought at the head of their troops. 昔日國王及其他的貴族們得遵守地位高則責任重的原則，於戰役中身先士卒。

## rapport〔 ræ'port , -'pɔrt 〕*n.* 關係

—— relationship characterized by harmony, conformity, or affinity

A common interest in gardening brought Molly and Loretta into closer *rapport.* 對園藝共同的愛好使茉莉及羅莉塔關係更密切。

## sangfroid〔 sɑ̃'frwɑ 〕*n.* 沉著；冷靜

—— coolness of mind or composure in difficult circumstances; equanimity

He played the game with perfect *sangfroid.* 他比賽時十分冷靜。

## savoir faire〔'sævwɑr'fɛr 〕*n.* 機智；隨機應變的才能

—— knowledge of just what to do; tact

You need both capital and *savoir faire* to be a successful entrepreneur. 想成為一位成功的企業家需要資本及機智。

Exercise：請由 **Group 3** 中，選出最適當的字，填入空格中。

1. Joel is tactful; he has plenty of _____.

2. Your physician may help you to obtain some relief from the _____ that accompanies a severe cold.

3. Instead of reducing his subordinates' salaries, the executive acted more nobly by cutting his own compensation substantially, in accordance with the principle of _____.

4. To do card tricks, you have to be good at _____.

第六章

5. If you get tired and bored on long train trips, try reading detective stories; they help to overcome _____.

【解答】
1. savoir faire 　　 2. malaise
3. noblesse oblige 　 4. legerdemain 　 5. ennui

## 【Group 4】

# 與説和寫有關的字

**adieu** 〔 ə'dju , ə'du 〕*n.* 再見

—— good-by; farewell

On commencement day we shall bid *adieu* to our alma mater.
畢業典禮那天，我們得跟母校說再見。

**au revoir** 〔,orə'vwɑr , ,orə'vɔr 〕*n.* 再見

—— good-by till we meet again

Since I hope to see you again, I'll say *au revoir* rather than adieu.
我希望能再見到你，所以我會說後會有期而不是再見。

**billet-doux** 〔'bɪlɪ'du 〕*n.* 情書

—— love letter

A timely *billet-doux* can patch up a lovers' quarrel.
一封適時的情書可以平息情侶間的爭吵。

**bon mot** 〔 bɔ̃'mo 〕*n.* 珠璣妙語；雋語

—— clever saying; witty remark

He often made us roar with laughter with a well-placed *bon mot*.
他經常以恰到好處的珠璣妙語使我們哄堂大笑。

**brochure**[6] 〔 bro'ʃur 〕 *n.* 小冊子

—— pamphlet; booklet

This helpful *brochure* explains social security benefits.
這本有用的小冊子解釋社會安全制度的好處。

**canard** 〔 kə'nɑrd 〕 *n.* 謠言;妄傳

—— false rumor; absurd story; hoax

It took a public appearance by the monarch to silence the *canard*
that he had been assassinated.
帝王出現於公衆之前,以平息他已被暗殺的謠言。

**cliché** 〔 kli'ʃe 〕 *n.* 陳腔濫調

—— trite or worn-out expression

Two *clichés* that we can easily do without are: "first and foremost"
and "last but not least." 兩種我們可以輕易不用的陳腔濫調是:「最先
也是最重要的是」及「最後但非最不重要的是」。

**entre nous** 〔 ɑ̃trə'nu 〕 *adv.* 不要跟別人說;只限我們兩人之間;
祕密地

—— between us; confidentially

The juniors expect to win, but, *entre nous*, their chances are not too
good. 三年級的學生想贏,但是你不要跟別人說喔,他們贏的機會不大。

**mot juste** 〔 mo'ʒyst 〕 *n.* 適當的字眼

—— the exactly right word

To improve your writing, try to find the *mot juste* for each idea
and avoid clichés. 爲了改進你的寫作,試著去找適當的字眼表達每一
個想法,避免陳腔濫調。

**précis** 〔 pre'si , 'presi 〕 *n.* 大綱;摘要

—— brief summary

Include only the essential points when you write a *précis*.
寫大綱的時候，只要把重點包括進去就可以。

## repartee 〔͵rɛpɚˈti 〕 *n.* 敏捷的應對

——— skill of replying quickly, cleverly, and humorously; witty reply

James Boswell admired Samuel Johnson's power of *repartee*.
詹姆斯・包斯威爾欽佩山繆・強森敏捷的應對能力。

## résumé[5] 〔͵rɛzʊˈme , ͵rɛzjʊˈme 〕 *n.* 摘要；履歷表

——— summary

The instructor asked for a *résumé* of the last lesson.
講師要求寫最後一課的摘要。

## riposte 〔 rɪˈpost 〕 *n.* 1. 機敏的應答；尖銳的反駁

2.【劍術】擋後還擊

——— 1. quick retort or repartee

    2. in fencing, a quick return thrust after a parry

Surprised to see him eating the apple core, I asked, "Won't it affect you?" "Pleasurably," was his *riposte*. 我看到他在吃蘋果核感到很驚訝，就問他：「這不會傷害你嗎？」他很機敏地回我說：「愉快的很。」

## tête-à-tête 〔ˈtetəˈtet 〕 *n.* 密談

——— private conversation between two persons

Before answering, the witness had a *tête-à-tête* with his attorney.
在回答問題以前，證人先與他的律師密談一番。

Exercise：請由 **Group 4** 中，選出最適當的字，填入空格中。

1. There are valuable hints on safe driving in this sixteen-page

    —————.

第
六
章

2. The expression "old as the hills" should be avoided because it is a(n) _____.

3. Investigation proved that the story was unfounded; it was just a(n) _____.

4. The manager went out to the mound for a brief _____ with his faltering pitcher.

5. Everyone supposes this diamond is genuine but, _____, it's only an imitation.

---

【解答】

1. brochure     2. cliché     3. canard

4. tête-à-tête     5. entre nous

---

## 【Group 5】

# 與情勢有關的字

**bête noire**〔ˌbɛtˈnwɑr〕*n.* 令人恐懼的人或事物

—— dreaded object or person; bugbear

She enjoyed all her subjects except mathematics, her *bête noire*.

她喜歡所有的科目，數學除外，那是她最怕的一科。

**carte blanche**〔ˈkɑrtˈblɑnʃ〕*n.* 全權；絕對的自主權

—— complete freedom to do something

The employer gave his secretary *carte blanche* in managing the routine affairs of the office.

雇主全權委託他的祕書處理辦公室的例行事務。

第
六
章

**cause célèbre** (ˈkoz͵seˈlɛbṛ ) *n.* 轟動一時的案件；有名的案例

—— famous case in law that arouses considerable interest; an incident or situation attracting much attention

The trial of John Peter Zenger, a *cause célèbre* in the eighteenth century, helped to establish freedom of the press in America.

約翰・彼德・山格的審判，一件在十八世紀轟動一時的案件，有助於建立美國的新聞自由。

**cul-de-sac** (ˈkʌldəˈsæk , ˈkʊl- ) *n.* 死路；死巷

—— blind alley

The house is located on a quiet *cul-de-sac*.

那個房子位於一條安靜的死巷。

**debacle** ( deˈbɑkl̩ , dɪ- , -ˈbækl̩ ) *n.* 慘敗；崩潰；垮台

—— complete failure; collapse; overthrow; rout

The *debacle* at Waterloo signaled the end of Napoleon's power.

滑鐵盧的慘敗象徵拿破崙政權的結束。

**fait accompli** (͵fɛtakõˈpli) *n.* 既成事實

—— thing accomplished and presumably irrevocable

Since Mother couldn't decide whether or not to buy the dress for me, I planned to buy it myself and present her with a *fait accompli*.

因為母親不能決定要不要買那件洋裝給我，我打算自己買下來，把既成的事實擺在她面前。

**faux pas** (͵foˈpɑ ) *n.* 失禮；失言

—— misstep or blunder in conduct, manners, speech, etc.

However, it turned out to be a *faux pas*, as Mother was quite offended.

然而，這件事變成一件很失禮的事，因為媽媽相當生氣。

第
六
章

**impasse**〔ɪmˈpæs, ˈɪmpæs〕*n.* 1. 僵局　2. 死路

—— 1. deadlock; predicament affording no escape

　2. impassable road

The foreman reported that the jury could deliberate no further, as
they had reached an *impasse*.

陪審團主席宣告陪審團已鬧成僵局，無法作進一步的商議。

**liaison**〔ˌlieˈzɔ̃〕*n.* 聯絡；接觸

—— bond; linking up

By joining the alumni association, graduates can maintain their
*liaison* with the school. 畢業生可藉著參加校友會，與學校保持聯絡。

**mélange**〔meˈlɑ̃ʒ〕*n.* 混合物；什錦雜燴

—— mixture; medley; potpourri

Our last amateur show was a *mélange* of dramatic skits, acrobatics,
ballet, popular tunes, and classical music. 上一次我們的業餘表演是
戲劇性幽默短劇、特技、芭蕾、流行歌曲，及古典音樂的大雜燴。

**mirage**〔məˈrɑʒ〕*n.* 海市蜃樓

—— optical illusion

The sheet of water we thought we saw on the road ahead turned
out to be only a *mirage*.

我們認為我們看見的前方路上的那一灘水，結果只是海市蜃樓而已。

Exercise：請由 **Group 5** 中，選出最適當的字，填入空格中。

1. Your flippant remark to Mrs. Lee about her ailing son was
　a(n) ————.

2. The inhabitants of the remote Eskimo village had practically
　no ———— with the outside world.

3. Mr. Briggs never concerned himself with hiring or dismissing employees, having given his plant manager _____ in these matters.

4. Despite seventeen hours of continuous deliberations, the weary negotiators still faced a(n) _____ over wages.

5. A(n) _____ is a short street closed at one end, so traffic cannot pass through it.

> 【解答】
>
> 1. faux pas  2. liaison  3. carte blanche
> 4. impasse  5. cul-de-sac

## 【Group 6】

## 與歷史和政府有關的字

**coup d'état** ('kude'ta ) *n.* 政變

—— sudden, violent, or illegal overthrow of a government

Napoleon seized power by a *coup d'état*.

拿破崙以政變的方式奪取政權。

**démarche** ( de'marʃ ) *n.* 策略;行動方針;政策之改變

—— maneuver; course of action, especially one involving a change of policy

Hitler's attack on Russia, shortly after his pact with Stalin, was a stunning *démarche*.

希特勒在與史達林簽約後不久攻擊俄國,是一項令人震驚的政策改變。

**détente** ( de'tɑt ) *n.* 緩和

—— a relaxing, as of strained relations between nations

An effective world disarmament treaty should bring a *détente* in international tensions.
有效的世界裁軍協定將帶來國際緊張情勢的緩和。

## entente〔ɑn'tɑnt, ã'tãt〕*n.* 諒解；協議

—— understanding or agreement between governments

Canada and the United States have a long-standing *entente* on border problems. 加拿大與美國對於邊界問題有長期的協議。

## laissez-faire〔ˌlɛse'fɛr〕*n.* 自由放任政策

—— absence of government interference or regulation

Adam Smith believed a policy of *laissez-faire* toward business would benefit a nation.
亞當·史密斯相信對於企業的自由放任政策會對國家有利。

## lettre de cachet〔'lɛtr̩dəka'ʃe〕*n.* 祕密逮捕令

—— sealed letter obtainable from the King of France (before the Revolution) ordering the imprisonment without trial of the person named in the letter

Dr. Manette was imprisoned through a *lettre de cachet*.
馬奈特醫生因為祕密逮捕令而被囚禁。

## rapprochement〔ˌraˌprɔʃ'mã〕*n.* 建立和睦關係

—— establishment or state of cordial relations

The gradual *rapprochement* between these two nations, long traditional enemies, cheered all Europeans.
素來互相敵對的兩個國家逐漸建立起和睦的關係，使所有的歐洲人都為之興奮。

## régime〔rɪ'ʒim〕*n.* 政權

—— system of government or rule

The coup d'état brought to power a *régime* that restored civil liberties to the oppressed people.

政變使一政權得勢，這政權讓受壓迫的人民重享公民自由。

Exercise：請由 **Group 6** 中，選出最適當的字，填入空格中。

1. Do you favor strict regulation of business or a policy of _____.

2. The tyrannical dictator was eventually overthrown by a(n) _____ effected by a strong military group.

3. The newly elected officials will face many problems left by the outgoing _____.

4. Our Bill of Rights protects us from such tyrannical abuses as were made possible by a(n) _____, a document ordering the imprisonment of a person without a trial.

5. Hopes for world peace rose sharply with reports of a(n) _____ in the strained relations between the two rulers.

---
【解答】

1. laissez-faire　　2. coup d'état　　3. régime
4. lettre de cachet　　5. détente

---

## 【Group 7】

## 與藝術有關的字

**avant-garde**〔 ɑvɑ'gɑrd 〕*n.* 先鋒；前衛（人物）

—— experimentalists or innovators in any art

Walt Whitman was no conservative; his daring innovations in
poetry place him in the *avant-garde* of nineteenth-century writers.
華特‧惠特曼並不保守，他在詩上面的大膽革新使他成為十九世紀的前衛
作家。

## bas-relief〔͵bɑrɪˈlif, ͵bæs-, ˈbɑrɪ͵lif, ˈbæs-〕 *n.* 浮雕

—— carving or sculpture in which the figures project only slightly
    from the background

The ancient Greek Parthenon is famed for its beautiful sculptures
in *bas-relief.* 古希臘的巴特農神殿以其美麗的浮雕雕刻而聞名。

## baton〔bəˈtɑn, ˈbætn̩, bæˈtɔ̃〕 *n.* 指揮棒

—— stick with which a conductor beats time for an orchestra or
    band

A downbeat is the downward stroke of the conductor's *baton,*
denoting the principally accented note of a measure.
強拍就是指揮的指揮棒向下指，表示一小節中主要的強音所在。

## chef d'oeuvre〔ʃeˈdoevrə〕 *n.* 傑作

—— masterpiece in art, literature, etc.

Many connoisseurs regard *Hamlet* as Shakespeare's *chef d'oeuvre.*
許多鑑賞家認為「哈姆雷特」是莎士比亞的傑作。

## denouement〔deˈnumɑ̃, denuˈmɑ̃〕 *n.* 1. 結局　2. 結果

—— 1. solution ("untying") of the plot in a play, story, or complex
      situation; ending

    2. outcome; end

In the *denouement* of *Great Expectations,* we learn that Pip's secret
benefactor is the runaway convict whom Pip had once helped.
在「孤星血淚」的結局裡，我們知道皮普的祕密恩人，就是他曾經幫助過
的那個逃犯。

**encore**〔'aŋkɔr , 'an- , -kor 〕*n.* 安可；再來一次；（應觀眾熱烈要求而）加演

—— repetition of a performance (or the rendition of an additional selection) in response to the demand from an audience

In appreciation of the enthusiastic applause, the vocalist sang an *encore.* 爲了答謝熱情的掌聲，那個聲樂家再唱一曲。

**genre**〔'ʒanrə 〕*n.* 1.（文藝作品之）類型 2. 風俗畫（以日常生活爲題材之寫實畫）

—— 1. kind; sort; category

2. style of painting depicting scenes from everyday life

The literary *genre* to which Poe contributed most is the short story. 愛倫坡最有貢獻的文學類型是短篇小說。

**musicale**〔ˌmjuzɪ'kæl 〕*n.*（社交性的）音樂會

—— social gathering, with music as the featured entertainment

At last night's *musicale* in my cousin's house, we were entertained by a string quartet.

昨晚在我堂兄弟家舉行的音樂會，以絃樂四重奏娛悅嘉賓。

**palette**〔'pælɪt , -ɛt 〕*n.* 調色盤

—— thin board (with a thumb hole at one end) on which an artist lays and mixes colors

After a few canvas strokes, the artist reapplies his brush to his *palette* for more paint.

在畫布上塗了幾筆後，藝術家又把畫筆在調色盤上沾一沾，以塗上更多的顏料。

**repertoire**〔'rɛpəˌtwar , -ˌtwɔr 〕*n.* 全部曲目；節目；全部才能

—— list of plays, operas, roles, compositions, etc., that a company or performer is prepared to perform

The guitarist apologized for not being able to play the requested number, explaining that it was not in his *repertoire.*

吉他手爲未能演奏要求的曲子而道歉，他解釋說那並不在他的曲目上。

**vignette** 〔 vɪnˈjɛt 〕 *n.* 小品文；短文

—— short verbal description; a literary sketch

James Joyce's *Dubliners* offers some unforgettable *vignettes* of life in Dublin at the turn of the century.

詹姆士‧喬依斯的作品「都柏林人」對世紀交替時的都柏林生活，提供了令人難忘的小品文。

Exercise：請由 **Group 7** 中，選出最適當的字，填入空格中。

1. After viewing the oil paintings, we turned our attention to another _____, watercolors.

2. A novel with a suspenseful plot makes the reader impatient to get to the _____.

3. If audience reaction is favorable, Selma is prepared to play a(n) _____.

4. Beethoven's Ninth Symphony is regarded by many as his _____.

5. By diligent study the young singer added several new numbers to her _____.

--- 【解答】 ------------------------------
1. genre      2. denouement      3. encore
4. chef d'oeuvre    5. repertoire

## 【Group 8】

# 與食物有關的字

**à la carte** 〔͵ɑlə'kɑrt 〕 *adj.* 單點的;依菜單點菜的   *adv.* 單點
—— according to the bill of fare; dish by dish, with a stated price
    for each dish
If you order an *à la carte* dinner, you select whatever you wish
from the bill of fare, paying only for the dishes ordered.
如果你晚餐是以單點的方式,就可以選擇價目表上任何你喜歡的項目,
而且只付所點的菜的價格。

**apéritif** 〔 ə͵perə'tif 〕 *n.* 餐前酒
—— alcoholic drink taken before a meal as an appetizer
Select a nonalcoholic drink, such as tomato juice, if you do not
care for an *apéritif.*
選一項不含酒精成份的飲料,如蕃茄汁,如果你不想要餐前酒的話。

**bonbon** 〔'bɑn͵bɑn 〕 *n.* 夾心軟糖;糖果
—— piece of candy

For Valentine's Day, Mother received a heart-shaped box of
delicious *bonbons*.
情人節的時候,母親收到一份心形盒裝的美味夾心軟糖。

**cuisine**[5] 〔 kwɪ'zin 〕 *n.* 烹飪 ( 法 );菜餚
—— style of cooking or preparing food
Around the corner is a restaurant
specializing in French *cuisine*. 轉角有一家專門做法國菜的餐廳。

【記憶技巧】
這是法文,所以發音很特別。

**demitasse** 〔'dɛmə͵tæs , -͵tɑs 〕 *n.* 小型咖啡杯;小杯黑咖啡
—— small cup for, or of, black coffee

Aunt Dorothy always takes cream with her coffee; she is not fond
of *demitasse*. 桃樂斯阿姨喝咖啡都會加奶油；她不喜歡喝黑咖啡。

# entrée〔'ɑntre , ɑ̃'tre〕*n.* 主菜

—— main dish at lunch or dinner

We had a choice of the following *entrées*: roast beef, fried chicken,
or baked mackerel.

我們從下列主菜中選擇一項：烤牛肉、炸雞，或烤鯖魚。

# filet〔fɪ'le , 'fɪle〕*n.* 肉片；魚片

—— slice of meat or fish without bones or fat

Because they contain no bones or excess fat, *filets* are more
expensive than ordinary cuts of meat.

因爲肉片沒有骨頭或多餘的脂肪，所以就比普通部位的肉貴一點。

# hors d'oeuvres〔ɔr'doevrə , -'dʌv〕*n.* 開胃菜；前菜

—— light food served as an appetizer before the regular courses
of a meal

Mother will need olives, celery, and anchovies for her *hors
d'oeuvres*. 母親需要橄欖、芹菜，及鯷魚做開胃菜。

# pièce de résistance〔,pjɛsdə,rezis'tɑ̃:s〕*n.* 1. 主菜

2. 主要項目；主要的作品

—— 1. main dish

2. main item of any collection, series, program, etc.

If you eat too much of the hors d'oeuvres, you will have little
appetite for the *pièce de résistance*.

如果你開胃菜吃多了，就沒有胃口吃主菜。

# table d'hôte〔'tæbḷ'dot , 'tɑbḷ'dot〕*n.* 套餐；定食

—— describing a complete meal that bears a fixed price

If you order a *table d'hôte* dinner, you pay the price fixed for the entire dinner, even if you do not have some of the dishes.

如果你晚餐點的是套餐，就得付所有菜的固定價錢，即使有幾道菜你沒吃。

Exercise：請由 **Group 8** 中，選出最適當的字，填入空格中。

1. Before dinner, our hostess brought in a large tray of appetizing
   _____.

2. Though this chef's style of cooking is quite interesting, it cannot compare with Grandmother's _____.

3. When I do not care to have a complete dinner, I order a few dishes _____.

4. My little sister was so fond of candy that she had to be restricted to one _____ after each meal.

5. If you like flounder but are worried about accidentally swallowing a fishbone, try _____ of flounder.

---
【解答】

| | | |
|---|---|---|
| 1. hors d'oeuvres | 2. cuisine | 3. à la carte |
| 4. bonbon | 5. filet | |

---

## 【Group 9】

## 與穿著有關的字

**bouffant**〔 bu'fɑ 〕*adj.* 膨鬆的
—— puffed out; full

School corridors and stairways would have to be widened considerably if all girls were to wear *bouffant* skirts.
如果所有的女孩都穿上蓬蓬裙，學校的走廊及樓梯都得拓寬了。

**chemise** 〔 ʃə'miz 〕 *n.* 寬鬆的洋裝
—— loose-fitting, sack-like dress
Though more comfortable than most other dresses, the *chemise* has often been ridiculed for its shapelessness.
雖然穿起來要比其他大部份的衣服都來得舒適，但那件寬鬆的洋裝還是以不成樣子而被取笑。

**coiffure** 〔 kwɑ'fjʊr 〕 *n.* 髮型
—— style of arranging the hair; headdress
Sally's attractive new *coiffure* was arranged for her by my sister's hairstylist.
莎莉那個吸引人的新髮型是我妹妹的髮型設計師為她設計的。

**corsage** 〔 kɔr'sɑʒ 〕 *n.* （女子洋裝上或套裝上的）裝飾花；胸花
—— small bouquet worn by a woman
At the Christmas season, ladies often adorn their coats with a holly *corsage*.
聖誕節的時候，女士們經常用冬青花束來點綴她們的外套。

**cravat** 〔 krə'væt 〕 *n.* 領帶
—— necktie
My cousin sent me a light blue shirt and a navy-blue *cravat*.
我表哥送我一件淺藍色的襯衫及一條深藍色的領帶。

**flamboyant** 〔 flæm'bɔɪənt 〕 *adj.* 色彩鮮豔的；浮誇的；火焰般的
—— 1. very ornate; showy
　　 2. flamelike

To add a touch of bright color to her outfit, Jane wore a *flamboyant* scarf.

為了在她的服裝上添加些許鮮明的色彩，珍圍上一條豔麗的圍巾。

## toupee〔tu'pe , -'pi〕*n.* 假髮

—— wig

The actor's baldness was cleverly concealed by a very natural-looking *toupee*.

演員的禿頭被一頂看起來非常自然的假髮巧妙地遮蓋過去。

## vogue[6]〔vog〕*n.* 流行；時尚

—— fashion; accepted style

Women's fashions change rapidly; what is in style today may be out of *vogue* tomorrow.

女士的流行式樣變化得很快；今天流行的也許明天就不合潮流了。

Exercise：請由 **Group 9** 中，選出最適當的字，填入空格中。

1. The excessive heat made George untie his _____ and unbutton his shirt collar.

2. After trying several elaborate hairstyles, Marie has returned to a simple _____.

3. On your visit to Mount Vernon in Virginia, you will be able to see the furniture styles that were in _____ in George Washington's time.

4. It was easy to identify the guest of honor because of the beautiful _____ at her shoulder.

5. The gowns in the dress salon range from sedate blacks to
_____ reds and golds.

┌─【解答】─────────────────────
│ 1. cravat　　　　2. coiffure　　　3. vogue
│ 4. corsage　　　5. flamboyant
└─────────────────────────

## 【Group 10】

# 各方面的字

**avoirdupois** 〔͵ævɚdə'pɔɪz , 'ævɚdə͵pɔɪz 〕 *n.* 重量；體重
—— weight; heaviness
Dieters constantly check their ***avoirdupois***.
節食者經常檢查他們的體重。

**bagatelle** 〔͵bægə'tɛl 〕 *n.* 瑣事
—— trifle
Pay attention to important matters; don't waste time on ***bagatelles***.
注意重要的事情；不要在小事上浪費時間。

**coup de grâce** 〔 kudə'grɑs 〕 *n.* 致命的一擊；（以免其多受痛苦）
慈悲的一擊
—— merciful or decisive finishing stroke
A sergeant unholstered his pistol and ran forward to give the ***coup
de grâce***.
警官解開手槍奔上前去，射出致命的一槍。

**façade** 〔 fə'sɑd , fæ'sɑd 〕 *n.* （建築物的）正面；表面
—— face or front of a building, or of anything

The patient's cheerful smile was just a *façade*; actually, she was suffering from ennui.

那病人愉快的微笑只是表面上的；事實上她倦怠的很。

**fête** 〔 fet 〕 1. *n.* 節日；慶祝會　2. *v.* 盛宴招待；款待

—— 1. festival; entertainment; party
2. to honor with a fête

Retiring employees are often *fêted* at a special dinner.

退休的員工經常被招待一頓特殊的晚餐。

**foyer** 〔 ˈfɔɪ‧e , ˈfɔɪɚ 〕 *n.* 門廳；劇場休息室

—— entrance hall; lobby

Let's meet in the *foyer* of the Bijou Theater.

讓我們在珠寶劇院的休息室會面。

**milieu** 〔 miˈljφ 〕 *n.* 周圍環境；出身背景

—— environment; setting

David found it much easier to make friends in his new *milieu*.

大衛發現在新環境裏交朋友簡單多了。

**parasol** 〔 ˈpærəˌsɔl 〕 *n.* 陽傘

—— umbrella for protection against the sun

In summer when you stroll on the boardwalk in the noonday sun, it is advisable to take along a *parasol*.

夏日正午陽光照耀下於海濱的木板路散步時，最好帶一把陽傘同行。

**par excellence** 〔 parˈɛksəˌlɑns 〕 *adj.* 最卓越的；出類拔萃的

—— above all others of the same sort (follows the word it modifies); unsurpassed

Charles Dickens was a raconteur *par excellence*.

查爾斯‧狄更斯非常善於講故事。

第六章

**pince-nez**〔ˋpænsˏne, ˋpɪns-〕*n.* 夾鼻眼鏡

—— eyeglasses clipped to the nose by a spring

Since they are held in place by a spring that pinches the nose,
*pince-nez* may not be as comfortable as ordinary eyeglasses.

因為夾鼻眼鏡是利用彈簧夾住鼻子以固定位置，所以它們戴起來不如一
般眼鏡舒服。

**raison d'être**〔ˋrezɔnˋdɛt〕*n.* 存在的理由；做某事的原因

—— reason or justification for existing

Abe is very fond of golf; he feels it is his chief *raison d'être*.

艾伯非常喜歡打高爾夫球，並認為那是他生存的主要原因。

**rendezvous**〔ˋrɑndəˏvu, ˋrɛn-〕*n.* 1. 會面的地點　2. 約會

—— 1. meeting place fixed by prior agreement
　　 2. appointment to meet at a fixed time and place

We agreed to meet after the test at the corner ice-cream parlor,
our usual *rendezvous*.

我們說好考試結束以後在轉角的冰淇淋店見面，那是我們約會的老地方。

**silhouette**〔ˏsɪluˋɛt〕*n.* 1. 剪影；側面影像　2. 輪廓

—— 1. shadow
　　 2. outline

I knew that Dad was coming to let me in because I recognized his
*silhouette* behind the curtained door.

我知道父親正走過來開門讓我進去，因為我認出簾幕門後他的影像。

**sobriquet**〔ˋsobrɪˏke〕*n.* 綽號

—— nickname

Andrew Jackson was known by the *sobriquet* "Old Hickory."

安德魯·傑克森以其綽號「老山胡桃」而知名。

**souvenir**[4]〔͵suvə'nɪr , 'suvə͵nɪr 〕*n.* 紀念品

—— reminder; keepsake; memento

To most graduates the senior yearbook is a treasured *souvenir* of high school days.

> 【記憶技巧】
> *sou* (up) + *venir* (come)
> (「紀念品」會使你的回憶
> 出現在腦中)

對大部份畢業生來說,高中畢業紀念冊是中學時代珍貴的紀念。

**tour de force**〔͵turdə'fors 〕*n.* 精心傑作;絕技

—— feat of strength or skill; adroit accomplishment

George's sixty-yard touchdown run was an admirable *tour de force* that won the game for us.

喬治持球跑了六十碼而觸地得分,實爲令人讚嘆之舉,並爲我們贏得這場球賽。

**vis-à-vis**〔͵vizə'vi 〕1. *adv.* 面對面地　2. *prep.* 與…面對面;與…相比

—— 1. face to face; opposite
　　2. when confronted or compared with

At the banquet table, I had the good fortune to sit *vis-à-vis* an old school chum. 在宴會桌上,我恰巧坐在一位老同學的對面。

Exercise:請由 **Group 10** 中,選出最適當的字,填入空格中。

1. Father brought me a print of the Lincoln Memorial as a(n) _____ of his visit to Washington.

2. When Paula was dieting, she would mount the scale morning and night in order to check her _____.

3. After school, I meet my friends at our _____ across the street.

4. Agnes is a mimic _____; no one in our club can do impersonations as well as she.

5. Because of his flaming hair, Harvey is popularly known by the _____ "Red."

6. The few small merchants who have survived the intense competition are fearful that the opening of another supermarket will be the _____ for them.

7. Our club is planning a(n) _____ to honor the outgoing president.

8. The first day at high school places the newly arrived pupil in a bewildering _____.

9. I did not recognize the hotel because its _____ and foyer had been modernized since my last stay there.

10. Winning the league pennant is an outstanding baseball achievement, but going on to capture the World Series in four straight victories is an even greater _____.

---

【解答】

| | | |
|---|---|---|
| 1. souvenir | 2. avoirdupois | 3. rendezvous |
| 4. par excellence | 5. sobriquet | |
| 6. coup de grace | 7. fête | 8. milieu |
| 9. façade | 10. tour de force | |

## REVIEW

Exercise 1：根據括弧中的提示，選出一個正確答案。

( ) 1. In serving the soup, the _____ (*clumsy*) waitress spilled
some of it on the guest of honor.

    (A) chic         (B) maladroit         (C) debonair

( ) 2. Monotonous repetition usually brings on _____
(*boredom*).

    (A) ennui         (B) éclat         (C) savoir faire

( ) 3. I'll be glad to give my opinion, but you must realize I am
no _____ (*expert*).

    (A) raconteur         (B) martinet         (C) connoisseur

( ) 4. A bibliophile is usually a _____ (*ardent adherent*) of
good literature.

    (A) protégée         (B) devotee         (C) repartee

( ) 5. We made a right turn into the next street, but it proved to
be a _____ (*blind alley*).

    (A) mélange         (B) cul-de-sac         (C) canard

( ) 6. The President was represented at the state funeral in Paris
by a special _____ (*diplomatic agent*).

    (A) ingénue         (B) bourgeoisie         (C) envoy

( ) 7. We had a _____ (*private conversation*) over a couple of
ice-cream sodas.

    (A) bête noire         (B) tête-à-tête         (C) mirage

第六章

( ) 8. Do not commit the _____ (*blunder*) of coming
unprepared to class.

    (A) faux pas     (B) impasse     (C) riposte

( ) 9. Today, my English teacher called on me for a _____
(*summary*) of yesterday's lesson.

    (A) rapport     (B) résumé     (C) brochure

( ) 10. Though awkward in sports, she has remarkable _____
(*skill*) at the piano.

    (A) sangfroid     (B) élan     (C) finesse

## Exercise 2：下列各題中，選出與斜體字意義最相近的答案。

( ) 1. prosperous *bourgeoisie*

    (A) elite     (B) entrepreneur     (C) middle class

    (D) citizenry     (E) officialdom

( ) 2. *flamboyant* jacket

    (A) debonair     (B) warm     (C) sanguinary

    (D) showy     (E) stylish

( ) 3. happy *denouement*

    (A) ending     (B) vignette     (C) milieu

    (D) event     (E) episode

( ) 4. sudden *démarche*

    (A) détente     (B) maneuver     (C) entrée

    (D) discovery     (E) aggression

( ) 5. attitude of *laissez-faire*

    (A) boredom     (B) equanimity     (C) eagerness

    (D) cordiality     (E) noninterference

( ) 6. enduring *entente*

    (A) influence    (B) understanding    (C) bitterness

    (D) cause célèbre    (E) entrance

( ) 7. serve *hors d'oeuvres*

    (A) à la carte    (B) appetizers    (C) desserts

    (D) pièce de résistance    (E) table d'hôte

( ) 8. join the *avant-garde*

    (A) gendarmes    (B) protégés    (C) devotees

    (D) underground    (E) innovators

( ) 9. request an *encore*

    (A) cancellation    (B) delay    (C) repetition

    (D) refund    (E) improvement

( ) 10. flavor *par excellence*

    (A) new    (B) unsurpassed    (C) spicy

    (D) mild    (E) inferior

Exercise 3：下列各題中，選出意義與其他三者無關的答案。

( ) 1. (A) face to face    (B) up to date

    (C) compared with    (D) vis-à-vis

( ) 2. (A) setting    (B) milieu

    (C) surroundings    (D) mélange

( ) 3. (A) pamphlet    (B) booklet

    (C) brochure    (D) silhouette

( ) 4. (A) category    (B) style

    (C) rate    (D) genre

第
六
章

( 　) 5. (A) par excellence 　　　　(B) exploit

　　　　 (C) tour de force 　　　　　(D) achievement

( 　) 6. (A) binoculars 　　　　　　(B) spectacles

　　　　 (C) pince-nez 　　　　　　 (D) camera

( 　) 7 (A) engagement 　　　　　　(B) rendezvous

　　　　 (C) adieu 　　　　　　　　(D) appointment

( 　) 8. (A) précis 　　(B) encore 　　(C) résumé 　　(D) summary

( 　) 9. (A) entente 　　　　　　　　(B) understanding

　　　　 (C) rapprochement 　　　　　(D) régime

( 　) 10. (A) apéritif 　　　　　　　 (B) appetizer

　　　　　(C) hors d'oeuvres 　　　　(D) denouement

Exercise 4：根據句意及所提示的字首，填入正確的字辭，每一個小
　　　　　　空格限填一個**字母**。

1. Albert introduced us to his f_ _ _ _ _ _ several weeks before
   they were to be married.

2. Try to find the m_ _ _ _ _ _ _ for your idea; if a word only
   approximates what you wish to say, reject it.

3. Don't spoil your writing with such a c_ _ _ _ _ as "the fly in
   the ointment" or "dumb as an ox."

4. Mae watched impatiently for the mailman; she was expecting a
   b_ _ _ _ _ _ _ _ _ from her fiancé.

5. He is the kind of painter who is always surrounded by a
   c_ _ _ _ _ _ of admirers and imitators.

6. She was as nervous as a d_ _ _ _ _ _ _ _ at a coming-out party.

7. A good p_ _ _ _ _ should contain fewer than a third of the number of words in the original.

8. Some employees regard the manager as a m_ _ _ _ _ _ _, but I have found him not too strict.

9. The prosecutor, it was charged, had made the trial into a c_ _ _ _ _ _ _ _ _ _ to further his political ambitions.

10. My mispronunciation of our guest's name was an embarrassing f_ _ _ _ _ _.

---

【解答】

| | | | | | | | |
|---|---|---|---|---|---|---|---|
| **Ex 1.** | 1. B | 2. A | 3. C | 4. B | 5. B | 6. C | 7. B | 8. A |
| | 9. B | 10. C | | | | | | |
| **Ex 2.** | 1. C | 2. D | 3. A | 4. B | 5. E | 6. B | 7. B | 8. E |
| | 9. C | 10. B | | | | | | |
| **Ex 3.** | 1. B | 2. D | 3. D | 4. C | 5. A | 6. D | 7. C | 8. B |
| | 9. D | 10. D | | | | | | |

**Ex 4.**

| | | |
|---|---|---|
| 1. fiancée | 2. mot juste | 3. cliché |
| 4. billet-doux | 5. coterie | 6. debutante |
| 7. précis | 8. martinet | 9. cause célèbre |
| 10. faux pas | | |

# 第七章
# 出自義大利文的英文字彙

> 拉丁文對英文的影響雖然不如法文，但仍然很重要。義大利對藝術豐富的貢獻，深深影響了西方國家的文化生活。很多關於音樂、繪畫、建築、雕刻和其他藝術的單字，都是來自義大利的外來語，這顯示了義大利文對英語的影響。

## 【Group 1】

## 有關歌聲的字

Group 1～10

**basso**〔ˈbæso〕*n.* 低音（lowest male voice; bass）

**baritone**〔ˈbærəˌton〕*n.* 男中音（male voice between bass and tenor）

**tenor**〔ˈtɛnɚ〕*n.* 男高音；次中音（adult male voice between baritone and alto）

**alto**〔ˈælto〕*n.* 1. 男最高音（highest male voice）
2. 女最低音（lowest female voice, the contralto）

**contralto**〔kənˈtrælto〕*n.* 最低的女低音（lowest female voice）

**mezzo-soprano**〔ˈmɛtsosəˈpræno〕*n.* 次女高音（female voice between contralto and soprano）

**soprano**〔səˈpræno〕*n.* 女高音（highest singing voice in women and boys）

**coloratura** 〔ˌkʌlərə'tjʊrə〕 *n*. 1. 花腔（ornamental passages〔runs, trills, etc.〕in vocal music） 2. 花腔女高音（soprano who sings such passages, i.e., a *coloratura* soprano）

**falsetto**〔fɔl'sɛto〕*n*. 1. 假聲（unnaturally high-pitched male voice） 2. 假聲歌手（artificial voice）

Exercise：請由 **Group 1** 中，選出最適當的字，填入空格中。

1. For her superb rendering of ornamental passages, the _____ soprano was wildly acclaimed.

2. The lowest singing voice is *contralto* for women and _____ for men.

3. Yodeling is a form of singing that requires frequent changes from the natural voice to a(n) _____.

4. Since Oscar's singing voice is between baritone and alto, he is classified as a(n) _____.

5. The highest singing voice is *soprano* for women and _____ for men.

```
---【解答】-----------------------------------
  1. coloratura      2. basso        3. falsetto
  4. tenor           5. alto
----------------------------------------------
```

## 【Group 2】

# 有關音樂作品速度節拍的字

**grave**[4]〔 grev 〕*adj.* 莊嚴而緩慢的（ slow〔the slowest tempo in music〕; serious ）

**largo**〔'lɑrgo 〕*adj., adv.* 極緩慢的（地）（ slow and dignified; stately ）

**adagio**〔 ə'dɑdʒo , ə'dɑdʒɪ,o 〕*adv.* 緩慢地（ slow; in an easy, graceful manner ）

**lento**〔'lɛnto 〕*adj., adv.* 緩慢的（地）（ slow ）

**andante**〔 ɑn'dɑnte , æn'dæntɪ 〕*adv.* 緩慢地；行板地（ moderately slow, but flowing ）

**moderato**〔,mɑdə'rɑto 〕*adj., adv.* 中板（ in moderate time ）

**allegro**〔 ə'legro , ə'lɛgro 〕*adj., adv.* 快速而活潑的（地）（ brisk; quick; lively ）

**vivace**〔 vi'vɑtʃɪ 〕*adj.* 生動的；活潑的（ brisk; spirited ）

**presto**〔'prɛsto 〕*adv.* 急速地（ quick ）

**prestissimo**〔 prɛs'tɪsə,mo 〕*adv.* 最快地（ at a very rapid pace ）

Exercise：請由 **Group 2** 中，選出最適當的字，填入空格中。

1. A piece of music marked ＿＿＿＿＿ moves more rapidly than one marked *presto*.

2. The slowest tempo in music, _____, is used in the opening measures of Beethoven's *Sonate Pathétique*.

3. *Annie Laurie* should be sung at a moderately slow but flowing pace, for its tempo is _____.

4. The _____ movement of Dvorak's *New World Symphony* is played in a slow and dignified manner.

5. The term _____ over the opening notes of *Sweet Georgia Brown* indicates that this tune should be played neither rapidly nor slowly, but in moderate time.

---
【解答】

1. prestissimo　　2. grave　　　3. andante
4. largo　　　　　5. moderato
---

## 【Group 3】

# 有關強弱的字

**crescendo**〔krə'ʃɛndo , -'sɛn- 〕*adj., adv.* 漸強的（gradually increasing〔or a gradual increase〕in force or loudness）
反 decrescendo

**decrescendo**〔ˌdikrə'ʃɛndo 〕*adj., adv.* 漸弱的（gradually decreasing〔or a gradual increase〕in force or loudness）
同 diminuendo〔dəˌmɪnjʊ'ɛndo 〕*adj.* 漸弱的　反 crescendo

**dolce**〔'doltʃe 〕*adj.* 悅耳而柔和的（soft; sweet）

**forte**〔'fɔrtɪ , -te 〕*adj.* 強音的（loud）　反 piano

**fortissimo**〔fɔr'tɪsə‚mo〕*adj., adv.* 最強的（地）（very loud）
　反 pianissimo

**pianissimo**〔‚piə'nɪsə‚mo〕*adj., adv.* 極弱的（地）（very soft）
　反 fortissimo

**piano**[1]〔pɪ'ɑno〕*adj., adv.* 弱音的（地）（soft）　　反 forte

**sforzando**〔sfor'tsɑndo〕*adj., adv.* 加強的（地）（accented）

Exercise：請由 **Group 3** 中，選出最適當的字，填入空格中。

1. The word _____ designates a familiar musical instrument, as well as a musical direction meaning "soft."

2. Ravel's Bolero rises to a dramatic climax by a gradual increase in loudness; few pieces have such an electrifying _____.

3. When a composer wants a chord played with a strong accent, he uses the term _____.

4. Mendelssohn's Scherzo has a _____ ending; it has to be played very softly.

5. A degree of loudness higher than *forte* is _____.

【解答】

1. piano　　2. crescendo　　3. sforzando
4. pianissimo　　5. fortissimo

第
七
章

【Group 4】

## 有關音樂效果的字

**a cappella** 〔͵ɑkə'pɛlə 〕*adj.* 無樂器伴奏的；團體清唱的（without musical accompaniment, as in an *a cappella* choir）

**arpeggio** 〔 ɑr'pɛdʒɪ͵o 〕*n.* 1. 和音急速彈奏（production of the tones of a chord in rapid succession and not simultaneously）2. 琶音（a chord thus played）

**legato** 〔 lɪ'gɑto 〕*adj., adv.* 圓滑的（地）（smooth and connected）

**pizzicato** 〔͵pɪtsɪ'kɑto 〕*adj.* 撥弦彈奏的；指彈的（direction to players of bowed instruments to pluck the strings instead of using the bow）

**staccato** 〔 stə'kɑto 〕*adj.* 斷音的；斷奏的（disconnected; abrupt; with breaks between successive notes）

**tremolo** 〔'trɛmə͵lo 〕*n.* 顫音（rapid〔"trembling"〕repetition of a tone or chord, without apparent breaks, to express emotion）

**vibrato** 〔 vɪ'brɑto 〕*n.* 抖音（slightly throbbing or pulsating effect, adding warmth and beauty to the tone）

Exercise：請由 **Group 4** 中，選出最適當的字，填入空格中。

1. By plucking the strings with his fingers, a violinist achieves a(n) _____ effect.

2. In Tchaikovsky's *1812 Overture*, the rapid and prolonged repetition of two tones produces a "trembling," emotion-stirring effect known as _____.

3. Some beginning piano students strike all the correct notes but fail to achieve a smooth and connected effect because they do not play them _____.

4. It is surely much easier to play the tones of a chord simultaneously than to play them as a(n) _____.

5. In Schubert's *Ave Maria*, the notes are smoothly connected, but in his *Marche Militaire* they are mainly _____.

【解答】

1. pizzicato    2. tremolo    3. legato
4. arpeggio     5. staccato

## 【Group 5】

# 有關作曲的字

**aria**〔ˋɑrɪə , ˋɛrɪə〕*n.* 詠嘆調;抒情調(歌劇及聖樂中有樂器伴奏的獨唱曲)(air, melody, or tune; especially, an elaborate, accompanied melody for a single voice in an opera)

**bravura**〔brəˋvjurə〕*n.* 1. 氣勢磅礡的樂曲(piece of music requiring skill and spirit in the performer)
2. 勇敢大膽的表現(display of daring or brilliancy)

**cantata**〔kænˋtɑtə〕*n.* 清唱劇(story or play set to music to be sung by a chorus, but not acted)

**concerto**〔kənˋtʃɛrto〕*n.* 協奏曲(long musical composition for one or more principal instruments)

**duet** 〔 dju'ɛt 〕 *n.* 1. 二重唱；二重奏（two singers or players performing together）
2. 二重唱或二重奏的歌曲（piece of music for two voices or instruments）

**finale** 〔 fɪ'nɑlɪ 〕 *n.* 終曲；最後樂章（close or termination; the last section of a musical composition）

**intermezzo** 〔 ˌɪntɚ'mɛtso , -'mɛdzo 〕 *n.* 1. 幕間劇（short musical or dramatic entertainment between the acts of a play）
2. 插曲（short musical composition between the main divisions of an extended musical work）
3. 間奏曲（a short, independent musical composition）

**libretto** 〔 lɪ'brɛto 〕 *n.* 歌劇劇本；歌曲歌詞（text or words of an opera or other long musical composition）

**opera**⁴ 〔 'ɑpərə 〕 *n.* 歌劇（play mostly sung, with costumes, scenery, action, and music）

【記憶技巧】
*oper* (work) + *a*（「歌劇」就是一件作品）

**oratorio** 〔 ˌɔrə'torɪo , ɑr- 〕 *n.* 神劇；清唱劇（musical composition, usually on a religious theme, for solo voices, chorus, and orchestra）

**scherzo** 〔 'skɛrtso 〕 *n.* 詼諧曲（light or playful part of a sonata or symphony）

**solo**⁵ 〔 'solo 〕 *n.* 1. 獨唱；獨奏曲（piece of music for one voice or instrument）　2. 單獨表演（anything done without a partner）

**sonata** 〔 sə'nɑtə 〕 *n.* 奏鳴曲（piece of music〔for one or two instruments〕having three or four movements in contrasted rhythms but related tonality）

**trio** 〔ˈtrio , ˈtraɪo 〕 *n.* 1. 三重唱；三重奏（ three singers or players performing together ）

2. 三重唱的樂曲；三重奏的樂曲（ piece of music for three voices or instruments ）

Exercise：請由 **Group 5** 中，選出最適當的字，填入空格中。

1. To perform in a(n) _____, one must be gifted both as a singer and as an actor.

2. Roberta refuses to do a solo, but she is willing to join with another in a(n) _____.

3. From the opening selection to the _____, we enjoyed the concert thoroughly.

4. Though there is orchestral accompaniment in a piano _____, the pianist is the principal performer.

5. The selection you played is unfamiliar to me, but its light and playful character leads me to believe that it's a(n) _____.

```
┌--- 【解答】 -----------------------------------
| 1. opera        2. duet          3. finale
| 4. concerto     5. scherzo
└----------------------------------------------
```

## 【Group 6】
# 與藝術有關的字

**cameo** 〔ˈkæmɪˌo , -mjo 〕 *n.* 浮雕飾物；硬石、貝殼上刻有不同顏色的浮雕（ stone or shell on which a figure, cut in relief, appears against a background of a different color ）　反 intaglio

**campanile**〔͵kæmpə'nilɪ 〕*n.* 鐘樓（bell tower）

**canto**〔'kænto 〕*n.*（長詩的）篇章（one of the chief divisions of a long poem）

**chiaroscuro**〔kɪ͵arə'skjuro 〕*n.* 1.（繪畫的）明暗對比（style of pictorial art using only light and shade）
2. 明暗對比的畫（sketch in black and white）

**cupola**〔'kjupələ 〕*n.* 1. 圓屋頂（rounded roof; dome）
2. 圓頂閣（small dome or tower on a roof）

**fresco**〔'frɛsko 〕*n.* 1. 壁畫法（art of painting with water colors on damp, fresh plaster）    2. 壁畫（picture or design so painted）

**intaglio**〔ɪn'tæljo , -'taljo 〕*n.* 凹雕；凹刻（design engraved by making cuts in a surface）  反 cameo

**majolica**〔mə'dʒalɪkə , -'jal- 〕*n.* 馬加利卡陶器（多彩而裝飾繁複的義大利原產陶器）（enameled Italian pottery richly decorated in colors）

**mezzanine**〔'mɛzə͵nin , -nɪn 〕*n.*（戲院裏）中層樓的包廂（intermediate story in a theater between the main floor and the first balcony）；（建築物兩層之間的）夾樓；夾層

**mezzotint**〔'mɛtsə͵tɪnt , 'mɛdzə- 〕*n.* 鋼線銅版雕刻法（picture engraved on copper or steel by polishing or scraping away parts of a roughened surface）

**patina**〔'pætɪnə 〕*n.*（銅器上的）綠銹；銅綠（film or incrustation, usually green, on the surface of old bronze or copper）

**portico**〔'portɪ͵ko , 'pɔr- 〕*n.* 門廊；柱廊（roof supported by columns, forming a porch or a covered walk）

**rotunda**〔ro'tʌndə〕*n.* 1.（有圓頂的）圓形建築物（round building, especially one with a dome or cupola）
2.（有圓頂的）圓形大廳（如美國國會圓廳）（large round room, as in the rotunda of the Capitol）

**stucco**〔'stʌko〕*n.*（粉刷牆壁用的）灰泥（plaster for covering exterior walls of buildings）

**tempera**〔'tɛmpərə〕*n.* 蛋彩畫法（method of painting in which the colors are mixed with white of egg or other substances, instead of oil）

**terra cotta**〔'tɛrə'kɑtə〕*n.* 1. 赤土陶器；陶俑（kind of hard, brownish-red earthenware, used for vases, statuettes, etc.）
2. 赤褐色的（dull brownish-red）

**torso**〔'tɔrso〕*n.* 1.（沒有頭和手的）人體軀幹雕像（trunk or body of a statue without a head, arms, or legs）
2. 人體軀幹（human trunk）

Exercise：請由 **Group 6** 中，選出最適當的字，填入空格中。

1. Because it is a large round room, the _____ of the Capitol in Washington, D.C., is ideal for an impressive ceremony.

2. The _____ my aunt wears has a carved ivory head raised on a light brown background.

3. A(n) _____ actually becomes a part of the wall on whose damp, fresh plaster surface it is painted.

4. The head of the statue was discovered not far from the place where its armless _____ had been found.

5. An antique increases in artistic value when its surface becomes incrusted with a fine natural _____.

6. The white of egg, or a similar substance, is used for mixing colors in _____ painting.

7. Read the fifth _____ of Scott's *Marmion* for a stirring description of young Lochinvar's elopement with fair Ellen.

8. The _____ applied to exterior walls of buildings is a mixture of Portland cement, sand, and lime.

9. In the morning we heard the sound of bells coming from the _____, a tall structure right next to the church.

10. The main building and the annex are connected by a(n) _____ that facilitates traffic between the two buildings, especially in bad weather.

```
┌── 【解答】 ─────────────────────────────┐
│  1. rotunda    2. cameo     3. fresco    4. torso    │
│  5. patina     6. tempera   7. canto     8. stucco   │
│  9. campanile  10. portico                           │
└──────────────────────────────────────────┘
```

## 【Group 7】

## 與人有關的字

**cognoscente** 〔͵kɑnjə'ʃɛntɪ〕 *n.* 鑑賞家 ( connoisseur )

**dilettante** 〔͵dɪlə'tæntɪ〕 *n.* 業餘的藝術愛好者 ( person who follows some art or science as an amusement or in a trifling way )

**maestro**〔'maɪstro〕*n.* 1. 名指揮家；名作曲家（eminent
conductor, composer, or teacher of music）
2.（藝術之）名家；大師（master in any art）

**virtuoso**〔ˌvɝtʃu'oso〕*n.*（藝術或演奏技巧上的）名家；大師
（one who exhibits great technical skill in an art, especially in
playing a musical instrument）

## 【Group 8】

# 描述人處境的字

**dolce far niente**〔doltʃefɑr'njɛnte〕*n.* 安逸；閒適（delightful
idleness）

**fiasco**〔fɪ'æsko〕*n.* 慘敗；大失敗；尷尬的結局（crash; complete
or ridiculous failure）

**imbroglio**〔ɪm'broljo〕*n.* 1. 困難的情況；錯綜複雜的局面
（difficult situation）　2. 糾紛（complicated disagreement）

**incognito**〔ɪn'kɑgnɪ'to〕1. *adv.* 隱姓埋名地；隱藏身份地（with
one's identity concealed）
2. *n.* 隱姓埋名（的狀態）（disguised state）

**vendetta**〔vɛn'dɛtə〕*n.* 仇殺；世仇（feud for blood revenge）

## 【Group 9】

# 有關食物的字

**antipasto**〔ˌɑntɪ'pasto〕*n.* 義式開胃菜（appetizer consisting of
fish, meats, etc.; hors d'oeuvres）

**Chianti**〔kɪ'æntɪ,'kjɑntɪ〕*n.* 基安蒂酒（一種義大利的紅葡萄酒）（a dry, red Italian wine）

**gusto**〔'gʌsto〕*n.* 愛好；滿腔熱情；由衷的高興（liking or taste; hearty enjoyment）

**pizza**² 〔'pitsə〕*n.* 披薩（large flat pie of bread dough spread with tomato pulp, cheese, meat, anchovies, etc.）

## 【Group 10】

# 一般性的字

**gondola**〔'gɑndələ〕*n.* 1. （威尼斯的）平底輕舟（boat used in the canals of Venice）
2. （飛艇、空中纜車等的）吊籃（cabin attached to the underpart of an airship）

**grotto**〔'grɑto〕*n.* 洞穴；石窟（cave）

**piazza**〔pɪ'æzə〕*n.* 1. （義大利的）露天廣場（open square in an Italian town）    2. 走廊；有頂迴廊（veranda or porch）

**portfolio**〔port'folɪ,o〕*n.* 1. 公事包（briefcase）
2. 部長或閣員的職位（position or duties of a cabinet member or minister of state）

**salvo**〔'sælvo〕*n.* 1. 同時發射（simultaneous discharge of shots）
2. 齊聲歡呼（burst of cheers, as in a *salvo* of applause）

**sotto voce**〔'sɑto'votʃɪ〕*adj., adv.* 輕聲的（地）（under the breath; in an undertone; privately, as in a *sotto voce* remark）

Exercise：請由 **Group 7～10** 中，選出最適當的字，填入空格中。

1. My old briefcase can hold more books and papers than this new _____.

2. The host filled his guests' wineglasses from a freshly opened bottle of _____.

3. The complicated disagreement about this year's budget is similar to the _____ we had about last year's budget.

4. Philip's cold prevented him from eating his dinner with his usual _____.

5. The versatile young musician has won fame not only as a conductor and composer, but also as a(n) _____ at the piano.

6. Because of the ridiculous failure of last year's amateur show, we are determined that this year's performance will not likewise become a(n) _____.

7. All eyes were riveted on the _____ as he raised his baton to begin the concert.

8. I did not hear what the proprietor said to the salesman, for they conferred _____.

9. The tourist relies on the taxicab in New York City and on the _____ in Venice.

10. While in prison, Edmond Dantès learned of an immense fortune concealed in an underground _____ on the island of Monte Cristo.

# REVIEW ★

**Exercise 1：選出正確答案。**

(　) 1. A(n) ＿＿＿＿ choir performs without accompaniment.

(A) a cappella　　　　(B) cantata

(　) 2. A ＿＿＿＿ is a musical composition requiring an entire orchestra, but featuring a solo instrument such as the piano or violin.

(A) sonata　　　　(B) concerto

(　) 3. When Ulysses returned ＿＿＿＿ to his palace, he was recognized by his dog Argus.

(A) incognito　　　　(B) falsetto

(　) 4. The anchored fleet welcomed the chief of state with a thunderous ＿＿＿＿.

(A) salvo　　　　(B) staccato

(　) 5. An impression made from an ＿＿＿＿ results in an image in relief.

(A) imbroglio　　　　(B) intaglio

( ) 6. The overworked executive longed for the _____ of a
  Caribbean cruise.
  (A) sotto voce            (B) dolce far niente

( ) 7. With the orchestra and balcony seats completely sold out,
  only a few _____ tickets are available.
  (A) mezzanine            (B) mezzotint

( ) 8. To achieve a smooth and flowing effect, my teacher
  advised me to play the first two measures _____.
  (A) tremolo              (B) legato

( ) 9. For an example of a crescendo from pianissimo all the
  way to _____, listen to Grieg's *In the Hall of the
  Mountain King*.
  (A) prestissimo          (B) fortissimo

( ) 10. A _____ sketch achieves its effects solely by shadings
  between black and white.
  (A) chiaroscuro          (B) terra cotta

Exercise 2：下列各題五個答案中，只有一個是斜體字的同義字或反義
  字，請選出來。

( ) 1. *canto*
  (A) pace        (B) lore        (C) solo
  (D) division    (E) cantata

( ) 2. *piano*
  (A) crescendo      (B) forte      (C) legato
  (D) decrescendo    (E) alto

第
七
章

(    )   3. *grotto*

     (A) cave           (B) terra cotta       (C) crash

     (D) trunk         (E) veranda

(    )   4. *cameo*

     (A) patina         (B) tempera        (C) intaglio

     (D) campanile     (E) bagatelle

(    )   5. *imbroglio*

     (A) disagreeable     (B) fiasco         (C) pianissimo

     (D) diminuendo     (E) agreement

(    )   6. *sforzando*

     (A) unstressed      (B) dignified      (C) brisk

     (D) sweet         (E) slow

(    )   7. *torso*

     (A) armless        (B) statue        (C) trunk

     (D) largo          (E) legless

(    )   8. *antipasto*

     (A) Chianti        (B) hors d'oeuvres   (C) piazza

     (D) gusto          (E) apéritif

(    )   9. *crescendo*

     (A) salvo          (B) pizzicato      (C) applause

     (D) diminuendo     (E) soprano

(    ) 10. *piazza*

     (A) pizza          (B) square        (C) town

     (D) rotunda       (E) column

第七章

Exercise 3：類比

( ) 1. DESSERT : ANTIPASTO
    (A) grave : prestissimo      (B) basso : soprano
    (C) entrée : hors d'oeuvres    (D) play : denouement
    (E) finale : overture

( ) 2. STAR : FILM
    (A) composer : sonata      (B) soloist : concerto
    (C) aria : vocalist      (D) drama : protagonist
    (E) actress : cast

( ) 3. COGNOSCENTE : DILETTANTE
    (A) uncle : aunt      (B) professional : amateur
    (C) odor : aroma      (D) ignoramus : connoisseur
    (E) artist : patron

( ) 4. INCOGNITO : IDENTITY
    (A) novel : pen name      (B) masquerade : disguise
    (C) pseudonym : authorship    (D) fiction : real
    (E) anonymous : unknown

( ) 5. TORSO : STATUE
    (A) trunk : tree      (B) dismember : intact
    (C) shard : vase      (D) atom : nucleus
    (E) violinist : orchestra

( ) 6. PATINA : TIME
    (A) white hair : age      (B) aging : wine
    (C) burn : acid      (D) mellowing : cheese
    (E) incrustation : dirty

第七章

(    ) 7. LENTO : TEMPO

       (A) gondola : canal        (B) papers : portfolio

       (C) Chianti : meal        (D) piano : volume

       (E) allegro : loudness

(    ) 8. ROTUNDA : CUPOLA

       (A) bottom : top        (B) dome : tower

       (C) edifice : dome        (D) room : building

       (E) base : mountain

(    ) 9. CANTO : LONG POEM

       (A) volume : encyclopedia

       (B) sergeant : commander-in-chief

       (C) music : poetry        (D) pianist : concerto

       (E) incident : full-length play

(    ) 10. CHORD : ARPEGGIO

       (A) salvo : performer

       (B) simultaneously : successively

       (C) chorus : conductor        (D) unit : series

       (E) presto : tempo

---

【解答】

| | | | | | | | | |
|---|---|---|---|---|---|---|---|---|
| **Ex 1.** | 1. A | 2. B | 3. A | 4. A | 5. B | 6. B | 7. A | 8. B |
| | 9. B | 10. A | | | | | | |
| **Ex 2.** | 1. D | 2. B | 3. A | 4. C | 5. E | 6. A | 7. C | 8. B |
| | 9. D | 10. B | | | | | | |
| **Ex 3.** | 1. E | 2. B | 3. B | 4. C | 5. A | 6. A | 7. D | 8. C |
| | 9. A | 10. D | | | | | | |

# 第八章
## 出自西班牙文的英文字彙

> 英文採用了許多西班牙文,應該不會令你驚訝。西班牙治理這個國家的廣大土地,包括佛羅里達州和西南部達數世紀之久。儘管西班牙的威望衰退了,事實上,今天中美洲和南美洲所有的地方和西印度群島、菲律賓群島,及其他極多的地方都說西班牙文。西班牙文是世界主要的語言之一,它當然對英語產生影響。

## 【Group 1】

### 有關人的字

Group 1～3

**aficionado**〔ə͵fɪsjə'nado〕*n.* 1. 熱愛者;…迷(person very enthusiastic about anything) 2. 運動迷(sports devotee)

**caballero**〔͵kæbəl'jɛro〕*n.* 1. 西班牙紳士(gentleman or gallant) 2.(美國南部)騎師;騎馬者(horseman)

**conquistador**〔kɑn'kwɪstə͵dɔr〕*n.* 征服者(conqueror)

**desperado**〔͵dɛspə'rado , -'redo〕*n.* 亡命之徒;暴徒(bold, reckless criminal)

**duenna**〔dju'ɛnə , ͵du-〕*n.* 少女的媬姆(elderly woman chaperone of a young lady; governess)

**gaucho**〔'gautʃo〕*n.* 高楚牧人(南美洲之牧人,爲西班牙人及印地安人之混血種族)(Argentine cowboy of mixed Spanish and Indian descent)

**grandee**〔grænˊdi〕*n*. 1. 大公（西班牙、葡萄牙貴族的最高爵位）
（nobleman of the highest rank）
2. 大官；大人物；顯貴之人（person of eminence）

**hidalgo**〔hɪˊdælgo〕*n*. 西班牙的次級貴族（nobleman of the
second class〔not so high as a *grandee*〕）

**junta**〔ˊdʒʌntə〕*n*. 1.（以武力奪取政權的）軍政府（a group of
military officers ruling a country after seizing power） 2.（中南
美洲的）議會；會議（council for legislation or administration）

**junto**〔ˊdʒʌnto〕*n*. 1.（政治上的）祕密結社（political faction）
2. 私黨；陰謀團體（group of plotters; clique）

**matador**〔ˊmætə͵dor, -dɔr〕*n*. 鬥牛士（鬥牛至最後階段，手持
劍刺死牛的主角）（bullfighter assigned to kill the bull）

**mestizo**〔mɛsˊtizo〕*n*. 混血兒（尤指拉丁民族與印第安族的）
（person of mixed〔usually Spanish and American Indian〕blood）

**peon**〔ˊpiən〕*n*. 1. 勞工；非技術工人（common laborer） 2. 被強
制勞役以還債的工人（worker kept in service to repay a debt）

**picador**〔ˊpɪkə͵dor〕*n*. 騎馬鬥牛士；鬥牛士的助手（於鬥牛開
始時，騎馬以槍刺牛使其發怒）（horseman in a bullfight who
irritates the bull with a lance）

**picaro**〔ˊpɪkəro〕*n*. 1. 流浪漢（vagabond〔A *picaresque* novel is
one that has a *picaro*, a rogue or vagabond, as the hero.〕）
2. 無賴（rogue; knave）

**renegade**〔ˊrɛnɪ͵ged〕*n*. 1. 叛徒（turncoat; traitor） 2. 叛教；
叛黨者（apostate〔deserter〕from a religion, party, etc.）

**señor**〔senˊjɔr〕*n*. 先生（gentleman; Mr. or Sir）

**señora**〔sen'jorə〕*n.* 女士；太太（lady; Mrs. or Madam）

**señorita**〔‚senjə'ritə〕*n.* 小姐（young lady; Miss）

**toreador**〔'tɔrɪə‚dɔr〕*n.*（騎馬的）鬥牛士（bullfighter, usually mounted）

**torero**〔to'rero〕*n.* 徒步的鬥牛士（bullfighter on foot）

**vaquero**〔vɑ'kero〕*n.*（美國西南部的）牧羊人；牧童（herdsman; cowboy）

Exercise：請由 **Group 1** 中，選出最適當的字，填入空格中。

1. The onetime Democrat who joined the Republican Party was regarded as a(n) ＿＿＿＿ by some of his former Democratic colleagues.

2. In the Old West, it was common for a stagecoach to be robbed by a(n) ＿＿＿＿.

3. A(n) ＿＿＿＿ is a nobleman of higher rank than a hidalgo.

4. Without an education or a skilled trade, you may earn little more than the wages of a(n) ＿＿＿＿.

5. The average fan attends two or three games a season, but the ＿＿＿＿ goes to many more.

6. Columbus was not a(n) ＿＿＿＿; he engineered no military conquests as Cortez in Mexico and Pizarro in Peru did.

7. The ＿＿＿＿ was chaperoned by her duenna.

8. The ruler ordered the arrest of all members of the ＿＿＿＿ involved in the plot against his regime.

9. Before slaying the bull, the _____ thrills the spectators by gracefully evading its charges.

10. The Spanish expressions for "Mr." and "Mrs." are _____ and _____.

【解答】
1. renegade    2. desperado    3. grandee
4. peon        5. aficionado   6. conquistador
7. señorita    8. junto        9. torero/matador
10. señor ; señora

## 【Group 2】

# 有關建築、穿著等的字

**adobe**〔ə'dobɪ〕*n.* 1. 泥磚；土坯（brick of sun-dried clay or mud）
2. 泥磚砌成的房屋；土坯屋（常見於美國西南部及墨西哥）
（structure made of such bricks）

**bolero**〔bə'lɛro〕*n.* 1. 波麗露舞（以三四拍子，稍快的速度，以響板擊打節奏來配合）（lively dance in ¾ time）
2. 波麗露舞曲（the music for this dance）
3.〔bo'lɛro〕*n.* 女用短上衣（short, loose jacket）

**bonanza**〔bo'nænzə〕*n.*（埋藏量）豐富的礦脈（accidental discovery of a rich mass of ore in a mine）

**bravado**〔brə'vɑdo〕*n.* 1. 虛張聲勢（pretense of bravery）
2. 逞強的行動（boastful behavior）

**cabana**〔ka'banja〕*n.*（海濱等處的）浴室（beach shelter resembling a cabin）

**castanets**〔͵kæstə'nɛts〕*n. pl.* 響板（hand instruments clicked together to accompany music or dancing）

**fiesta**〔fɪ'ɛstə〕*n.* 宗教節日；假日（religious holiday; any festival or holiday）

**flotilla**〔flo'tɪlə〕*n.* 小艦隊；小船隊（small fleet; fleet of small vessels）

**hacienda**〔͵hɑsɪ'ɛndə〕*n.* 大莊園；大牧場（large ranch）；大農場（plantation）；莊園住宅（the main house on a hacienda, where the owner lives）

**incommunicado**〔͵ɪnkə͵mjunɪ'kɑdo〕*adj.* 被單獨監禁的；不得與他人接觸的（deprived of communication with others）

**mantilla**〔mæn'tɪlə〕*n.* 1. 連披肩的頭紗（woman's light scarf or veil）　2. 女用小披肩（cloak or cape）

**olio**〔'olɪ͵o〕*n.* 混雜物；雜燴；什錦菜（mixture; hodgepodge; medley）

**peccadillo**〔͵pɛkə'dɪlo〕*n.* 輕罪；小過失（slight offense）

**poncho**〔'pɑntʃo〕*n.* 龐喬斗蓬；南美人的披風式外套（large cloth, often waterproof, with a slit for the head）

**pueblo**〔'pwɛblo〕*n.* 普魏布勒印地安人的村莊（Indian village built of adobe and stone）

**siesta**〔sɪ'ɛstə〕*n.* 午睡（short, rest, especially at midday）

**tortilla**〔tɔr'tija〕*n.*（墨西哥）玉米薄餅（thin, flat, round corn cake）

Exercise：請由 **Group 2** 中，選出最適當的字，填入空格中。

1. Have you ever seen graceful Spanish dancers do the bolero to the accompaniment of clicking _____.

2. For every prospector who struck a(n) _____, there were countless others whose finds were disappointing.

3. Cheating on an examination is no _____, but a serious infraction of ethics.

4. You may be surprised to learn that a house made of _____ can last for more than a hundred years.

5. The ruffian's defiant challenge turned out to be mere _____, for when I offered to fight him, he backed down.

6. Our Latin American neighbors celebrate a(n) _____ by wearing brightly colored costumes and by singing and dancing.

7. By midafternoon, the whole _____ of fishing vessels had returned to port with the day's catch.

8. A gaucho often carries a(n) _____, which he uses as a blanket or wears as a cape.

9. When the afternoon heat is most intense, Carlos takes a short _____ before resuming his work.

10. Mexicans are very fond of the _____, a thin, flat, round cake made of corn.

【解答】
| | | |
|---|---|---|
| 1. castanets | 2. bonanza | 3. peccadillo |
| 4. adobe | 5. bravado | 6. fiesta |
| 7. flotilla | 8. poncho | 9. siesta |
| 10. tortilla | | |

## 【Group 3】

# 有關地方、動物等的字

**arroyo**〔əˈrɔɪo〕*n.* 易乾涸的小溪；旱谷（watercourse; small, often dry, gully）

**bronco**〔ˈbraŋko〕*n.* 北美野馬（half-wild pony）（= *broncho*）

**burro**〔ˈbɝo , ˈburo〕*n.*（馱貨用的）小毛驢（small donkey used as a pack animal）

**canyon**[3]〔ˈkænjən〕*n.* 峽谷（deep valley with high, steep slopes, often with a stream flowing through it; as the Colorado River in the Grand *Canyon*）

**indigo**〔ˈɪndɪˌgo〕*n., adj.* 1. 靛藍色（的）；深紫藍色（的）（deep violet blue）　2. 產靛之豌豆科植物（plant yielding a blue dye）

**mañana**〔mɑˈnjɑnɑ〕*n.* 明天（tomorrow）

**mesa**〔ˈmesə〕*n.* 台地（flat-topped rocky hill with steeply sloping sides）

**mustang**〔ˈmʌstæŋ〕*n.* 北美野馬（bronco）

**pampas**〔ˈpæmpəz〕*n.* 彭巴斯草原；南美大草原（尤指阿根廷）（vast, treeless, grassy plains, especially in Argentina）

**sierra** 〔 sɪ'ɛrə 〕 *n.* 齒狀山脈；山峯如鋸齒狀直立的山脈 ( ridge of mountains with an irregular, serrated 〔 saw-toothed 〕 outline )

Exercise：請由 **Group 3** 中，選出最適當的字，填入空格中。

1. A Hopi Indian village was secure against enemy attacks because it was built on top of a steeply sloping, flat-topped _____ .

2. The blue dye formerly obtained from the _____ plant can now be made artificially.

3. Do today's work today; don't postpone it to _____ .

4. In desert areas of Mexico and our own Southwest, the _____ is used for carrying heavy loads.

5. The _____ in Argentina are famous for their cattle, corn, and wheat.

┌─ 【解答】 ────────────────────────┐
│ 1. mesa        2. indigo       3. mañana │
│ 4. burro       5. pampas                 │
└──────────────────────────────────────┘

 **REVIEW** ★

Exercise 1：選出正確答案。

( ) 1. The _____ has become an institution in climates where the oppressive midday sun makes activity difficult.
    (A) fiesta      (B) vendetta      (C) bourgeoisie
    (D) siesta      (E) bolero

第八章

( ) 2. To maintain anonymity, the leader of the junto employed
a _____.
(A) lackey      (B) grandee      (C) pseudonym
(D) mantilla      (E) peon

( ) 3. _____ are Argentine cowboys who inhabit the _____.
(A) Gauchos…pampas      (B) Caballeros…mesas
(C) Desperadoes…sierras      (D) Vaqueros…pueblos
(E) Picaros…adobes

( ) 4. A famous painting by Murillo depicts a smiling señorita
looking down from a window with her mantilla-clad
_____ by her side.
(A) protégée      (B) aficionado      (C) duenna
(D) grandee      (E) fiancé

( ) 5. Benedict Arnold was the _____ American
Revolutionary general whose plot to surrender West Point
resulted in a _____.
(A) patriotic…vendetta      (B) renegade…coup d'état
(C) brilliant…junto      (D) turncoat…fiasco
(E) apostate…détente

Exercise 2：下列各題五個答案中，只有一個是斜體字的同義字或反義
字，請選出來。

( ) 1. *duenna*
(A) duet      (B) biennial      (C) chaperone
(D) twosome      (E) fiancé

( ) 2. *indigo*
(A) needy      (B) sugar      (C) clay
(D) native      (E) blue

第八章

( ) 3. *peccadillo*

    (A) erroneous     (B) groundhog     (C) alligator

    (D) petty officer     (E) serious offense

( ) 4. *olio*

    (A) grease     (B) mixture     (C) fuel

    (D) page     (E) confusing

( ) 5. *grandee*

    (A) peon     (B) river     (C) niece

    (D) dam     (E) canyon

( ) 6. *aficionado*

    (A) zeal     (B) actress     (C) enthusiast

    (D) trifler     (E) fictional hero

( ) 7. *conquistadors*

    (A) discoverers     (B) conquests     (C) explorers

    (D) conquerors     (E) unvanquished

( ) 8. *renegade*

    (A) infidel     (B) desperado     (C) rogue

    (D) villain     (E) turncoat

( ) 9. *arroyo*

    (A) dart     (B) gully     (C) mesa

    (D) waterfall     (E) bronco

( ) 10. *siesta*

    (A) holiday     (B) sojourn     (C) fiesta

    (D) vigil     (E) nap

第八章

## Exercise 3：類比

( ) 1. MATADOR : PICADOR
  (A) bravado : courage
  (B) coup de grâce : initial blow  (C) overture : finale
  (D) preface : conclusion  (E) toreador : torero

( ) 2. BONANZA : MINER
  (A) legacy : heir  (B) crop : farmer
  (C) diploma : student  (D) jackpot : gambler
  (E) bull's-eye : marksman

( ) 3. ADOBE : PUEBLO
  (A) settlement : Indian  (B) cabana : beach
  (C) terra cotta : clay  (D) seaport : flotilla
  (E) concrete : turnpike

( ) 4. OLIO : INGREDIENT
  (A) concerto : instrument  (B) medley : air
  (C) potpourri : confusion  (D) entrée : dessert
  (E) aria : opera

( ) 5. SIERRA : CANYON
  (A) soprano : bass  (B) arroyo : mesa
  (C) indigo : red  (D) grandee : hidalgo
  (E) monarch : retinue

第八章

----【解答】----------------------------------------------

**Ex 1.** 1. D  2. C  3. A  4. C  5. D

**Ex 2.** 1. C  2. E  3. E  4. B  5. A  6. C  7. D  8. E
  9. B  10. E

**Ex 3.** 1. B  2. D  3. E  4. A  5. A

# 第九章
# 字彙的舉一反三 — 衍生字

## 何謂衍生字（Derivative）

　　一個字在加上字首、字尾…等變化型式之後，可產生出許多新的字，這些新的字就叫衍生字，譬如：

| 字首（Prefix） | | 字 | | 衍 生 字（Derivative） |
|---|---|---|---|---|
| with | + | hold | = | withhold（抑制） |
| (back) | | | | (hold back) |

| 字 | | 字尾（Suffix） | | 衍 生 字（Derivative） |
|---|---|---|---|---|
| literate（識字的） | + | ly | = | literately（有文化修養地） |
| (educated) | | (manner) | | (in an educated manner) |

| 字首（Prefix） | 字 | 字尾（Suffix） | | 衍 生 字（Derivative） |
|---|---|---|---|---|
| semi | + literate + | ly | = | semiliterately（半文盲地） |
| (half; partly) | | | | (in a partly educated manner) |

　　現在讓我們再仔細地討論衍生字的各種型式：

## 1. 加上字首成衍生字

**規則：** 加字首時，不要刪減字母。保留字首和本來單字的所有字母。

| PREFIX | WORD | DERIVATIVE |
|---|---|---|
| dis + | similar（相似的） | = dissimilar（不相似的） |
| dis + | organized（有組織的） | = disorganized（雜亂無章的） |

| | | |
|---|---|---|
| un | + natural（自然的） | = unnatural（不自然的） |
| un | + acceptable（可接受的） | = unacceptable（不能接受的） |
| inter | + related（相關的） | = interrelated（互相關聯的） |
| inter | + action（行動） | = interaction（互動） |
| mis | + spelled（拼字） | = misspelled（拼錯的） |
| mis | + informed（通知） | = misinformed（被提供錯誤消息的） |

**Exercise 1：在第三欄中寫出加上字首後的衍生字。**

| I. PREFIX | II. WORD | III. DERIVATIVE |
|---|---|---|
| 1. over | + ripe（成熟的） | = ＿＿＿＿＿＿＿＿＿ |
| 2. dis | + integrate（整合） | = ＿＿＿＿＿＿＿＿＿ |
| 3. un | + necessary（必要的） | = ＿＿＿＿＿＿＿＿＿ |
| 4. anti | + aircraft（飛機） | = ＿＿＿＿＿＿＿＿＿ |
| 5. in | + audible（聽得見的） | = ＿＿＿＿＿＿＿＿＿ |
| 6. under | + rated（評價） | = ＿＿＿＿＿＿＿＿＿ |
| 7. fore | + seen（看見） | = ＿＿＿＿＿＿＿＿＿ |
| 8. extra | + ordinary（一般的） | = ＿＿＿＿＿＿＿＿＿ |
| 9. un | + noticed（注意到） | = ＿＿＿＿＿＿＿＿＿ |
| 10. with | + held（握住） | = ＿＿＿＿＿＿＿＿＿ |
| 11. e | + migrate（遷移） | = ＿＿＿＿＿＿＿＿＿ |

12. mis + spent（花費） = _____

13. over + estimated（估計） = _____

14. dis + interred（埋葬〔屍體〕）= _____

15. semi + circle（圓） = _____

16. un + nerve（神經；勇氣） = _____

17. pre + existence（存在） = _____

18. dis + solution（解決） = _____

19. extra + curricular（課程的） = _____

20. un + navigable（可航行的） = _____

21. over + run（跑；蔓延） = _____

22. in + appropriate（適當的） = _____

23. semi + autonomous（自治的） = _____

24. dis + satisfied（滿意的） = _____

25. un + abridged（刪節） = _____

26. micro + organism（生物） = _____

27. re + entry（進入） = _____

28. inter + relationship（關係） = _____

29. sub + ordinate（縱座標） = _____

30. retro + actively（活躍地） = _____

【解答】

| | | |
|---|---|---|
| 1. overripe（過熟的） | 2. disintegrate（使瓦解） | 3. unnecessary（不必要的） |
| 4. antiaircraft（防空的） | 5. inaudible（聽不見的） | 6. underrated（被低估的） |
| 7. foreseen（可預見的） | 8. extraordinary（不尋常的） | 9. unnoticed（沒被注意到的） |
| 10. withheld（抑制） | 11. emigrate（移出） | 12. misspent（浪費的） |
| 13. overestimated（高估的） | 14. disinterred（挖出〔屍體〕） | 15. semicircle（半圓形） |
| 16. unnerve（使緊張） | 17. preexistence（前世） | 18. dissolution（溶解） |
| 19. extracurricular（課外的） | 20. unnavigable（不能航行的） | 21. overrun（〔雜草〕蔓延於） |
| 22. inappropriate（不適當的） | 23. semiautonomous（半自治的） | 24. dissatisfied（不滿意的） |
| 25. unabridged（未刪節的） | 26. microorganism（微生物） | 27. reentry（再進入） |
| 28. interrelationship（相互關係） | 29. subordinate（下級的） | 30. retroactively（有追溯效力地） |

第九章

# 2. 加上字首 UN 或 IN 成衍生字

加上字首 UN 或 IN 後，成否定意思，例如：

PREFIX　　　　WORD　　　　　DERIVATIVE

un ＋ remunerative（有利益的）＝ unremunerative（無利益的）
(*not*)　　　(*gainful*)　　　　　(*not gainful*)

in ＋ tangible（可觸摸的）　＝ intangible（不可觸摸的）
(*not*)　(*capable of being touched*)　(*not capable of being touched*)

如果你不確定到底要加 UN 或 IN，就查閱字典。

**IN 的變化型式：**

1. *l* 之前，IN 轉變成 IL，如 *illegal*（非法的）, *illiterate*（不識字的）等。

2. *b, m* 或 *p* 之前，IN 轉變成 IM，如 *imbalance*（不平衡），*immature*（不成熟的）, *improper*（不適當的）等。

3. *r* 之前，IN 轉變成 IR，如 *irrational*（不理性的）, *irresistible*（不可抗拒的）等。

另外兩種較少見的否定字首是 DIS，如 *disagreeable*（令人討厭的），和 A，如 *atypical*（非典型的）。

Exercise 2：將第二欄的字加上適當的否定字首（在第一欄中）*in, il, im,* 或 *ir*，然後將完成的否定字填入第三欄中（如第一行中的例字）。

| I. NEGATIVE PREFIX | II. WORD | III. NEGATIVE WORD |
|---|---|---|
| 1.   in   + | gratitude（感激的） = | ingratitude（忘恩負義） |
| 2. _____ + | patiently（有耐心地） = | _____ |
| 3. _____ + | responsible（負責任的） = | _____ |
| 4. _____ + | equitable（公正的） = | _____ |
| 5. _____ + | moderate（適度的） = | _____ |
| 6. _____ + | literacy（識字） = | _____ |
| 7. _____ + | replaceable（可替代的） = | _____ |
| 8. _____ + | consistently（一致地） = | _____ |

9. ＿＿＿＿ + personal（個人的） = ＿＿＿＿＿＿＿＿＿＿＿＿

10. ＿＿＿＿ + legible（易讀的） = ＿＿＿＿＿＿＿＿＿＿＿＿

11. ＿＿＿＿ + plausible（貌似可信的） = ＿＿＿＿＿＿＿＿＿＿＿＿

12. ＿＿＿＿ + articulate（口齒清晰的） = ＿＿＿＿＿＿＿＿＿＿＿＿

13. ＿＿＿＿ + material（物質） = ＿＿＿＿＿＿＿＿＿＿＿＿

14. ＿＿＿＿ + reversible（可逆的） = ＿＿＿＿＿＿＿＿＿＿＿＿

15. ＿＿＿＿ + security（安全） = ＿＿＿＿＿＿＿＿＿＿＿＿

16. ＿＿＿＿ + liberal（自由的） = ＿＿＿＿＿＿＿＿＿＿＿＿

17. ＿＿＿＿ + perceptibly（能察覺地） = ＿＿＿＿＿＿＿＿＿＿＿＿

18. ＿＿＿＿ + flexible（有彈性的） = ＿＿＿＿＿＿＿＿＿＿＿＿

19. ＿＿＿＿ + relevant（相關的） = ＿＿＿＿＿＿＿＿＿＿＿＿

20. ＿＿＿＿ + moral（道德的） = ＿＿＿＿＿＿＿＿＿＿＿＿

第九章

【解答】

| | | |
|---|---|---|
| 1. ingratitude（忘恩負義） | 2. impatiently（不耐煩地） | 3. irresponsible（不負責任的） |
| 4. inequitable（不公平的） | 5. immoderate（無節制的） | 6. illiteracy（不識字） |
| 7. irreplaceable（不能替代的） | 8. inconsistently（不一致地） | 9. impersonal（沒有人情味的） |
| 10. illegible（難讀的） | 11. implausible（令人難以置信的） | 12. inarticulate（不善言辭的） |
| 13. immaterial（非物質的） | 14. irreversible（不可逆的） | 15. insecurity（不安全） |
| 16. illiberal（不自由的） | 17. imperceptibly（不可察覺地） | 18. inflexible（無彈性的） |
| 19. irrelevant（不相關的） | 20. immoral（不道德的） | |

# 3. 加上字尾成衍生字

規則：加字尾時，不要刪減字母，保留原來單字的所有字母和所有字尾，但原字字尾是 *y* 或是不發音的 *e* 時例外。

| WORD | SUFFIX | DERIVATIVE |
|---|---|---|
| accidental（意外的） | + ly | = accidentally（意外地） |
| drunken（喝醉的） | + ness | = drunkenness（酒醉） |
| banjo（班卓琴） | + ist | = banjoist（班卓琴師） |
| ski（滑雪） | + ing | = skiing（滑雪） |

Exercise 3：將正確的衍生字填入第三欄中。

| I. WORD | II. SUFFIX | III. DERIVATIVE |
|---|---|---|
| 1. govern（統治） | + ment | = _____ |
| 2. tail（尾巴） | + less | = _____ |
| 3. synonym（同義字） | + ous | = _____ |
| 4. radio（無線電） | + ed | = _____ |
| 5. unilateral（單方面的） | + ly | = _____ |
| 6. ego（自我） | + ism | = _____ |
| 7. sudden（突然的） | + ness | = _____ |
| 8. room（房間） | + mate | = _____ |
| 9. ski（滑雪） | + er | = _____ |
| 10. foresee（預見） | + able | = _____ |

第九章

11. solo（獨奏）　　　　+　ist　　=　_____

12. beach（海灘）　　　+　head　=　_____

13. head（頭）　　　　　+　dress　=　_____

14. book（書；帳簿）　　+　keeper =　_____

15. Hindu（印度教的）　+　ism　　=　_____

┌─ 【解答】 ─────────────────────┐

1. government
（政府）

2. tailless
（無尾的）

3. synonymous
（同義的）

4. radioed
（用無線電發送的）

5. unilaterally
（單方面地）

6. egoism
（自我中心主義）

7. suddenness
（突然）

8. roommate
（室友）

9. skier
（滑雪的人）

10. foreseeable
（可預見的）

11. soloist
（獨奏者）

12. beachhead
（灘頭堡）

13. headdress
（頭飾）

14. bookkeeper
（簿記員）

15. Hinduism
（印度教）

└─────────────────────────────┘

# 4. 字尾為 y 的字如何形成衍生字

規則 1：如果 *y* 之前是個子音，加字尾前先改 *y* 為 *i*。

| WORD | SUFFIX | DERIVATIVE |
|------|--------|------------|
| hurry（趕快） | + ed | = hurried（匆忙的） |
| spicy（辣的） | + est | = spiciest（最辣的） |
| heavy（重的） | + ness | = heaviness（重） |
| greedy（貪心的） | + ly | = greedily（貪心地） |

例外 1：字尾加 *ing* 時，*y* 不變。

hurry（趕快）　　　　+　ing　　=　hurrying（匆忙）

falsify（偽造） ＋ ing ＝ falsifying（偽造）

例外 2：記下這些特殊的例外：dryly（乾燥地）, dryness（乾燥）,
shyly（害羞地）, shyness（害羞）, babyish（嬰兒般的）,
ladylike（淑女的）。

規則 2：*如果 y 之前是母音，加字尾前 y 不改。*

betray（出賣） ＋ al ＝ betrayal（出賣）
convey（傳送） ＋ ed ＝ conveyed（傳達）
joy（高興） ＋ ful ＝ joyful（高興的）

例外：daily（每天）, laid（放置）, paid（支付）, said（說）。

Exercise 4：將正確的衍生字填入第三欄中。

| I. WORD | II. SUFFIX | III. DERIVATIVE |
|---|---|---|
| 1. decay（腐爛） | ＋ ed | ＝ _____ |
| 2. fancy（幻想） | ＋ ful | ＝ _____ |
| 3. stealthy（隱密的） | ＋ ly | ＝ _____ |
| 4. foolhardy（有勇無謀的） | ＋ ness | ＝ _____ |
| 5. magnify（放大） | ＋ ing | ＝ _____ |
| 6. plucky（有勇氣的） | ＋ est | ＝ _____ |
| 7. defy（公然反抗） | ＋ ance | ＝ _____ |
| 8. overpay（付給…過多） | ＋ ed | ＝ _____ |
| 9. accompany（陪伴） | ＋ ment | ＝ _____ |

第九章

10. costly（昂貴的） ＋ ness ＝ _____

11. ceremony（典禮） ＋ ous ＝ _____

12. deny（否認） ＋ al ＝ _____

13. momentary（片刻的） ＋ ly ＝ _____

14. crafty（狡猾的） ＋ er ＝ _____

15. display（展示） ＋ ed ＝ _____

16. bury（埋） ＋ al ＝ _____

17. contrary（相反的） ＋ wise ＝ _____

18. oversupply（供應過多） ＋ ing ＝ _____

19. harmony（和諧） ＋ ous ＝ _____

20. worry（擔心） ＋ some ＝ _____

第九章

【解答】

| | | |
|---|---|---|
| 1. decayed（腐爛的） | 2. fanciful（幻想的） | 3. stealthily（隱密地） |
| 4. foolhardiness（有勇無謀） | 5. magnifying（放大的） | 6. pluckiest（最有勇氣的） |
| 7. defiance（公然反抗） | 8. overpaid（付給…過多） | 9. accompaniment（附屬物） |
| 10. costliness（昂貴） | 11. ceremonious（講究禮節的） | 12. denial（否認） |
| 13. momentarily（短暫地） | 14. craftier（更狡猾的） | 15. displayed（展示的） |
| 16. burial（埋葬） | 17. contrariwise（反之亦然） | 18. oversupplying（供應過多的） |
| 19. harmonious（和諧的） | 20. worrisome（令人煩惱的） | |

Exercise 5：下列各題各有四個空格，第一格是原形容詞，請完成其他的衍生字。

I. ADJECTIVE　　　II. ADJECTIVE(-er)　　　III. ADJECTIVE(-est)

IV. ADVERB(-ly)　　　V. NOUN(-ness)

1. clumsy（笨拙的）　　clumsier（較笨拙的）　clumsiest（最笨拙的）
   clumsily（笨拙地）　clumsiness（笨拙）

2. _____　　noisier（較吵的）　　_____
   _____　　_____

3. _____　　_____　　sturdiest（最健壯的）
   _____

4. _____　　_____　　_____
   uneasily（不自在地）_____

5. _____　　_____　　_____
   _____　　greediness（貪心）

6. flimsy（薄弱的）　_____　　_____
   _____

7. _____　　wearier（較疲倦的）　_____
   _____

8. _____　　_____　　heartiest（最真摯的）
   _____

9. _____   _____   _____

warily（謹慎地）   _____

10. _____   _____   _____

_____   unhappiness（不快樂）

---

【解答】

1. 一

2. noisy          noisiest         noisily          noisiness
  （吵鬧的）      （最吵的）        （吵鬧地）       （吵鬧）

3. sturdy         sturdier         sturdily         sturdiness
  （健壯的）      （較健壯的）      （健壯地）       （健壯）

4. uneasy         uneasier         uneasiest        uneasiness
  （不自在的）    （較不自在的）    （最不自在的）   （不自在）

5. greedy         greedier         greediest        greedily
  （貪心的）      （較貪心的）      （最貪心的）     （貪心地）

6. flimsier       flimsiest        filmsily         flimsiness
  （較薄弱的）    （最薄弱的）      （薄弱地）       （薄弱）

7. weary          weariest         wearily          weariness
  （疲倦的）      （最疲倦的）      （疲倦地）       （疲倦）

8. hearty         heartier         heartily         heartiness
  （真摯的）      （較真摯的）      （真摯地）       （真摯）

9. wary           warier           wariest          wariness
  （謹慎的）      （較謹慎的）      （最謹慎的）     （謹慎）

10. unhappy       unhappier        unhappiest       unhappily
  （不快樂的）    （較不快樂的）    （最不快樂的）   （不快樂地）

---

## 5. 字尾爲不發音的 e 的字如何形成衍生字

規則 1：*所加的字尾若以母音開始，則原字尾的 e 去掉。*

| WORD | | SUFFIX | | DERIVATIVE |
|------|---|--------|---|------------|
| love（愛） | + | able | = | lovable（可愛的） |
| use（使用） | + | age | = | usage（用法） |
| produce（製造） | + | er | = | producer（製造者） |

例外 1：*以 ce 或 ge 結尾的字，在加以 a 或 o 開頭的字尾時，e 要保留。*

notice（注意到） + able = noticeable（引人注目的）
advantage（優點；利益）+ ous = advantageous（有利的）

例外 2：*記下這些例外*：acreage（畝數）, mileage（哩程數）, singeing（把…微微燒焦）, canoeing（划獨木舟）, hoeing（用鋤頭耕作）, shoeing（使穿鞋；給（馬）釘馬蹄鐵）。

規則 2：*所加的字尾若以子音開頭，則原字最後的 e 保留。*

| WORD | SUFFIX | DERIVATIVE |
|------|--------|------------|
| excite（使興奮） + | ment | = excitement（興奮） |
| care（小心） + | ful | = careful（小心地） |
| fierce（兇猛的） + | ly | = fiercely（兇猛地） |
| complete（完整的）+ | ness | = completeness（完整） |

例外：acknowledgment（承認）, judgment（判斷）, argument（爭論）, awful（可怕的）, duly（恰當地）, truly（真地）, wholly（完全地）, ninth（第九的）。

Exercise 6：在第三欄中填入正確的衍生字。

| I. WORD | II. SUFFIX | III. DERIVATIVE |
|---------|-----------|-----------------|
| 1. depreciate（貶值） | + ion | = _____ |
| 2. survive（存活） | + al | = _____ |
| 3. suspense（懸疑） | + ful | = _____ |

4. fatigue（疲勞）　　　　+ ing　　= _____

5. censure（責備）　　　　+ able　　= _____

6. acquiesce（默認）　　　+ ent　　= _____

7. nine（九）　　　　　　+ th　　= _____

8. hostile（有敵意的）　　+ ity　　= _____

9. malice（惡意）　　　　+ ious　　= _____

10. dawdle（遊手好閒）　　+ er　　= _____

11. reverse（顛倒）　　　　+ ible　　= _____

12. immaculate（潔淨的）　+ ly　　= _____

13. spine（脊椎）　　　　　+ less　　= _____

14. outrage（暴行）　　　　+ ous　　= _____

15. demote（降級）　　　　+ ion　　= _____

16. homogcnize（使均質）　+ ed　　= _____

17. recharge（充電）　　　　+ able　　= _____

18. abate（減少）　　　　　+ ment　　= _____

19. emancipate（解放）　　+ or　　= _____

20. dispute（爭論）　　　　+ able　　= _____

21. whole（整個的）　　　　+ ly　　= _____

22. provoke（激怒）　　　　+ ing　　= _____

23. argue（爭論）　　　+ ment　=＿＿＿＿＿＿＿＿＿＿

24. fragile（脆弱的）　　+ ity　=＿＿＿＿＿＿＿＿＿＿

25. replace（取代）　　　+ able　=＿＿＿＿＿＿＿＿＿＿

---

【解答】

| | | |
|---|---|---|
| 1. depreciation（貶值） | 2. survival（存活） | 3. suspenseful（提心吊膽的） |
| 4. fatiguing（令人疲勞的） | 5. censurable（該責備的） | 6. acquiescent（默認的） |
| 7. ninth（第九的） | 8. hostility（敵意） | 9. malicious（懷有惡意的） |
| 10. dawdler（遊手好閒的人） | 11. reversible（可逆的） | 12. immaculately（潔淨地） |
| 13. spineless（無脊椎的） | 14. outrageous（殘暴的） | 15. demotion（降級） |
| 16. homogenized（均質的） | 17. rechargeable（可再充電的） | 18. abatement（減少） |
| 19. emancipator（解放者） | 20. disputable（有爭論餘地的） | 21. wholly（完全地） |
| 22. provoking（令人生氣的） | 23. argument（爭論） | 24. fragility（脆弱） |
| 25. replaceable（可取代的） | | |

---

# 6. 字尾加 **ly** 成衍生字

加上 *ly*，形容詞可變成副詞：

| ADJECTIVE | | SUFFIX | | ADVERB |
|---|---|---|---|---|
| brave（勇敢的） | + | ly | = | bravely（勇敢地） |
| calm（冷靜的） | + | ly | = | calmly（冷靜地） |

例外：若形容詞以 *ic* 結尾，則加 *ly* 之前要先加 *al*。

heroic（英勇的）　 + *al* + ly 　 = heroically（英勇地）
specific（特定的）　 + *al* + ly 　 = specifically（明確地）

注意：大部分以 *ic* 結尾的形容詞都有另一個以 *ical* 結尾的型式。
如 philosophic（哲學的）和 philosophical（哲學的），
historic（歷史上重要的）和 historical（歷史的）等。

Exercise 7：把下列的形容詞改成副詞。

　　　　ADJECTIVE　　　　　　　　ADVERB

1. overwhelming（壓倒性的）＿＿＿＿＿＿＿＿＿＿＿＿

2. normal（正常的）　　　　＿＿＿＿＿＿＿＿＿＿＿＿

3. interscholastic（校際的）　＿＿＿＿＿＿＿＿＿＿＿＿

4. mutual（互相的）　　　　＿＿＿＿＿＿＿＿＿＿＿＿

5. amicable（友善的）　　　＿＿＿＿＿＿＿＿＿＿＿＿

6. conspicuous（引人注目的）＿＿＿＿＿＿＿＿＿＿＿＿

7. economic（經濟的）　　　＿＿＿＿＿＿＿＿＿＿＿＿

8. outspoken（直率的）　　　＿＿＿＿＿＿＿＿＿＿＿＿

9. graphic（生動的）　　　　＿＿＿＿＿＿＿＿＿＿＿＿

10. incontrovertible（無爭論餘地的）＿＿＿＿＿＿＿＿＿

11. punctual（準時的）　　　＿＿＿＿＿＿＿＿＿＿＿＿

12. exclusive（獨享的）　　　＿＿＿＿＿＿＿＿＿＿＿＿

13. unwary（不小心的）　　　＿＿＿＿＿＿＿＿＿＿＿＿

14. chronic（慢性的）　＿＿＿＿＿＿＿＿＿＿＿＿＿＿＿

15. synthetic（合成的）　＿＿＿＿＿＿＿＿＿＿＿＿＿＿＿

16. intermittent（間歇的）　＿＿＿＿＿＿＿＿＿＿＿＿＿＿

17. manual（手工的）　＿＿＿＿＿＿＿＿＿＿＿＿＿＿＿＿

18. heavy（重的）　＿＿＿＿＿＿＿＿＿＿＿＿＿＿＿＿＿

19. infallible（不會犯錯的）　＿＿＿＿＿＿＿＿＿＿＿＿＿

20. frantic（瘋狂的）　＿＿＿＿＿＿＿＿＿＿＿＿＿＿＿＿

---

**【解答】**

1. overwhelmingly
（壓倒性地）

2. normally
（通常）

3. interscholastically
（校際地）

4. mutually
（互相地）

5. amicably
（友善地）

6. conspicuously
（醒目地）

7. economically
（在經濟上）

8. outspokenly
（直率地）

9. graphically
（生動地）

10. incontrovertibly
（無可爭辯地）

11. punctually
（準時地）

12. exclusively
（專門地）

13. unwarily
（不謹慎地）

14. chronically
（慢性地）

15. synthetically
（以合成方式）

16. intermittently
（間歇地）

17. manually
（手工地）

18. heavily
（猛烈地）

19. infallibly
（絕對地）

20. frantically
（瘋狂地）

---

Exercise 8：寫出正確的加 *ic* 的形容詞，及再加 *ally* 的副詞，如以下兩個例子：

| I. NOUN | II. ADJECTIVE(-ic) | III. ADVERB(-ally) |
| --- | --- | --- |
| democracy<br>（民主政治） | democratic<br>（民主的） | democratically<br>（民主地） |

| optimism<br>（樂觀） | optimistic<br>（樂觀的） | optimistically<br>（樂觀地） |
|---|---|---|
| 1. autocracy（獨裁政治） | _____ | _____ |
| 2. stenography（速記） | _____ | _____ |
| 3. antagonist（反對者） | _____ | _____ |
| 4. pedagogy（教育學） | _____ | _____ |
| 5. economics（經濟學） | _____ | _____ |
| 6. astronomy（天文學） | _____ | _____ |
| 7. pediatrics（小兒科） | _____ | _____ |
| 8. bureaucracy（官僚政治） | _____ | _____ |
| 9. autobiography（自傳） | _____ | _____ |
| 10. symmetry（對稱） | _____ | _____ |

【解答】

1. autocratic, autocratically（獨裁的/獨裁地）
2. stenographic, stenographically（速記的/速記地）
3. antagonistic, antagonistically（反對的/反對地）
4. pedagogic, pedagogically（教育學的/教育學方面）
5. economic, economically（經濟上的/在經濟上）
6. astronomic, astronomically（天文學的/天文學上地）
7. pediatric, pediatrically（小兒科的/在小兒科方面）
8. bureaucratic, bureaucratically
　　（官僚政治的/官僚作風地）
9. autobiographic, autobiographically
　　（自傳的/以自傳的方式）
10. symmetric, symmetrically（對稱的/對稱地）

第九章

# 7. 要重覆字尾的衍生字

**規則 1：** *所加字尾的第一個字是母音，而原字又是單音節時，要重覆最後子音。*

| WORD | SUFFIXES | DERIVATIVES |
|------|----------|-------------|
| run（跑） | + ing, er | = running, runner（跑者） |
| stop（停止） | + ed, age | = stopped, stoppage（停止） |
| wet（濕的） | + er, est | = wetter, wettest |

**例外 1：** *如果最後的子音前面有兩個母音，則不必重覆最後子音。*

| sail（航行） | + ed, ing | = sailed, sailing |
|------|-----------|-------------------|
| kneel（跪下） | + ed, ing | = kneeled, kneeling |

**例外 2：** *如果最後的子音前面是另一個子音時，不必重覆最後子音。*

| halt（停止） | + ed, ing | = halted, halting |
|------|-----------|-------------------|
| ask（問） | + ed, ing | = asked, asking |

**規則 2：** *所加的字尾以母音開頭，而原字的重音節在最後時，要重覆最後的子音。*

| re′fer<br>（參考） | + ed, ing, al | = referred, referring,<br>referral（參考） |
|------|---------------|-------------------|
| trans′mit<br>（傳送） | + ed, ing, er | = transmitted, transmitting,<br>transmitter（發報機） |
| read′mit<br>（重新接納） | + ed, ing, ance | = readmitted, readmitting,<br>readmittance（重新接納） |

注意：此規則不適用於當最後的子音不在重音節時。

'credit　　　　　　+ ed, ing, or　= credited, crediting,
（將…記入貸方）　　　　　　　　　 creditor（債權人）

'limit（限制）　　+ ed, ing　　= limited, limiting

'offer　　　　　　+ ed, ing, er　= offered, offering,
（提供；報價）　　　　　　　　　　 offerer（報價人）

例外 1：此規則不適用於最後的子音前有兩個母音的情況。

contain（包含）　+ ed, ing, er　= contained, containing,
　　　　　　　　　　　　　　　　　　container（容器）

recoil（退縮）　　+ ed, ing　　= recoiled, recoiling

appeal（吸引）　 + ed, ing　　= appealed, appealing
　　　　　　　　　　　　　　　　　　（有吸引力的）

例外 2：此規則不適用於最後的子音前有另一個子音時。

condemn　+ ed, ing, able　= condemned, condemning,
（譴責）　　　　　　　　　　 condemnable（應受譴責的）

conduct　+ ed, ing, or　　= conducted, conducting,
（進行）　　　　　　　　　　 conductor（指揮）

例外 3：此規則不適用於重音節回到第一音節時。

re'fer（參考）　　　+ ence　　= 'reference（參考）

de'fer（使延期）　 + ence　　= 'deference（尊重）

in'fer（推論）　　 + ence　　= 'inference（推論）

但是：ex'cel（勝過別人）— 'excel*l*ent（優秀的）。

Exercise 9：在第三欄中寫出正確的衍生字，務必小心拼字。

　　　I. WORD　　　　II. SUFFIX　　III. DERIVATIVE

1. concur（同時發生）　　+ ing　　= ＿＿＿＿＿＿＿＿

2. entail（使必要） + ed = _____

3. abhor（痛恨） + ent = _____

4. flat（平的） + er = _____

5. retract（縮回） + able = _____

6. refer（參考） + al = _____

7. dispel（消除） + ed = _____

8. deter（阻礙） + ent = _____

9. ungag（解除禁止發言） + ed = _____

10. drum（鼓） + er = _____

11. elicit（引出） + ing = _____

12. imperil（危害） + ed = _____

13. absorb（吸收） + ent = _____

14. defer （推遲） + ence = _____

15. propel（推進） + ant = _____

16. inter（埋葬） + ing = _____

17. append（附加） + age = _____

18. covet（覬覦；垂涎） + ous = _____

19. discredit（使丟臉） + ed = _____

20. adapt（適應） + able = _____

21. cower（畏縮） + ing = _____

22. disinter（挖出屍體） + ed = _____

23. pilfer（偷竊） + er = _____

24. slim（苗條的） + est = _____

25. excel（勝過別人） + ent = _____

---【解答】--------------------------------

1. concurring
（同時發生的）

2. entailed
（使必要）

3. abhorrent
（令人憎惡的）

4. flatter
（奉承）

5. retractable
（可縮回的）

6. referral
（參考）

7. dispelled
（消除）

8. deterrent
（妨礙的）

9. ungagged
（解除禁止發言）

10. drummer
（鼓手）

11. eliciting
（引出）

12. imperiled
（危及）

13. absorbent
（有吸收力的）

14. deference
（尊重）

15. propellant
（推進的）

16. interring
（埋葬）

17. appendage
（附加物）

18. covetous
（貪圖的）

19. discredited
（名譽掃地的）

20. adaptable
（能適應的）

21. cowering
（畏縮）

22. disinterred
（挖出屍體）

23. pilferer
（小偷）

24. slimmest
（最苗條的）

25. excellent（優秀的）

第九章

**Exercise 10：依所給的字完成三個衍生字。**

1. regret（後悔） _____ing _____ed _____ful

2. sin（犯罪） _____ing _____ed _____er

3. patrol（巡邏） _____ing _____ed _____man

4. occur（發生） _____ing _____ed _____ence

5. adjourn（使延期） ＿＿＿＿ing ＿＿＿＿ed ＿＿＿＿ment

6. flip（輕拋） ＿＿＿＿ing ＿＿＿＿ed ＿＿＿＿ant

7. transmit（傳送） ＿＿＿＿ing ＿＿＿＿ed ＿＿＿＿er

8. profit（獲利） ＿＿＿＿ing ＿＿＿＿ed ＿＿＿＿able

9. defer（使延期） ＿＿＿＿ing ＿＿＿＿ed ＿＿＿＿ment

10. dissent（不同意） ＿＿＿＿ing ＿＿＿＿ed ＿＿＿＿er

11. protract（延長） ＿＿＿＿ing ＿＿＿＿ed ＿＿＿＿or

12. spot（看見） ＿＿＿＿ing ＿＿＿＿ed ＿＿＿＿er

13. commit（委託） ＿＿＿＿ing ＿＿＿＿ed ＿＿＿＿ment

14. excel（勝過別人） ＿＿＿＿ing ＿＿＿＿ed ＿＿＿＿ence

15. recur（再發生） ＿＿＿＿ing ＿＿＿＿ed ＿＿＿＿ent

第九章

---- 【解答】 ----------------------------------------
1. regretting, regretted, regretful（後悔/後悔/後悔的）
2. sinning, sinned, sinner（犯罪/犯罪/罪人）
3. patrolling, patrolled, patrolman（巡邏/巡邏/巡邏警察）
4. occurring, occurred, occurrence（發生/發生/事件）
5. adjourning, adjourned, adjournment（延期/延期/延期）
6. flipping, flipped, flippant（輕拋/輕拋/輕率的）
7. transmitting, transmitted, transmitter（傳送/傳送/發報機）
8. profiting, profited, profitable（獲利/獲利/有利可圖的）
9. deferring, deferred, deferment（使延期/使延期/延期）
10. dissenting, dissented, dissenter（不同意/不同意/反對者）
11. protracting, protracted, protractor（延長/延長/量角器）
12. spotting, spotted, spotter（看見/看見/監視人）
13. committing, committed, commitment（委託/委託/承諾）
14. excelling, excelled, excellence（勝過別人/勝過別人/優秀）
15. recurring, recurred, recurrent（一再發生的/再發生的/一再發生的）

# 8. 一些麻煩的衍生字

　　沒有簡單的規則能告訴你什麼時候要使用 *able* 或 *ible*，*er* 或 *or*，*ant* 或 *ent* 等。因此以這些麻煩的字尾結尾的字必須個別去記。平時應養成習慣多利用字典。

　　1. 加 *able* 或 *ible*。熟記下列的形容詞：

<table>
<tr><td colspan="2">ABLE</td><td colspan="2">IBLE</td></tr>
<tr><td>①</td><td>demonstrable（可證明的）</td><td>①</td><td>credible（可信的）</td></tr>
<tr><td>②</td><td>impregnable（堅不可摧的）</td><td>②</td><td>fallible（易犯錯的）</td></tr>
<tr><td>③</td><td>indisputable（無可爭辯的）</td><td>③</td><td>flexible（有彈性的）</td></tr>
<tr><td>④</td><td>memorable（難忘的）</td><td>④</td><td>illegible（難讀的）</td></tr>
<tr><td>⑤</td><td>navigable（可航行的）</td><td>⑤</td><td>incontrovertible（無可爭辯的）</td></tr>
<tr><td>⑥</td><td>returnable（可歸還的）</td><td>⑥</td><td>invincible（無敵的）</td></tr>
<tr><td>⑦</td><td>serviceable（合用的）</td><td>⑦</td><td>plausible（似真實的）</td></tr>
<tr><td>⑧</td><td>tenable（有道理的）</td><td>⑧</td><td>reprehensible（應受指責的）</td></tr>
<tr><td>⑨</td><td>unmanageable（難管理的）</td><td>⑨</td><td>resistible（可抵抗的）</td></tr>
</table>

　　注意：*以 able 結尾的形容詞，名詞字尾是 ability，以 ible 結尾的形容詞，名詞以 ibility 結尾。*

<table>
<tr><td>ADJECTIVE</td><td>NOUN</td></tr>
<tr><td>impregnable（堅不可摧）</td><td>impregnability（攻不破）</td></tr>
<tr><td>flexible（有彈性的）</td><td>flexibility（彈性）</td></tr>
<tr><td>venerable（可敬的）</td><td>venerability（值得尊敬）</td></tr>
<tr><td>invincible（無敵的）</td><td>invincibility（無敵）</td></tr>
</table>

第九章

2. 加 *er* 或 *or*。熟記下列的名詞：

| ER | OR |
|---|---|
| ① consumer（消費者） | ① aggressor（侵略者） |
| ② defender（保衛者） | ② censor（審查員） |
| ③ foreigner（外國人） | ③ creditor（債權人） |
| ④ mariner（水手） | ④ debtor（債務人） |
| ⑤ observer（觀察者） | ⑤ governor（州長） |
| ⑥ philosopher（哲學家） | ⑥ originator（創始者） |
| ⑦ reporter（記者） | ⑦ possessor（所有人） |
| ⑧ subscriber（訂閱者） | ⑧ progenitor（祖先） |
| ⑨ sympathizer（同情者） | ⑨ speculator（投機者） |

注意：*ate* 結尾的動詞變為名詞時，以 *or* 結尾，而不是 *er*。

| VERB | NOUN |
|---|---|
| demonstrate（示威） | demonstrator（示威者） |
| liberate（解放） | liberator（解放者） |

3. 加 *ant* 或 *ent*。熟記下列的形容詞：

| ANT | ENT |
|---|---|
| ① brilliant（燦爛的） | ① complacent（自滿的） |
| ② buoyant（有浮力的） | ② decent（高尚的） |
| ③ flamboyant（豔麗的） | ③ eloquent（口才好的） |
| ④ flippant（輕浮的） | ④ eminent（卓越的） |
| ⑤ fragrant（芳香的） | ⑤ iridescent（彩虹色的） |
| ⑥ malignant（惡性的） | ⑥ obsolescent（即將廢棄的） |
| ⑦ nonchalant（漠不關心的） | ⑦ pertinent（恰當的） |
| ⑧ poignant（令人痛苦的） | ⑧ potent（強有力的） |
| ⑨ relevant（相關的） | ⑨ recurrent（一再發生的） |
| ⑩ vacant（空的） | ⑩ repellent（令人厭惡的） |

第九章

注意：*以 ant 結尾的形容詞變成名詞時，以 ance 或 ancy 結尾。*

*以 ent 結尾的形容詞變成名詞時，以 ence 或 ency 結尾。*

| ADJECTIVE | NOUN |
|---|---|
| nonchalant（漠不關心的） | nonchalance（漠不關心） |
| eloquent（口才好的） | eloquence（口才） |
| vacant（空的） | vacancy（空房） |
| decent（高尚的） | decency（得體） |
| brilliant（燦爛的；聰明的） | brilliance（光輝；才華） |
| complacent（自滿的） | complacence（自滿） |

## Exercise 11：填空

1. inflex____ble（無彈性的）

2. ten____ncy（租賃）

3. vehem____nce（激烈）

4. benefact____r（恩人）

5. self-reli____nce（自力更生）

6. vis____bility（能見度）

7. dispens____r（藥劑師）

8. relev____nce（關聯）

9. infall____bility（無錯誤）

10. unchange____ble（不變的）

11. collaborat____r（合作者）

12. impregn____bility（攻不破）

13. reflect____r（反光裝置）

14. curr____ncy（貨幣）

15. correspond____nce（通信）

16. contend____r（爭奪者）

17. imperman____nt（非永久性的）

18. irrevers____ble（不可逆的）

19. inaccess____bility（難接近）

20. depend____nt（依賴的）

第九章

```
┌─── 【解答】 ─────────────────────────────────────┐
│   1. i      2. a      3. e      4. o      5. a      6. i    │
│   7. e      8. e      9. i     10. a     11. o     12. a    │
│  13. o     14. e     15. e     16. e     17. e     18. i    │
│  19. i     20. e                                           │
└────────────────────────────────────────────────────────────┘
```

Exercise 12：寫出下列各名詞的形容詞。

| NOUN | ADJECTIVE |
|---|---|
| 1. capability（能力） | capable（有能力的） |
| 2. urgency（緊急） | |
| 3. resistance（抵抗） | |
| 4. infallibility（無錯誤） | |
| 5. subservience（卑躬屈膝） | |
| 6. compatibility（相容） | |
| 7. eminence（卓越） | |
| 8. truancy（逃學） | |
| 9. audibility（可聽見） | |
| 10. opulence（富裕） | |
| 11. inconstancy（多變） | |
| 12. malevolence（惡意） | |

13. indefatigability（不疲倦） _____

14. observance（遵守） _____

15. cogency（說服力） _____

16. adaptability（適應性） _____

17. incandescence（白熱） _____

18. unavailability（不可獲得） _____

19. compliance（順從） _____

20. transiency（短暫） _____

【解答】

| | | |
|---|---|---|
| 1. capable（有能力的） | 2. urgent（迫切的） | 3. resistant（抵抗的） |
| 4. infallible（全無錯誤的） | 5. subservient（卑躬屈膝的） | 6. compatible（相容的） |
| 7. eminent（卓越的） | 8. truant（逃學者） | 9. audible（聽得見的） |
| 10. opulent（富裕的） | 11. inconsistent（不一致的） | 12. malevolent（有惡意的） |
| 13. indefatigable（不知疲倦的） | 14. observant（善於觀察的） | 15. cogent（有說服力的） |
| 16. adaptable（能適應的） | 17. incandescent（白熱的） | 18. unavailable（不可獲得的） |
| 19. compliant（順從的） | 20. transient（短暫的） | |

第九章

## Exercise 13：寫出正確的衍生字。

| I. VERB | II. NOUN (-er, -or, -ent, -ant) | III. NOUN (-ion, -ence) |
|---|---|---|
| 1. transgress（違反） | transgressor（違反者） | transgression（違反） |
| 2. _____ | _____ | dependence（依賴） |
| 3. _____ | correspondent（通訊記者） | _____ |
| 4. consult（請教） | _____ | _____ |
| 5. _____ | _____ | exhibition（展覽） |
| 6. _____ | observer（觀察者） | _____ |
| 7. intercept（攔截） | _____ | _____ |
| 8. _____ | _____ | opposition（反對） |
| 9. _____ | immigrant（移入的移民） | _____ |
| 10. collaborate（合作） | _____ | _____ |

【解答】
1. ─
2. depend, dependant (dependent)（依賴/受扶養的家屬）
3. correspond, correspondence（通信/通信）
4. consultant, consultation（顧問/諮詢）
5. exhibit, exhibitor（展覽/展覽者）
6. observe, observation（觀察/觀察）
7. interceptor, interception（攔截者/攔截）
8. oppose, opponent（反對/反對者）
9. immigrate, immigration（移入/移入）
10. collaborator, collaboration（合作者/合作）

Exercise 14：寫出正確的衍生字。

| I. NOUN | II. ADJECTIVE | III. ADVERB |
|---|---|---|
| 1. happiness（快樂） | <u>happy（快樂的）</u> | <u>happily（快樂地）</u> |
| 2. ＿＿＿＿＿＿ | courageous（勇敢的） | ＿＿＿＿＿＿ |
| 3. ＿＿＿＿＿＿ | ＿＿＿＿＿＿ | amicably（友善地） |
| 4. immaturity（不成熟） | ＿＿＿＿＿＿ | ＿＿＿＿＿＿ |
| 5. ＿＿＿＿＿＿ | original（最初的） | ＿＿＿＿＿＿ |
| 6. ＿＿＿＿＿＿ | ＿＿＿＿＿＿ | coherently（前後一致地） |
| 7. benevolence（慈善） | ＿＿＿＿＿＿ | ＿＿＿＿＿＿ |
| 8. ＿＿＿＿＿＿ | harmonious（和諧的） | ＿＿＿＿＿＿ |
| 9. ＿＿＿＿＿＿ | ＿＿＿＿＿＿ | stubbornly（頑固地） |
| 10. proficiency（精通） | ＿＿＿＿＿＿ | ＿＿＿＿＿＿ |
| 11. ＿＿＿＿＿＿ | legible（易讀的） | ＿＿＿＿＿＿ |
| 12. ＿＿＿＿＿＿ | ＿＿＿＿＿＿ | unanimously（全體一致地） |
| 13. shyness（害羞） | ＿＿＿＿＿＿ | ＿＿＿＿＿＿ |
| 14. ＿＿＿＿＿＿ | weary（疲倦的） | ＿＿＿＿＿＿ |
| 15. ＿＿＿＿＿＿ | ＿＿＿＿＿＿ | insecurely（不安全地） |

第
九
章

16. autonomy（自治）_____ _____

17. _____ logical（合邏輯的）_____

18. _____ _____ outrageously（殘暴地）

19. consistency（一致）_____ _____

20. _____ hostile（有敵意的）_____

【解答】

1. —
2. courage, courageously（勇氣／勇敢地）
3. amicability, amicable（友善／友善的）
4. immature, immaturely（不成熟的／不成熟地）
5. origin, originally（起源／起初）
6. coherence, coherent（一致性／一致的）
7. benevolent, benevolently（慈善的／慈善地）
8. harmony, harmoniously（和諧／和諧地）
9. stubbornness, stubborn（頑固／頑固的）
10. proficient, proficiently（精通的／精通地）
11. legibility, legibly（易讀性／易讀地）
12. unanimity, unanimous（全體一致／全體一致的）
13. shy, shyly（害羞的／害羞地）
14. weariness, wearily（疲倦／疲倦地）
15. insecurity, insecure（不安全／不安全的）
16. autonomous, autonomously（自治的／自治地）
17. logic, logically（邏輯／合邏輯地）
18. outrage, outrageous（暴行／殘暴的）
19. consistent, consistently（前後一致的／前後一致地）
20. hostility, hostilely（敵意／有敵意地）

Exercise 15：寫出正確的衍生字。

| ADJECTIVE & OPPOSITE | ADVERB & OPPOSITE | NOUN & OPPOSITE |
|---|---|---|
| 1. mature（成熟的） <u>immature（不成熟的）</u> | <u>maturely（成熟地）</u> <u>immaturely</u> （不成熟地） | <u>maturity（成熟）</u> <u>immaturity（不成熟）</u> |
| 2. ＿＿＿＿＿＿＿ impatient（不耐煩的） | ＿＿＿＿＿＿＿ ＿＿＿＿＿＿＿ | ＿＿＿＿＿＿＿ ＿＿＿＿＿＿＿ |
| 3. ＿＿＿＿＿＿＿ ＿＿＿＿＿＿＿ | dependently（依賴地） ＿＿＿＿＿＿＿ | ＿＿＿＿＿＿＿ ＿＿＿＿＿＿＿ |
| 4. ＿＿＿＿＿＿＿ ＿＿＿＿＿＿＿ | ＿＿＿＿＿＿＿ incompetently （無能力地） | ＿＿＿＿＿＿＿ ＿＿＿＿＿＿＿ |
| 5. ＿＿＿＿＿＿＿ ＿＿＿＿＿＿＿ | ＿＿＿＿＿＿＿ ＿＿＿＿＿＿＿ | plausibility （貌似真實） ＿＿＿＿＿＿＿ |
| 6. ＿＿＿＿＿＿＿ ＿＿＿＿＿＿＿ | ＿＿＿＿＿＿＿ ＿＿＿＿＿＿＿ | ＿＿＿＿＿＿＿ irresponsibility （不負責任） |
| 7. legible（易讀的） ＿＿＿＿＿＿＿ | ＿＿＿＿＿＿＿ ＿＿＿＿＿＿＿ | ＿＿＿＿＿＿＿ ＿＿＿＿＿＿＿ |
| 8. ＿＿＿＿＿＿＿ inflexible（無彈性的） | ＿＿＿＿＿＿＿ ＿＿＿＿＿＿＿ | ＿＿＿＿＿＿＿ ＿＿＿＿＿＿＿ |

第九章

9. _____ formally（正式地） _____

_____ _____ _____

10. _____ _____ _____

_____ unimportantly _____
（不重要地）

【解答】

1. ─
2. patient, patiently, patience, impatiently, impatience
（有耐心的/有耐心地/耐心/不耐煩地/不耐煩）
3. dependent, dependence, independent, independently,
independence（依賴的/依賴/獨立的/獨立地/獨立）
4. competent, competently, competence, incompetent,
incompetence（有能力的/有能力地/能力/無能力的/無能力）
5. plausible, plausibly, implausible, implausibly, implausibility
（似真實的/似真實地/不像真實的/難以置信地/不像真實）
6. responsible, responsibly, responsibility, irresponsible,
irresponsibly（負責任的/負責任地/責任/不負責任的/不負責任地）
7. legibly, legibility, illegible, illegibly, illegibility
（易讀地/易讀/難讀的/難讀地/難讀）
8. flexible, flexibly, flexibility, inflexibly, inflexibility
（有彈性的/有彈性地/彈性/無彈性地/缺乏彈性）
9. formal, formality, informal, informally, informality
（正式的/拘泥形式/非正式的/非正式地/非正式）
10. important, importantly, importance, unimportant,
unimportance（重要的/重要地/重要性/不重要的/不重要）

# 第十章
# 關係字及類比字

## 1. 字的關係

　　字義類比是 GRE 語文能力單元的第二部份，通常有 10～15 道題左右。此類型問題主要在考你對字義的了解程度，因此你很可能會看到一些不常見或較難的單字。不過由於字與字之間都有關係可循，所以只要小心找出其中關係，還是可以做出有根據的猜測。現在就讓我們來討論字和字之間的關連性。

## ROBIN : BIRD（知更鳥：鳥）

　　ROBIN 和 BIRD 的關係是什麼？ROBIN（知更鳥）是鳥的一種，BIRD 是鳥的總稱。設前者為 A，後者為 B，則 A 屬於 B。下面我們來探討幾組字的關係。

## MINE : COAL（礦場：煤）

　　MINE（礦場）是 COAL（煤）的出處（source），設前者為 A，後者為 B，則 A 是生產 B 的地方。

## SPADE : DIGGING（鏟子：挖掘）

　　SPADE（鏟子）是 DIGGING（挖掘）的工具，設前者為 A，後者為 B，則 A 是做 B 的工具。

## TEMPERATURE : THERMOMETER（氣溫：溫度計）

　　TEMPERATURE（氣溫）要用 THERMOMETER（溫度計）來度量，設前者為 A，後者為 B，則 B 為測量 A 的工具。

## MEEK : SUBMIT（溫順的：順從）

　　MEEK（溫順的）就會 SUBMIT（順從），設前者為 A，後者為 B，則 AB 為同義字關係，要注意 A 是形容詞，B 是動詞。

| WORD PAIR | RELATIONSHIP |
|---|---|
| PAUPER : MEANS<br>貧民：財富 | A lacks B.（A 缺少 B） |
| FOUNDATION : EDIFICE<br>基礎：雄偉的建築物 | A supports B.（A 支持 B） |
| WATCHMAN : THEFT<br>看守人：竊盜 | A guards against B.（A 防守 B） |
| BLINDFOLD : VISION<br>蒙住眼睛：視力 | A interferes with B.（A 干擾 B） |
| LITERATE : READ<br>識字者：閱讀 | One who is A can B.<br>（A 的人能 B） |
| ILLNESS : ABSENCE<br>疾病：缺席 | A may cause B.（A 可能造成 B） |
| SEIZING : TAKING<br>抓：拿 | A is a sudden, forcible form of B.<br>（A 是 B 中一種猛然有力的形式） |
| GREGARIOUS : COMPANY<br>群居的：同伴 | One who is A likes B.<br>（A 的人喜歡 B） |
| PEBBLE : STONE<br>小圓石：石頭 | A is a small B.（A 是小 B） |
| PAINTER : EASEL<br>畫家：畫架 | A uses B in his work.<br>（A 工作時使用 B） |

## 2. 字義類比問題

　　字義類比粗略可分大─小，部分─整體，原因─結果，普通
─特殊，工具─使用方式／使用者等關係，本章將討論更密切的
關係。請看下例：

**PREFACE : INDEX**

 (A) tool : drill      (B) departure : trip

 (C) famine : drought    (D) appetizer : dessert

 (E) water : well

〔詳解〕PREFACE（序言）和 INDEX（索引）的關係，前者位
於書前，後者位於書後，(D) 的 appetizer 是正菜前所上
的開胃菜，dessert 是餐後甜點，所以這題應該選 (D)。

Exercise 1：在下列各字組中，選出和題目大寫字組有類比關係的一
     組，將 **A, B, C, D** 或 **E** 填入空格中。

(   ) 1. NEEDLE : STITCH ::

  (A) shears : prune     (B) rake : mow

  (C) spade : level      (D) stake : bush

  (E) wrench : soak

(   ) 2. FATHOM : DEPTH ::

  (A) calorie : temperature   (B) search : treasure

  (C) minute : time      (D) dive : surface

  (E) base : height

(   ) 3. DAM : FLOW ::

  (A) research : information   (B) laws : justice

  (C) reporters : news     (D) autocracy : liberty

  (E) education : opportunity

(   ) 4. FOREST : TIMBER ::

  (A) magnet : filings     (B) art : museum

  (C) quarry : stone      (D) clay : earth

  (E) zoo : spectators

第十章

( ) 5. NECK : BOTTLE ::

    (A) bonnet : head         (B) rim : wheel

    (C) roof : cellar         (D) metal : leather

    (E) chain : link

( ) 6. TYRO : EXPERIENCE ::

    (A) despot : power         (B) razor : sharpness

    (C) craftsman : skill         (D) coward : courage

    (E) farewell : welcome

( ) 7. GRAVEL : PIT ::

    (A) oil : well         (B) cement : sand

    (C) tunnel : cave         (D) asphalt : road

    (E) crest : mountain

( ) 8. FACULTY : TEACHER ::

    (A) congregation : clergy     (B) crew : foreman

    (C) act : play         (D) choir : singer

    (E) election : candidate

( ) 9. KITTEN : CAT ::

    (A) ewe : lamb         (B) tiger : cub

    (C) seedling : flower         (D) fawn : deer

    (E) napkin : towel

( ) 10. MICROSCOPE : BIOLOGIST ::

    (A) horoscope : scientist     (B) medicine : druggist

    (C) lens : photography

    (D) telescope : astronomer

    (E) spectacles : optometry

第十章

(　) 11. LIEUTENANT : OFFICER ::

    (A) actor : understudy      (B) moon : planet

    (C) veteran : newcomer

    (D) sophomore : undergraduate

    (E) passenger : conductor

(　) 12. BIRTH : DECEASE ::

    (A) takeoff : flight      (B) negligence : dismissal

    (C) opera : finale      (D) dawn : sunset

    (E) competition : defeat

(　) 13. FOG : VISION ::

    (A) superstition : ignorance   (B) evidence : testimony

    (C) malnutrition : growth    (D) rain : overflow

    (E) vigilance : safety

(　) 14. PLANT : HARVEST ::

    (A) factory : equipment    (B) launch : decommission

    (C) sow : irrigate      (D) clump : shrub

    (E) mishap : carelessness

(　) 15. COD : FISH ::

    (A) immunity : disease     (B) band : trumpet

    (C) mutiny : authority     (D) penalty : offense

    (E) pneumonia : illness

【解答】

| 1. A | 2. C | 3. D | 4. C | 5. B | 6. D |
|------|------|------|------|------|------|
| 7. A | 8. D | 9. D | 10. D | 11. D | 12. D |
| 13. C | 14. B | 15. E | | | |

在 EXERCISE 1 中我們討論了有類似關係的字組,請再看下列的例子:

BANKRUPTCY : PROFIT ::

(A) population : housing     (B) fatigue : effort

(C) congestion : space     (D) memory : knowledge

(E) flood : thaw

BANKRUPTCY(破產),PROFIT(利潤),破產是利潤虧損的結果。我們來看五組字組:

(A) population(人口),housing(住宅),兩者是人和住所的關係。

(B) fatigue(疲倦),effort(努力),前者是果,後者是因,兩者是因果關係。

(C) congestion(阻塞),space(空間),阻塞是因為空間不足的結果。

(D) memory(記憶力),knowledge(知識;理解),兩者為同義字關係。

(E) flood(洪水),thaw(冰、雪的融化),冰、雪融化會造成洪水,兩者是因果關係。

由此可知答案應選(C)。

Exercise 2:以下的練習較練習 1 來得困難。如果你在所給的字組中不能馬上找出適當的答案,試著照上面的方法,分析彼此間的關係,必能找到相關的字組。

(    ) 1. SOLVENT : PAY ::

(A) indigent : thrive     (B) innocent : acquit

(C) loyal : adhere     (D) punctual : tardy

(E) lavish : economize

( 　 ) 2. ANTISEPTIC : BACTERIA ::
　　(A) soldier : nation 　　　　(B) hair : scalp
　　(C) pseudonym : author 　　(D) prescription : cure
　　(E) education : ignorance

( 　 ) 3. INTERMEDIARY : SETTLEMENT ::
　　(A) belligerent : peace
　　(B) prosecutor : conviction 　(C) adherent : pact
　　(D) strife : recess 　　　　　(E) rumor : discovery

( 　 ) 4. GENEROUS : FORGIVE ::
　　(A) pliable : yield 　　　　　(B) spineless : resist
　　(C) opinionated : change 　　(D) conspicuous : hide
　　(E) impatient : delay

( 　 ) 5. DISTANCE : ODOMETER ::
　　(A) weight : scale 　　　　　(B) heat : barometer
　　(C) quiz : knowledge 　　　　(D) map : compass
　　(E) clock : time

( 　 ) 6. GUILTLESS : BLAME ::
　　(A) unbiased : prejudice 　　(B) bankrupt : debt
　　(C) sincere : honesty
　　(D) apprehensive : worry
　　(E) verdict : acquittal

( 　 ) 7. AUTOMATON : ORIGINALITY ::
　　(A) ambassador : good will 　(B) pioneer : foresight
　　(C) hothead : equanimity 　　(D) guest : hospitality
　　(E) benefactor : generosity

第
十
章

(   ) 8. CONJUNCTION : CLAUSES ::
    (A) barrier : neighbors       (B) paragraph : phrases
    (C) door : hinges            (D) bridge : shores
    (E) preposition : nouns

(   ) 9. IRREVOCABLE : ALTER ::
    (A) irreproachable : trust     (B) available : obtain
    (C) audible : hear
    (D) intelligible : comprehend
    (E) pressing : defer

(   ) 10. SMOG : POLLUTANTS ::
    (A) fog : travel           (B) wars : destruction
    (C) ambition : diligence
    (D) contagion : disinfectants
    (E) exhaustion : overwork

(   ) 11. MANACLE : MOVEMENT ::
    (A) sailor : crew          (B) pendant : chain
    (C) gag : speech          (D) manual : information
    (E) invalid : vigor

(   ) 12. EROSION : WATER ::
    (A) earthquake : destruction   (B) ocean : wine
    (C) inauguration : presidency
    (D) aging : time          (E) solid : liquid

(   ) 13. ARISTOCRAT : COUNT ::
    (A) flower : leaf          (B) senator : voter
    (C) professional : amateur    (D) civilian : soldier
    (E) insect : ant

第十章

( 　) 14. DESPOTIC : DOMINEER ::

　　(A) disgruntled : rejoice　　　(B) cordial : rebuff

　　(C) timorous : withdraw　　　(D) aggressive : tremble

　　(E) malcontent : cooperate

( 　) 15. HOLD : VESSEL ::

　　(A) tail : airplane　　　(B) vault : security

　　(C) site : edifice　　　(D) garage : vehicle

　　(E) basement : house

```
---【解答】-------------------------------------
  1. C      2. E      3. B      4. A      5. A      6. A
  7. C      8. D      9. E     10. B     11. C     12. D
 13. E     14. C     15. E
```

## 3. 交替型式的類比問題

　　有一種交替型式的類比問題，題目給的是第一組字組和第二組字組的第一個字，你必須在所給的字當中選出一個最恰當的字。下列的練習就要介紹你這種型式的類比問題。

**Exercise 3**：選出最恰當的字，把 **A, B, C, D** 或 **E** 填入空格裏。

( 　) 1. *Justice* is to *judge* as *health* is to _____.

　　(A) lawyer　　　(B) nutrition　　　(C) physician

　　(D) disease　　　(E) jury

( 　) 2. *Dentist* is to *teeth* as *dermatologist* is to _____.

　　(A) heart　　　(B) feet　　　(C) eyes

　　(D) skin　　　(E) lungs

(   ) 3. *Quart* is to *gallon* as *week* is to _____.

    (A) pint         (B) year         (C) liquid

    (D) month       (E) measure

(   ) 4. *Horse* is to *stable* as *dog* is to _____.

    (A) leash       (B) curb         (C) bone

    (D) muzzle      (E) kennel

(   ) 5. *Pear* is to *potato* as *peach* is to _____.

    (A) carrot      (B) cucumber    (C) nectarine

    (D) melon      (E) tomato

(   ) 6. *Composer* is to *symphony* as *playwright* is to _____.

    (A) essay      (B) cast        (C) novel

    (D) drama     (E) copyright

(   ) 7. *Friction* is to *rubber* as *repetition* is to _____.

    (A) skill       (B) novelty     (C) literacy

    (D) memory    (E) knowledge

(   ) 8. *Pond* is to *lake* as *asteroid* is to _____.

    (A) moon      (B) comet      (C) planet

    (D) orbit      (E) meteor

(   ) 9. *Bear* is to *fur* as *fish* is to _____.

    (A) seaweed    (B) fins        (C) scales

    (D) water      (E) gills

(   ) 10. *Condemn* is to *criticize* as *scalding* is to _____.

    (A) boiling     (B) warm       (C) freezing

    (D) combustible  (E) burning

第
十
章

( ) 11. *Pearl* is to *oyster* as *ivory* is to _____.

    (A) piano         (B) crocodile         (C) tusks

    (D) elephant       (E) tortoise

( ) 12. *Sheep* is to *fold* as *bluefish* is to _____.

    (A) boat           (B) line           (C) bait

    (D) school        (E) shoal

( ) 13. *Drama* is to *intermission* as *conflict* is to _____.

    (A) feud           (B) truce

    (C) reconciliation     (D) intervention     (E) stage

( ) 14. *War* is to *hawk* as *peace* is to _____.

    (A) eagle         (B) gull          (C) dove

    (D) falcon        (E) owl

( ) 15. *Ballistics* is to *projectiles* as *genealogy* is to _____.

    (A) exploration     (B) lineage         (C) minerals

    (D) causes        (E) missiles

( ) 16. *Pistol* is to *holster* as *airliner* is to _____.

    (A) fuselage      (B) hangar         (C) runway

    (D) fuel           (E) landing

( ) 17. *Frugal* is to *waste* as *infallible* is to _____.

    (A) dread         (B) save          (C) criticize

    (D) prosper       (E) err

( ) 18. *Toothpaste* is to *tube* as *graphite* is to _____.

    (A) pencil        (B) lead          (C) coal

    (D) cable         (E) tar

第十章

(　　) 19. *State* is to *traitor* as *plant* is to _____.

    (A) soil           (B) absorption         (C) leaf

    (D) pest          (E) moisture

(　　) 20. *Spot* is to *immaculate* as *name* is to _____.

    (A) autonomous     (B) illiterate

    (C) anonymous     (D) dependent     (E) illegible

【解答】

| | | | | | |
|---|---|---|---|---|---|
| 1. C | 2. D | 3. D | 4. E | 5. A | 6. D |
| 7. A | 8. C | 9. C | 10. A | 11. D | 12. D |
| 13. B | 14. C | 15. B | 16. B | 17. E | 18. A |
| 19. D | 20. C | | | | |

心得筆記欄

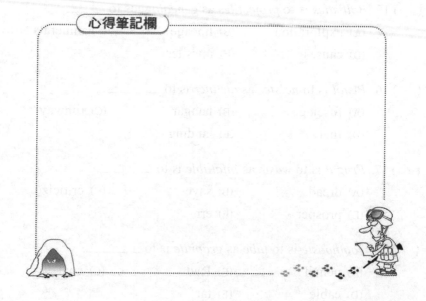

第十章

# 單字索引

單字索引

單字索引

# Vocabulary 22000
## 字彙 22000

附錄音 QR 碼 售價：280 元

| | | |
|---|---|---|
| 修　　　編 / 劉　毅 | | |
| 發 行 所 / 學習出版有限公司 | ☎ (02) 2704-5525 |
| 郵 撥 帳 號 / 05127272 學習出版社帳戶 | |
| 登 記 證 / 局版台業 2179 號 | |
| 印 刷 所 / 裕強彩色印刷有限公司 | |
| 台 北 門 市 / 台北市許昌街 17 號 6F | ☎ (02) 2331-4060 |
| 台灣總經銷 / 紅螞蟻圖書有限公司 | ☎ (02) 2795-3656 |
| 本公司網址 / www.learnbook.com.tw | |
| 電 子 郵 件 / learnbook@learnbook.com.tw | |

2022 年 1 月 1 日四版一刷

ISBN 978-986-231-467-8

趁著年紀輕，記憶好的時候，
熟悉重要單字，一生受用。

單字永遠學不完，
唯有使用，才不會忘記，
要使用、使用，不斷地使用。

劉毅老師在「快手」和「抖音」
有一千多個視頻，
可以在網上跟著劉毅老師學習。

我們有「網紅英語2000句」，
及「英文三句金寶典①②」，
可以用裡面的句子，
在網上和劉毅老師一對一交流。